BEHIND THE COVER

ALYSE PALSULICH

KAPOW is an imprint of THE POLYETHNIC PUBLISHING
United States of America

KAPOW is an imprint of The Polyethnic Publishing, LLC.

BEHIND THE COVER

The Polyethnic Publishing, LLC

e-mail: contact@thepolyethnic.com
www.thepolyethnic.com

Printed in the United States of America

First Paperback Edition, October 2017
Front Cover Illustration and Design © 2017 by Allison Li
Interior Design by Nicole Lambert
Edited by Alyssa Barber

ISBN-13: 978-1-946105-20-2
ISBN-10: 1-946105-20-1

Dedicated to my dad, for all of the late-night tea.
And my mom, for teaching me it's okay to laugh.

01 | One Word

-Charlotte-

Fate has a twisted sense of humor. One day, you're gushing about an awkward first kiss, and the next, you're shaking at a funeral. But I'm getting ahead of myself, as I often do.

One word changed my entire life, just one word.

Spy.

If it weren't for that word, I would have grown up learning how to jump rope instead of tying and escaping knots. Or finger painting rather than discovering what ingredients make the best invisible ink. I suppose, some things are the same. Like all children, my mother had to teach me what's safe to eat and what wasn't. If it smelled funny, or didn't pass the POTW (Poisoned or Tampered With) tests don't put it in your mouth.

Don't get me wrong, I'm not complaining. Without being a "spy" I'd never have complete control over an empty bowling alley, which would be more fun if I were, you know, *bowling*. As tempting as it is to grab a ball and hurl it down the lane at breathtaking speeds until demolishing a neat triangle of pins, I can't allow my attention to dissipate for even a moment.

The sole door swings open (note I said door, not entrance/exit) with a quiet hiss of air. Even as my demeanor remains constant, my muscles and brain tense in preparation. After a quick scan of the room, I remind myself of my options.

Most accessible assets: phone, chairs, bowling shoes, cleaning spray, knife.

Most dangerous weapons: bowling balls, broken glass in trash, steel bars, again, knife.

Every good spy knows you're only as good as what you've got, and I came ready. I have been preparing for this moment my entire life. My first mission, and it just walked through the door.

Miss High Heels doesn't seem surprised when I slip the knife to her throat. Instead, a cool smile crosses her cheeks as she presses her finger to the knife's edge, pushing it away. A drop of blood pools on the tip of her finger, but neither of us move to clean it.

She's attempted to conceal her identity through large sunglasses and a hat covering her face and hair. It's all put to waste as her driver's permit flashes from the inside of her purse pocket when she pulls out a tube of cherry red lipstick. Yet again I ask if I want to go through with this.

"Miss Richards, is it?" Her voice carries the authority of an experienced leader while she looks like a spoiled high school student.

"Yes. It's nice to meet you, Miss Thomas." She stops in surprise before returning her lipstick to her purse. No personal information concerning her identity had been provided through our emails, but knowing information is a *major* part of my job.

"How can I be certain that you're worthy of this assignment?" Even with her face covered, it's easy to catch her expression harden. Part of me wants to laugh, but I swallow down emotions to stay professional.

"You are Claire Emery Thomas," I start, ready to prove myself with this practiced speech, "even though you're only eighteen years old, you've dropped out of nine elementary schools, middle schools, and high schools. You may have changed your name for private reasons, but your relation to your *extremely* wealthy father, has not changed. In fifth grade, you 'accidently' spilled wine on the Australian Prime Minister's plans for a partnership with the US." I pause dramatically, this girl never stood a chance. Once something's on the internet, it never leaves. "And, you're smarter than the spoiled rich girl everyone seems to think you are." I lean back in my chair as a bright red smile slithers across her flawless skin.

"I'm impressed." Confidence is one of the strongest components in a spy's arsenal, but arrogance is their greatest enemy. My expression remains a steady mask. "Are you ready for the case?" She slides a blank folder across the table.

"You already sent me this," I comment, glancing through the text. "What you haven't told me is why. Why do you want me to find this man? With all the money you have laying around I'm sure you could pay anyone to find him."

"Let's just say it goes deeper than that, and my reasoning is my own. It is not something you need to know." Her sharp reprimand snaps me back to reality. This is really happening. "Do you accept this case?"

Thirty long seconds pass. I examine my nails and take my time as to insinuate I have plenty of cases and could easily discard hers. What she doesn't know is that this is my one and only chance. My chance at the big leagues, and I plan to use it. Any uncertainty leaves with the finality of my words. "I accept."

"Wonderful. I'll expect timely updates." Her navy dress sways against her heels as she strides elegantly toward the door. She stops before leaving and winks over her shoulder. "This should be interesting."

02 | Yours, Mine, Ours

-Emily-

My hand trails in the water leaving swirls of bubbles and the river gurgles its quiet response. For now, it looks like it might end up being my only company. Normally, it annoys me when he's late, but today I'm okay with a small break from the busy world. Days are ticking away to the end of summer.

Heavy breathing intrudes upon my thoughts even before a twig snaps from the weight of his foot. "I'm...so...sorry!" I look up to discover a head of dark brown hair bobbing above the bushes. The blonder tips are slicked against his cheek and forehead from sweat, long enough to cover his stormy blue eyes.

I shout back to him, "I was wondering if you forgot."

"As if that's possible. My agent wouldn't release me from a tedious meeting and my driver was slow hitting every red light." He groans, gesturing like that's his biggest problem as he sits next to me. Our knees bump into each other, but neither of us moves away.

"Listen to yourself," I chuckle. "*Your* agent. *Your* driver." My voice takes on a sarcastic tone as I nudge him with a grin.

"Well, I brought something that was going to be for *us* but maybe now it will just be *mine*." Ben wiggles his eyebrows and hops up onto our tree. Its branches separate at the ground only to reunite a few feet into the air with a curvy shape. As we've grown up sitting in the middle section, it's bent downward creating a heart shape.

"Wait, no! I take it back." I support my hands against the branch before jumping up next to him. "What is it?"

"Just this." His arm moves into view revealing a crushed and melted Snickers bar.

"My favorite," I cheer before pulling it out of his grasp. As I open the wrapper, gooey chocolate melts across my fingers. I break off a piece of my Snickers and hand it to him in a sacred manner. We eat in silence, the only noise belonging to the stream flowing by.

For a second, Ben looks like he's considering wiping his hands against his new jeans. He changes his mind and hops down to wash in the water. Even without my asking, he cups a small pool between his hands and brings it over to the tree so I can rinse away my own chocolate.

"Being the great best friend I am." Ben pauses to wink at me. I shake my head allowing a few giggles. "I brought you two gifts." He reaches into his pocket to display a thin box.

I raise an eyebrow before pulling off the crinkled paper. The corners aren't perfect and the bow is lopsided. I slide off the bow, placing it on his forehead, before gently ripping open the paper. "Ben. This is worth, like, a hundred dollars." I shift the CD case causing light to catch and flash away in a cascade of colors.

He laughs. "Not nearly that much. And I've been meaning to give one to you. It just took a while to figure out how to sneak the disk past Rob."

I can't help laughing with him at the thought of his scrawny agent trying to stop Ben. "Thank you, I can't wait to listen to it."

He rubs at his neck as it burns bright red like it always does when someone talks about his music. "I hope you like it." His phone buzzes and he passes me an apologetic look when he reads it. "I have to go, Rob wants me to go give an interview with Krystal."

"So soon?" I grouse, keeping a sarcastic tone.

"We can talk tomorrow, how 'bout at my house?" He offers, passing me a quick hug.

"Fine. Just know I'm expecting more Snickers." I wiggle my finger warningly as he pulls away.

"Always." He turns and runs back through the bushes.

"Try not to get that designer jacket stained, it's starting to smell like sweat," I shout behind him, though that's impossible with his strong cologne. Companies are requiring he show off their products in exchange for their sponsorship, which Rob is always on the lookout for. Most of the time they're top of the line items teenagers would pay a fortune for, but I'm not loving this perfume scented cologne.

"I guess I'll be a trend setter," he calls back over his shoulder, with a final wink before disappearing into the forest.

"As if you aren't already," I mutter, cradling the disk between my fingers.

After a few minutes, my phone buzzes letting me know mom wants me inside. I take my time walking back, kicking my feet through stray leaves. When I look up a trail of smoke stains the sky like a map leading to my house.

A wave of panic passes over me as I stumble into a sprint pushing through tree branches. "Oh my gosh. Oh my gosh. Oh my gosh," I mumble under my breath. I haven't ran this hard since the pacer test. Three more trees. Two. One.

I break through the wall of forest, my hands dropping to my knees.

BEHIND THE COVER

A barbecue.

I sprinted for a *barbecue.*

Mom turns around and waves at me with a spatula or whatever it's called. "You gave me a heart attack," I grumble and slump down into a chair next to her. "I thought the smoke was coming from our house."

A blush fills my cheeks as my mom laughs. "Well, maybe these burgers. How was your day honey? Did you have fun with Ben?"

"Yeah, it was great."

"Oh good." Mom places a plate of burnt hamburger patties on the table. I open two hamburger buns and she lays a patty in each.

"These taste like charcoal," I groan. Dad had always been the better cook. After devouring my burger, I ask, "Can I go inside and get ready for bed? I'm really tired."

"Sure honey, sweet dreams." She kisses my forehead and I go to my room.

Before settling into bed, I place Ben's CD into my computer and stream his new album. A notification pops up on my phone letting me know I have a follower request on Instagram.

Booklover321 has requested to follow you. Accept or Decline?

In their bio it states that they'll be going to Simplot High this year, just like me. I accept their request and follow them back. Cuddling in my blankets with Ben's voice flowing through my ears and a possible new friend, I can't help but think tomorrow's going to be a good day.

03 | Everyone Loves Hawaiian

-Charlotte-

"Miss me?" Most people claim to have an annoying voice in their head whether it belongs to a conscience or their own crazed thoughts. I literally have a voice in my head: *Nick Richards.*

"Obviously not. Otherwise I would have opened communications with you," I shoot back, but he chuckles.

"So you did miss me." It isn't hard to imagine the cocky grin crossing his face. "Why else would you have replied?" He drawls through my earpiece. Through the years, I've concluded that brothers are more trouble than they're worth. Especially mine.

"To tell you to shut up. I have some important business to attend to."

"Important business? Now this wouldn't have anything to do with your meeting at the bowling alley, would it Charlie?" I stop walking. He wasn't supposed to know about that, no one was.

"How did you-" I regret the question the moment it leaves my mouth, mentally chastising myself.

"You may be a field agent, but I am a techno genius." He says cockily, the clacking of his keyboard echoing in my earpiece. "All I had to do was pull up the trackers and connect your earpiece to my account so I could open the sound stream and botta-bing, botta-boom, a third member joined your meeting."

"Great," I grumble under my breath. Now he'll never leave.

"What're you doing?" A crunching noise erupts in my ear and I cringe in response.

"Nick, turn off the speaker if you plan on eating." The crunching stops. "I'm about to plant some bugs and cameras in Mrs. Parker's house."

"I'm lost, rewind." Nick may be a tech nerd, but when it comes to the actual mission, he's about as helpful as a five-year-old (the youngest official spy was six). That's why I'm the one doing all the work.

"The target's daughter is Emily Parker who lives with her mom, his wife. Interesting fact, they never divorced. Even though he's been gone for ten years they're technically still married. So that's the best place to start gathering info." I pick up speed to a jog while pulling my hair into a high ponytail.

Current cover: athletic girl going for daily run.

"And how do you plan on doing that?" Nick slurps on a drink.

"There aren't any cars in the driveway, and according to traffic cam videos, Emily and her mom always park out front. Meaning that the house is empty."

"So, what, you're going to break into her house? That sounds like a great plan." I don't miss the sarcasm in his voice.

"I know right." I wait for the mailman to turn the corner of the street before opening the gate to Miss Parker's backyard. Though their trusting nature has made things easier, I would appreciate some sort of challenge.

After securing a laser trip line (just light, not an actual burn-your-skin-off laser) to the gate, I slide my drawstring bag off my shoulder and onto her back patio. Her backyard is more extensive than I'd originally thought. The well-kept lawn and flower gardens ebb into a forest without an obvious end.

Note to self: possible hidden back entrance to backyard.

I grab a handful of bugs and cameras out of my bag and set to work. One on the bottom of the bench. Another in the corner of a worn-out soccer net. A waterproofed bug in the flowerpot.

My hands gradually empty when a slow creaking like that of an old house disrupts my mission. I grab my bag while rolling under a grove of bushes.

"Em? Is that you?" A wrinkled face framed by pale hair pops over the fence. "I've got tomatoes that're ripe for the picking. Would you like some?" She looks around the yard once more before shrugging and returning to her house.

A collection of crushed leaves just beyond my bush catch my eye and I recognize a path of cracked twigs and dirt. While I scuff the dirt to cover my own marks, I notice remaining prints all appear to be from the same two people (same shoe sizes and stride lengths). Perhaps they belong to Emily and her mom? Or is there another regular?

If this path weren't so well-used I would have needed to check my bearings once or twice by now. Green and brown melt together throughout my surroundings, with the echoing of a nearby stream ever changing. It sounds and appears as though I've left behind all traces of the city and entered a hidden jungle. Abruptly, the trail ends as the stream crosses my path.

My eyes trace the intricate designs of roots up to a trunk that splits in two before joining into a single, leafy spiral, creating a heart shape. I place one camera on the left and a bug on the right.

"Nice work." Ah, so the pest returns. "I'd recommend finding your way back home. Grocery trips only last so long."

"Right. Thanks Nick."

"I would use some of your spy tricks to get home ASAP. Otherwise your chances of getting caught increase exponentially," he says matter of factly, the scientist in him making its routinely appearance.

"Aw, is someone worried about me?" I coo while sprinting back to the house.

"No. Not you exactly." His tone becomes similar to that of a robot. "If you get caught then it becomes my job to rescue you before Kriss finds out what's going on and kicks both our butts. And I, for one, am not interested in extra P. E." Kriss' version of P.E. is excruciating, but gets us into shape. Last time I had to race her car for a two mile curving expeditions, and wasn't allowed to stop until I won or had completed fifteen reps. It's times like those that make me question my choices, but it's times like now that remind me I was made for this life.

I slip back through the gate and continue running until I reach a small diner at the entrance of the target's neighborhood.

Nick goes offline while I take a quick stop in the bathroom, change from my jogger disguise to a Pizza Hut delivery uniform and grab a pizza I stashed here previously. I wonder if anyone noticed the slight scent of marinara earlier. Nick comes back online the moment I make my way back to the house.

"What do you think you're doing?" He shouts in my ear, his voice growing as panicky as a robot can.

"For someone so smart you can be *so* clueless sometimes," I retort. "What kind of surveillance would it be if I only bugged the outside of their house?"

"Wait, so you're-"

"Uhuh, 'bout time you caught up." I smirk.

"Oh." He starts to talk again but I silence him with a harsh *shhhh* as I ring the doorbell, taking note of the silver Honda minivan out front.

A minute passes. Then another. After three my hand reaches forward to knock when the door slides open.

"Hello?" A confused voice meets my ears before I see her face.

"Pizza delivery?" I respond with an equally questioning tone. I examine her dark wavy hair and thinned body shape, taking a mental image for later. Even though Mrs. Parker may be a more direct line to her husband, it would be much more difficult to obtain information from her than her daughter. And if the husband and wife are in a fight, there's a greater chance that the husband is still speaking with the daughter over the wife.

Cover: Embarrassed, teenage pizza delivery bum.

"I don't think we ordered any pizza," she murmurs, then calls out, "Em? Did you order a pizza?"

Emily Nicole Parker. Layered honey brown hair. About five foot six. Brown eyes. Freckles. Little to no makeup. No extraordinary physical traits aside from scarred knees. She smiles kindly, and from that smile I know this case is in the bag.

"Um, I don't think so. But Ben was acting weird today so I wouldn't be surprised if he got it for us." She looks up at me. "Is it Hawaiian?"

"It is," I confirm, thank goodness I used Nick's program to search through past purchases. Besides, everyone likes pineapple.

She and her mom share a smile and say, "Ben."

"So this is the right place?" I ask doubtingly though I already know the answer.

"Yup, we're, uh, sorry about all the trouble," Emily comments as I slide the pizza box into her arms.

"No problem-o, but do you think I could use your bathroom? I wouldn't normally ask-" Mrs. Parker cuts me off with a wave of her hand.

"Of course! Go down the hall, turn left at the end, and it'll be the first door to the right." She's making this almost too easy.

"Thank you." I remove my shoes and head into said hallway while they walk in the opposite direction toward the dining room (I found a map of their house on a real estate website).

Rather than go straight to the bathroom, I run my hand along the hallway walls and inside the doors to each of the rooms, laying down an invisible wire embedded with listening/recording devices. After five rooms, I've covered this entire half of the house and rush to make my way back. To my luck their dining room is on the opposite side of the house so I get to continue the wire through every room. Though my quick search comes up empty handed without evidence toward Mr. Parker, I've gathered plenty of intel. Like how there's not a single picture with Emily's dad, and most of Emily's own pictures are of these later years after he abandoned them.

"Thanks again. I just wanted to let you know I'm leaving," I call out through the doorway to their dining room.

"No, thank you," Emily's mom yells back through a mouthful of pizza.

I complete the wire circuit over the doorframe and leave. Outside of her house rests a car, except I don't recognize it. As in there's no brand or recognizable traits. It's like it was made to blend in with its silver coloring and tinted windows which makes it all the more suspicious.

In my ear Nick shouts, "Hurry up and get in!"

Without a moment's hesitation, I casually stroll up to the vehicle and sit in the passenger's seat. Nick and I may tease each other, but when it comes down to it we've got each other's backs. At least, I think we do.

"So," Nick starts once I'm situated and we're speeding home, "what do you think?"

"It's cool," I comment flippantly. Right now I'm more concerned with checking the audio hookup than his new toy. My fingers flip through the wires connecting the audio to his speakers for reception.

"Cool? No. I don't think you understand just how 'cool' this is." His green-grey eyes flash in the sunlight, reflecting his passion. "This is the future of vehicles: automatic, close to frictionless-"

"Nick," I interrupt, growing further irritated with the wires as the speakers remain silent, "do you even have a license?"

A mischievous grin pulls at his mouth revealing Cheeto-filled teeth. "That's the best part." I flinch as he lifts his hands from the wheel. "I synced the controls with traffic cameras and as many visual maps as legally available. Then, I—"

"Nick."

"Okay, maybe they weren't all legal. I mean-"

"Nick. Richards."

"Fine! *Half* of them were legal. You happy? As I was saying the best part of this car is that it drives itself."

Luckily, he finishes before I get the chance to flip him out of his seat and jump in. "I'm only asking one more time: do you have a license?"

"Hmm, did I take Driver's Ed *and* pass the tests? No. Do I have a license? Yes."

I don't bother continuing this conversation. "So why did I get the honor of your chauffeuring? Just a test run?" Giving up, I throw myself back against my seat. This whole attempt was a failure if I can't get these stupid machines to work. My first official run, busted by technology.

"Partly that and partly the fact that Kriss is going to be home in approximately two point six one minutes." Nick pauses, and reaches over into my lap grabbing the wires. He swaps two of them, and ties three together resulting in the speakers buzzing to life. I pass him a relieved smile.

"And how long until we're home?"

"One point seven four minutes."

We stop at a red light and a blue corvette pulls up next to us. Two girls around our age, but of higher popular status and wealth, roll down their windows. They begin to flirtatiously wave and wink. One even goes so far as to flash her phone number and signal "call me!"

I can't understand other girls seeing Nick as "hot." Plus, if they knew him, his personality would cancel out any positive outer appearance. We have completely different hair as mine is fire engine red and his is sandy yellow with streaks of light green left over from an experiment gone awry. Both our faces are sprinkled with freckles, his eyes hold a grey green quality where mine are more of a blue green. He's a couple of inches taller than me, but what I lack in height I make up for in strength which, dare I say it, he could use one or two more workouts a week. Or any workouts at all, for that matter.

Somehow Nick doesn't notice the girls, as he often doesn't, and continues his happy chatter about his latest invention.

The light turns green and we pull into our neighborhood leaving the confused girls to their average lives. Maybe not *average* considering the car they're driving, but anything's more normal than us.

"Twenty-five seconds earlier than predicted," Nick comments absentmindedly and types some information into a tablet he made years ago.

Before entering the house we verify our fingerprints, shoeprints, and irises. "Someday someone's going to want to break into our house and they're going to chop off our fingers and cut out our eyes just to get through the front door," I complain.

I reach to the door but it opens on its own accord. As I turn to ask Nick about his upgrades to the house technology my eyes meet those of Kriss.

"About time you two showed up."

04 | Sparks

-Emily-

Once upon a time, Ben was still an unknown nerd. I was the cool one in the relationship. Well, as cool as I'd ever be. That all changed one night when I posted a video of Ben's singing to YouTube and shared it on Instagram. Then Clarisse reposted it. Her uncle saw it and showed Rob who got Ben his first major contract. The next day when we arrived at school, *everyone* had heard Ben's singing. It wasn't long after that until his first album came out and the rest is history.

With this sudden boom in popularity, Ben's family gained more money in a month than his parents made in three years. They no longer had to live in the worn-down house next door to me. Even through Ben's protests to moving, his parents bought a *huge* house. If we weren't in Boise, Idaho, I would call it a mansion. The purchases didn't stop there. His parents hadn't grown up with any money to spare, and this completely new idea overtook their lives. Before they knew it, the debt they gained was more than they had ever owned. For years to come Ben and I worked together through the night helping him earn back that money with his music.

I shake my head, dismissing the whirlwind of memories. I knock on his double French doors and they open to a tall, well-groomed man with a mustache. *Do all butlers have mustaches?* "Miss Emily."

"Edwin, I told you to call me Em." I step inside.

"Of course, Miss Em." He bows again.

Laughing, I ask, "Where's Ben?"

"His music room, Miss Em."

"Thank you." As I walk toward the music room I shout, "It's just Em! No Miss."

Though I'm yet to memorize the entire building, I know where all of Ben's favorite rooms are. The music room is at the top of his list. It's like a mix of a recording studio and a Jr. High band room: even messier if possible.

I tiptoe up behind him and throw my hands over his eyes. "Guess who."

"Em?" He grabs my hands, pulling them away from his face along with a grin.

"How'd you guess?"

"Who else has hands that smell like Snickers?"

"Guilty." I pull up a chair and grab my guitar. "I listened to your new album last night."

"What did you think?" He bites his lip in anticipation.

"Well..." I trail off and his tanned face pales instantly. My legs swing back and forth between the legs of the chair as I start to laugh. "I'm kidding, it's amazing, as usual. My favorite song was Sparks."

"Would you like a live performance?" He offers, moving toward me.

"Only if I get to play the guitar."

"I'd never have it any other way." His lips curve upward.

A silly grin lights up my face as I strum my fingers across the strings. I may not be a professional, but I've been taking lessons and improved greatly, if I do say so myself.

After a few measures of me getting used to the song,

Ben begins to sing.

"You asked me what I thought of you,
When I first fell head over heels.
Well I can't lie when I began to pursue." His voice is scratchy as though it hasn't been warmed up. The lyrics might not be the smoothest, but knowing they're his own words more than makes up for it.

'Cause when those sparks started flyin'
I knew I was decidin'
You're the one,
The only one,
My one true love." With the quick beat I can't help but join in. Ben chuckles but changes his pitch to match mine. The song speeds up.

And now I know it's meant to be.

Yes you and me, it's our destiny. My voice cracks loud enough to awaken the dinosaurs making both of us laugh our way through the final lines.

We can't stop our groovin'
No we've got to keep on movin'."

"Ooooooooooh, oh, oh oooh."

A new voice vocalizes. A voice that gives me a headache the second I hear it. I stop playing and singing.

"Hey Krystal," Ben says, clearing his throat.

"Hi babe, did you forget about our date?" She leans in to kiss his cheek but Ben ducks away, resulting in a brief frown tainting her pinched face.

"What date?" He asks, confusion leaking into his voice.

"Ugh, you promised me you'd remember." Her whining voice is even worse than her singing voice. Think polished nails on a chalkboard.

"If there was something to remember, I would. If you really want to, we can do it tomorrow. Right now I'm hanging out with Em." Ben keeps his tone calm yet firm.

"But babe-"

"I told you to stop calling me that."

"Fine, *Ben*, we don't get to hang out, especially with all the time you spend with that *normal* girl," Krystal whines, stabbing her finger towards me. I push her finger back at her, but keep quiet.

"I would hardly call her normal." I punch him and he laughs. "But I do enjoy spending time with her. She's my best friend and our relationship is purely professional."

She gives an annoyed squeal and stomps out of the room. *Diva much?* I place my hand on Ben's arm before he can stand up. "Let me go talk to her."

"Okay," he replies and walks me to the door.

It doesn't take long to find her glossy black dyed hair flipping over her shoulder. We're so different it's almost funny that we're the two major girls in Ben's life. I have dirty blonde hair, and she has black. She's tall and I'm short. Her makeup is done to perfection and I'm lucky if I remember to swipe on some lip gloss. She has stunning blue eyes and I have average brown. "Hey."

"Oh, it's you." She flips her hair again and rolls her eyes. "What do you want?"

"To see if you're okay. Boys can be stupid, even Ben."

"His only stupid decision is choosing you over me," she snaps, crossing her arms.

"It's not like we're dating or anything." I groan, looking up at the ceiling.

"*Sure*. Keep telling yourself that honey." A deceptive look slithers across her face. "It doesn't matter. I'll get him soon enough. Enjoy him while you can."

"What are you talking about?" So not just annoying, but crazy too. Great.

"Ben will be mine. Enjoy him while you can because soon I doubt you'll even be friends. Let alone best friends." She flips her hair a final time before sauntering down the hallway.

BEHIND THE COVER

"Wrong way," I shout.

"Right, thanks." She turns around and marches the other way.

05 | Family Secrets

-Charlotte-

Kriss cocks her eyebrow and places her hand on her hip. "How was the meeting?"

"Does everyone know about my secret meeting?" I sigh in exasperation.

Popping her hip to the side, Kriss rolls her eyes. "When you live in a family of spies, your business is everyone's business. In other words: there are no secrets."

She winks and strides into our small kitchen. "I got your favorites b-t-dubs."

If any other adult were to attempt to mimic teenagers, I would be annoyed. But when Kriss does it, it's a part of her laughing at the world she's trying to save. In a totally "see how stupid it sounds" kind of way. To be honest, Kriss has reached such a high status of the honored popularity level entitled "cool" it doesn't matter what she does. She's going to be awesome.

Her son, on the other hand, is the opposite of cool.

As if to prove my point, Nick stumbles into the kitchen tripping over his untied shoelaces about a dozen times. When he finally manages to seat himself at our mini bar he's already gasping for breath. All the while he was attempting, unsuccessfully I might add, to hide his new remote control. I pity anyone stuck with him as a field partner.

I can't help but scoff at how loudly Nick's feet slap against the floor in his getaway attempt. The door leading to his basement haven slides shut barely missing his nose making him stumble back. Nick turns to glare at me, but I shrug innocently and pass the look on to Kriss.

"Nick, is there something you'd like to show me?" She leans back against and runs a finger through her dark waves of hair.

"Nope. Not a thing. Nothing at all. In fact, I was just heading downstairs to get back to work on fixing that voice decoder you were asking me about. Whoever busted it, busted it up really well. I mean, the internal structure is completely fried!" As Nick grows more animated and really gets into his white lie, his body language also becomes enthusiastic. So enthusiastic that his hand holding his remote-control flies into the air as he illustrates his point on how there was way too much current for such simplistic resisters. *Amateur.*

"Not a thing, huh?" Kriss steps next to Nick and uncrosses her arms to grab the remote. "This looks pretty new. Wonder when you made this when there was hardly enough time to work on my busted-up voice decoder, which yes, I was the one who damaged it. Then again I'd prefer to lose a voice decoder than a partner."

Nick's eyes grow wide, "What in the name of Percy Jackson happened?" Geek *and* nerd.

Kriss looks over at me and winks. "That is a secret entitled to field agents. There are some things behind the scenes never sees."

"Like what?" Nick steps back in the kitchen, his mouth agape.

"Didn't I just say it's a secret?" Kriss' voice is confident but not cocky. Whenever she talks it sounds like you're playing a mind game with her.

"But you also said that there are no secrets in this family." Nick smiles with a voice more cocky than a nerd during finals.

"Let me rephrase that: there are no secrets left unsolved in this family. I'm sure you'll one day solve it." She hands back the remote and Nick cradles it carefully. "Would you like to know something behind the scenes does see?"

"What?" Even as his hands evaluate the wellbeing of the remote, his eyes are intent upon Kriss.

She leans in close to his ear and whispers, "The dishes."

"Do I have to?" Nick groans.

"Well, it was either that or grounded from the lab for a week." Kriss examines her flawless nails nonchalantly. "Your choice."

"Dishes, here I come," Nick grumbles. "Will you at least put the remote on my work table? Who knows what could happen to it in this wet disaster waiting to happen."

"I'll do it," I offer and place a spoon in the sink next to him. Water splashes threateningly close to his precious contraption and I pretend not to notice the daggers he's sending me.

"I'll accompany you." Kriss grabs the remote as I open the door for her by inputting my birthday.

Our home is one of the most average houses (by appearance at least): single story, varying shades of tan and brown, small kitchen, small bedrooms, two bathrooms (which is *not* a good idea with two girls and one fretful teenage boy), you get the point. The major exceptions of our house are my personal office (hidden in my walk-in closet) and Nick's basement lab. Anything that's Kriss' and, therefore, off limits to us, is as well.

When we got the house, the basement wasn't finished so the dividers, or lack thereof, were really the outlines of walls framed by wooden poles. Naturally we decided the basement would be Nick's terrain for his crazy experiments. Over time he renovated by getting parts from who knows where to upgrade everything. Now the room looks like an actual mad scientist work space-not that he's far from it.

As we near the bottom of the stairs the walls transform from the clean tan color to wore down wood covered in years' worth of marks and, eventually, a metallic gleam. Rather than create a normal laboratory with added shelving and the likes, Nick built desks and shelves into the walls themselves. Even the clear glass windows provide a view of the frozen compartments and an oven next to those.

If someone were to randomly venture into this lab they would think it to be a mess. I know better. His lab is a symbol of Nick's mind itself. At first glance, the disaster of electronics and computer-generated designs appear random, but with closer observation an organized pattern can be found. At least, that's what Nick assures Kriss and me. I've never had time to waste on the kangaroo project.

Kriss and I make our way to Nick's main workbench where her voice decoder is resting. Her lips slide into a smile as she examines her poor device. It's the computer version of a dissection table. Wires and components are carefully arranged around the small box with an array of tools nesting beyond those. An outer shell, disguised as a sunglasses case, is split into three parts waiting at the end of the metal table. Kriss sighs dramatically.

"You didn't think he'd actually finish it, did you?" I place his remote in a small circle of empty space.

"Originally I knew he'd finish it. In a timely manner I wasn't so certain. Especially since I knew he wouldn't be able to stop himself from adding his own updates. Once I learned about his kart I figured it'd be placed on the backburner." I follow her eyes to a dusty cabinet holding his first major invention: a Lego maid to clean his room. My smile quickly matches Kriss'.

"The kart is pretty cool," I offer. "Some girls even attempted to, uh, flirt with him at a stoplight."

"Oh really?" Kriss' eyes sparkle like a gossiping teenager. Sometimes I wonder if she was forced to grow up too early or has never really grown up. "And how did he respond?"

"He didn't. I don't think he even realized they were there." My brother can be completely oblivious.

"Uhuh, 'course he didn't. He's not you." I warm at Kriss' compliment and turn to retreat to my room. She stops me by placing a hand on my shoulder and twisting about so we're facing each other. "Do I get to hear about your meeting or do I have to figure out what happened on my own?"

I do my best imitation of Kriss' confident nonchalant attitude and wave my finger. "There may not be any secrets left unsolved in our family, but I'm going to enjoy this as long as I can. I really want to do this on my own, ya know?"

"I do." Kriss ruffles my hair in a "that's so adorable" kind of way before warning, "But remember this is a fickle game we play, and I've been a player in it much longer than you. Meaning that other people have been playing it longer than me. So, stay on your toes."

"I know, thanks Kriss."

"That's my girl," Kriss collects her voice decoder and steps towards the back of the room. There's probably another exit I'm yet to discover back there. "And Charlie?"

"Yes?"

"I'm proud of you." My face beams brighter than the sun.

06 | That's Creepy

-Emily-

BEN: saaaave me!!!!!

ME: what?

BEN: krystal wants us to give each other makeovers!

ME: you got yourself into this mess, good luck hotshot

BEN: goodbye

BEN: if I never see u again my wills hidden in our old tunnel :'(

I can't help but laugh at Ben's unfortunate situation, even if he totally ditched me. Every Sunday before the new school year Ben and my parents would give us our school shopping money before dropping us off at the mall to buy everything we needed for the year. It was a good thing too, because Ben needed someone to explain to him that just because an entire outfit is neon that doesn't mean it matches.

Today my mom made me go shopping to get me out of bed, though it's not nearly as fun without Ben. At least he's here in the spirit, or...the texting spirit.

I pick up a purple blouse before shoving it back on the shelf.

"Yeah, not your color."

"Excuse me?" I turn to find a boy with short, curly black hair and green eyes.

"That shirt. It doesn't compliment you. Though you'd rock it in this dress." He holds up a light blue and white dress that would fall just above my knees.

"Thanks for the help." I take the dress and turn to leave.

"Third period, Whitmer bio." He blurts out.

"What'd you say?" I turn around to catch him leaning against a clothes rack on wheels. It rolls backward causing him to fall through a bunch of hangers. Spurts of laughter push through my lips as I lean down to help him up.

"Last year we had biology together during third period. Can't say I'm surprised you don't remember me. You were too busy with your famous boyfriend." At that statement, I release his hand allowing him to stumble his way up to standing.

I blush in embarrassment, I can't even remember this guy's name. I wish he'd just leave me alone. "He's not my boyfriend and never was."

"Good to know, Emily. Now I'm going to help you find some decent clothing for your sophomore year." Creepy much?

"You are?" *Not.*

"I am." I shake my head at the absurdity of it all.

"I'm warning you now that if you try to kidnap me I have nine-one-one ready to go." I wave my phone in the air as if to prove a point.

He laughs, and pulls his hands out of his pockets. "I'll be sure to keep my hands where you can see them."

"You'd better," I threaten but it's an empty threat. I

guess it could be nice to shop with someone rather than feel like a complete loser on my own. Then again, this guy could be an even bigger loser than me. Doubtful, but possible.

He looks down at my bags and asks, "What do you have so far?"

"A couple shirts and jean shorts."

He slaps his hand across his face, "you're *so* lucky I took pity upon you. You need some serious help." He grabs my hand attempting to drag me into a store but I pull away and wag my finger.

"Nine-one-one, remember?"

"Ugh, fine," he groans. "Come in here, okay?"

"Okay." He smiles and holds open the door of H&M thus beginning our shopping adventure.

We go through shirts, skirts, shorts, pants, dresses; if you can name it I tried it. I don't think I've ever spent such a high percentage of my back to school money on clothes. Guess I won't spend much time browsing the office supplies.

After about three hours of shopping, I can't take it anymore. "Time for a break!"

"Aren't girls supposed to like shopping?" He asks, confused. I think he's having more fun than me.

"I'm just not in the mood," I grumble.

"Fine, I'll buy you a snack."

He leads me to the food court where we buy Jamba Juice smoothies. I sip mine awkwardly, trying to be quiet. It's only now I realize how messy Ben and I are around each other. Normally we'd be having a contest to see who could finish first, or combining different amounts of our smoothies to find the perfect flavor.

I've been pounding my brain trying to figure out who this guy is. He looks so familiar, and knows exactly what to say to get me to laugh. Maybe we worked together on a bio project?

"And then I jumped off the cliff." He sighs and shakes his head. "Emily, are you even listening?"

"Mhmm, something about jumping off a cliff," I comment, swirling my straw around my smoothie.

"Okay, well it's your turn to tell me about yourself." He lets go of his smoothie and leans down on his elbows. Automatically, I pull back.

"What do you want to know?" I raise my eyebrow.

"Everything." He grins. "Well maybe not everything—"

"My name's Emily Parker and my favorite color is yellow. I love Snickers more than all else and would prefer not to talk about myself." I interrupt, spewing information like a volcano.

"I'll keep that in mind." He rubs his chin.

"Why do you keep saying stuff like that? *That's good to know'*? and *'I'll keep that in mind'*? FYI that's creepy."

"Because I want to get to know you. Everyone does. You're Emily Parker. Best friend of Ben Adams. Even your names go well together," he scoffs, shaking his head. "Anyway, if you need someone cool to hang out with beyond Biology projects, I'm there."

He must be joking. It's Ben they really want to know, not me. I'm just the means to get to him. "It's nice of you to say those things, but I've already got a best friend and we're not in bio anymore. Sorry."

"I wouldn't be so sure. That Krystal girl and him are on the cover of every other magazine. And this year's chemistry, we could be lab partners," he calmly replies as though stating a well-known fact. Maybe for him, it is. "Let me help you, what's your number?"

A part of me flinches at his words. Who does he think he is? As a thought crosses my mind a smile graces my lips. I dig around my purse for a piece of paper and he hands me a pen with which I scribble out a number.

"I'll see you tomorrow." He winks, taking the torn paper.

"Sure. Bye Creeper." I grab my bags and leave, hiding a grin. No way do I plan on wasting any more time with him.

On my way out of the mall I receive a picture of some sparkly pink nails.

ME: nice job!! Not bad for the first time! Krystal will have fun showing them off ;)

BEN: they aren't hers

ME: OH. MY. GOSH. I can't wait to see everyone's reaction at school tomorrow!

BEN: uh yah. hey I'm at the tree could u hurry?

ME: I'll be there in a sec

I rush home, throw my bags in my room, and sprint out to our tree. Ben's sitting on a low branch, swinging his legs with an uneasy look on his face.

"Do you have any idea how to get this stuff off?" He timidly waves his newly painted nails in front of me.

I smile and pull nail polish remover out of my pocket. "I thought you'd want this."

"You're my hero." He hugs me after I climb up next to him.

"Of course I am." I roll my eyes. "So why did you want to see me?"

He bites his lip, looking anywhere other than my eyes. "I'm, umm," the rest of his sentence is so quiet I can't make it out. What's going on with him? He's never been one to be tongue-tied.

"Ben, what's up?"

"I," he draws out the one sound rather than finish his sentence.

"Come on, I'm your best friend. You can tell me anything, and we both know I couldn't hate you forever. Nothing's worse than that Halloween you stole all of my Snickers." I attempt a joke.

"Okay then I'm just going to say it." He takes a deep breath and finally looks me in the eyes. "I'm moving." My smile drops.

"You're getting a new mansion?" I brush his bangs out of the way to get a better read on his clouded blue eyes.

"N-no. Well yes, but not what you think. I'm moving out of Idaho to San Diego." He covers his face with his hands.

My mouth drops open. "What? Why? You can't! I won't let you! Have you talked to your mom about this? Forget that, have you talked to my mom about this? There's no way you're serious." Cold laughter coughs out of my throat. My head drops down as a single tear trickles down my cheek.

His fingers nudge my chin upwards, but it's my turn to look away. "Em, please listen to me. I don't have much of a choice. If I stay here, then my music could come to an end. They've been saying for months that I'm a liability, and my parents..." He stops swinging his legs, wringing his hands together. I place my hand over his until he continues, "They haven't been happier in years. For the first time they've gone an entire week without fighting." Something catches in my throat as his voice breaks, "Em, say something, please."

"When do you leave?"

"Tomorrow." I lean into his chest, allowing the tears to come. This could be the last time I'll see him, and all I'll remember is that stupid cologne.

07 | Assistant

-Charlotte-

Never have I felt at such a loss. Control is the one thing I need. I *have* to be in charge. Me not being in control is like a puppy without energy: fearful and dead inside. How on earth Nick convinced me to place my control and trust in his hands, I'll never know. Though if he dares to let me get hurt I will not hesitate to roundhouse him to a time before electronics.

My face flattens as I run into a wall.

That's it, I can't take this anymore. I slide my hands up to my eyes and quickly tug at the rag acting as a blindfold.

"Charlie, you promised you wouldn't!" Nick complains as he pushes my hand away and pulls the rag back into place. "It's just for a little while longer, I won't even let you run into more walls."

"Gee, thanks," I mutter sarcastically. "Are we at least almost there?"

"Yeah." A slight breeze whooshes across my face as a door slides open. "After you." Nick places his hand on my back and guides me through the doorway. In all honesty, I would probably be better at finding my way without his help.

Mud squishes between my toes and a branch whacks my face. "Thanks Nick, you're a real help."

"Sorry about that, but we're seriously almost there. Just a few more steps." Even with the blindfold and long route to get here, I know exactly where he's taking me. Hinges squeak as he pushes open an old door. The bottom of the door scrapes across the floor causing me to cringe. You would think he could take the time to fix such irritating minor grievances. A wave of dust mites hit us as we enter the room and a damp scent sneaks into my nose. "You can take it off now."

I pull off the cloth and roll my eyes. "The shed. Big surprise. You know I have some work I need to get done today; I don't have time to waste messing around. If you want to play childhood games you'll have to wait for another day."

"The shed isn't the surprise." Nick steps to a table hidden in the back corner of this small room and whips off a table cloth. Light seems to appear out of nowhere as it gleams on the metallic objects flashing in my eyes. "This is the surprise."

Nick's smile grows wider when I carefully inspect the items. "What are these things?" My voice comes out sharper than I meant.

"Gifts. Kinda a congrats for making it this far and good luck thing. I've been working on these for a while, and I figured you'd be the perfect test subject. I mean, they'll be pretty helpful out in the field." He shudders at the mention of a field agent's work.

I pick up a small oval shaped object with a pointy bit that extends when the top is pressed down. "A pen?"

"A pen." Nick nods in confirmation then begins his sales pitch. "But not just any pen! Please notice that in addition to the button on top there is a slide on the side, ha! Slide on the side, that rhymes. Anyway, also notice how it twists off into two smaller pens as well, like so." He demonstrates by taking the pen from my hands and pulling the top one way and the bottom the other way. Even though he said that by splitting it into two parts it would become two pens, they don't look like pens.

"So, what do these do?" I ask with a bored tone to my voice. If all he's surprising me with is a pen, I really need to get back to work.

"Well, this half." He holds up a cylinder with a cap on one end. "Has invisible ink if you pop off the cap and if you push the button here a black light makes it appear. And this half is actually a camera that takes images of whatever the pen is tracing." Nick smiles smugly as I briefly allow a hint of impressment to infiltrate my expression.

Next, I grab a latex glove, like the ones worn at a doctor's office. "Put it on," Nick encourages me. When I place the glove on my hand it disappears completely by welding to the shape of my hand.

"Woah." I turn my hand back and forth. If you look closely you can see a slight glimmer of light reflecting off my hand, but that's the only giveaway. "What does this do?"

"You know how difficult it is to get a proper fingerprint? And then there are those tricky locks where you have to get a copy of so and so's fingerprint and then recreate it just to get in. Well worry no more. With this glove, you can easily scan a partial fingerprint and get a full fingerprint. I used the national database of prints and logical reasoning based on different types of fingerprints. Anyway, to scan a fingerprint just hold your thumb and ring finger together for about twenty seconds then press your pointer finger on the print."

"Nick, this is actually really cool." I follow his instructions and the glove heats up a little as I press my thumb to my ring finger. "So just by touching the print it goes where?"

"Well, you could then directly activate it onto the glove

so that the glove changes from your fingerprint to the new one by squeezing your thumb and pinky fingers together." My finger appears to transform before my very eyes twirling into a new pattern with different scratches and ridges from my own. Nick is getting good at what he does, like, *really* good. I wouldn't be surprised if he was known as the next Einstein. "Or, you can save it to this database." He picks up a thick, purple book.

When he drops it into my hands I'm surprised by how light it is and almost toss it into the air. A look of caution flares in his eyes, but he holds his tongue for once. I automatically turn to the back cover to search for a summary; a fantasy book about a poor little witch. My fingers scroll through the pages and it looks to be a normal novel. However, I of all people should know better than to judge a book by its cover.

"Turn to page one fifty-four." Nick instructs. At first it appears to be an average page describing the sisterhood of a princess and witch, but then the words begin to jump off the page. Literally. They twist and bend as they lift into the air and hover above the book changing from a child's story to a holographic database. With my still gloved hand I begin to manipulate the words moving through files and opening various websites.

"Nick, you're the best. Thank you so much!" I hug him and collect the items in my arms.

"Yeah, I kinda am. The rest are pretty self explanatory and instructions for them can be found in in the DB, I mean database." He stops me once I've grabbed everything on the table. "Hold on a second. I may be the best, but that doesn't mean I dish out my work for free."

Of course, there's a catch. I groan, "Alright, what is it?"

"In exchange for me creating all these awesome inventions and anything else you might need for your mission, I would like to be your coworker."

"You mean, partner?" He nods his head releasing laughter from my throat. "That's a good one. You as a field agent. *Ha!* Besides, this is my mission. My first one. My *own*. Thanks, but no thanks."

"I don't mean as a field agent. Charlotte, it's always a good idea to have a partner back at base for backup. What if you need help out there? I can even help come up with strategies and such for you and manipulate the cameras and please." He widens his eyes creating the most adorable face. Even though he's a year older than me, I often feel as though I'm the older sibling. I have to break eye contact when I shake my head no. "Fine. No inventions for you then." Nick holds out his hands.

A good agent always considers every option.

I look down in my arms at his amazing gadgets. These could be very useful. Nick's also right; having backup at base is a good idea. Just, why does it have to be Nick? Sure, he's a genius at times, but not at the right times about the right things. Not to mention he annoys the crap out of me. My eyes trail back toward the book...

"Oh alright. You can be my *assistant* in this case. And for the record, that's called blackmail, not surprises."

"Yes!" Nick cheers and pulls me into a tight hug. I pluck his arms from me and walk back to the house. Nick skips up next to me jumping higher and higher with each step exerting more energy than he has in weeks. I decide to test my new gloves and press my finger to the scanner using Nick's print to enter the house. It works perfectly.

When he trails me into my room I consider slamming the door on him and claiming I need to change, but he's going to be a part of this at some point so I might as well get it over with. I place the DB on my green bedspread and take the rest of the stuff to a door next to my bookshelf. It opens to my own private office.

My office is much smaller than Kriss and Nick's work

spaces, but it's big enough to hold my computer, source papers, and anything I might need for a cover. I sit on a giant ball substituting a chair and power up my computer. Nick makes himself at home by using a pile of pillows from my bed as his own couch. He leans over my shoulder staring at my computer. I push his face back with my hand. "You know." his voice is muffled beneath my fingers. "I could speed up your processor for you. Or better yet, build you a new one."

"My computer's fine, thank you."

"If you say so. What are we doing right now?"

"I'm planning how I'm going to get started on the mission today." My email pops open along with my case file.

"Is this it? Is this the actual case info?" Nick's voice is filled with excitement, and a little nervousness as he leans forward again. This time I don't push him away. "Can I read it?"

"You're going to have to if you want to work with me." I roll my eyes and print out a copy for him. His knees jerk up and down in anticipation. He grabs at the paper so roughly I fear it might rip.

"This is it? This is all she gave you to work with?" I quietly smirk as his expression drops to disappointment, but as something clicks in his brain he lights up again. "It's incredible what we're going to do with such little info. Okay, so mission goals." He pulls out a smart device to take notes. "According to the client's wishes, we need to discover the whereabouts of a man named Tom Parker. Honestly Charlie this doesn't sound like much of a case. Just a family disagreement"

"Sure...on the surface it's exactly that. But beneath? Who knows? Maybe this is a huge break for me. If I do well enough I might even get to be a part of Kriss' branch of the agency." There, I've said it. My goal and dream. People say it's a bad thing to say your goals out loud, but people are often wrong.

"Keep dreaming Miss Optimist." Nick taps a button on his screen and I roll my eyes again in order to hide my blush. "What's today's plan?"

"Using audio recordings, which I'm sure you've been listening in on-"

"Guilty as charged."

"Emily is visiting the mall. I've deduced that my best chance at finding Mr. Parker is to get close to his daughter. It's very likely that out of anyone, he'll make contact with her." I explain while Nick listens intently jotting something down on his device every now and then. "Anyway, I'll be making a trip to the mall."

"Sounds like a good plan. How can I help?"

"Well I was going to ask if you could get the mall's security system under your control, but that might be a little difficult for you." I smile at him, offering up the challenge. "Oh, and an employee outfit wouldn't hurt."

"I'm on it." Nick salutes me and marches out of the room; he's a man on a mission. On *my* mission.

Eventually I'll have to come up with a permanent cover for this case, but today I just need to fit in as an average mall going citizen. First things first: I need to hide my fiery red hair with an average brown wig, otherwise everyone would remember me. What do girls wear now anyway? Short skirts? Tight skinny jeans? Leggings? Leggings have been popular on social media so I pull a simple black pair from a hanger. Boise summers are hot, but the mall can be somewhat chilly so it wouldn't be unthinkable for me to wear a cute blue sweater. To finish off the average teen girl look I slide on a pair of tan sandals and add extra eyeliner in a swirly pattern I saw on YouTube.

I pass Kriss on my way to the door where Nick is

waiting, "How do I look?" I do a little twirl. "Did I capture the teen style of today?"

"Straight out of Vogue." Kriss winks at me and sips her coffee.

Nick looks me up and down, though I can't quite place the look on his face. "I wouldn't exactly say you look *normal* but close enough. Let's go."

I look to Kriss for help, but she doesn't reply as her eyes twinkle with laughter. "Have fun, and remember don't get caught."

Nick and I reply in sync, "We won't."

His new car is waiting out front glimmering in the sunlight. When I close the door a little too hard, Nick glares at me without comment. I don't waver, but attempt to give him an apologetic glance. If I apologized verbally then he would get a point up in the game of sibling rivalries, which I could never knowingly give up.

"Do you hear it?"

"Hear what?" I've been so consumed in my thoughts I hadn't even realized we didn't talk the entire drive.

"Exactly. She's silent. Quieter than a mouse." Nick grins at me and I notice he's relaxing back in his seat with his hands behind his neck.

"Well, this is my stop." I open the door and slam it closed as he points his hand at me. The speaker in my ear crackles to life with his voice but I tune it out. I'm in charge and he's my assistant. When I need his help, I'll let him know. A smile creeps across my lips; this could be fun.

I open the book to page one hundred and fifty-four, using my gloved hand to pull up Emily's audio files. At 10:23am her mom forced her to come out of her room. Soon after an argument of obligations ensued resulting in Emily giving in. Thirty minutes later they were exiting their house to venture to the mall. I check my watch: 11:32am. Emily should be arriving any minute now. Nick could be of use.

"Use the mall's parking lot security cameras and tell me when a silver Honda minivan with a license plate 1A 004B arrives." I command hoping he's paying attention.

"Wow, that's a tall order without a please."

"Nick." My tone is a warning within itself.

"Hey, at least I know you aren't doubting my skills." He starts to hum Jingle Bells under his breath as the tapping of his fingers on a device. Christmas music already? I'll never understand how a mind like his works. "And here it is. Just pulled in near the Cheesecake Factory. You should grab me a piece if you get a chance."

"Unlikely, thanks." Of all the stores in that section of the mall I'd assume she's going to H&M, they're the most popular in the teenage department for Boise. I hasten my speed and formulate a plan in my head. What could I really learn from this excursion?

For starters, Emily's mannerisms on her own. How people behave without others judging them can really define a person. As much as some might claim certain attributes are natural actions without any reason to define them, I've learned otherwise. A person might always tuck her hair behind her ear when nervous because she wants to enhance her senses, meaning opening her hearing up would be useful. Or a boy might scratch his head when thinking because it stimulates his brain through action. Some unconscious activity can even be caused by unconscious observations of others. That's why a child might not have the same appearance as their parents but one could still note the similarities of both people. With a little research I can use these characteristics to learn much more about Emily.

Perhaps I can also discover some more concrete details like an email or phone number. She's somehow managed to keep her information private from the internet which in today's culture is quite the feat.

H&M comes into view and I slow my pace to a more casual speed. All my senses kick into gear. This is my first major step of my first ever real mission. A shiver runs down my spine and back up. Since I first received the email outlining my task I've been shoving my excitement into the back of my mind. With every passing moment, it fought against me to resurface, but I'm good at fighting my emotions. Maybe a little too good because it just transformed into a pile of nerves and plummeted down into my stomach.

The thought of failure never crossed my mind. Me and failure don't even belong in a sentence together. Except for right now. Right now with my mind processing everything from the distant scent of salty burnt pretzel to my mixed up feelings in my stomach.

Chaos starts to creep into the back of my mind driving me to a complete stop when Kriss' words echo quietly. *One thought tips the balance and one focused thought is worth a hundred thoughts.*

Not the most poetic line ever, but it does the job. I focus on one word: Emily. Then expand that: attain details about Emily. And continue from there until there isn't any room left for nerves or excitement.

I let a sigh of relief escape my lips. That's never happened before, and it can't ever happen again. Slip-ups like that are not okay.

Finally, I enter the store. With one quick scan my surroundings are imprinted in my memory and to my right stands a girl with layered hair cascading from blonde to brown. When she turns around our eyes lock for what my watch claims to be a second: Emily Parker.

Rather than approach Emily I walk in the opposite direction towards the cash register all the while keeping an eye on her from the back of my head. Apparently, Emily wasn't the only person with back to school shopping in mind as H&M is a madhouse full of teenage girls with a sprinkle of boys. The crowd only thickens the closer I get to the register.

A smile of relief overtakes the cashier's when her eyes lock with mine as my feet continue walking in her direction.

"You're the new girl, right?" At first I want to say no way and jump out of this mess. Then my instinct points out what a golden opportunity this is.

"Yes, I am." Her hopeful expression expands to the rest of her body while her hands are working the cash register and folding a shirt into a bag.

"It's great to meet you, Bryn, especially now. Well, it's not the best circumstances for you to start, but it's a perfect break for me." She turns back to the customer and smiles offering them a good day. "Here's the crash course on cashier one-oh-one, though I'm sure you already know most of this. Since it's your first day you won't be allowed near the register but just roam about the store, replace clothing items to their proper places, and help any poor people stuck with changing room duty. Oh, and here's your nametag!" She pokes a pin through my shirt and nods in approval.

"Sounds good." I thank her and get to work. Not exactly her work. More like my work disguised as her work. But work nonetheless.

Luckily for me, everything is a mess. Not a single pile of sweaters or shorts lay untouched, so I can venture anywhere in the store without seeming out of place. Now it's time to move in closer to the target.

She's still moping about in a poor mood left over from her argument with her mother. Every now and then she'll pick up a shirt or skirt and roughly shove it back into place so I trail her from a distance cleaning up her mess. Her phone buzzes and she stops to look at it and her fingers go flying. Even her face lights up when I assume she's replying to a text message. I have to get in closer to get a peek.

I step in closer preparing to do one of the oldest tricks in the book. She shifts back without really paying attention as I walk forward causing her to stumble giving me the perfect opportunity to catch her. As I help her regain her balance I catch a look at her phone; Ben's name is at the top of her screen with an emoji sticking its tongue out. In the split second I get, I read the texts summarizing that he's the reason she's alone today. I save this information in a part of my brain to examine later.

"I'm sorry," Emily comments once we're both returned to stable positions. I find this somewhat funny as it was my fault the collision occurred and I would never apologize about something that wasn't my fault.

"It's no problem at all." I remember my cover as an H&M employee and quickly jump back into the role. "Is there anything I can help you with? It's only my first day, but I'll be happy to help you in any way necessary." I'd assume that if it really were my first day I would attempt to explain my mishap using the first day on the job excuse.

"Oh, I'm okay. I mean I'm just browsing, thanks though." She's obviously trying to end the conversation so I step back.

"Okay! You know where to find me if you need any help." I flash her a Disney approved smile and head to the changing rooms.

With one hand I slip my nametag into my pocket and with the other I grab an array of shirts. Surprisingly there's only one or two people in line to try something on and a robust worker quickly makes work of getting everyone to an appropriate changing room. When it's my turn he asks, "How many clothing items?" I hold up my three shirts in response. "Great! You'll be in this room right here." He holds out his arm like an escort. I nod my head crisply in thanks and pull the curtain silencing the rest of the world.

Before I can forget any of what just happened, I pull out my gloves and DB and enter exactly what happened including direct quotes from her text messages. Once I'm done, Nick's voice shouts in my ear.

"Did you just make contact with the target?" His voice is full of excitement. "Isn't it one of the biggest rules not to make contact with the target but to let the target make contact with you?"

"Well, for starters we kind of made contact with each other. Plus, I can do so if there's a necessary piece of evidence attainable, which there was, or if it's as a separate cover that there's a hundred percent chance of the target not recognizing you as your main cover, which again, there was. So actually I was following all of the rules." I pause with a smile. "Besides, the very first rule of being a field agent is that all rules can be bent for different cases."

"Uhuh, of course. Though your reasoning is much less than concrete I'll let it pass."

"Nick, you're the assistant I'm the leader. So, do you plan on helping me or just being a distraction?" I ask with my voice sharpened by irritation.

"Yada yada yada. What do you need?"

"Look in the DB, I just updated the case file." I give him a second to read what I've added before continuing. "From her text messages would you agree that it's safe to assume and therefore forward to my associate that Ben is close to the Parker family-maybe even a part of the family. It's a possible theory that her father reached out to him as well."

"I agree with you about all of those assumptions, especially because you're the one with training about human emotions and not me. However, if you're solely basing these assumptions on that one conversation about

Ben not going with Emily to the mall, I would have to disagree, because honestly what guy would want to spend his day in the mall?"

"A guy who's truly in love?" I suggest, but he's right. I'm a fact seeking spy, not myth making paparazzi. "If I happened to get both Ben and Emily's phone numbers, would you be able to retrieve their other conversations?"

"I'm pretty sure that's illegal." Nick rebuffs and I almost laugh.

"When has that ever stopped you?"

"Good point. But this is more than illegal, that would be violating their personal lives which I'm not okay with. Now, if you got me the phones themselves I could download an application that would only tell us when they mention certain topics. It will take me a day or two to program the app, but I think this would be preferable."

"You're right," I agree grudgingly. As badly as I want to get information back to Miss Thomas, it's more important that the information is good. "Could you tell me when the target leaves?"

"Sure, she already did," Nick says calmly and takes a bite of who knows what in my ear. I don't even bother to lecture him on his eating habits.

"What? Why didn't you tell me? Where did she go?" I collect my shirts and little number tag that the employee had handed me and exit the changing room. As I leave the store my eyes flitter to the girl who provided my employee cover trying to assist three customers at once. Poor girl, hopefully the real Bryn shows up soon.

"She's all the way in Gap now. Wow, girl moves fast. I almost had a hard time keeping up with her on the mall cams. She just entered the store so you have plenty of time to catch up. Wait, don't you have to stay out of sight now? Otherwise she'll see you and be all like 'wait, aren't you an H&M employee'?" I roll my eyes at Nick's naivety. Obviously, I can't approach her again. That would create a lasting memory which could be the downfall of this entire case.

"Nick." I raise my voice as though I'm talking to a baby. "Since I have no intention of blowing my cover I clearly can't talk to her. Today's mostly about *observing*. Do you understand?" He doesn't even bother to respond which only makes me laugh harder. If you don't laugh at your own jokes, then who will?

At least Nick's info was correct. I walk into Gap and stand next to a row of sweatshirts in front of a mirror with Emily showing clearly in the reflection. When she picks up an ugly maroon purple I can't help but think we have *very* different clothing taste. Unless my cover was an elderly blind lady I would never wear a shirt like that.

Apparently, I'm not the only one watching her. A handsome dark-haired boy steps up behind Emily with a dress as cautiously as if he were nearing a bomb. Interesting. Are they friends? No. Emily proves they're not friends when she jumps around in shock and looks him up and down. She pulls out her phone and waves her arm towards him in a supposedly threatening manner (truthfully, she looks like a three year old trying to boss her parents around). Things become even more interesting when this mysterious boy leads Emily out of Gap. He attempts to grab her hand, but Emily quickly pulls away with a glare.

"Nick, do we have a mike on the target? And do you know who just talked to her?"

"Unless you recently hooked up a bug on the target, which you unfortunately didn't, we have no audio. Now this boy, his name is Zack Albert Taylor by the way, has attended the same school as the target since fifth grade. They had all of their elementary school classes together and every elective. Even a few core classes. That's one reason I'm surprised she acted as though they'd never even met."

"Sounds like a classic Gale and Katniss."

"What?" No modern culture at all.

"*Hunger games*? He probably has had a secret crush on her for the longest time, but she's been blind to it. In fact, she hasn't even noticed who he was."

"Oh, yeah. I can only imagine what that would feel like."

The more stores they stop by the more relaxed Emily becomes. Zack does most of the talking filling their time with what appears to be jokes and sarcasm only supporting my theory. Luckily for her, he saves her wardrobe choices and seems to be enjoying shopping more than Emily herself.

I walk past the couple keeping a decent distance between us with my eyes trained on the floor ahead of me. For once Zack isn't making a smart remark, but offering to take Emily out for a smoothie. She nods her head in agreement and I slip out to the front of the store. I don't need to watch them in line; I've seen enough today to get a great grip on both of their personalities.

Emily: a strong-willed girl who hasn't been subjected to real life, except for some unfortunate circumstances. She's been living in her own little world with her family and Ben. One of her biggest fears is being alone. Very innocent.

Zack: also stubborn and sarcastic. He's very charismatic and athletic, the kind of boy that's naturally popular. Even though one would think they'd know him, I doubt they would. He's the type of person to keep everything internal and only reveal his true self if on accident. The person he wants you to see is a carefree, hardcore jock.

This boy could bring an entirely new part to the case if

I play my cards correctly.

They finally make it out of the store and I walk past their backs sliding my hand across the bottom rims of both their shirts placing the bugs. Neither one even bothers to look back at me. "Nick, open up lines A-1 and A-2."

"Did you seriously just mike them? Sweet. You could probably come back now and we could listen to it together." Nick's voice is practically pleading. I want to keep up with the surveillance, but I also feel bad for Nick. He's been sitting in a car all alone for hours just to help me.

"Fine, it could be nice to get a second set of ears." Kindness sibling point for me and the score is 1-0 with me in the lead.

I sadly watch Emily and Zack make their way to the cafeteria before returning to Nick. Sure enough, Nick's so bored he's simply sitting there blowing a tape roll back and forth. One time he inhales a little too hard and it rolls back into his mouth resulting in him coughing it back up. I choose this moment to enter the car which only makes his cheeks grow an even brighter shade of red.

"How's the audio going?"

"Boring, as you can see, er, hear." He turns up the volume and Zack's voice echoes around the car.

"What did I miss?"

"Nothing at all. Literally all that's happened is Zack reminiscing about their old Biology projects. They weren't even good projects. Like I never took Biology, but I could still have topped their projects."

Zack's voice grows louder as he says, "And then I jumped off a cliff."

"Bio projects, huh?" I raise an eyebrow at Nick, and he shrugs in response.

"Emily are you even listening?"

"Mhmm, something about jumping off a cliff," Emily

replies.

"Okay, well it's your turn to tell me about yourself." Zack turns the tables. Nick and I share a look: this is perfect!

"What do you want to know?" Emily sounds defensive, but that's nothing new.

"Everything." Zack tries to backtrack. "Well maybe not *everything*-"

"My name's Emily Parker and my favorite color is yellow. I love Snickers more than all else and would prefer not to talk about myself."

"Sassy," Nick comments with a smile.

"Shhh." I glare at Nick fighting back my own smile.

"I'll keep that in mind," Zack continues.

"Why do you keep saying stuff like that? *'That's good to know'*? and *'I'll keep that in mind'*? FYI, that's creepy."

"Because I want to get to know you. Everyone does. You're Emily Parker. Best friend of Ben Adams. Even your names go well together. Anyway, if you need someone cool to hang out with beyond Biology projects, I'm there." Somebody's not cocky at all.

"It's nice of you to say those things, but I've already got a best friend and we're not in bio anymore. Sorry." Nick turns to me and mouths *sassy*.

"I wouldn't be so sure. That Krystal girl and him are on the cover of every other magazine. And this year's chemistry, we could be lab partners." Zack's voice remains even, though I bet that comment stung. He's good at keeping his cool, could make a good agent.

"Maybe. Anyway, I have to go. Thanks for the smoothie and help."

"I'll see you tomorrow."

"*Sure.* Bye Creeper." The conversation clicks to an end as Nick silences Zack's line and turns down Emily's.

Nick shifts the car into drive without a word. The drive

back is quiet since I'm entering everything we learned into the DB occasionally asking for his opinion. Mostly Nick just agrees with me rarely adding in his own thoughts. We wait in our driveway for a second so I can finish a sentence when the speakers crackle with sounds.

"Do you have any idea how to get this stuff off?" It's a male voice, though more distant.

"I thought you'd want this," Emily replies. Nick shoots me a confused look.

"Emily must be meeting Ben after the nail polish incident," I explain.

"You're my hero!" Ben's voice returns.

"Of course I am. So why did you want to see me?"

"I'm, umm." Ben doesn't finish his sentence. Nick looks to me with expectation of my irritation. I hate it when people mumble. It shows a weakness in character in my opinion.

"Ben, what's up?"

"I..." He doesn't finish. Again.

"Come on, I'm your best friend. You can tell me anything, and we both know I couldn't hate you forever. Nothing's worse than that Halloween you stole all of my Snickers."

"This girl is great! Sassy, Snickers, what more could one want?" I roll my eyes and Nick and I both laugh, but we're cut short by Ben's voice.

"Okay then I'm just going to say it. I'm moving."

"You're getting a new mansion?"

"N-no. Well yes, but not what you think. I'm moving out of Idaho to San Diego." This. Is. Perfect. With the loss of a key person in her life, Em is going to be awfully lonely, and vulnerable.

"What? Why? You can't! I won't let you! Have you talked to your mom about this? Forget that, have you talked to my mom about this? There's no way you're serious." It sounds like she's coughing into the mike or there's some odd interference.

"Em, please listen to me. I don't have much of a choice. If I stay here, then my music could come to an end. They've been saying for months that I'm a liability, and my parents-they haven't been happier in years. For the first time they've gone an entire week without fighting." Nick looks over at me with a solemn expression I can't read. "Em, say something, please."

"When do you leave?"

"Tomorrow." Excitement runs through my body resulting in me accidentally slapping Nick in a high five attempt.

How many agents get a perfect piece of information on the first day?

I am nailing this case.

08 | First Day Alone

-Emily-

My heart broke once before when I lost my dad and sister, but Ben sewed it back together. This time I'm going to have to do it myself.

We were texting but he lost connection half an hour ago so his updates about him and Krystal have come to an end. At least his texts were making me laugh, mostly at Krystal's expense. One can only hold in beans for so long.

Even with my argument that attending school would be damaging to my mental health, mom held firm that it would be good for me. I waited for the bus (alone), sat on the bus (alone), and am now entering the gateway to destruction aka school (alone).

As I walk down the hallway I lose count of how many sideways glances I receive. With Ben by my side, I never noticed, but now there isn't anything to preoccupy me beyond my thoughts.

A girl steps in front of my path, twirling lock a of blonde hair around her finger. A bubble of gum pops between her lips as she sneers, "Where's your, like, lover boy? Or did he finally realize he's been wasting his time." I recognize this girl to be Clarisse; the ex-best friend who has a love/hate relationship with the entire school. She's great if you're on her good side. Not so much if you're on her bad. Guess which side I'm on. As long as Ben's with me she leaves me alone, but now there's nothing stopping her.

"Get over yourself Clarisse." I'm not in the mood to deal with her and her fake eyebrows.

"Get over myself, ha! He was only friends with you because, umm, what was I saying?" She's not dumb, especially when plotting your demise, but Clarisse isn't the best with words.

Kade steps in for her. "She means he was only friends with you out of pity. Right babe?" His short black hair is already spiked up in sweat. I can't help but laugh at how little he's changed. Everyone else is trying to present themselves as a new, *cooler*, version of their Jr. High selves. But all that's changed for Kade is that he finally fits in that old basketball jersey. Unfortunately, even his abs can't make up for his jerky attitude-and girlfriend.

"Right!" Clarisse smiles at Kade as though he's the first drop of rain in a drought.

"I'll believe it when the words actually come out of her mouth," I retort, motioning in her direction.

"That's why I'm-" She begins to finish her sentence, but I'm already walking away. I don't need this.

"Look at his funny ears!"

"And did you even hear his high voice?" Their words succumbed to chirps of laughter.

"It's not funny. He's nice and smart and sometimes funny, but only when he tries to be." They just cackled harder so I walked up and kicked them.

"Thanks," he whimpered quietly as they stalked away.

"That's what I'm here for." I smiled, wrapping an arm over his shoulder. Looks like it was time for me to get some new friends.

My memory fades as I walk away. It's been a long time since second grade. No one would dare laugh at Ben's voice now and his hair covers his ears. Sometimes I miss the days when things were honest rather than creeping behind people's backs with words sharper than knives.

The toe of my new shoe stubs against the edge of a desk causing me to grab my foot and jump around like a fool. A quiet snicker floats through the air to my ears and I notice I'm not alone. At least there's only one girl sitting at a desk. Then again, she has her phone out with the camera directed right at me. I'd kindly remind her of our school's policy against recording without permission, but I don't need to fall even lower on the social status scale.

Sighing I drop into a seat next to the window as my shoulders slump down. I shuffle through my backpack in search of my phone, cursing the creator of dresses for not creating pockets as well. After my mom's and my argument I only had two minutes to throw on some clothes and get to the car. I grabbed the outfit on top of my pile: the blue and white dress the creepy guy first showed me. If my mom was going to force me to go to school my feet were at least going to be comfortable so I decided my new white tennis shoes would be okay. Now I'm not so sure. When I go down in flames in popularity I'll have to let my mom know it's all her fault for forcing me to go to school today.

There! I finally find my phone and power it on. Great. Just great. Since Ben and I were texting all night I only have thirty percent battery left. I battle my options of sitting here doing nothing and looking like a complete dork or using up my phone battery. The second wins. I swipe through my limited number of apps to Instagram where my notifications are blown up by first day selfies.

Using my phone camera, I adjust my unruly hair. The layers look more like a lion's mane, but I snap a picture anyway. With the new Instagram filter, I can at least cover some of my face through animated makeup.

I can't help but smile as I hit post with a feeling of

accomplishment. Even more than that, a feeling of normalcy. My phone buzzes twice as I receive a series of notifications. Ben liked my photo and commented *Good luck today! Wish I was there.* Me too Ben, me too.

The chair scrapes next to me as a groan blows out of my lips. "You again?"

"Me again. I told you I'd see you today," he says giving me a sideways grin. He props his legs up against the desk, pushing his seat back until it's on the verge of tipping over.

"A creeper and a stalker," I comment, ticking off the titles with my fingers.

"We were having some great bonding time yesterday." As if to prove his point, he reaches his arm over my shoulders. My head snaps in his direction and for a brief second it almost looks like his expression morphs into one of anxiety. He cocks an eyebrow, as if to ask for permission to continue the physical contact. In response I puff out my cheeks and throw his arm away from me. "Until I tried texting your number, that is."

I turn away, covering my laughter through the palm of my hand. "Oh, really?"

"Somehow that contact signed me up for a series of cat facts." The guy shakes his head, but continues smiling. "Took me about thirty texts to block them."

"Sounds fun," I say before turning back to my phone to reply to Ben.

Right as I duck down a tennis ball flies over my head. It bounces against the wall in sync with the ringing of the bell until Creeper catches it.

"Ball," the teacher commands, and Creeper tosses it back to her. She's tall, but looks like she could be a student herself with wavy brown hair and matching eyes. "Hello class. I'm Miss Hobs, your Accelerated English Nine teacher. I'm all about having fun, trust me, I'm the most fun teacher you'll have in this joint. But to keep that up, some of you suckers actually have to work." She walks around and hands out an assignment:

Write what you think Mrs. Hobs is like as a person using context clues from your first impression of her, her classroom, etc.

"You may work in groups no less than two and no more than two. In other words, work in partners." She smirks and pops her hip out to the side. Our class is quiet, still shell-shocked at the whirlwind that is Miss Hobs. "Well, what are you waiting for? Get to work."

"Let's get to work, partner." Creeper winks at me, already standing up.

"Who exactly do you think you are?" I ask, staying put. All around the room old friends are reuniting and new friendships are forming.

"The only other person without a partner." He's right. "I think she's a bit of a control freak. Just look at the way Miss Hobs demands the attention of a room. And her posters: *Percy Jackson, Harry Potter, Lord of the Rings, Star Wars*, definitely a geek."

"I prefer the term nerd," I mutter indignantly, but write down his comments anyway.

"Fine, nerd, whatever."

"I bet she's athletic too, why else would she have such a great arm?" I try to contribute.

"Maybe she likes to give failing students death by tennis ball?" His straight face almost makes me laugh. Almost.

"Because that makes sense." I look past him to the rest of our class. "I think we're done."

He grabs my paper and turns both of ours in. As soon as the bell rings I dash into the zoo of a hallway.

Since it's the first day of school, today's a half day and all the classes are short. Our school works differently from most; instead of having six or seven classes a day, you only have three long ones. Each of these classes count as two semesters worth of credits, and then you switch all three classes second semester. At least, that's my understanding of it.

Using my class schedule as a guide, I make my way into room 210. A maze of lab tables are set up in the back covered in who knows what, until I reach the front of the classroom. According to the seating chart I'm between Aubrey, Clarisse's friend, and Zack Taylor.

Just as the bell finishes ringing Mr. Taylor himself dashes into the seat next to me. I drop my head onto the desk in front of me. "You're Zack?" I ask without looking up.

"Yes, yes I am. Feel free to wear the name out, it was always yours to say." He winks as I turn my head to meet his eyes.

"I think I prefer Creeper." I nod my head and the teacher steps to the front of the classroom. "Creeper will do just fine."

09 | Cover: New Girl

-Charlotte-

"What's so important that you had to wake me up at." Nick pauses to rub his eyes and get a better view of my clock. "No way it's ten!"

"It isn't. My clock is four hours and twenty-eight minutes ahead. It helps me keep my brain sharp," I comment absentmindedly while slipping on some earrings. Light reflects off of the diamonds into Nick's eyes causing him to flinch away.

"So really it's five thirty-two. See? What human in their right mind would get up at this time? Or worse, force another human to get up this early?" Nick grumbles and throws himself on my newly made bed. I frown at the wrinkles appearing around his body like ripples in a lake.

"Apparently the Boise School District along with every high schooler in it, that's who. So does my outfit fit the cover?" I turn to show off my too short shorts and loose shirt that barely reveals my shoulders.

Cover: enthusiastic, optimistic ninth grade girl who just moved to Boise from Florida. Excited about everything and looking to make some new friends. Determined to have a good school year. Appearance of blonde hair, makeup and popular clothes.

"I'd say so, and nice hair dye by the way." He looks me

over once more. "But do they really allow all of that, *skin,* to show?" Nick wrinkles his nose when he says skin and turns back around onto my bed pretending to sleep with a pillow tucked under his chin. He looks like a giant teddy bear.

"Officially, no. Unofficially it's better than what most girls are wearing today." Quietly, I step next to Nick who's starting to drift into dream world and clap my hands next to his ear. I snicker as he jumps straight up. He narrows his groggy eyes at me in annoyance to which I smile innocently back. "Do you have my schedule for today? I mean, you did remember to enroll me, correct?"

"Correct, Miss Bryn." Nick holds out my papers and I quickly snatch them away.

"Bryn? Why Bryn?"

"Isn't that what your cover was yesterday? Now you have a memory to go with it." Nick smirks as though he just solved the case. In turn, I slap his arm and he recoils in pain.

"Are you kidding me? What if Emily saw my nametag yesterday and recognizes me today?" I groan. This is *not* how I wanted to start off.

"Trust me, she didn't. Oh, and you should probably stop calling her Emily, everyone calls her Em." Nick yawns. "Do you need anything else, or can I go back to sleep?"

"A ride to school would be nice. Also, make sure all of the audio equipment is set up correctly; today we need to save everything."

"Done. Just type the school's address into my car and you're gone. Make sure you don't get a scratch on her or I will personally injure you." Nick can't physically harm me, but he can create chaos through technology.

When I enter the kitchen for a quick bite of breakfast I spot a note sitting on the fruit basket.

Have a good first day Charlie! I'm sure you'll do

great, but don't forget to have a little fun as well.
Love always,
Kriss

I smile and tuck the note into my pocket. Kriss always knows exactly what to say, but she doesn't need to worry about me having fun. For me, work is fun. Being a spy and helping save people is the best thing I could be doing. Granted, this case might not be the "save the world" type, but it could be my first step into the doorway of great missions.

Carefully opening the door to Nick's car, I place my backpack in the passenger seat and type in the school's address. Within moments I'm on my way.

Yesterday I sent Miss Thomas an update with details from my short surveillance trip explaining my theories and plan of action, but she's yet to respond. Hopefully today I'll capture some information that will warrant a reply from her.

It becomes obvious I'm nearing the school when the crowds of teenagers grow. Even as they walk in crowds there are small divisions between them, and the vast majority have their heads locked down onto their phones. The smart car pulls into a parking spot right in front of the school.

Not only am I holding my class schedule, but also Emily, I mean *Em's,* as well. First period she has English while I have Spanish, which should be a breeze since I fluently speak French, German, Mandarin, and Spanish. Second period we have Chemistry together and I chose to have an open third period to get a little extra work time.

A cool breeze blows against me when the doors open so I breathe in deeply welcoming my new cover. I end up coughing as a disgusting mixture of sweat, axe, and perfume fill my nostrils. Gross.

At first the hallway is completely empty, but as I

continue to the center of the building I find the entire student body collected in the small space. I've never seen so many people in one spot. A smile splits my face as I realize how perfect this situation is. I'm literally trained for slipping in and out of crowds, this couldn't have been better had I planned it.

It's only been a few minutes but I already know the small group in the center of the room must be the popular kids. The further from the center, the further down the social food chain ending with the poor little geeks scrambling between bodies to get to class early. Confidently, I stroll toward the popular group with a smile on my lips and a skip to my step. So far, so good.

There they are: the royal couple. At the center most position of the entire school stands a girl with a tight belly shirt and white shorts even shorter than my own pulling at her hips. An arm rests across her shoulders leading to her guy with a self-confident smirk defining him even more than his baggy basketball shorts and jersey.

"Hi. I'm new here, my name's Bryn!" I stick out my hand practically bouncing up and down on the balls of my feet. To add energy to my voice, all of my sentences start to end in exclamation marks.

"Uh, hi. I'm Clarisse." She raises a penciled-on eyebrow. Her thoughts are painfully obvious as she judges me, trying to decide if I'm worth her time. Another boy walks up and attempts to grab my hand which is now resting by my side. I pretend not to notice and perk up even more by swinging my arms from side to side.

"Hey babe, you're smoking." Mentally I want to sidekick this pompous jerk back to his childhood for a quick review of manners, but I've got to keep with my cover. So instead I grin at him and step away.

"Thanks! I'm *so* excited to start school here! Well, not actual school, but, like, the social part." The tan haired jerk now tries to hook his arm over my shoulders and my hand is halfway up to his face to slap it before I chastise myself. I need to fit in if I want Em to start hanging out with me.

"Then you're gonna wanna stick with us. Unless you plan on dropping status." Clarisse's boyfriend says.

"Plus you're so hot you're only gonna fit in here." He touches my arm and pretends to sizzle. I turn away while coming up with an excuse to leave when Em enters my view.

A frown tugs her features downward and she pulls her arms in tight. To my surprise she tries to step away from this group, but Clarisse and her boyfriend intercept her escape route.

"Where's your, like, lover boy? Or did he finally realize he's been wasting his time." Clarisse smirks, drawing laughter from the surrounding crowd.

"Get over yourself Clarisse," Em growls and attempts to continue walking.

"Get over myself, ha! I'm surprised he could, umm, what was I saying?" Real articulate Clarisse. Thank goodness Em doesn't appear to hang out with these people, because I don't think I could take such stupidity for long.

"She means he was only friends with you out of pity. Right babe?" Her boyfriend finishes for her.

"Right!" Clarisse and her boyfriend smile at each other then turn back to Em.

"I'll believe it when the words actually come out of her mouth." Em retorts pushes through the group. This time they let her as the warning bell starts to leave.

I pull the jerk's arm off my shoulders and shove him away. "It was great meeting you all, but I have a class to get to."

Clarisse gives me a funny look, but no one says anything as I trail Em's path.

She walks into a classroom one door over from mine. I

want to talk to her, but I can't be late for class. Nothing good could come from drawing attention to myself. One of the biggest points of being a spy is hiding in plain sight.

Before entering Spanish I peek over my shoulder to see Zack walking into the same class as Em. His face lights up the moment his eyes focus on something. I'd be willing to bet he just found Em. That relationship might be helpful.

The bell rings signaling the start of class. "Hola estudiantes. Mi llamo Señor Juan." A male voice resonates across the room, but a small man stands up front holding a dry erase marker.

Half the class stumbles over their poor accents as they attempt to reply in Spanish while the other half doesn't even bother to reply. I can't help but roll my eyes. As Señor Juan begins to talk about our goals for the school year I slowly begin to zone out of his class and focus on my case.

Clarisse and her group have power in this school, so it would be a positive to stay in their good graces. Something was off between her and Em. Their history shouldn't be too hard to figure out.

Señor Juan dismisses us into the crazed hallway where I follow Em to Chem.

The class is called to order by a tall, wispy old man, but everyone's still standing around talking. Eventually, students begin to pay attention when he hands out packets the size of short stories. He says we can work in groups, but doesn't require it. At least, I think that's what he said his voice is nearly too quiet to hear.

I look at Em considering my options, but Zack makes the decision for me as she begrudgingly accepts his invitation to work together.

I gasp in surprise as a hand grabs mine and pulls me backwards. I twist around and see the jerk from earlier. "Partners?" He asks, but doesn't wait for my response when he turns around and flips through the packet.

Everyone seems to be working in partners, and I don't want to stick out so I follow him to the back of the room. I let him do the work of discovering the names of equipment throughout the lab while I sit back and watch Em and Zack.

"Did you get that babe?" The boy turns back to me with a white powder coating his face and light brown hair.

"Sure did, Santa." He scrunches up his face in confusion then touches his cheek with his pointer finger collecting some powder.

"I really hope that wasn't poisonous." Genuine concern leaks through his voice before he laughs it off.

"Pretty sure it isn't." I look at his packet and attempt to read his messily scribbled name. "Braydon?"

"Brandon," he corrects and continues to wipe off the powder. We're about to get back to work (me spying and him working) when a sharp crashing noise grabs our attention.

"Creeper!" Em shouts at Zack.

"What? I was just going to wipe off some dust." Zack smiles deviously.

I look back at Brandon. "Who are they?"

"Who?" He asks blankly, pulling out the next item on our list.

"The people who just dropped the beaker." I roll my eyes.

"Oh, them." Brandon rubs the back of his neck. "I dunno either of them real well. Clarisse hates Em since she stole Ben from her and Zack is more of the more mysterious type. For some reason the girls seem to like 'im." Brandon looks at me and his face drops. "Oh no you don't! Not you too. You can't like him."

"Of course, I don't." I think for a second then look back at Brandon as class is dismissed. "Actually, that isn't a bad idea. Not a bad idea at all."

Since I don't have another period, I let the crowds dissipate before leaving school. It's strange walking around the halls without anyone else here. Less intimidating and a lot smaller.

Nick's just now groggily making his way around the kitchen trying to find breakfast. "How is she?" He asks.

"Your car is fine," I grumble letting annoyance sharpen my voice. Being in the hectic school environment is completely draining, and my day isn't over-not even close. Here Nick is bumbling around looking as though he just got up. I'd be amazed if he managed to turn on the audio equipment. "So what's going on right now with Em?"

"Her and Zack were just excused from Drama, so I thought I'd go get something to eat." Okay, maybe he did bother to turn on the audio. Surprise must show on my face because he replies. "Did you think I wouldn't do it? I have no intentions of succumbing to an early death by you. And I would like to keep my role in this case."

"Great." I grab a cheese stick and head over to our family's main office. We each have a personal computer, but the shared one contains the most storage. While Nick opens today's audio files I lounge back in a spinney chair and let my mind relax for a moment. It's not often that I stop thinking, but after dealing with hormonal teenagers all day I think I deserve a break. By the time Nick has everything set up I've almost dozed off.

He clicks open the file for a mike I placed on Em today in Chemistry. I expect to hear the rumbling of a bus and cacophonous voices in the background, but instead a stuffy silence fills our speakers. I raise a questioning eyebrow at Nick to which he shrugs his shoulders and continues scooping Lucky Charms from his bowl. If it were me eating a soupy disaster Nick would be on me in a second, but for some reason it's okay for him to eat in the office.

A sudden swoosh enters our airwaves followed by a

slight humming, not electronic, but human. Em must bend right where the mike is because a crunching sound fills my ears causing both Nick and me to cringe. "May I have this dance?" Em asks. Odd, I thought she was alone. I turn to Nick.

"Could you find the location of Em using my bug and use that to turn the school's cameras on?"

"Just a sec." He taps the keyboard so quickly I wonder if he's pushing random buttons. "The location, and the cams." All four of his computer screens display the same video of Em bending over with a gold dress pressed against herself bowing and holding out her hand.

A warm feeling penetrates my chest; she looks like a child. Em reminds me of the childhood I never had. I loved my childhood (what kid wouldn't love learning how to defuse a bomb and put it back together?). But a pang of sadness reverberates in me calling for all the Disney movies and father daughter dances I missed. Silliness was never an option for me, why bother wasting my time with something I'd never need?

An older man enters the camera pulling the scene to a close. Em stumbles backwards and tucks the dress to the side as though embarrassed to be caught. Before I get to hear their conversation my phone pings with a message.

Miss Thomas' name appears at the top of my screen. An odd giddiness spreads across my face as I open her message certain that she'll be congratulating me for my information. My stomach drops when I see what she sent.

"What is it?" Nick asks with a concerned expression.

"She sent me this." I hold up my phone for Nick to see.

Keep working. I expect something major by the end of next week. Keep learning more about Em, she's vital to this story. Don't get cocky.

10 | Gains and Losses

-Emily-

CRASH.

Light flickers off the shards of glass from Creeper's beaker accident. We weren't supposed to touch anything, just write down the names in our packets. But *nooo* Creeper just had to practice his juggling with the glass beakers the moment I looked away. He's the most infuriating, annoying, immature guy I've ever met. And the worst part is how the other girls fawn over him. all fawn over him, encouraging his antics.

"What class do you have next Emily?" He drawls.

I sigh, but tell him anyway, "Drama."

"I didn't take you to be the acting type, except for you pretending not to like me." He winks and I turn away from him.

"Why do I have to like someone?"

"Guess you-" He's interrupted by the bell ringing, "Crap. Gotta run."

BEN: how r u doing

ME: Between Creeper, broken glass, and drama FANTASTIC

BEHIND THE COVER

BEN: that bad

ME: Drama's good because Creeper's not in it

BEN: aren't u happy i made u take it :)

BEN: wait, who's creeper?

ME: I'll call you after school, we can talk then

BEN: fine but i want answers

Giggling, I slip my phone in my purse and walk into the theater. Into a person to be more accurate. "Oof! I'm so sorry I—oh." I cut off my apology when I see who it is.

"Would you, like, look where you're going. Or are you too busy texting your mom?" Clarisse and her crew snicker. "Now get out of my way!" She moves to hit me, but Kade grabs her arm. That's a little violent for just a run in, isn't it?

"I was actually texting Ben," I snap back.

"Oh, well," she tries to come up with a comeback but a confused haze overtakes her face. She ultimately decides it best to stomp off. Even her boyfriend seems to have a hard time not cracking up as she stumbles on her high heels.

Our instructions are written on the board commanding we answer the questions on our papers then sit quietly. I don't even see our teacher. There's only one question:

Where are you?

That's it? I quickly scribble down *the drama room of Simplot High School in Boise, ID,* and relax back in my seat. Like everyone else in the room, I pull out my phone and start to browse Instagram.

Most of my feed is filled with pictures of Ben, but

there's only one that he actually posted. In the picture Krystal is leaning over to kiss his cheek, but he's blocking her lips with the palm of his hand. I comment with a few emojis as a stream of words displays at the top of my screen. By tapping on them my app opens a direct message between BookLover321 and me.

BookLover321: Hey! How's your first day?

Me: Great, you?

It's crazy to think that this person on the other side of their screen is somewhere in this building. I could know them.

BookLover321: I'm doing fine. Bored. But fine.
Me: Haha same

BookLover321: Lol

BookLover321: It's only the first day and I want school to be over

Me: XD

I look around, but no one's doing anything aside from a group of boys throwing paper airplanes. Clarisse and Aubrey are using their phones to adjust their makeup before snapping selfies. Kade leans over Clarisse's shoulder, mimicking Ben and Krystal's post. Even before the end of class, everyone's out the door to avoid the end of school rush.

My mom texts me warning she's going to be about fifteen minutes late so I wander around the theater. Gold glitter winks at me from a star on a changing room reminding me of those in movies. It doesn't sound or look like anyone's around so I slip into the room. Squeaking echoes from the door's old hinges.

The room's a mess, but a beautiful mess. A variety of dresses, hats and props are scattered around the ground. I hold up a glimmering sun colored dress similar to that of Belle in *Beauty and the Beast* and search for a mirror. After shuffling my way across the room, I find a mirror toward the back. It's a full body mirror with gold swirls accenting the brim. Across the center a web of cracks stretches outwards from a knife embedded in the mirror itself. *What happened here?*

A crown rests to the side of my feet that I place on my head while I twirl with the dress pressed against me. For a moment I feel like a princess. Free of my problems. No more bad days or Creepers or annoying popular girls. All that's missing is my prince.

"May I have this dance?" I lower my voice in a begging manner and bend down upon one knee.

"Hmm, I'm not sure." My voice returns to normal for princess me as I rub my chin thoughtfully in a very unprincessy manner.

"Oh, please my lady? Never have my eyes had the pleasure of such beauty. It would be of the greatest of honors to be Em's prince."

"When you put it that way of course I have to." I stand and dance around the room to a silent song.

Slow clapping puts an end to my act. "Emily, I believe it is. You are in my third period drama, correct?"

"Umm yes, sir." I turn to find an older man. He has a small layer of white fuzz along his chin and cotton like hair. His coco colored skin is stretched tight over his tall body illustrating his many years through wrinkles. I can only imagine how red my face burns in embarrassment.

"Glad to know I have such a passionate actress. Maybe

we'll find a way to perform a play containing a princess."
He winks at me.

"Oh, I don't know about that, you don't have to change
anything for me, I mean-" My phone buzzes. "I have to go.
See you tomorrow." I sprint out the school's front doors
and into my mom's minivan.

She's on the phone for the entire ride talking to some
couple who found their happily ever after and planning the
big day. Yup, my mom's a wedding planner. While she's
chatting away about the big day, I'm just glad I don't have
to talk about mine.

Once we're home I attempt to call Ben but he doesn't
pick up, so I leave a voicemail instead.

"Hey, why aren't you answering? How was your
day? Mine was fine. Creeper is just this creepy kid who was
in my Bio class last year and found his way into my first
and second periods. Drama was weird today. Please pick
up. I don't like talking to myself. I'll tell you all the fun
details when you call me back. Anyway, I miss you. Bye."

Once I'm done I decide to check out the latest news,
and surprise, surprise, Ben's the first thing to pop
up. There are about a dozen articles about his big move. On
every single one is a picture. A picture that steals my breath
before I take it. The picture is of Ben and Krystal kissing.
Not only that, I think...I think he's enjoying it. I recognize
the little wrinkles that appear along the edges of his eyes
when he's happy.

Krystal's promise echos in my ears and I slam my eyes
shut.

Crack!

"Emily Nicole Parker, what was that?" My mom
exclaims from down the hall. She slams open the door to
find me curled up in a ball on my bed. "Oh honey, what's
wrong?"

"It's B-" I change my mind mid-sentence; Mom

doesn't need to know about my boy issues. "I just had a bad first day."

She picks up my phone and wraps her arms around me. I nuzzle my face into her hair as she says, "I'm sorry honey, but please don't take it out on your phone next time. Is there anything I can do?"

"No, but thanks." She stays a while longer before returning to her work.

I slide my finger over the now cracked screen of my phone, powering it on to see BookLover321 sent me a message.

BookLover321: How was your first day?

Me: It was fine until I saw my best friend making out with some other girl

BookLover321: Oh no! You ok?

Me: Fine now just hurt

BookLover321: I bet, I'm sorry :(

Me: Thanks but it was a stupid thing to be upset about

BookLover321: I'm always here to talk :)

Maybe I don't have to do this by myself.

11 | Sidelines

-Charlotte-

Today I need it to be perfect. Dark, worrisome circles under my eyes are not acceptable. Neither is my slight acne breakout from stress. Or my seemingly permanent frown. Bryn would have enticing makeup layered over flawless skin with an ever-present smile building up her energy. I apply an extra layer of sparkly strawberry pink lip gloss before returning to the mirror. My hands naturally comb through my now blonde hair that I spent forever straightening. It's odd seeing straw blonde instead of my vibrant red curls, and my face feels as though it's gained five pounds. When I look at my reflection it's all worth it. Not because I look "hot," which I do, but because I am the best Bryn that has ever walked the earth. Sorry H&M Bryn, but there's a new Bryn in town. Granted, I would prefer my usual kick butt look, but this works too.

It's only my second day in the field, but it needs to be a big one. It must be a *perfect* one. After Miss Thomas' negative comments yesterday I spent the entire night coming up with probable scenarios (though they became less probable as the night went on) and how I would react. My plan today is to casually bump into Em during lunch, after second period, and introduce myself as the new girl from Florida looking for a friend. Seeing how lonely Em was yesterday, even dropping her standards low enough to hang out with a creepy guy the entire day, she'll jump at the chance.

After slinging my yellow backpack over my right shoulder, I peek into Nick's room. He's rolled onto one side with his knees pulled up to his bare chest with one arm. With his other arm he's supporting his thumb leading into his mouth. A ratty old Mike Wazowski lays below his messy hair superseding a pillow. As he softly inhales and exhales a dribble of drool crawls in and out of his mouth smearing across poor Mike. Nick's so cute when he's asleep-so cute it's embarrassing. I pull out my phone and snap a picture before deciding to let him sleep.

"Cover up those-oh never mind. You're wonderful anyway," Nick mumbles around his thumb then pulls Mike in tight and twists over. Him and those computer dreams.

And I'm up 2-0 in sibling points. That kind of blackmails got to be worth something, not to mention I let him sleep in.

Letting him sleep in, however, also means I have to hurry to stay on schedule. Luckily for me, Nick left his computer logged on after a long night of going over audio and video recordings. Otherwise I'd have to type in his overly complicated password then attempt to find the correct programs. No thank you.

My fingers slowly tap at the keyboard copying the code Nick left on a sticky note in his neat handwriting. *Thank God* I stuck with field work, I am *not* a math person. A ping emits from the computer when I hit enter and all four screens subdue to darkness. Hopefully I did that right.

Kriss left me another note, only this time it's taped to Nick's control panel. He would be absolutely enraged if he saw something sticky touching his invention. I can't help but chuckle at the idea of angry Nick: jaw set as stone, angry eyes twitching back and forth, mouth moving without words and his hands a flurry.

Once I've entered the school's address I read Kriss' note printed with her curly writing.

Yesterday was a hard day, but it's only the beginning. Today's a new day and it's the continuation. So is tomorrow. You haven't reached the end yet, so the destination is in constant change. Don't worry so much. Fun. Remember?

Love Always,

Kriss

Easy for her to say. She's everything I could ever want to be. Intelligent, athletic, and most of all an experienced and sought-after agent. What I would give to have thousands of dollars sitting over my head. Even a few hundred would be nice.

I cringe as Simplot High School's campus comes into view. Almost anything sounds better than going to school. I can't believe it's only the second day.

I construct my features into a smile when I join my classmates in Spanish. A carefully drawn conjugation box resides on the board alongside a list of Spanish verbs. This class is going to be so easy I almost wonder if I'll regret taking it. Perhaps I'll switch to cooking or something at semester.

As the class mumbles along *yo, tu, ella, nosotros, vosotros, ellos y ustedes* my gaze wanders to my classmates. I don't recognize a single face aside from yesterday's class, meaning none of them are part of the popular group. Clarisse and her *chicas* are probably practicing eloquent French with lovely pastries.

I stare dumbly at a darkly tanned boy with a mop of frizzy curls bowled up on the top of his head as the class seems to be laughing in his direction.

"What did you just say, Caleb?" Señor Juan jerks towards him streaking green marker across the board onto the wall.

"Fo real do, dis class is finna boring."

"Do you think that's Spanish?" Señor Juan stares at Caleb blankly, genuinely confused. I want to smack my head against my desk.

"Are you thick? Imma speaking English."

"As an expert at both languages." A group of boys in the back of the class snicker. "I am quite certain 'finna' is not English."

"Ever heard of 'slang'?" Caleb creates air quotes with his fingers mimicking Señor Juan. That same group of snickering boys crow in encouragement.

"Would you just shut up already?" I slap my hand against my book and turn to the boys. "It's bad enough we have to come to this blasted place, but I don't need to feel my IQ drop ten points every time you idiots open your mouths."

For once, they actually do shut up. In fact, the entire class does as they turn back around to stare at me mouths agape. In an attempt to salvage my cover, I light up my face with another silly smile and blush deeply.

Señor Juan gauchely clears his throat and returns to our lesson. For the rest of class I'm the ideal Bryn student. I constantly bounce up and down in my chair and reply to all of his questions with a bubbly but poor Spanish accent and curl my hair around my finger.

I'm first out of the door even before Señor Juan excuses us with my cheeks ablaze.

Brandon saddles up next to me a little too close for my liking as we walk to Chem. Em is a mere four quick steps ahead of me and it would be so easy to just bump into her now. No. I have to wait. I have to stick to the plan.

"Dude, you're even hotter when you're yelling." Brandon pulls half of his lips into a grin while I collect the rest of our items in our packet.

"What are you talking about?" Even though I'd love to express my annoyance of him through my voice I keep it light.

"In Spanish? You totally roasted Caleb. 'Bout time too, we were sick of him thinking he's good enough to hang with us." Brandon holds up a hand for a high five, but I twirl around it grabbing a graduated cylinder. I toss it to him which he catches and writes the name.

"So, you didn't think I was too mean?" Making my eyes as big and begging as possible, I look up at Brandon.

"No! Of course not. It was great." He rubs his neck then points to me smirking again. "You were great."

"Aw thanks. Glad to hear it." I rock back and forth on my heels then pivot. "Be right back."

I have no intention of being "right back" but instead continuing with the items on the other side of the classroom near Em and Zack. It's clear that Zack's trying extra hard to make Em laugh with all his witty and sarcastic comments. He even directs some at himself, but the most Em can muster up is a complacent smile. A reddish pink color outlines her eyes giving proof to her previous crying. I'll have to ask Nick about this later. Hopefully he was up soon enough to focus a camera on them.

Eventually Em says, "Excuse me, but I've gotta go to the bathroom."

"Right. Of course. Take your time." Zack smiles at her and runs his fingers through his dark hair as Em speed walks away. Immediately Aubrey and another girl I recognize from Clarisse's crew appear next to Zack offering to help him out. He looks sadly after Em for a moment before turning to them. "Ladies."

They pull him over to their table leaving me alone. Brandon joins me with a confused expression on his face as usual. "What're you doing?"

"They had the Bunsen Burners." I shrug and casually hold up the cord.

"Oh, cool." Relief floods across his face. I would hate to have my expressions displayed so openly.

Em doesn't return until the very end of class. At first she heads over to Zack, but a girl grabs his arm and Em turns the other way. It's almost sad watching these two doomed lovers as a quiet thought tugs at the back of my mind. I push it back for later.

"You are coming to Kade's party, right? It's gonna be a blast," Brandon confirms when we're excused from class.

Seeing Em exit the classroom, I quickly reply, "Of course." And dash out after her not really knowing what I agree to.

I lose Em to the masses, but her bright blue backpack catches my eye and I zone in on her. My pace quickens as I move into the target weaving in and out of people without a problem. Six steps to go.

Five.

Four.

Three.

Two.

A hand clamps against my mouth muffling my scream as I'm submerged into darkness.

12 | A Look in the Past

-Emily-

"Em! Em wait up." I slowly turn around half expecting to see Creeper, but to my surprise I'm greeted by Kade. My frown deepens as I turn to leave though I stop when his hand appears on my shoulder.

"What do you want, Kade?" I groan.

"I was going to invite you to my party tonight." He leans over as he catches his breath. You would expect an athlete to be in better shape. "It's kind of a welcome to school type thing. Not everyone's invited so I'd prefer for you not to talk about it."

"What about, like, oh what's her name, umm Clarisse?" I twirl my hair around my finger and imitate her voice filling it with giggles.

"What about her?"

"She hates me." I say with a *duh* tone of voice.

"She hates everybody," He states blankly.

"What about you?"

"She just hates me less." Kade shrugs.

"Okay, see you there." I laugh. "Where exactly is there?"

He hands me a scrap of paper. "Here's my address and if you have any questions just text that number." He smiles and confidently walks away.

BEHIND THE COVER

A party? Me? *No thanks.*

I arrive in English just before the five-minute bell rings, as does Miss Hobs. She 'tsks' her tongue at the half empty class. "Extra credit to those of you here, as you should all arrive at least five minutes early."

Miss Hobs can't start with half the class missing, so I pull out my phone.

BookLover321: You look awfully pretty today! :)
Me: Aw thanks
Me: How can you see me?

I look around in excitement, is BookLover321 in my class?

BookLover321: On your story
BookLover321: Gotta go ttyl

Right, I forgot about that.

I lazily doodle in my new notebook. I find myself shading in his eyes before I realize I drew Ben. I really miss him, but he clearly doesn't miss me. Why else wouldn't he reply to my texts or calls?

Dimples appear at the stroke of a pencil followed by laughter crinkles near his eyes. He's wearing his soccer uniform and in the background, if you look hard enough, you can see me slide tackling Krystal. Ben and I used to play soccer every season, but it's been at least a year since we last kicked a ball around. I wish I could say the drawing were a real memory, but Krystal would never let her high heels touch dirt so I have to be creative.

"Nice drawing." Minty breath brushes against my cheek and I jump into attack mode. My hand whacks his face away from mine. "What the heck Emily?"

"Do not place your face that close to me. *Ever.*

Understand, Creeper?" I place my hand in a prepared attack position. Creeper quickly pulls away giving me my space so I let my body relax.

"Sorry, I didn't mean to invade your space," he apologizes. "It's really a nice drawing. Let me guess, that's Ben, you, and Krystal?" He squints to see all the details.

"Yup." I smile proudly at my work. I'm not a practiced artist, but it's still fun to sketch.

"Do you play soccer?" His eyes twinkle with an idea.

"Yes." I draw out the word and raise an eyebrow. "Why?"

"Soccer tryouts are this week. You should totally go!" His eyes light up with an expression so hopeful he reminds me of a young child.

"How 'bout totally no. I'd rather not give Clarisse another reason to laugh at me." As I turn to put the paper away for later, I see a black eye forming where I hit him.

"What are you looking at? Beside my beautiful face of course." He grins and whips his head causing his bangs shift across his brow.

"Nothing. And your 'beautiful face' is giving me a headache." I push him trying to look away from the bruising.

His hand covers his heart. "I'm wounded!" More than he knows.

"Get over yourself," I laugh.

Miss Hobs returns and slams the door shut as the last ring of the bell echoes throughout the classroom locking out any tardy students. "I expect you to all arrive at least five minutes prior to the start of class, got it? Good.

"Now that that's out of the way let's get started. Last night I was very entertained reading what you all thought based on your first impressions." She gives Creeper a pointed smile; I can only imagine what he wrote. "And it was nice seeing a bit of your personalities. For our very first unit you will be writing essays about your six-year-old selves." The whole class groans. "But today you will only be writing down information and outlining. The essay will be due at the end of next week. Use the papers on your desks to get started."

She leans back in her chair and turns on Pandora. While I expect some older classical music or *The Cure*, latest pop hits start playing.

The neon green paper catches my attention:

Though I called this an essay, it will be more of a short story about your life as a six-year-old. Be as creative as you want, I really hope to see where you are in writing and learn your "voice".

Day 1: write down ten memories from when you were six. Expand three of them into real scenes such as that of a book. Brainstorm how you can connect these three memories into your essay. This is a CREATIVE writing assignment.

Ten memories, that should be easy enough...

1: Super Tuesdays
2: Snickers
3: Father and Sister
4: Kidnapped
5: Broken Window
6: Box Wars
7: Bird Nest
8: Muddy Days
9: First Crush
10: Swollen Hand

"I can only imagine what some of those are," Creeper says peeking over my shoulder. His eyebrows raise as he continues reading. "Who was your first crush?"

"Keep your eyes on your own paper." I glare at him.

"You looked like you were stuck, so I was going to help you out. I am the genius in our relationship after all." He shrugs, leaning back in his seat.

"First off, there is no relationship between you and me. Secondly, what kind of 'genius' advice could you give me?" I whisper fiercely only getting angrier as he chuckles.

"Choose one that makes you laugh, one that makes you cry, and one that fills you with a lovey feeling." He cockily raises an eyebrow before turning back to his desk. "I'll take that by the way. If there's no relationship, there's no hateful relationship either."

"Uhuh," I grumble. His advice was actually helpful. When he turns I can't help but catch sight of his eye; my muscles tense at the sight of blue and purple puffing out. So much for his beautiful face.

I choose one that makes me laugh first: Broken Window.

Crystals of snow were sprinkled across his hair like sugar on a cupcake. Shivers ran through my body from the cold through my coat, mittens and scarf. Ben attempted to hide his cold to look "manly" but I knew he was freezing too. Though it didn't happen often, our parents had made us ride the bus that day. And in turn, wait for the bus. To distract myself I looked around and found myself staring at a sparkling icicle dangling from the roof of Ben's house. "Isn't that pretty?" I commented.

"Do you want it?"

"Yes!" I smiled, not thinking about how he'd get it. Ben picked up an icy rock and began to aim, "I don't know if this is a good idea..."

"Of course it is. Don't be a baby. I have good aim." The rock flew from his hand right into the window.

BEHIND THE COVER

"Oops."

"Ben, your mommy's gonna kill you!"

"No she's not," he picked up another icy rock.

"What're you doing?"

"Getting you that icicle." This time it cracked the ice cycle, and the window. He ran and caught the icicle with a goofy grin on his face. "Here it is!"

"That was the most stupidest thing you've ever done." I took the icicle anyway.

At lunch that day his mother had called us both into the office where she lectured Ben for being so stupid as to throw the rock not once, but twice. She made him, and therefore us, clear all of the driveways and sidewalks in our neighborhood of snow and ice in punishment.

Ben can't help but blush and grimace whenever icicle or snow is brought up, which has always proven to make me laugh. I'll never let him live that one down.

My next story always puts a warm feeling in my chest, though I'm not completely sure why: Swollen Hand.

We were on the bus to the water treatment center for a field trip when Ben had a great idea.

"Hey Em," he said, "do you wanna play tennis?"

"You can't play tennis on the bus silly." I laughed, didn't he know anything?

"Not tennis with courts and stuff. I mean tennis with your hands."

"You mean where you slap each other?"

"Yeah!"

"No."

"Oh, c'mon! Are you scared you're gonna lose?"

"No."

"Then let's do it!"

"Fine." Ben was a much more stubborn six-year-old than me and I knew I'd end up playing.

We both started off softly hitting each other's' hands,

then he really began to slap hard. I clenched my teeth and refused to show a reaction. My hand grew numb soon after which made it easier. After about thirty minutes my hand had lost all feeling and slipped out of his when he slapped mine. "No fair! I didn't try to move it. I want a rematch!"

"Uh, Em?" His face had a sickened expression on it.

"What?"

"Your hand, it's big'n'floppy."

"WHAT?" I tried to move it, but it just flopped down onto my thigh. Speaking of which, it was the size of my thigh!

"I'm so so so sorry Em! Do you want ice? Snickers? A kiss to make it feel better?" I made him do all three of those things. For the next week he was practically my slave while I couldn't write or eat properly and he had to make up for it all.

It always makes me happy thinking about how much Ben cared for me during those weeks. I may have gotten sick on Snickers, but what did it matter with my best friend at my side?

For my final story I choose my father and sister, that was a really hard time I always tear up thinking about. I place the tip of my pencil against the paper, but something holds me back. I shake away the feeling. I'm okay.

Not many people know that I had a sibling once. A little sister whose name was Maree. She was two years younger than me, but lots of people mistook us for twins. There was always a smile on her face, even though she had the hardest life of anyone I know. She had leukemia. But no matter what kind of treatments she had gone through she would always have a joke for you.

My father was a doctor whose job was to heal people

with leukemia, and Maree was his best patient. Whenever someone would be going through a really hard operation, she'd be right there to help them along and cheer them up.

When I was six her conditions worsened greatly. She had to stay at the hospital full time and Mom and Dad wouldn't even let me see her because they thought it would scare me too much. One day they came home with a paper. It said: knock knock, who's there? Emmie, Emmie who? Emmie. The best sister I could ever ask for, I love you. Goodbye.

I didn't understand at first, then my mom explained that this was the last thing she dictated before the operation where she died.

It was supposed to be one of those operations where it was a life or death situation with the fairy tale ending, but that's not what happened. My dad had been the doctor who operated on her, so I know it was the best it could've been and nothing could have stopped it from happening. But that's not how my dad saw it. For about a week he stayed in his room, depressed from guilt. Then he couldn't take it anymore and gave up. He quit his job, said goodbye to Mom and me, and, well, that's as much as I know.

I don't really remember much after that. All I do remember is one night when it was particularly bad and Ben was sitting there trying to get me to pull off my cover by bribing me with Snickers. After a while he just sat there rubbing my back and letting me cry. Once I finally did take off my blanket he made a promise to me. "I will never leave you. That's what BFF means. Best Friend FOREVER. I promise to always be there for you, my favorite girl."

A tear drips down my cheek. Why would I ever do something like this? I try so hard not to remember, to be the girl I'm supposed to be. I need to do something different. I'm about to throw my paper in the trash when Creeper grabs my arm and stops me.

"It can't be that bad," he says in a joking manner.

I just shake my head and place the wrinkled piece of filth in the recycling. When the bell releases us it takes me a wobbly minute to stand and go to Chem.

I promise to always be there for you, my favorite girl.

What was I thinking?

13 | Awkward Encounters

-Charlotte-

2-1 point for Nick.

Before his eyes caught mine and his hot breath flew across my ears with a harsh *shhhh* I flipped him over my shoulder onto the ground while delivering a few well-placed kicks. Even once I realized it was Nick I provided a few extra bruises.

"What do you think you're doing?" I shout, not bothering to keep my voice down. With everyone herding to the cafeteria or parking lot I'd be amazed if someone heard me. "You're ruining the mission."

"I'm saving your butt, that's what." Nick glares at me, but continues tugging me to the back of the janitor's closet.

"Saving me? From what? Getting much needed intel?" I cross my arms as I transition into a sitting position on top of him. He doesn't even bother attempting to move out from under me.

"No! Look at that." Nick pulls out his tablet and opens an app with little symbols on it.

"Okay?" I push the screen back at him and move to exit the closet. "That's great, but in case you didn't notice, I have a case to solve. Oh, and you're done being my partner." That causes him pause, but then he comes back his voice as imploring as ever.

"Charlie, please just listen to me. Something's going on. This symbol here." He stabs his finger at the screen. Now that I look closer I can see it has a map of the school with code flowing throughout it. Nick's finger is pressed down atop a circle cut in half by a diagonal line with a leaf shape inside it. "No one else should have any symbols appearing. Only you and me. This program reveals coded trackers used by agents like Kriss. She had these two embedded in our ankles when we were little." He points to a pair of glasses next to what looks like a howling wolf. I wonder why she'd choose a wolf for me. "Plus the new symbol has been following you all day aside from class time and she was closing in on you right when I got here, and I was worried."

"Nick, I'm sure it was just an overprotective parent or some guy who's obsessed with piercings. Trust me, it's no big deal. If someone were tracking me, I would've noticed by now." The symbol moves past our door and I feel Nick relax below me.

"If you say so, but I'm not so sure." I smile at Nick's concerned expression, but then remember he ruined my chance to bump into Em.

"You're still off the case after this interference. I didn't get any new information today, and don't know how I can make up for it. My client won't be happy." With all the situations, I came up with last night I never imagined I'd be trapped by Nick in a janitor's closet; this almost deserves two sibling points.

"I've got an idea, c'mon." While I'm lifting my leg from Nick a loud creak interrupts us followed by pale light.

A couple emerges falling into the room tangled in each other's arms. Nick and I turn to each other sharing a disgusted expression. Nick clears his throat, but the couple doesn't reply as they're too focused on each other. He clears his throat again, but they still don't notice. In fact, they move closer and closer to Nick trapping him in a corner. For a second I consider leaving Nick in this uncomfortable situation as payback for taking away my plan, but ultimately decide to be a good sister. 3-1. "Hey Clarisse."

Clarisse jumps away from her boyfriend in surprise, then smiles at me. She looks back and forth between Nick and me with her smile growing like a vine. "Hi Bryn. Sorry, we didn't know this room was taken." She grins at me after looking Nick up and down. "Nice job."

"Oh-we're not-no." Nick's face blanches in embarrassment at the very thought.

"Thank you." I grin at Clarisse and cut Nick off. "But you can have it."

"Hey, you *have* to go to the party tonight. It's going to be, like, a blast!" Clarisse offers grabbing onto her boyfriend's arm. He doesn't even react when her nails dig into his skin. "I know Brandon was excited to invite you but, oh well." She looks around, her eyes glossing over. "You have to come to the party tonight! Even though Brandon wanted to invite you, oops. Guess I spilled the beans." Nick and I exchange a confused glance, but Kade seems unperturbed. I continue like she didn't just repeat herself.

"He did, and I will be going. Though I don't have the address, could you text it to me?" I hand over my phone and she quickly enters her contact with a heart emoji next to her name. "Thanks."

"No problem. We'll see you there." Clarisse gives me a quick hug then Nick and I make our exit.

Nick looks at me warily. "Well, that was weird," I comment.

"Clarisse or you being so...girly." I glare at him.

"You say that like it's a bad thing."

"It's just different. Nice jeans by the way-though I'm

pretty sure jeans are for over your skin." I laugh at his protectiveness. Ripped jeans aren't generally my style, but I thought it would be a good fit for Bryn.

Nick struggles to walk through the crowd tripping on foot after foot. He attempts to apologize to every person he bumps, but eventually loses track. I look away from him for a moment, but when I look back he's gone. Without missing a beat I check over my shoulder, lock my eyes on Nick's messy hair, and twist to my right around a pair of giggling girls. My hand clasps his as I pull him next to me. "So, where are we going?"

"Miss Hobs' classroom." Nick nods to the right at the B hallway.

The number of students decreases until we enter her classroom where it reaches zero. Miss Hobs has abandoned her class during lunch period leaving us free to search.

"What exactly are we doing in here? It's not too late for me to try to introduce myself to Em." I lounge back against the table group I believe belongs to Em and Zack.

Rather than respond, however, Nick walks back toward the entrance of the classroom and plunges his hand into the recycling bin. He rummages around for a bit then pulls out a clenched fist. When he opens his hand a small ball of wrinkled papers emerges. Before he can ruin this too, I grab the paper away.

Em's name is neatly written in the top right corner along with titles for each of the papers. Silently, my lips mouth the words while I read through these stories from Em's life. I don't even bother replying and tackle Nick with a giant bear hug. He stumbles back a few steps as though he doesn't realize what's going on, then gradually melts into the hug by wrapping his arms around my stomach and tucking his chin into my shoulder.

"This means I'm back on the case, right?" His voice comes out slightly muted by my shoulder.

"Yes. Yes, it does." I laugh.

"You really are taking this cover seriously, and Bryn is such a girl," Nick murmers when I finally pull away.

"Thanks...I think. What prompted you to say that?"

"Your perfume. It smells really nice." Nick's voice grows softer. He's not the best at comments. He's more of the upfront, cold hard facts type of guy. I smile back at him.

"Thank you." I let him lead us through the hallways to the parking lot now that it's mostly empty. "How did you get here? I mean, I took your precious baby."

"Kriss drove me." It would be a lie for me to say I'm not jealous. One drawback from being on a case means that I won't get to spend as much time with Kriss. I'm really going to miss her training.

Once we're home, Nick retires to the office to review video like the good little assistant he is and I flop down onto my bed. Sleep threatens to overtake my body even though it's only four in the afternoon. I'm quickly jerked into consciousness by the buzzing of my phone.

CLARISSE: Cant wate 2 c u at the party! <3

I scoff at her poor English, but respond nonetheless.

ME: Ditto :)

I do not want to go. I'd rather redo summer boot camp than go to a high school party pretending to like all these people.

My thoughts are interrupted by my phone buzzing yet again, but from a different number.

UNKNOWN NUMBER: Hey hot stuff

ME: Hello?

UNKNOWN NUMBER: You'd better be all dolled up 4 da party tonight cause were gonna be da bomb

ME: BRANDON

BRANDON: it's true u getting ready?

ME: Yah, so go away!

Rather than text me, a phone call comes through. Instantly I hit decline, but he calls again. And again. *And again.* After the fifth call I groan in exasperation and accept.

"Yo!" Yup, definitely Brandon.

"Hi. Brandon, I need to get ready, so can you please stop calling me?" I figure through the phone my voice will sound the same whether I put energy into it or not.

"Wait, I called you so you could talk *and* get ready. See? Perfect."

"Sure, I'm just not going to reply to you."

"Then I'll do all the talking. I do like to talk." I'm halfway tempted to throw my phone into the office and let Nick deal with Brandon.

Ever since Nick's comment on my ripped jeans I've become self-conscious about them, so I quickly change out of my current outfit and into a pale white spaghetti strap dress that falls down to my mid-thigh with a tan belt around my waist. Though the top part presses tight to my skin, the bottom hangs loosely around my legs. I even have matching tan sandals. Totally a Bryn outfit.

Brandon's voice reemerges from the silence of my closet when I return to my room. I guess he's been talking to himself for a while.

"After school today Clarisse was talking about how you and some guy were in a hot make out session, but I obviously didn't believe her. You couldn't have. Not when you've got a guy like me waiting to party with you tonight."

"Brandon," I start, but don't even know how to finish. Should I allow the rumor of my "hot" boyfriend? That would just be awkward. I can only imagine trying to explain to Nick that Clarisse wants to go on a double date with us.

"Yes dear?"

"It's really weird changing and putting on makeup with you talking so I'm going to hang up now. Please don't call or text me. Buh-bye!" I hit end call before he gets the chance to comment on the changing bit.

After my primping this morning, at least I don't have to worry about too much makeup. I quickly add a little more blush and call it good. Girly Bryn would use this chance to display some of her jewelry so I grab a pair of golden hoop earrings and matching chain necklace with a heart intertwined at the bottom.

I look up the address on my phone and discover the house is within walking distance. Since I didn't get much exercise today (aside from slightly beating up Nick) I choose to walk over to Kade's house.

It's true what they say about Boise; it really is a desert. During summer the heat can be unbearable for the toughest of creatures while in the winter even a penguin would shy away at the freezing temperatures. Right now we're stuck toward the end of a heatwave. So, even though it's seven thirty at night, the temperature is still at eighty-three degrees Fahrenheit. I can't wait for fall.

I'd imagine Bryn to be the party type girl, so I enter Kade's two story house without hesitation or knocking. They didn't keep this party a secret, that's for sure. It looks like our entire grade is spread throughout

Kade's house laughing and jamming out to loud rap and hip hop. I walk confidently into the main room in hopes of finding Em, but to no avail. Clarisse is again in the center of everything, but she leaves her position to take me by her side and offer me a diet coke. When I politely decline, we continue over to Kade.

"Glad you made it. And I know I'm not the only one." Kade nods his head in Brandon's direction, who's yet to notice my arrival. In a last-ditch effort to avoid his attention, I move onto the dance floor. Bryn is totally a dancer. Every time I hear Brandon's voice behind me, I move further and further into the crowd of sweaty teenagers until I find myself breaking through near the entrance.

The door opens and a small body squeezes through, looking phased at the new environment. Even with the intense body odor surrounding me and lack of space, a smile creeps across my lips. Nick puts a voice to my thoughts in my earpiece, "The target is entering the building."

14 | Searching

-Emily-

Bzzzz! Bzzzz! Bzzzz!

My finger runs smoothly over my phone's power button. This device has helped me through the hard times, but broken me even more. Should I risk answering? There's always the off chance that Ben had a good reason for not answering earlier and I could use some cheering up.

Before I can change my mind yet again I hold the phone up to my ear. "Hello?"

"Em! Oh, I'm so glad you answered, I want to tell you everything." It's not difficult to imagine his sparkling eyes and giant goofy smile.

"That's great, but could I talk first?"

"But I-"

"Seriously Ben." He must be able to hear the daggers in my voice for he stops talking. "Why didn't you answer the phone yesterday?"

"That's what you're mad about? I was preparing myself for a lot worse," he chuckles, "Rob stole my phone. He said I was 'obsessing over it'."

"Oh." *Should I ask about the picture?* "Didn't you have some huge welcome party?"

"Yeah, it was fine. Not the best, not the worst."

"Who was there?"

"Taylor Swift, Jon Cozart, and-dude, you should've seen how jealous Krystal got when Jennifer Lawrence stopped by. At one point she couldn't take the fact that I was giving Jen so much attention for her birthday so Krystal grabbed me and kissed me. The camera's got it all on tape, though they happened to miss the part where she blushed furiously later and apologized."

"Haha, that sounds a little more than 'fine'." Even I can hear the insincerity in my voice.

"What's wrong?"

"Nothing's wrong." Everything is wrong. It's not fair that those people got to put their manicured paws all over him when he was my friend and I'm left to suffer alone.

"Something's definitely wrong. Are you jealous?" I could practically see him wiggling his eyebrows.

"No. Why would I be jealous?"

"You are *so* jealous!" My cheeks are heating up, I need to change the subject.

"Anyway, I need to go."

"You're not getting away that easily. Besides, you still need to tell me about this Creeper." His voice grows hoarse when he says Creeper.

"He's just this kid who has been stalking me lately. It started at the mall when you skipped out on shopping and he's continued sticking to me tighter than glue at school since we have two classes together. At first it was super annoying, but he's the only one who really bothers to talk to me, so it's better than nothing." I leave out BookLover321, because I'm not even sure what's going on there.

"He sounds suspicious. Be careful Em, I don't want you getting hurt. And I'm sure that people want to talk to you. I mean, there are plenty of nice *girls* in your classes you could be friends with." Now who's jealous?

"Like Clarisse?"

"She's not so bad." I roll my eyes at that.

"She insults me every time we talk. Or at least tries to."

"Well, she's better than that, that Creeper." I laugh out loud at his flustered voice. He's always been a little overprotective when it came to me and other guys.

My mom's voice comes from downstairs, asking if I'm ready for the party. I shout "almost" and turn back to Ben, "I've got to go. Let's talk again tonight, okay?"

"Wait, what's going on?"

"I have a party. I really need to leave."

"Look who's popular now. Wait, is Creeper going to be at this party?" I blush at his words. "Just kidding. Have fun and I'll be waiting to hear about it. I promise Rob won't steal my phone tonight."

"Bye Ben."

"Bye Em."

When my phone buzzes off, I scan my room in hopes of finding something suitable to wear. With my clothes scattered across my bed, floor and every other imaginable surface I'm lucky to find a pair of nice white pants and cute ocean blue top. I think Creeper picked this outfit out for me.

"You look very pretty," my mom comments on my way out the door.

"Thank you." I smile and give her a quick hug before leaving.

It doesn't take long to find Kade's house. A line of parked cars leads the way to a house with music pouring out the doors and windows. I look down at the paper in my hands to double check the address, and sure enough, I'm here. Shadows move across the dimly lit windows and a small crowd of teens are flowing in and out of the door.

"Um, excuse me." I politely try to push past a pair of girls joined at the hip. They don't notice me, but move just enough that I can squeeze through a small crack in the door.

The atmosphere hits me like a brick wall the second I enter the house stopping me in my tracks. For a second, it's too overwhelming and my senses shut down. A moist texture to the air breaks me from my trance in a shiver of disgust. There's a reason I don't go to these things.

I scoot away from the masses into a more secluded corner and pull out my phone. It's only now that I see our error: BookLover321 and I hadn't set a meeting place.

Me: Are you here?

BookLover321: Yes

Me: Where should we meet?

I tap my foot against the ground waiting for a response. A familiar scent enters my nose making me to look up. Kade's dark eyes meet my own. "Welcome to the party."

"Thanks." I glance around at what looks like our entire graduating class. "I thought this was supposed to be a smaller party?"

"When word gets out, word gets out," Kade says with a shrug. He doesn't look concerned. A boy I don't recognize stumbles into us, then looks up with a dazed expression.

"My man!" He mumbles, doing one of those guy handshakes with Kade. "Blowing party, dude."

"Thanks," Kade chuckles, righting the boy and sending him on his way. "You don't look like you're having much fun."

"I'm just looking for someone." I wrap my arms around myself like that will somehow protect me from all the commotion going on. If only Ben were here, he's better in these social situations.

"Who? Maybe I can help you find them." Kade looks like he's genuinely interested.

"I'm fine, but thank you." Kade and I have had classes together for as long as I can remember, but we never got to know each other. The extent of our relationship was a fifth-grade sleepover where Clarisse admitted her first crush. No one was allowed to go near him; Kade was Clarisse's property.

"If you need anything, let me know," Kade offers and moves past me to a new crowd.

BookLover321: Meet me in the kitchen

Me: On my way

Turning around everything looks the same as everywhere else: many teens chatting, a few dancers, and loud music. Maybe I should have taken Kade up on his offer.

I push up onto my toes to see over the crowd, but remain a few inches too short. As I jump into the air, the bottom of my shoe slides against a puddle of liquid. I prepare for a collision course with the ground that never comes. Instead, my body collapses into another who in turn hits the floor.

"Hey!" A female voice exclaims, irritation evident in her voice. I pull my face away from her dark curls and untangle myself. "Watch where you're going."

"Sorry, Aubrey." I grimace at the sight of the contents of her now empty soda can covering my white pants. She declines my hand, pushing herself off the ground. "Do you know where the kitchen is by any chance?"

"Duh," Aubrey says, rolling her eyes. A look of disgust pulls her features together as she looks down on me visually taking apart my appearance. I can't help but feel like a worm being pulled at in a bird's nest. "Follow me, I need to wash off now thanks to you."

"Sorry about that," I mumble. People move out of her way purely by her glare. Aubrey guides me through a doorway and the environment calms instantly.

Excitement bubbles up in my chest at the thought of meeting the ever elusive BookLover321. At first, it looks like no one's in here, until I see her. "Clarisse?" My voice comes out almost as a shriek.

"What?" Clarisse turns around with a bored expression until she sees our appearances. "Oh my gosh, what happened here?"

"Emily here tackled me." Aubrey brings her lips into a pout, before her tanned cheeks puff out in laughter. Though there's a certain quality lacking. "Kidding! There was just a little dancing incident."

"Oh," Clarisse murmurs, raising an eyebrow. Aubrey shakes her head in a way I can't read as Clarisse dampens a paper towel. They communicate without saying anything, just like Ben and I do. We wouldn't even have to look at each other. As they turn away I pull out my phone and shoot a message to BookLover321 asking where they are.

Centered in a conversation founded on laughter, Clarisse and Aubrey return to the main room quickly forgetting the girl who jumped out of the background. At least, I hope so.

A part of me wants to stare at my screen until I get a response, but the dark soda stain between my legs is of greater importance. My lips part in a groan as the stain only darkens when I scrub at it. What if BookLover321 happens to be a really cute guy? Doubtful, but possible. Even if they aren't a cute guy, what kind of person would stay to chat with a girl covered in soda?

Five paper towels and a buttload of soap later, I give up. BookLover321 still hasn't replied. Instead they left me on read and added a video of the party to their story. So now I have issues keeping online friends in addition to real ones. Go me.

Bracing myself for the trip back outside, I push through the door right into another person. "I'm so sorry," I exclaim. "I don't know why I'm so clumsy today."

"No, no. It's my fault." A blonde-haired girl looks over at me as she brushes her shirt off. She holds out her hand with a smile. "I'm Bryn."

"Em," I reply, shaking her hand.

"Oh my gosh, that was *so* formal." Bryn laughs and I quickly join her. Remembering my stain, I hold my hands down in front of my legs. "Sorry, I'm new here, and totally out of my zone."

"You're all good," I say with a grin. She's practically jumping out of her skin with all her energy. "But I'm actually on my way out."

"Mind if I join you?" She blushes, adding tone to her freckled pale cheeks. "I was actually just leaving myself."

"Sure." We start to walk away, but Bryn grabs my arm and drags me into a sprint. "What's going on?" I ask between hurried breaths.

"I'm just, er, avoiding someone." She checks her shoulder and we slow to a walk. I follow her line of sight to a boy twisting around with his hands cupping his mouth.

"I see you've met Brandon," I conclude with a wink.

"Unfortunately," Bryn groans, throwing her head back. Once we're three houses away, we can finally talk without yelling.

"So, where are you from?" I try to start a conversation. As lame as my attempt was, Bryn responds with the same energy as earlier.

"Florida. It's so different here. Like I can't get over how dry the air is, I feel like I have a perpetual cold." Her bracelets cling against each other as she flips her hand to the side to animate her words.

"Haha, really? I-" I cut myself off with a gasp. "Over here, it's my turn to avoid someone." No fricken way, he really is a stalker. Bryn and I move off the sidewalk behind a tree just as I make eye contact with Creeper across the street. Something shoots down my chest as I feel a tap against my shoulder. Bryn and I turn like children caught with our hands in the cookie jar to Creeper with his arms crossed and foot tapping against the ground.

"I was on my way to the party, but I get the feeling this will be way more interesting." He raises a dark eyebrow, amusement sparkling in his eyes.

"Aren't you a little late?" Bryn shoots back, mimicking his posture.

"The party don't start till I walk in." We continue walking with Bryn to my right and Creeper to my left.

"Maybe," Bryn starts, smiling mischievously, "if I hadn't been there."

Creeper nods in in approval. "I like her. What's her name?"

Before I can reply, Bryn answers for herself, "My name is Bryn."

"I'm-"

"I don't really care." She cuts Creeper off with a solemn expression. After a few awkward moments, she breaks into a grin. "I was just joking. Geez, you Idaho people need to lighten up."

"I'm Zack Taylor," Creeper replies. I wait for a smart-aleck comment that never comes.

"Bryn is new here, she just moved from Florida, isn't that neat?" I offer.

"Sure." Creeper nods his head. "You know, I'm surprised. I didn't think you were the partying kind of girl."

My cheeks light up an angry red. "Oh? Excuse me for not being what you wanted."

BEHIND THE COVER

"I just meant that-" Creeper throws his hands up and his expression softens.

I raise an eyebrow. "What exactly did you mean?"

"That I thought you were." His hand combs through his curls leaving them messy. "I dunno, different. Not a bad different or anything, just different."

"Oh, well, this is my stop." I gesture toward my front door and step away from the two. "I'll see you at school, I guess."

"Of course, you will." And there's the Creeper I know. He winks flashing his teeth in a grin.

"See you!" Bryn reaches over to give me a surprise hug. After Ben and I got close, I never had a good girl friend. Maybe it's time I look beyond the internet.

"See you." I wave bye, and step into the house, quietly closing the door behind me.

It might have been great meeting Bryn, but BookLover321 has some answering to do.

Me: Where were you?

BookLover321: ...

Me: I waited forever!!!

BookLover321: I'm sorry!!!! I got distracted and once i was there you weren't

BookLover321: Can I tell you a secret?

Me: Sure

BookLover321: A voice told me not to

BookLover321: I swear I'm not crazy please believe me

Me: Really?

I don't really know how to react. If she's going to come up with an excuse, she needs something better than "A voice told me not to."

BookLover321: Yes, I'm sooooo sorry

Me: I'll forgive you, but can you answer a question?

BookLover321: Yes

Me: Who are you?

Read.

15 | Music Taste

-Charlotte-

I lazily run my fingers through my hair and recline against a chair. My permanent Bryn smile is pulling hard on my cheeks, though it's finally becoming more natural. School hasn't been too miserable, especially since the homework is minimal compared to my original amount for training with Kriss.

The chair slides to the side making me jump though I land on the balls of my feet with my weight shifted to the toes in preparation. Granted, the biggest fight I could get here is with Clarisse and that's using the term "fight" loosely.

"Hey hot stuff, haven't seen you in a while." Brandon leans in next to me. I look up to see his eyes shaded by sunglasses with a baseball cap resting on his head. He's wearing a camouflage jacket over the usual athletic attire. The Charlie in me wants to scoff and roll my eyes, but I've got to step it up for Bryn.

"We saw each other yesterday." I grin at him. "What's up with the getup?"

"Oh, Clarisse. I'm going totally Romette and risk my entire social status to hang out with you babe, 'cause we're meant to be." Right. Aubrey and Clarisse were pissed after I blew them off to go see Em at the party. "Don't worry, it shouldn't last too long. They'll get over it."

"You mean Romeo?" I giggle.

"Exactly. See? You even speak my language." He leans in to hug me right as Zack walks up behind him.

"Whatcha doing Bryn?" He casually asks like we're overnight friends. Brandon doesn't look back, but drops to the floor and crawls away under the table. Zack looks at him, concerned.

"Just talking. Not much else to do in this class." I shrug and sit atop the table swinging my feet back and forth until they kick Brandon in the butt pushing him forward.

"Good point. Anyway, I came over to ask if you'd want to go visit Em after school. You guys seemed to really hit it off last night, and I thought it would be nice for her to have a little company. You know, with her one and only friend gone."

I nod my head. "Sure, sounds fun." I had considered not coming today with Em home sick, but Nick convinced me to go anyway. The bell rings and I stare at him, waiting to move. "Don't you have to go to class?"

"Not really," he shrugs, "you?"

"Nope."

"Great, we can go visit Em now." Zack turns and exits the classroom without asking my input. Then again I suppose Bryn wouldn't expect him to ask as she'd be skipping ahead of him.

"So, can you drive?" I ask once I've caught up to him.

"I can't, but my older sister can. She's a senior has plenty of open periods. I texted her earlier and she said she'd be here." He turns until his eyes land on a silver Toyota Avalon. "Right there in fact."

We walk over to the car and he holds open the door for me as though he's a gentleman. In the driver's seat sits a girl who looks like an older female version of Zack, only much prettier. Light glistens off her lips as she silently mouths the words to a post she's reading on her phone.

Zack sneaks into the seat behind her and presses his hands over her ears and she screams. She mutters under her breath before growling, "Zack."

"Hey sis! Great to see you."

"Wish I could say the same." It's funny how similar their interactions are to Nick and me, yet so different. He'd never dare to touch my head without my permission and if I repeated Zack's actions to him Nick would probably gasp or squeal. "Is this your girl you've been going on about?"

"One of them." Zack looks over at me with a grin on his face then buckles back into his seat.

"Hm, blonde hair so not Em," she muses as though thinking it over while exiting the parking lot. "Hi Bryn, I'm Enida. It's nice to meet you."

"It's nice to meet you too!" I've never heard of the name Enida, might make a cool cover someday. Though it is original and therefore memorable.

"I guess we're off to the Em's place then. Mind plugging in the address Zack?" She smiles and turns on the radio. I quickly recognize this to be one of Ben's latest hits called *Sparks*. To test my theory (I'd almost call it a fact by now) that Zack likes Em, I peek back to see his reaction.

"Can we please turn this crap off? This music's for little girls who desperately want to fit in," Zack grumbles, crossing his arms. I see his glaring reflection in the window.

"I happen to like it. He has a great voice. Plus, he used to live in Boise, did you know he was in your grade at our school?" Enida asks.

"I wish I could forget."

"He's just jealous that Em and Ben are besties," I crow and Enida raises an eyebrow.

"It all makes sense now."

"Shut up."

"Hey! I can't believe you didn't get me his signature," Enida says indignantly. "No more rides for you."

"You are the most embarrassing sister ever," Zack groans.

"I do my best," she reminds him then clicks open the car locks. "Do you need a ride back?"

"No way. Em's mom has us covered." Zack practically sprints from the car like he's being chased by the cops.

"Are you sure? I-" The door slams shut. "Well, like I said it was a pleasure to meet you. Hopefully I'll see you again."

"Hopefully," I agree and exit the car in a much more ladylike fashion. Their comments only confirmed my plan of action.

Mrs. Parker opens the door as we walk up and welcomes us with a smile. "It's so kind of you to come-"

"Creeper! Bryn!" Em steps next to her and waves excited. "What are you doing here?"

"Emily, I thought we moved pass Creeper," Zack jokes as we step into their house.

"You'll always be Creeper, what're you talking about?" She winks. For a sick girl, she seems to have a lot of energy.

"I'm going to go start on dinner, have fun." Mrs. Parker waves goodbye and moves into the kitchen. Her head pops back with a mischievous expression. "But not *too* much."

"Of course not," Zack agrees, nodding his head fervently. Em and I exchange a glance, which he catches. "What?"

"Like you don't know," Em replies. Her lips pucker together as she reaches toward her midsection. "I'll be right back."

Zack runs his fingers through his hair and looks up at me. "What should we do?"

BEHIND THE COVER

I glance around before settling on a couch. The TV is playing music, so I turn the volume up to provide Em with some privacy and pat the couch next to me motioning for Zack to sit down. He glances over where Em disappeared before joining me. As the couch sinks down I naturally slide into him, but neither of us move away. "Hello there."

Zack offers me a half smile in response. A minty scent brushes off him as he shifts over that smells vaguely of gum. "Last night was fun."

"It was," I agree. After dropping off Em, Zack walked me home and we had a get to know each other conversation. "I was worried about making friends here."

"You're doing great so far. I mean, if I'm in your life then things have to be good." My hair flips into his face as I shake my head in laughter.

"What's so funny?" A smile splits Em's face with her hands planted on her hips. She shifts her weight over and raises an eyebrow.

"Just Zack being Zack." I shrug.

"I think we've reached the limit of Zack jokes for the day."

"But those are my favorite kinds." Em pouts before breaking into a grin as she pulls a CD out of her pocket. "This was a gift from Ben, that I think you'll like." She slides it into the one of the TV players and the song plays.

"This is *Sparks*, right?" I ask with a sneaking smile I look over to Zack.

"Yup." Em nods her head and sits down next to Zack.

"Yeah Zack, what do you think?" I laugh. My chin rests upon my fist and I configure my features into an interested expression.

"It's a nice song." Zack smiles painfully at us.

"Really? That's not what you said earlier. I distinctly remember you saying-"

"Bryn, you have an excellent memory." Zack cuts me

111

off again. Em has a funny look on her face but laughs anyway.

My earpiece crackles to life as Nick's voice enters my ear. "Charlie, be nice to the poor guy." It's only now that I realize Nick has been listening in on the entire scene. "He's your ticket in."

"Don't worry about me," I reply. Em and Zack turn to stare at me with curious eyes. "I mean, er." Nick is shouting random covers in my ear to fix my mistake, but none of them make sense. "Do you guys do any sports?"

Zack continues to stare while Em says, "Ben and I used to play soccer. But, like, everyone played soccer at some point here."

"I'm one of those who actually stuck with it." Zack jerks a thumb at his chest clearly proud of himself. "Team captain on Rush. Soon to be captain on high school."

"I've always wanted to play," I say with a sigh.

"You have?" Nick asks in my ear, recognizing the truth to my voice. I shrug, hoping he's found a camera with the right angle to watch.

"Well tryouts are coming up soon, you should come with Em and me."

"I don't think I can try out, there's a reason I quit," Em explains gently. "But you should Bryn."

"I don't know about that." I don't see how this could help in my case, but it would be fun. Maybe I could explain it as extra exercise.

"I'll make a deal with you," Em starts with a sparkle in her eye. "If you try out, I'll go to every one of your games."

I shift uncomfortably in the couch. On one side, I've always wanted to try a sport. On the other, this is my chance at life. Nick interrupts me before I can argue, "Go for it. Charlie, you've earned it, and it'll be extra time with Em. Maybe even her mom." He was already to 3-3 in sibling points, but I think he deserves another one just for that. I must be losing my game.

"Please?" Em begs, pressing her hands together.

"Fine." She practically jumps out of her chair when she cheers. "Hold on, don't hurt yourself."

"Or make yourself sick," Zack adds.

"Is it bad for me to be happy? After Ben left and, well, just Ben I guess, I thought I'd be alone, but maybe not." Em smiles at me with her giant brown eyes. Her words cut through me, but maybe after this we can become real friends. I scoff at myself for even thinking such a thing. Everyone knows all relationships end the moment the case is cleared. Too bad though, she's really starting to grow on me. Zack too for that matter.

16 | The Game We Call Life

-Emily-

My mom's always been a germaphobe. Whenever Maree or I were sick, she'd lock us up in our rooms and keep us secluded. For years my dad tried to help her get better about it, and yesterday was the fruit of his work. I still can't believe she let Bryn and Creeper come over.

My alarm beeps, alerting me that it's time to get up though I've been up for hours in anticipation. Within minutes my mom's already in my room. "How are you feeling?"

"Great, in fact, I think I'm good enough to go to school." Her expression drops instantly.

"I don't think it's a good idea, you were up most of the night sick. Your body might not be able to handle it, not to mention the emotional stress." She collects trash from around my room and wet towels in a small basket.

"Mom, it's just one of those twenty-four-hour things. I'm fine." I look up at her imploringly. "I can't skip school."

"It's not skipping if you're sick." My mom stops cleaning and sets down the basket. She narrows her eyes examining me. "Aren't you supposed to be begging to stay home?"

"I found two friends, and I can't lose them. I can't lose anyone else." I look straight into her eyes as she softens

114

finally understanding. "Please Mom."

"Fine. You can go for lunch and third period." She leaves my room with the basket pressed against her hip.

Mom and I used to go to a counselor together, though I suspect it was more for my benefit than hers. After a few sessions, Dr. Thansely explained that mentally I would never be the same. That I would most likely have a challenging time with relationships and loss. A wound healed by time, but I suspect Ben leaving reopened it.

I shuffle through my closet for a few minutes, before settling on a pair of jean shorts and sweatshirt. After packing my backpack with work from yesterday, I head over to the kitchen. I sit down at our island table where a plate is stacked with a dozen pancakes. I lick my lips in anticipation growing from the enticing smell. "Mom, this looks so amazing."

"Thanks." She fills another plate with the last batch and turns off the stove. "Try one."

Not bothering with a fork or knife I grab a pancake and layer on the whipped cream. To keep from spewing food out of my over filled mouth, I give my mom two blue thumbs   up.

When she takes a bite it looks as though she's reliving an old memory, but all she says is, "They're pretty good." Mom passes me a napkin and I wipe my face off. She disappears into the pantry and reemerges with a jar of Nutella.

"We have Nutella?" I shout in surprise.

"Would you like some?" She holds it out to me which I gratefully take.

"Thanks." I scoop out a large spoonful slathering it all over my pancakes then licking the spoon.

"So, I was thinking you might like to spend the day together until I take you to school."

"That sounds great. What do you want to do?"

"I was thinking a game day."

"Life?"

"I'll clean up in here while you go get the game set up." I shove the rest of my pancakes into my mouth and head down the hall to a closet. Along the way I drag my hand along the wall humming one of Ben's and my songs. A bump pushes my hands up causing me to stop. It feels like a wire, but I can't see anything. As I move my finger along the bump, it continues in both directions all along our wall. That's weird; I've lived here my entire life and never noticed it.

We haven't had a game day in forever, and when I reach the closet *The Game of Life* box is all the way at the top resting on a pile of dusty boxes. I stand on my tiptoes, but for once Creeper was right: I am short. Cautiously, I place a foot on the bottom shelf and push down to test the strength. It supports me so I stand on it with both my feet. With one hand, I hold a shelf at my chest level. With the other I reach up and grab the nearest corner of *The Game of Life*. I tug on it and yank it into my hand. Unfortunately, I forgot about the laws of gravity and friction.

The rest of the boxes that were supporting *The Game of Life* come tumbling down barely missing me. I hop down to examine the damage. The flap to one of the boxes is hanging open, so I pull over the other flap and look inside

.This must be where Mom hid all of Dad's old things. Pictures of him are carefully wrapped and stacked next to folders. Mom's voice sounds from down the hall so I return the boxes to their original positions after grabbing one of the folders. I make a quick stop in my room and bury it in my underwear drawer where no one will look then return to our living room.

"Did you find it?" My mom asks, sitting on top of a pile of pillows. Across from her is another pile just for me.

"Yup, just a little dusty. We haven't played in forever."

I sit down and blow a layer of dust of the top of the box.

"I'm beginning to lose track of time." She shakes her head, and I notice new wrinkles around her eyes. "I'm pretty sure I remember the rules, but it might be safer for you to be the banker." She points a remote at our TV and turns on Pandora.

"Okay, but if we forget I might make up the rules," I warn her and settle into place. "What color car do you want?"

"Blue." I set up each of our cars with a tiny pink person seated in the front seats.

Neither of us are competitive so all rules gradually are replaced with our own and we completely forget about the whole winner/loser thing. My car quickly fills up with triplets and once I add in a grandpa to my family (I landed on the husband square again in my second round through) a trailer is necessary. My mom has chosen to refrain from obtaining any family members to avoid the college squares, so she's about ten times wealthier than me. Then again, I'm in debt to my grandfather character as he had enough money saved to pay me off. We've all but forgone the original game.

My mom glances down at her phone in surprise, but tries to hide it with a smile. Not trusting her poor lying skills, I pull out my own phone to discover I only have fifteen minutes left until the end of chemistry. "Mom!"

"Yes honey?"

"This was your plan the entire time."

"Spending quality time with my daughter?"

"We're going to be late," I grumble scattering the piles of money while attempting to clean up the board.

"Well, you're so late now maybe it would be best to just wait until tomorrow." She leans down next to me and collects the tiny buildings.

"Nuh-uh. Nice try, but I still have a little lunch and

drama."

"Your food is on the table. Go grab your backpack and I'll get the car going."

I want to glare at her the entire drive over, but she has a shuffle of my favorite songs playing and I don't have it in me to be angry while *Stitches* is playing. The worst I can do is leave the car without telling her to have a good day.

I enter the cafeteria and sit at my usual table in the back. The bell rings soon after unleashing a horde of teenagers. As per usual, Creeper slips past person after person making his way to the front of the sandwich line. He even winks at the older lunch lady making her blush as she gives him an extra scoop of pickles.

Normally there's a girl or two hanging on his arms, but today he's alone when he sits down at my table with a loud sigh. He rubs his eyes and groans then looks up. "Em, what are you doing here?"

"Oh, I don't know. It's not like this is my school or anything."

"Haha, very funny." He grabs my lunch bag and starts looking through it. "You know what I mean."

"I was sick, not dead." I shrug then take a couple of his pickles. "Besides, tryouts are after school today and I'm going to watch Bryn to make sure she holds up her end of our deal."

"I don't like you coming back so early." Creeper pulls out a Snickers bar and bag of pancakes.

"Gee, glad to know I'm so appreciated." I take his sandwich as payment and open my Snickers first.

"Again, you know what I mean." Creeper rolls his eyes but stops halfway through when he bites into a pancake. "Thwis iwth amathing." Soggy indigo crumbs spurt out of his mouth right as Bryn walks up.

"That. Is. Disgusting." She shakes her head and moves from Creeper's side of the table to mine. "Nice to see you again Em!"

"Thanks, you too." I turn to Creeper who's in the middle of shoving another pancake down his throat. "That is how you should've greeted me."

The bell rings causing a slight frown to touch Bryn's normally smiling lips. "I don't understand how they think that's enough time for us to not only get our food, but eat it." She gestures toward Creeper. "See what it causes?"

I crack up as Creeper tries to talk, but can't with his mouth full. "I don't suppose you have drama next, do you?"

Bryn frowns looking down at her food. "No, I actually have a free period."

"Oh, see you at tryouts then." I steal my lunch bag back from Creeper and clean up his mess while he attempts to clean himself up.

"Almost forgot about that." Bryn waves goodbye as she joins the crowd leaving the cafeteria.

I stand to join her but Creeper grabs my wrist. He instantly let's go with fear engraved across his features, but I smile letting him know it didn't hurt so he holds it again. "What're you doing, Creeper?"

"I'm going to be your guide." He stumbles out of the bench before quickly righting himself.

"Uh huh, good luck with that." I try to walk past him but he hastens his speed to match mine. "But you're not in Drama." Creeper walks with his arms stretched in front of me like a bird clearing the hallways.

"I am now."

When we reach the Drama room he steps back, allowing me in first.

A buzzing in my pocket catches my attention. BookLover321 is back to texting me again, though they still remain anonymous. I smile at their comment on my shorts being cute, but not as cute as my smile. I can't tell if they're flirting, or a supportive friend.

Hands press against my back in support and I look up into Creeper's green-grey eyes. "Are you planning on actually opening the door or skipping class? 'Cause if you're skipping I have some great ideas, like there's this movie I've really been wanting to see—"

"Of course I'm not skipping." I see his excitement change into laughter. "There, the door is open. Happy?"

"Not really, but I should've known you weren't the kind of girl to go skipping."

"Obviously." I trade my phone for a textbook in preparation for my homework. According to Creeper, I didn't miss a thing yesterday. Since Creeper is apparently a teacher's aide (TA) this class period, he's been hanging out in drama with me. Or so he says.

"You're so boring," Creeper sits backward on the seat in front of me. "Homework, seriously? Do you have nothing better to do?"

"Do you?"

"As a matter of fact I do."

Before I can ask him what, we spot Clarisse and Kade making their way to my section of the audience. Until the teacher, Mr. Matchen, steps to the front of the theater. I breathe a sigh of relief as he says, "Clarisse and Kade, sit down immediately." They look pretty gob smacked that he knows their names and instantly find some seats. In fact, the entire class stops what they're doing to straighten up.

Mr. Matchen raises a questioning eyebrow at Creeper. "And who might you be?"

"Zack." There's a defiant tone to his voice.

"Zachary what are you doing in here? I don't see your name on my class list."

"It's just Zack." Creeper glares back causing laughter to stir in my stomach. "And there must be a mistake. Check again."

"I can assure you there is no mistake and I will be the

one giving the commands, not you. Are you certain this is your class? That you aren't a TA for Senior Verde?" There's a mysterious twinkle to Mr. Matchen's eye. I can tell I'm going to like this class, even if it's off to a late start.

"I'm sure," Creeper replies, though his voice is a little less defiant and more nervous.

"We'll clear this up after class." He turns to everyone. "Here is a schedule for our upcoming play: *The Secret Garden*." A paper lands in my hands:

Friday, September 2nd: Auditions for The Secret Garden

Thursday, October 27th 7:00pm: Dress rehearsal of The Secret Garden (In front of school)

Saturday, October 29th 7:00pm: Performance of The Secret Garden (In front of parents and other guests)

Mr. Matchen waits for us to finish reading before talking again. "And here is the script for *The Secret Garden*. You all must audition for at least one part unless you plan on being one of the stagehands and costume or makeup artists. If you do plan on being a stagehand speak to me once today's lesson is complete. For the remaining week, you have time to prepare the scene for your audition."

There are only about twenty parts meaning that at least a third of the class are going to be stagehands or in charge of costumes and makeup. Since all the girls are going to want to be the main character, Mary, I decide to go with the supporting role of Martha. This is only our first play, and we still have plenty to go. I haven't forgotten his promise of a future princess play.

"Mr. Matchen!" Calls out the squeaky voice of Clarisse. "I, like, don't get it. How are we supposed to memorize all of this in less than a month! I can barely remember what I had for lunch, let alone a, oh what do you call it?"

"Firstly, I will require you raise your hand before speaking. Secondly, just worry about the lines for your audition at the moment. It will come easily after all of the practicing we'll get done."

For the rest of class I practice Martha's part with Creeper, who tells me he's planning on transferring into Drama so he might as well practice too. He wants to get the part of Dickon, the lead male, but is also going to audition for a supporting role just in case. It's pretty fun when we get into the acting, and one time he flails his arms in his audition scene where he and Mary meet with him throwing a fit, accidentally throwing his pencil across the room.

"Time for tryouts," Creeper cheers dancing around next to me.

"You know what, I think I might stay here for a while." My mind flashes back to the special room I had discovered which sounds much more inviting than the flurries of judgmental teenagers outside.

"No way. I don't care if I have to drag you out there." He looks at me daringly and I stare right back.

"You might have to." I cross my arms and walk to my seat with my backpack. As soon as I have all of my stuff neatly tucked inside, my stomach flips as my body is thrown over his shoulder. "What do you think you're doing?" I screech.

"Carrying is easier than dragging." I can hear a goofy grin in his voice. He puts me down once we're outside near the locker rooms.

"Fine, I'll go. But only because I never want you to carry me like that again," I put on my hands on my hips with a glare on my lips. I'd probably look a lot more intimidating if he wasn't five inches taller than me.

"That's my girl. C'mon, we both know you enjoyed it."

"I'm not your girl!"

BEHIND THE COVER

"That's my young woman." He winks before running off to the guys' tryouts.

I walk over to the other field and sit down under a shady tree as Coach Simmons shouts for the girls to begin juggling. I catch Bryn's eye and we exchange a quick wave before she gets to juggling. With nothing else to do but watch, I count Bryn's low bounces off her feet until the coach calls them in.

They pass around for a bit where it became apparent who has and hasn't played soccer before. I cringe every time someone kicks the ball with their toe. At first Bryn spends some time watching the other girls, then jumps into a group who knows what they're doing. She stumbles around some before getting her feet under her. Luckily, the coach doesn't spend too much time on passing.

"Separate into backs, mids, and forwards." Every time Coach Simmons talks it sounds like she's yelling. She directs the group with her finger sending two teams to the field.

Bryn takes her place at attacking mid in the center of the action with a fiercely determined expression on her face. Coach Simmons doesn't even need a whistle; she just shouts, "Go!" and the scrimmage starts.

Bryn's forwards lose the ball instantly, so she drops into a position to win it back when the other team passes it right into her feet. She begins to dribble, and blows past the first girl who tries to stop her. After faking a pass to an outside mid who is lagging far behind the play, she sprints past her next defender running at goal. She cuts her first touch in, then shoots and just like that the score's up 1-0.

My jaw drops. I thought she said this was her first time.

The rest of the scrimmage continues the same way so I cast my gaze to Creeper's tryout every now and then. Whenever I look over I can't see what's going on, only a bunch of physical plays which normally ends up with someone on the ground.

The tryout concludes with Bryn scoring her sixth goal (I think), but Coach Simmons stops her before she can leave. They exchange a few words then Bryn comes running up to me.

"I'm in! Coach said she wasn't supposed to tell the rosters until tomorrow, but I played so well she had to tell me." Bryn's grin is contagious. Her face is lit up brighter than New York on New Year's.

"Great job! Though I'm not surprised." Once she collects herself, we walk over to Creeper's tryout. "We should celebrate. Want to have a movie night at my house tonight?" I offer.

"Sure." She cheers, her voice light and bubbly.

"Feel free to come over whenever you feel like it. This is going to be fun." I try to match her enthusiasm. She gives me a quick hug before leaving.

I check my phone for messages while walking over to Creeper's tryout:

BEN: how was your day?

ME: Good, but missing you :/

BEN: let's video later, I have a surprise ;)

Before I even reach the field I'm enveloped in his arms. He smells of grass, sweat, and a lot of hard work.

"I made varsity!"

"Bryn did too." He pulls me even tighter before letting go. "Bryn and I were going to have a movie night tonight to celebrate, wanna come?"

"Um, of course!" Creeper nods.

"Great. Now you're my ride home to help me

celebrate."

"Sounds good." A troublesome smile lights up his face and he shoves me over his shoulder.

"I said never to do this to me again!" I shout into his arm.

"But we're celebrating, and I'm giving you a ride home."

When he finally puts me down I'm standing in front of a rather beat up red ford truck. He doesn't even bother to open or unlock the door until he's all situated in his seat, so I slam the door extra hard when I sit down.

Without asking permission I plug my phone in and start playing music from my Favorites playlist.

"What is this, teen weekly?" He asks as *Mercy* by Shawn Mendes begins to play.

"Don't dis my music," I say indignantly. He just shakes his head as I dance the rest of the ride.

When we get home I realize I forgot to ask my mom about the whole movie night thing, "Crap."

"What?" Creeper asks.

"I kinda forgot to ask my mom about all of this." Little does it matter though, because as soon as I walk into the kitchen with Creeper by my side my mom's eyes soften and her lips form a gentle smile.

"I was wondering if we could have a movie night tonight in celebration of him making the varsity team? Bryn is going to come too if that's okay." I cross my fingers behind my back and smile up at her.

"Of course it's okay. Congratulations! Just tell me ahead of time in the future. I'll go buy some popcorn, ice cream, and Snickers." She hugs me and whispers, "We're even now?"

I nod, and let go of her.

"Want to see my room?" I offer when the silence becomes uncomfortable.

"I feel like this is such a major step in our relationship." Creeper holds his hand over his heart and gasps dramatically.

"Drama geek," I say, shoving him.

We sit down on my green bedspread and he nods in approval, "your room's nice, and totally you."

"What is that supposed to mean?"

"Shawn Mendes and Ben Adams posters? Disney snow globes? Totally you." I can feel a blush of embarrassment heat my cheeks.

"At least it's organized." I don't tell him it's been a mess for weeks up until this morning when my mom cleaned it while I was taking a relaxing, long shower.

"Creepily so." He walks over to my bookshelf. "I'm almost afraid to touch anything." Yet he picks up a picture of my parents, sister and me I found in the file from this morning. It was right after she was born. "I didn't know you have a sister."

"I don't." I grab the picture and put it back.

"Oh." It's clear he doesn't know what to say so I step in.

"Let's find some movies to watch." I guide him back downstairs and into our basement where our theater room is. One wall my mom and I painted with a special white paint outlined in black wood working as a screen. I pull back a velvety curtain to reveal our large collection of movies.

"Woah." Creeper exhales then starts to look through them, pulling one out every now and then.

I can't help but peek at his choices; *Ironman 3, Ferris Bueller's Day Off, and Napoleon Dynamite,* "I get to pick the next three and then Bryn chooses the first one we watch."

"Fine, but if you choose Disney for every movie I may leave now." Creeper warns, touching his finger to the tip of my nose.

"Of course not," I roll my eyes, "you haven't earned the privilege of a Disney marathon with me." I pull out *Mulan, Parent Trap,* and *Pitch Perfect.*

"I sure hope Bryn has decent taste in movies."

"If she does I guess yours won't matter."

"Whatever," he says and places our selections in a pile next to the DVD player while I clean up the rest of the movies.

Upon hearing the opening and shutting of a door we return to the kitchen to find my mom, Bryn, and plenty of snacks. "Thanks mom, you're the best."

"Take care of Em here." I groan as she chuckles.

"Of course ma'am," Creeper says with a sweet voice at the same time Bryn says, "Of course Ms. Parker." They blush and look down at their feet. We carry the snacks down to the theater room.

"Here are some movies and we already decided you get to choose, Bryn." I place all six movies before her.

"If you guys insist." She carefully evaluates each title and chooses *Mulan.*

"I've been set up," Creeper complains, but he doesn't sound too disappointed.

"Who wouldn't want to watch Mulan? It's not even a Disney princess movie. It's about a girl who kicks butt and saves China." That determination and excitement from tryouts returns to Bryn's eyes, and with how Creeper's staring at her, I'm willing to bet he noticed too.

"Fine. I'll watch it, but only if I get the tub of mint chocolate ice cream."

"That's my favorite too!" Bryn exclaims.

"I guess we'll have to sit together then." He takes the mint chocolate and plops onto a large, one person rocking chair.

"Fine. I guess we will." Bryn pushes him to the very

edge and sits down in the small space. "I'm still waiting for the entire story behind the nickname. I think there's something you left out."

Creeper opens his mouth. "I—"

"He's just a very creepy guy, as I'm sure you've learned," I interrupt; I've gotten pretty good at interrupting him.

She laughs without holding back, her laughter resembling those bells from *The Polar Express*. It's obvious that she's the kind of girl who doesn't really care what others think. Creeper shoots me a glare, but I ignore it as I insert the *Mulan* disk and turn off the lights.

It's kind of lonely sitting on my couch away from Bryn and Creeper. Bryn and I sing along to all the songs as loud as our vocal cords will allow. Even though he made fun of us for it, I'm pretty sure Creeper joined in at *Be a Man*.

I finally silence my phone after its constant buzzing from Ben's video calls.

A ringing ensues and I cringe realizing I must have switched it to ring instead of silence, "I'm so sorry guys, I don't know what's wrong with my phone."

"It's not your phone, be back in a sec," Bryn chirps stepping outside. When she comes back in she says she has to go home and gives Creeper and I a hug.

The credits begin to roll and I say, "Sooo, you and Bryn?"

Creeper raises his eyebrow, "somebody's jealous?"

"As if."

"Uh huh, well don't worry. She's very pretty and I love her enthusiasm." He winks before turning back to our pile of movies. "Can I choose the next?"

"Sure." I glance at the door where Bryn left.

"*Napoleon Dynamite*."

"Fine." After I put the movie into the DVD player I join him on his couch.

BEHIND THE COVER

"Couldn't stay away?" He whispers into my ear.
"You wish," I add on, "Zack."

17 | Who Uses Instructions Anyway?

-Charlotte-

Music throbs through my ears as I jot down theories from my experience earlier today. Ever since tryouts I haven't been able to stop smiling. The rush that came with running by people with a ball back on my foot was beyond anything I've ever felt. I can still imagine the feeling of people attempting to get something, anything on me but not being able to. From my legs kicking up and down off the back of my bed to my head bobbing every part of me is filled to the brim with euphoria. Who would've thought that one of the best parts of my first case would be getting to play soccer?

My ears suddenly feel naked when the music disappears and I look up to meet Nick's rainy grey eyes. There isn't any room left for irritation with all my happiness so I just smile at him.

He looks at me like he's checking out an injured patient. "Sorry, I knocked, but I guess you didn't hear me. I came in in case it was an emergency, sorry," Nick mumbles like he's afraid I'm going to attack him.

I grin and pull him down onto the bed next to me popping one of my earbuds into his left ear and the other in my right. "This song is great, I think you'd love it."

"Yeah, it is." He shakes his head in disbelief causing the earbud to dislodge and fall onto my bed. "Bryn is really rubbing off on you, isn't she?"

"I'm just in an incredible mood thanks to you." His eye bulge a bit.

"Me?"

"Yes, you. Soccer was amazing, I made varsity in case you didn't hear, and then I got to spend the night with Em and Zack which cemented my plan." I shift into a sitting position and pull my legs up to my chest placing my phone to the side. Nick moves the DB into the cleared space and opens it up to page one fifty-four making my most recent notes to appear before us.

"I'm glad that I made you happy." He smiles at me and we share a special sister-brother moment, but it quickly comes to an end when he says, "Where am I at in the sibling points?"

"Four to three. Your favor," I groan.

Nick begins to bow in a mocking fashion. "Thank you, thank you. You may hold your applause until the end." I softly shove his shoulder and he stops with an amused sparkle lingering in his eyes. "Anyway, tell me everything and most importantly; tell me about this genius plan you have."

"Well, I'm sure you were watching my tryout somehow." Nick shrugs innocently. "And I played phenomenally well. Coach Simmons stopped me and told me privately that I made varsity while I was leaving to meet Em. Both Zack and I made varsity so Em offered to have a movie night in celebration."

"You should've invited me." Nick feigns a pout.

"I didn't know you were such a huge fan of *Mulan*." I shrug, flicking my fingers through the DB scrolling through articles. "There was some serious bonding time over Mint Chocolate Chip ice cream between Zack and me."

"And that is good how?" Nick asks fiddling around with my earbud.

"I have learned at least two things in my high school experience." I pause for dramatic effect. "First, we live in the now. Everything is right now permanent, but you and I both know how quickly that can fall apart."

"Are you referring to Easter of three years ago?" Nick asks. I slowly nod my head and we both shiver. "Okay, but what does this have to do with anything?"

"I'm getting there," I grouse and roll my eyes. "As I was saying, the moment that little social wall crumbles it's Pompeii take two, and I'm not just talking about pimples. From my research and recent experience, when a girl explodes, she needs someone to talk to and spew about. Drama unfolds and the truth comes out."

"You talk about this like you aren't a teenage girl." Nick shakes his head at me.

"I'm different."

"Trust me, I know." He pauses and I can see the gears turning in his head as he considers my plan. At first disgust is the only emotion playing on his face then his thoughtful scientific on and finally understanding. "As crazy as this sounds, I suppose it could work as long as you play your cards the right way."

"I always do." My voice is smugger than I mean it to be while coming off my happiness high. As my thumb and pointer finger move further apart in the air in the air the article clears up and I move it so that Nick can read it properly. "This explains it all, do you want a copy?"

"It's okay, I can access it now that it's saved in your history." His hand falls to his lap, drumming against a box. "I have a new invention for you if you'd like to see it."

"Of course, I'd like to see it. As long as it doesn't blow up in my face."

"It's been difficult for me to keep up with you using

only audio and there are times when we wish we could pause your memories and go through exact details so I came up with these." Nick pops open the box revealing two small half circles filled with water. "These are special contacts with video cameras and access to the DB. That means that not only is everything you see when wearing these stored inside the DB, but I can pull up documents for you to see too."

I take the contacts in my hands and shift them around until sunlight reflects off them in a way that the tiny threads of wiring are barely visible. I've got to give it to him, Nick knows his stuff. "That's really cool, thank you."

"No problem." He leans over my shoulder as I continue adding notes to the database. Using the fingerprint function of the gloves I had obtained full fingerprints for Em, Mrs. Parker and Zack through our two nights together. Now we know none of them have alternative aliases.

Mr. Parker's name pops up with about a dozen question marks (courtesy of Nick). "Did you ever find anything else on him?"

"Nope, but as you requested I have stayed within the legal and non-intrusive ramifications. If you extended my barriers, however, I might have actually found something."

"Well, if you do just don't tell me." I roll my eyes. An intense growling gurgles against my back and I snap my eyes to Nick. "What. Was. That?"

"Oh, I'm hungry." He shrugs as if this is a normal thing and reclines backwards.

"Then go get some food."

"Come get some food with me." His voice is pleading and with all the work I've put in today I think I deserve a break.

"Fine." I clean up my DB and scattered evidence along with my new contacts and follow Nick out of my room into the kitchen. "What do you want to eat?"

"Pumpkin." Nick's eyes stray to the pantry as he licks his lips. "Or cake."

"Pumpkin?" I lean down to stretch my legs after sitting for so long and see a cake mix on the floor in the pantry. "If you really want we can make a pumpkin cake. It'll cost you a sibling point though."

"Deal." He holds out his hand and I take it dragging him into the cooking area. I tie an apron over my new Twenty One Pilots sweatshirt while tossing another one to Nick. "Did you have to give me the *My Little Pony* one?" He whines.

"Kriss did get that for you. After all, you were the one who was obsessed not me."

"I don't recall." Nick looks down at the ground and hides behind the pantry door. I pull it open with one hand dangling my phone in front of him.

"I do, as does my phone's memory. Would you like to see?"

"No thanks. Let's get baking." He grabs three cans of pumpkin and tosses them to me. Each one I catch in time while juggling the others. He flings over a bag of chocolate chips and finally the cake mix, which lands on my head. I manage to balance it all like an acrobat.

Nick picks up the eggs and moves as though to throw them, but I stop him with a warning glare. Instead he gets the milk and bowl. "Where are the instructions?"

"Must've gotten thrown out with the box." I shrug. "That's okay. No one actually uses them anyway."

"Then what do we do?"

"First we wash our hands." I race to the sink before he gets the chance. After I'm done taking my own sweet time with the hot water I flick the switch cold and toss my used towel on his head.

"What now?" Nick wrings his hands out with the towel

and neatly folds it over the faucet head.

"The dry ingredients, so all the stuff in the bag. Then we stir in some eggs and milk. Lastly come the pumpkin and chocolate chips." I rip open the bag with my hands and dump the powdery ingredients into the mixing bowl. "Oh, and could you preset the oven?"

"What temperature?"

"I don't know, whatever you think will work."

"Uh, okay." He bites his lip. I watch as his hands start to move to his tablet, but return to the oven.

A plume of powder puffs into the air as I mix the flours, salt, sugar and whatever else was in that bag together. Nick brings forward the eggs and cracks them into the bowl dropping broken shells into the mix. Since I'm stirring with my hands anyway, I pull out the pieces. Crunchy pumpkin cake doesn't sound all that appetizing. The batter starts to look like actual cake batter once he pours in the milk. Finally, he dumps in both cans of pumpkin and the entire bag of chocolate chips making the batter looks like an asteroid belt. "I have an idea; what if we put in some cinnamon too? Then it would have that fall flavor."

"I like it." Nick grabs the cinnamon container and turns it upside down. Except, he forgot to check the tightness of the lid and both it and the filter fall into the mix along with a waterfall of cinnamon. "There's no going back now."

His face wrinkles up like he's about to sneeze so I place my finger under his nose stopping it. He smiles at me gratefully then both of us dig out the cap and filter then continue squishing together all the different ingredients until the oven beeps. We tip the batter into the cake pan and place it in the oven.

"How long should we wait?" Nick asks with a white timer in his gooey hand.

"Normally I think we take it out once we're done cleaning everything up. It's like a magical correlation based on effort or something."

"You just killed the science side of me." He cringes, closing his eyes.

"You're welcome." I wink and slide my finger along the edge of the bowl to gather the remaining batter. Ignoring warnings of salmonella poisoning I savor the flavor. Mostly I had chocolate chips in the taste, but I think that was for the better. Nick follows suit and an expression of joy fills his face.

"This is going to be great," he states then picks up the rest of the trash laying around. We wait a couple more minutes before pulling the cake out of the oven. It's risen and dried out proven by the cracks running along the top.

I use a knife to cut the cake into thirty second pieces and place two on our napkins. Nick and I look at each other then take a bite at the same time.

I've never tasted something so terrible. We both splutter out the...thing (I wouldn't call it food) and rush to get water. The very center was gooey, but the outside was dry as sand with random groups of cinnamon spread throughout it. Even the chocolate chips were messed up from being burnt.

"Maybe it was just the first bite," Nick says, determined to get something good to eat. He shoves the rest of his piece into his mouth but spits it all out again. Only this time, he spat it all over me.

"You did not just do that." My voice is venomous. I grab one piece of cake per hand and round so that I'm facing him full on.

"Sorry," he squeaks and backs away slowly. When I raise my arm to throw he sprints behind the table yet I still manage to hit him with both pieces. They explode like tiny bombs into the air leaving the moist part hanging on Nick's forehead and back. On his way to the other side of the kitchen, he grabbed half of the cake and is now pelting me with his own mini bombs. I quickly arm myself with the rest and use the pan as a shield.

Even with the shield he hits the top of my head and arms. Though once we run out of cake and stand to survey the damage, it's clear more harm came to him and his *My Little Pony* apron.

The door to the house slams shut and we exchange a look of pure horror. "This is unexpected." Kriss grins at us, lifting her sunglasses above her eyes to get a full view.

"Uh, we made cake," Nick offers gesturing towards the splatters all over him.

"I can see that. First, I have something to tell you." Kriss completely blows off the situation. We walk into the living room, though Nick and I stay standing while she lays across a white couch. "I'm going to ignore what just happened because it might change my mind, but that means you both have to be more responsible from now on."

"Yes ma'am." Nick and I say in unison looking down at our toes.

"I've got a job out of town and since you're both working so hard on your case I was going to leave you alone here. I know I've done it before, but this time is different. You'd be alone for weeks, maybe even a month. Do you understand?"

"We do," Nick and I say in unison, again.

"What are your thoughts?"

"We can do this," I promise, moving my eyes so that I'm looking straight into hers. "We'll make sure everything stays neat and excel in whatever we're doing."

"That's what I wanted to hear." She walks over and rubs our hair then grimaces at the cake between her fingers. "Now go clean up."

Once Kriss is gone, Nick and I turn to each other and

start cracking up. Between heaving laughter, Nick says, "Best...Cake...Ever." I can't help but agree with him.

18 | Sharing Trust

-Emily-

BookLover321: Hey

Me: Hi! What's up?

BookLover321: Just lunch like veryone else in Simplot

BookLover321: *everyone

Me: Haha, yeah guess so

BookLover321: Did you see Aubrey's outfit?

Me: CUTE

BookLover321: Eh i guess

"What's so interesting on your phone?" Creeper asks, dropping his tray onto the table.

"Just Instagram." I shrug, putting my phone in my pocket. All I've learned is that BookLover321 admitted to being a female. "Are you going to eat those sweet potato fries?"

"You can have them." He turns his tray towards me,

brushing his hand against mine, "And I need a nickname for you. If you're going to call me Creeper then I get to return the favor."

"Sure," I mumble through a mouthful of fries. I swallow before continuing, "But it has to be something original. Not 'babe' or 'bae'."

"I could call you shortie." He grins and puts his hand to his chin, "I mean you only come up to about here."

I push his hand away, "I'm not *that* short. You're just abnormally tall. I'm average."

"Hi guys!" Bryn exclaims sitting down next to me, "What's cooking?"

"Uh, what?" Creeper asks.

"What's going on? Or in dude language, 'sup bro?" She does that little hair flip thing all the guys seem to be obsessed with and we laugh.

"Now you're speaking my language, but the hair flip should be like this." He flips his hair in what appears to be the same way as Bryn.

"Uhuh," she says uncertainly. "Anyway, are you excited for practice tonight?"

"Don't remind me," Creeper mutters.

"What's wrong Zack?"

Since Creeper puts his head in his hands I answer for him, "While girls have been having fun practices, the boy have had fitness sessions. Our friend Creeper has been doing a little more eating and a little less working out than he should."

His head pops up. "It's awful. Wait, did you just say we're friends?" Creeper squints one eye and looks over at me.

"If it's that bad, then you probably need it," Bryn comments.

"My six pack would say otherwise. Wanna see? I'll show you right now if you want." He begins to pull up his shirt causing Bryn and me to exclaim our disgust. "Fine, your loss." He shrugs and takes our finished trays to the garbage.

Bryn smiles and scoots closer to me now that Creeper's gone. "Can I tell you a secret?"

"Of course." I reach over and put my hand over hers.

"I may have been exaggerating my feelings of dislike towards Zack's abs." *Not* what I was expecting.

"Okay." My voice cringes a little without my meaning to.

"I mean, what I'm trying to say is that I think I might like him." *Oh.*

It takes me a second to process this additional information but once I do I throw my arms around her.

"So you're okay with this, right? You seem pretty close and I don't want to invade..." she trails off.

"It's fine, more than fine, it's great."

"Oh good." She pauses and lets a goofy smile light up her eyes. "Do you think he likes me?"

"If he doesn't, he's going to. You're way too pretty and nice for him not to. And you know what? Tonight we're going to have a special planning session. It could be at your house if you want!" I'm getting more and more eager.

"That sounds amazing! But not at my house." She almost sounds like she's snapping at me, but I see her apologetic expression and don't press the issue.

"Okay, at mine then. Only now you'll have to do deal with my mother and her excitement at my newfound socialness. If I keep having friends over, my mom's going to suspect I'm popular." I wink and we laugh.

"Great!"

"What's great?" Creeper is about to sit down when the bell rings. He raises his eyebrow but Bryn and I clamp our mouths shut.

"Girl talk?" He asks while we make our way to drama

class.

"Something like that," I reply and share a conspiratorial glance with Bryn.

He opens the door for me and bows, as has become tradition. As we walk and sit down I have a sudden awareness of his proximity. His minty breath I've come to recognize and those gold speckles in his green eyes. I'm going to have to be careful when he and Bryn are dating to not accidentally get between them.

Before class lets out Mr. Matchen reminds us that we only have a few days until auditions. Between soccer, homework and hanging out with Creeper and Bryn I haven't had much time to practice.

When the bell releases us, I duck away to avoid Creeper throwing me over his shoulder and hurry to my locker without another word. I sense him before I see him and slam my locker shut.

He intercepts me on my way to the fields. "Did I do something wrong? I thought things were going well, I mean you even called us 'friends'." He runs his hand through his hair.

"You didn't do anything." I bite my tongue, searching for the right words to explain without revealing Bryn's secret. "Let's try to be a little more distant, okay? We're still friends but, we need to back off a bit."

His hands clench then let go. "Fine. I can do that. We're just friends, like always."

"Yeah, exactly." I awkwardly pat him on the back.

Practice goes by in a blur, I barely process anything. Bryn catches my eye a couple of times with a worried look to ask if I'm okay.

Things are finally back to normal now that Bryn and I are messing around in my room. "Red or pink?" She asks, pulling out two bottles of nail polish. I'm reminded of when Ben and Krystal painted each others nails. Speaking of which:

Blip. Blip. Blip. My computer starts to beep. "Should I answer?"

"Who is it?" Bryn asks.

"Ben."

"Go for it."

I hit the answer button while Bryn and I settle onto my bed with my laptop between us. Ben's face suddenly fills the screen, "Hi, Em!"

"Hey, Ben," I giggle.

"Is that someone with you?" He squints on the screen.

"Yup, Bryn. Remember, she's the girl who was at the movie night? And made varsity soccer?"

"The movie night with that creep." This time Bryn's the one giggling at his aggressive tone of voice. I knew I wasn't imagining it.

"Exactly, and tonight we're going to get Bryn a date with 'that creep'." When Bryn starts to blush I realize I probably shouldn't have said that. "I'm sorry Bryn, I'm new to all of this girly stuff. I'm so used to telling him everything."

"It's okay, maybe he can help us." Bryn looks hopefully to Ben.

"You'll *need* my help if you want to succeed. Especially if she has a hand in it." He gestures in my general direction.

"Hey!" I shout, offended. We haven't gotten to spend any time together lately.

"Wow, the famous Ben helping plan how I'm supposed to get a date." Bryn shakes her head. "This is crazy, you know that, right?"

"You will soon learn-" Ben starts.

"That everything about us is crazy," I finish, and it almost feels like he's back home.

"Then let's get started," Bryn exclaims.

"It's go big or go home, right?" Ben pauses to let us nod. "So instead of asking him out on some boring date, why not go for homecoming?"

I slap my head. "Why didn't I think of that?"

"Because I'm the genius here, obviously." He rolls his eyes. "No offense Bryn."

"None taken. And I love your idea. Now we just have to come up with a plan."

"That's my specialty." I smile deviously. Or at least try to, maybe it isn't so devious since Ben cracks up. "I actually have a good idea!"

"Oh, this is going to be interesting," Ben snickers.

My back hurts from bending over and my mind may be complete slush, but nothing can beat this feeling of accomplishment. Bryn went home a few hours ago, but Ben and I talked a while longer catching each other up with our lives.

Now that Mom's in bed and everyone else is gone, exhaustion is kicking in. I flop back on my bed, then turn to my side flicking on my phone.

BookLover321: Wanna play a game?

Me: Sure

BookLover321: What about 20 Qs?

Me: Okay! You can go first

BookLover321: Something no one knows about you

I have to stop and think about this. Ben knows pretty much everything; is there anything I haven't told him?

BEHIND THE COVER

Me: This is kinda embarrassing (embarrassed emoji)

BookLover321: it's okay what happens herestays here

Me: when I was little I had this dream of becoming a famous singer (ironic, right?) and made a video of *Call Me Maybe* and posted it online and it's sooo embarrassing

BookLover321: lol that's great!

Me: I'll let you start easy, favorite food?

BookLover321: Yogurt parfait :P first kiss?

Me: ughhh, this is ACTUALLY embarrassing. Like no one can know this...

Me: So back in elementary school Clarisse and I were best friends super close, but she claimed Kade. Right after that he kissed me (Covering eyes emoji) sooo bad. I didn't mean to idk if he did either,

Me: But elementary school kisses don't count anyway

I can't believe I told her that. Sometimes it's so much easier to get things off your back to someone when you aren't looking them right in the face. And if I did know who this anonymous person is, I doubt I could look them in the eyes next time I see them. As I wait for a response, I find it difficult to breath. What if they're friends with Clarisse and Kade?

BookLover321: Totally, I can imagine that XD

Me: Single or taken?

BookLover321: Taken

That doesn't narrow it down much, people switch between taken and single every other day.

BookLover321: Best idea yet?

Me: Posting Ben's music on YouTube. Though I really miss him, I wish he didn't have to leave

If I hadn't done that, maybe Ben and I would still be neighbors, but there's no way he'd be happy.

Me: What did you mean by the voice that one time?

BookLover321: idk, theres just a voice that tells me things like in my head

BookLover321: sometimes theres more than one its confusing

BookLover321: What's your biggest regret?

Me: My dad leaving.

I hadn't realized the truth of this until I typed it out. My fingers pause for a moment before hitting send, do I really trust this stranger with this information? Yes. I might not know their name, but I know who they are. They were there for me even when others weren't. They were thinking of me and wanted to talk to me. She provided a self-confidence I didn't know I had. My fingers brush against the family picture.

BEHIND THE COVER

Me: Sometimes I wonder if part of it was my fault. I always seemed to remind him of what he lost

I drum my fingers against my phone, waiting for a response. Three little dots fade darker then lighter representing her typing. A yawn escapes my lips as my eyelids drop for a final time tonight.

19 | Dimethylene Blue

-Charlotte-

Yet another packet now lies before me along with the rest of my classmates. A collective groan emits from our lips as we flip through the fact filled pages determining our further slogging and cramming. The worst part of all is that the due date is a mere two weeks away; at least I have Nick who will be more than happy to help. Whenever I show him my chemistry packets he scoffs at the elementary level of it and chastises me that I should know this stuff. Nonetheless, he completes it without fail every time.

A tight squeal of irritation severs through the downcast room dragging our collective attention to Clarisse. She slaps the packet down on the lab table spreading her palm against it. Kade attempts to calm her, but once Clarisse is throwing a fit she's as powerful as a whirlwind and nothing will stand in her winds. "We're supposed to do this *entire* packet?"

"We'll do it in class," the teacher says, though his voice resembles a whisper.

"But that's, like, more work than we've had to do the entire year with our other classes."

Em's missed most of class today, and Nick slept in so I have no way of discovering her whereabouts. Instead, I've taken her seat at Zack's side. He leans over to my ear and whispers, "This is what she did in drama too."

"Drama queen," I say and roll my eyes. Zack laughs in response, but is surpassed by creaking of heads turning.

"What did you call me?" Clarisse hisses eyes flashing.

"Just queen." I grin at her. *WWBD?* What would Bryn do?

"That's right which means that I make the rules. Do you know what happens when people break rules?" I stare right back into her eyes as though we're in a staring contest. She blinks. "They're punished, and guess who broke the rules at a certain little party?"

My expression is that of pure innocence until our teacher clears his throat. While we were distracted, he moved to the back of the lab and set up stations with different chemicals. He waves at us and I'm the first to jump out of my seat with Zack's hand in mine. Our teacher assigns us to a station with a bottle of chemicals next to beakers filled with water pointing to the lab instructions in our packet.

Zack pops the chemicals from one hand to the other shifting it around like a juggler preparing an act. While I'm scanning through the packet, the chemicals gain a name. "Zack, stop that." I grab the chemicals out of his hand.

"I knew what I was doing, don't worry about me, babe." He swipes at the chemicals, but merely brushes against my hand.

"Oh yeah? Then what is this?"

"Chemicals." Zack leans back against the table having no packets on it.

"I meant what kind of chemicals." I roll my eyes. Brandon looks at me sadly from across the room where he's been forced to work with one of Clarisse's friends. It almost makes me feel bad until he winks and signals *call me*. "This is filled with dimethylene blue."

"Cool. Blue's a great color. Can I have it back now?"

"My child, you clearly don't know what dimethylene blue does." I place a pair of gloves on my hands then take off the lid and extract a droplet. From that droplet, I only release a fraction into the water and it overflows blue into the sink. The liquid is a vibrant blue continuing for minutes from the chemical.

"Intense." Zack nods his head in respect and turns on the faucet so that the water starts to drizzle into the drain yet a blue stain remains on the sink. I'm tempted to scrub the blue away, but remember that it would take days if not weeks of scrubbing to clear it.

Zack pulls out his phone and looks up at me, his eyes wide with concern. "We need to go, now." He grabs my hand and drags me past the teacher out of the lab.

"Where are we going?"

"To find Em." He holds his phone up to his ear, and the green light from his call reflects off his cheek. "Em, where are you?" I can't hear her response, but Zack does. "We'll be right there. Don't worry." Without missing a step, he slides his finger around his phone and passes it over to me.

What I see stops me in my tracks. Zack catches his phone as it slips from my fingers. On Clarisse's Instagram she posted a video of a younger Em dancing and singing to a silent tune, but a series of words pass over the images. *Do you really know Emily Parker?*

"What is this?" I ask darkly.

"That's what we're going to find out." Zack grinds his teeth together. "Em's near the fields."

As we get closer, I can see Em's small body rocking back and forth against her usual tree. Her head is pressed between her knees to cover the tears I'm sure are there. We sit down on either side of her and wrap her in our arms.

"Did you see?" Her voice is soft and damaged, but she doesn't look up.

"Not yet," I answer. "Should we?"

"If you want." Em sniffles and peaks over to watch with us. Or maybe more accurately, watch our reactions.

Zack starts the video:

Probably not. You probably don't know that she goes after guys that aren't hers. Don't believe me? Ask Kade, or Em herself. Or just keep watching.

For a second the video switches over to Zack throwing Em over his shoulder. I turn in surprise, but Zack remains steely.

But that's just the beginning. She guilt tripped her dad into depression until he couldn't take it any longer.

The younger Em dancing transforms into a picture of her and her dad.

We all know of her relationship with Ben Adams, but what we didn't know is how deep her jealousy goes. If she could, she would do anything to take away his fame. Her jealousy pushed him all the way to California.

A video of Ben singing merges into Em's video until it's just Em. I'm not sure how *Call Me Maybe* could come across as menacing, but it somehow does.

Do you know Em as well as you think? Slide over for even more.

The video draws to a close, but it's not the end. To the right of it are screenshots of messages with Em, and quotes about conversations with her. Below is Clarisse's commentary tearing Em's character apart as best she can.

Zack and I exchange a look, but Em is the one who talks. "Well? Are you mad at me?"

"Mad?" Zack and I repeat in shock.

I shake my head. "Clarisse is the only one we should be mad at."

Em finally looks up to meet our eyes. Hope hides in the corners behind walls of tears. "Really?"

"Emily Nicole Parker," Zack starts, lifting her chin

until they're face to face. "You are perfect. This is a load of crap. Everyone who knows anything knows the kind of person Clarisse is and who you are. And if they don't? They don't deserve you, anyway."

"That's the thing, they aren't all lies." The slight smile Zack had planted shriveled. "You can see the proof yourself."

"Words can be twisted to mean anything, that's all this is," I try to explain. "Like Zack said, you are more than this. Anyone I'd allow to be my friend is a pretty great person."

At last Em's face breaks into a smile. "You mean that?" Zack and I nod. "I guess as long as you two are by my side I'm all good."

"Exactly," Zack and I pull her in for one more hug but are interrupted by an announcement over the school speaker system: *Emily Parker, please come to the main office.*

We escort Emily back into the school and return to Chemistry. Even though they keep their eyes trained on us, our classmates don't come too close.

A devious smile slithers across my face causing Zack to lift a questioning eyebrow. "How would you like to get a little revenge?"

"Revenge?" His voice is filled with curiosity and malice. "Do tell."

"Is it true that Kade's on the varsity soccer team just like Clarisse is on volleyball?" I query, searching drawers for a ziplock bag. Tweezers. Magnets. Toothbrushes. I don't even know what. There they are.

"They do. Please explain." Zack continues following me around the room as I grab a funnel from another group's experiment.

"Clarisse showers after volleyball at the same time as the soccer girls. Trust me, she takes *forever*. Does Kade shower in the guy's locker room as well?"

"Yup. Now I would simply love to hear more of this revenge you mentioned." Zack leans his shoulder against the cabinet while crossing his arms. A hair sticks straight up after he flips his bangs.

"Perfect. So next period we're going to have to skip lunch, and head over to the locker rooms instead. I assume you know how to open up a shower head?" He nods, I'd love to hear an explanation for that. I lean in closer to his ear and whisper my plan like elementary girls gossiping.

"Excellent. I love it." He grins and we return to chemistry where we each fill our own little bag with dimethylene blue.

Class ends soon after. With the general population flowing to the cafeteria, Zack and I move in the opposite direction. The crowd parts for him while he winks and flirts as I swim through like water slipping through cracks in dirt. Eventually, the crowd thins out the closer we get. I look to the left door and nod to Zack then walk through the right when he returns the action.

I walk past the lockers to the shower area and pull out a new pen Zack made for me that's as many tools as I could ever want in one. The shower head gets stuck halfway through coming off, but with enough of a struggle it pops off. I open the little bag slightly, place a funnel into it, and poor the chemical into the dry pipe with utmost care. A smudge got on the finger of my glove so I waste no time in pulling off the gloves and throwing them into the waste basket along with the bag and funnel. Not my best work, but I doubt anyone will bother to check up on it. Plus, there aren't any fingerprints or cameras in here so there's no way to trace it back to me. Someone should readjust the camera outside so that it can capture who's coming in and out of the locker rooms.

For me the process only took a few minutes, but the

same can't be said for Zack. By the time he finally comes out of the boy's locker room lunch is almost over. My jaw drops as he stumbles out. "What are those?"

He guiltily looks down to his shoes which are covered in a layer of blue as well as his hands. Behind him lays a trail of blue foot prints with highly distinguishable designs. "I dropped some and the floor was still wet. Don't worry, the tiles are so stained with other...stuff that no one will notice."

"Yeah, I know they won't notice that, they're guys. What they will notice are *blue* shoe prints."

"Oh, maybe. I tried to clean it off my shoes, but that didn't work out so well." He holds out his blue fingers and I shake my head. What a maladroit.

"Take off your shoes and hide them under a bush, we'll take care of them later. For now, let's cover up those tracks." The paper towel roll squeaks like an old door as I rotate it to remove dozens of pieces. I soak my pile and place one piece over each shoe print. Right now I'm hoping that the guys won't question a mess of paper towels and toilet paper plastered to the floor. It's definitely better odds than the blue at least.

We return outside just as the bell rings. "You have to go to class and help Em." I say.

"Of course." Zack picks up his shoes as I casually stroll over to the parking lot where Nick's waiting.

"Good luck," I say and swing halfway into Nick's car.

"I'll keep you up to date." He shoves his hands into his pockets with the shoes dangling by the strings.

"Good." The door slams shut, but I leave the window open.

"And Bryn, thanks. I had a great time with you, not to mention it's about time someone put Queenie in her place. Nothing is okay with what she did today."

"I look forward to it." The window rolls up.

BEHIND THE COVER

Nick gawks at me. "I turned off the livestream for twenty minutes and everything happens. Do I even want to know?"

I smile in response.

20 | Homecoming Troubles

-Emily-

My hair tickles my cheek while the wind whispers in my ear. Even the sun winks from above the crossbar. The *tweet* of a whistle pushes me out of the perfect moment. Bryn calculatingly jogs up to the ball. Her eyes find the left corner while her hips lean in the same direction. Bryn's foot, however, pushes the ball to the right corner of the net. My brain must manufacture the *swhish* of the ball hitting the net for there's no way I could hear it over the cheering. The final blaring of the whistle makes the cheers grow louder.

Bryn's flooded by teammates. My eyes catch Creeper's. He's standing on the sideline next to me with my mom to my left. His hair is plastered to his forehead, from the wind, but nothing could draw back from his smile.

The team's mini celebration ends at Coach Simmons.

She gives a speech and the team cheers back in excitement. They push Bryn forward causing even more whooping and hollering.

"What a way to start the season, huh Em?" Zack says, putting his arm over my shoulders, which I quickly shrug out of.

"It was great," I smile, hugging myself.

Bryn jogs over to us with a smile, her lips pulled wider

than I've ever seen. "The game? It was pretty great."

"You know what was great? Your PK was great! That was amazing, you have to teach me how to do that."

"Haha, sure," Bryn replies.

Zack reaches toward me to flip me over his shoulder, but the glares of our peers stops him in his tracks. I cower into myself avoiding eye contact. Everywhere I turn my head there's another mask of disgust staring down at me.

"So, party at my place?" Bryn asks, sneaking me a look once we're all packed into my mom's minivan. Today's the day. Our plans are set into motion awaiting its key guests.

I watch Zack's eyes and am surprised to find him already looking at me. He flashes a smile and I flick my head in Bryn's direction.

"I need to grab a few things, then I'll be right over," I promise Bryn.

"Fine, but hurry back." I'm not actually going to be there when she asks him, I'll only be part of the celebration.

The animated conversation dies down as we near Bryn's house and Creeper and Bryn get out of the car. They thank my mom again and Bryn makes me promise to hurry before we leave.

"Zack asked me to give you this." My mom reaches over the seat and hands me a very familiar ugly, purple shirt.

"He thinks he's so funny." My mom passes me a weird look, but doesn't ask.

I grab a little gift I bought Bryn from my room, and decide to change into the purple shirt just to give Creeper a laugh. When I unroll the shirt a small piece of paper falls out. In typed lettering it says:

A smoothie's always refreshing right after soccer, isn't it? Here's five dollars to get one.

Taped onto the note is a five-dollar bill.

What's going on?

I jog downstairs and find my mom waiting in the car.

"Ready to go?"

"Umm, yeah." I glance at the time. "But first could we stop at the mall?"

"If you want. Zack did give me some money for gas." Mom looks down at me with a mysterious glint to her eye.

That boy is going to be in major trouble when I find out what's going on. My mom starts to walk away to give me my space to do what I have to do.

We haven't discussed the Instagram incident yet, and I'm fishing for time. I think mom's trying to figure out what to say, or how to say it. When the vice principal explained what happened to my mom, she made me go out to the car and wait for her. Still, this car ride continues the silence before the storm. "I'm going to stop by the bookstore quickly, okay?"

"Okay, I'll be over near the food court. My phone will be ready if you need me." I promise.

The large man with a thick mustache smiles at me and I order a pineapple smoothie.

"Here you go," he says exchanging the smoothie for my five-dollar bill. He grimaces before speaking again, "You wouldn't happen to be Emily, would ya?"

"I am, why?" I gawk up at him as he rubs his fingers through his mustache.

"Oh good! I'm tired of asking every pretty girl who paid with a five-dollar bill. Anyway, this is for you." He hands me another paper.

"Thank you," I say and walk over to a table. Slurping my smoothie, I open yet another typed note:

Hope you're having fun so far. Once you've finished your smoothie it's time to go looking for a fake hidden collection of plants.

I shake my head in confusion. "A fake hidden

collection of plants?" What's that supposed to mean? I guess a collection of plants could mean like a greenhouse, or a garden. Wait, hidden, secret? Secret garden? And fake...a play would be a fake secret garden? So maybe this could be leading me to the drama room? I text my mom asking her to take me to school and she says she'll meet me at the car. I dearly hope I'm right.

After another silent car ride, I'm standing outside the school. Which is closed. Meaning it's all locked. What do I do now?

I scan the building and see a flash of light in one of the windows. I walk over to the window and see that it belongs to the drama room. Neatly sitting in the corner of the widow is a hand drawn sketch of some stick figures messing around on a swing set, slide and teeter totter.

My mom is patiently waiting in the car and I feel bad, but I have to ask, "Mom, can we make just one more stop?"

She patiently smiles at me, "Of course. Where to?"

"The park," these two words taste bitter on my tongue and fill my stomach with a sense of dread, but I can't quit now. I look at my phone; Bryn's already asked Creeper. I wonder how he responded. Did he give her a quiet yes with one of his adorable smiles? Did he shout out yes and throw her over his shoulder? Did he twirl her round and round? I already know Bryn will squeal and tackle him with all of her might.

The park appears before us. "Thanks mom," I say and slowly open the door. A rope is hanging next to a swing from with a sign saying, "Pull me." I tug on the rope and a recording starts to play. "Emily, will you come with me to homecoming?" My breath catches at his voice. "You're my closest friend. You drive me crazy when you're around, but when you aren't around I can't stop thinking about you. So...will you go to homecoming with me? Take your time to answer, but at least think about it."

I brush away tears I hadn't realized were collecting while his message ends. Why him? Why did Zack have to go and do this? He's crazy. But maybe, just maybe, it's a good kind of crazy. The kind of crazy that can grow on you. I can't say yes for Bryn...Oh, Bryn. What's going on at her house?

21 | Invitation Take Two

-Charlotte-

The balloons are kind of a flop, but at least the streamers are nice. Zack looks at me like I've sprouted horns when we walk into my house (we deactivated the alarms and such). "Nice decor."

"It's for you silly," I exclaim and hand him a balloon. He shakes it around in his hands and a piece of chocolate vibrates around it like a drum.

"Thanks." Zack's jaw clenches in and out as he squeezes the balloon between his fingers until it pops. A bite sized Butterfinger falls into his hands. "Thanks again."

"There's much more where that came from, but first-" Nick enters the room with a collection of helium filled balloons tied together. Nick's trying to smile and be supportive, but he can't move past the protective brother stage. His expression reminds me of Eeyore from *Winnie the Pooh* attempting to be positive. I act as middle grounds and pass the collection of over filled balloons from Nick to Zack. "Take these."

Curiously, Zack keeps his jovial air by tossing the balloons from hand to hand and shaking one next to his ear. His grin slackens into a slight pout. "What, no more candy?"

"Just pop it already!" I giggle shoving his shoulder.

Nick glares at me and speaks into the comm.

"Never knew someone was such a girly-girl," He mocks.

"Shut up." I clench my jaw.

"What did you say?" Zack asks, running a hand through his hair. Something's making him nervous. Wonder what it is. The number of balloons in this room, the obvious tension flowing from Nick, the missing Em, who knows?

"I didn't say anything. Now just hurry up and pop those balloons," I command pushing the balloons in his face.

He puts his hands up in mock surrender and pulls the balloons down to his chest level. They keep moving downwards where they end up underneath his butt. He lays down flattening them until muffled booming explodes one by one as the balloons pop. When Zack stands up the words '*will you go to homecoming with me*' are spread across the flattened carpet. Only, they actually are in the mixed-up order of '*to me will homecoming you with come.*' Nonetheless the message is clear enough.

In a classic Bryn move I jump onto him wrapping my arms around his neck, squealing as though I'm a little girl. He casually catches me and puts me back on the ground. A grin pushes up the edge of his lips. "I've got to go to the bathroom."

"Oh, okay." I nod my head fervently in understanding. "Hurry back though."

Zack doesn't meet my eyes as he walks to the hallway. Once he's out of earshot I pull Nick in next to me and whisper in his ear. "Open the link to the bathroom sound bug."

Nick's way ahead of me and his fingers are already flying across his tablet pulling open the sound app. Within moments Zack's echoing voice bursts into my earpiece.

"Pickup. Pickup already Emily." The dial tone stops and Em's voice enters.

"H-hello?" She sounds terrified.

"Em, did you?"

"I did." Nick looks at me and mouths *what* I shake my head in equal confusion.

"And?"

"Zack, you're a great friend, but, uh, I think you and Bryn-"

"Yeah, of course." They pause. Nick smiles at the awkward conversation and I punch his shoulder. I don't understand this boy.

"So, Bryn and you. Great."

"Exactly. I guess I'll see you on Monday then."

"Monday." They pause and Zack turns on the faucet. "Bye Zack."

"Bye Emily." He turns off the water and the phone buzzes off. Nick taps the tablet and silences our earpieces. We exchange a few quick glances conversing over what could have just happened. By the time Zack's back in the living room we're still drawing up a blank.

Zack looks at me with sadness piercing through his eyes, but the rest of him is a mask of happiness. If I really were Bryn I wouldn't have a clue there's anything going on with him. He wraps one arm around my waist and pulls me into a hug and blows a wave of hair over my shoulder when he says, "I will gladly take you to homecoming." Something resonates through me as I bounce up and down in supposed excitement.

"You have no idea how much this means to me," I squeal in his ear making him pull back while keeping his arrogant grin. Zack may be hot, but there's more to him than what meets the eye.

"As excited as I am, I really need to get home. Thank you, Bryn, I look forward to seeing you again." Zack squeezes me once more before releasing.

"Oh, but Em isn't even here yet! She has to see." I hate how whiny I sound, but it's Bryn's voice not mine. Zack opens his mouth to counter, but I pull out my phone and pretend to have a text from Em. "I guess she can't make it. Well, then I hope you have a nice night. I'll see you Monday? Unless you wanted to hang out this weekend." I trail off and look up to his eyes.

"That's okay." He says too quickly. "That is, I have a lot of stuff going on this weekend."

"Ah, sounds like very important stuff." I reach up on my tiptoes and kiss his cheek then lead him out the door. "Have a good weekend."

"You too." Zack doesn't miss a beat and kisses my cheek back. He really is a great actor, maybe if I ever need a replacement for Nick.

Speaking of, Nick's face is contorted in a pout when I return. We start picking up the balloons without a word only sounding the occasional popping when we decide to eat a chocolate. Once everything's cleaned up we go to our unofficial mission headquarters in my room.

Nick brings the audio recordings back up in the DB and replays them three times until we decide there's nothing left to decipher. Something definitely happened between Em and Zack that included Bryn without including Bryn. All I know for sure is that it's creating more drama than I could've hoped for.

After Nick and I go over possible, but not plausible, situations including but not limited to an invitation of some sort, a gift, anxiety, or medical issues, I relax back onto my bed snuggling up to my pillows. It's been a long day, and though I had a phenomenal soccer game, I would prefer to get some sleep over revisiting everything that's happened.

Nick lays down next to me with his eyes inches away

from mine. It's crazy how different we are, yet through it all we're the closest team there'll ever be: sister and brother.

"What do we do now?"

"We wait."

22 | To Be or Not to Be...

-Emily-

"Hello?"

"Ben! Thank you so much for picking up."

"What's going on?" Concern leaks through his voice. "Are you okay?"

"Do you remember how we totally planned Bryn's homecoming invitation?"

"Yup, it was tonight, right?"

"Yup."

"How'd it go?"

"I don't know."

"What?" I can imagine him frowning as he tries to figure out what's going on.

"Well, when I was freshening up after the game I found a note. It lead me to another note, and that one lead me to another one and so on. The final one lead me to this park where there was a tape recorder and Zack asked *me* to homecoming!"

"Woah, slow down. Who is this *Zack*?" Ben's voice is all defensive. I knew I could rely on him for help.

"Zack is Creeper." He mumbles something too quietly for me to hear. "What?"

"Nothing. What are you going to do now that he asked you to homecoming? Oops, I mean his *recording* asked you to homecoming."

"I said no, obviously."

"Oh, well, that's good." He pauses and I move into my bathroom to start brushing my teeth. "I saw something on Instagram."

"Ben, please stop. I don't want to talk about it." I spit out the toothpaste and snap into the phone.

"Isn't this something we need to talk about?" He sounds confused, but hurt too.

"If you think so," I concede as I pull a band out of my hair and onto my wrist. My hair falls in waves as I lean over and brush it out before starting a braid. "Which part?"

"One, are you okay? And two what did she mean by the part about you and me?"

"One, yes. Bryn and Zack were there to help me. And two." I exhale sharply. It's only been a few weeks, yet things are changing between us. How long am I supposed to go without seeing Ben? "There was a girl who started messaging me on Instagram and I thought we were becoming good friends, but obviously not. Clarisse took my words and twisted them to sound how she wanted." I quote back what Bryn and Zack said. What I've been repeating to myself over and *over* again. "Are we all good?"

"I am if you are." An unspoken apology is set in those words, and I accept it gratefully. "I've been thinking," he starts.

"Uh oh. That's never good." I finish my routine and return to my bedroom. The purple shirt lays on my bed and I consider falling asleep in it. Choosing not to, I throw it into the back of a drawer.

"That hurts Em." We both laugh. It feels good to laugh with Ben again. "I don't know how much longer I can go without seeing you, so I sent some plane tickets in the mail for you, your mom, Bryn, and Creep to come visit." He inhales sharply before continuing. "Would you like to come visit?"

"I'm glad to say yes at least once tonight!" Does he really have to ask? I can't help my beaming face.

"Great! It's over the long weekend, so we can spend the most amount of time together. I thought it would be cool to meet Bryn after all our planning, and I had to check out Creep and make sure he's good enough to be your friend. Is that okay?"

"That sounds perfect."

"I hate to say this, but I have to go. Just remember that whatever happens, you still have me."

"I know Ben. I know. And you always have me."

"Hey Em?"

"Yeah?"

"I love ya."

"I love you too, Ben."

I've yet to see Creeper or Bryn since the mess of homecoming invites, but we didn't have plans to meet over the weekend. I can only hope that things will be normal. I talked to Bryn who was ecstatic about Creeper accepting, at least nothing seemed wrong with her. I wonder if Creeper told her anything.

I stretch back in my seat and my eyes glance upon Creeper on the other side of the room. As he enters the Chem lab, his head is bowed down and his hands are in his pockets, is he embarrassed? I doubt it.

"Hey," he says, sitting down next to me.

"Hi."

"Listen, about the homecoming invitation, I meant as friends, and I stepped way outta place-"

"Creeper, slow down. Actually, no, stop. Everything's fine. We're friends, right?" I'm not going to lie, his explanation doesn't sound like what the tape said, but I'm not going to press the matter.

"Right."

I send him a smile in return since class is starting. Thank goodness, for the rest of our Chem everything goes on as usual.

I anxiously wait at the lunch table for Bryn and Creeper. Even through the crowded cafeteria it doesn't take long for me to spot them holding hands and smiling. When they do sit down they sit extremely close together. I'm not the only girl in the cafeteria frowning.

Up until this point I hadn't noticed Clarisse, Kade and their friends have been absent from school. Now, they one by one march into the cafeteria with their heads held high. Correction *blue* heads held high. Snickers erupt in small crowds as they make their way to their center table. Normally Clarisse's clothes are barely noticeable leaving little to the imagination, but today she's wearing skin-tight jeans and a sweater. Even with the extra clothes her face is a vibrant shade of blueberry blue matching her hands. All their hair was clearly dyed back to somewhat natural colors, but nothing could've saved their skin.

I cover my mouth to smatter my giggles, though Bryn and Creeper wink at each other and high five. "What is going on?"

"I have no idea." Creeper shrugs.

Clarisse storms over to our table and points an extremely blue finger with angry red nails in my face. "You!" She accuses.

"Me?" I repeat, confused.

"You did this to get back at me!"

"Did what?"

"Did wha—" she starts to repeat but shakes her head in anger. "*This!*" Clarisse thrusts her hands up and down then back and forth at the blue people.

"Oh, you mean the Smurf thing. That wasn't me. I wasn't even here on Friday. I left early after a certain *incident."*

"Who else would do this to me? Everyone else loves me," Clarisse snarls. She looks back at Kade. He stumbles forward.

"Right. Everyone loves her." He grabs her hand and a crowd of supporters gathers behind then.

"Guys, stand down." Creeper gets up waving his hand. "It wasn't Emily, like she said; she was at her house. Besides, she hasn't even thought of revenge."

"Why Zack, are you choosing her side?" Aubrey purrs, swishing her eyelashes up and down.

"I'm choosing the side of basic human rights." Creeper place his hand on my shoulder and girls sitting off to the sides at tables nod their heads in agreement. Even the cafeteria ladies resemble bobble heads even if they have no idea what's really going on.

"Then I guess you aren't on her side." Aubrey winks.

"Really try thinking hard on that. Do you believe you're human? Clarisse wasn't smart enough to make that video on her own." Part of the student body agrees through shouting while her portion gasps in disgust. Clarisse snorts and for a second it looks like she's considering attacking me. With a pat from Kade, she turns on her heel while stomping back to their table.

Once everything quiets back down, well I guess it actually becomes louder with chatter, I lean toward Bryn and Creeper. "What really happened?"

"Like Zack said, we don't know a thing." Bryn smiles innocently. She's sweet to try, but needs to work on her lying skills.

"C'mon, I know you better than that. I believe you got revenge on my behalf." I look at them pleadingly.

"Oh, alright. Maybe I have an idea of what happened." Creeper concedes. "We may have put chemicals in the showers to dye the guys soccer team and cheerleaders."

I gasp in shock, but also amusement. "You did that! How could you?"

"That's nothing from what's to come." Creeper glares over at them.

"It was nothing." Bryn grins.

"What am I going to do with you?" I laugh looking back at the Smurfs.

"I have plenty of ideas." Creeper winks at me. I gasp in disgust and slap his cheek. "What was that for?"

"You have a lot to learn about being a boyfriend."

"A what?" Creeper's face is blank in confusion as he looks back and forth from Bryn to me and back again. Bryn and I exchange a pitiful expression and sigh in unison. He really is as clueless as Jar Jar Binks.

"A B. O. Y. F. R. I. E. N. D. Also known as a boyfriend. A boy who is dating a girl." I elaborate.

"I know what a boyfriend is." Creeper rolls his eyes his eyes. "I'll try to step it up."

"Good," I say.

"Great." Bryn smiles with a light blush. She glances at Creeper from under her eyelashes, but he doesn't seem to notice as he's staring at me. "But we can take things slowly if you want."

"Okay, wanna hang out tonight?" Creeper asks. I mouth *good job* at him and smile.

"Sure. What should we do?"

"What about laser tag?" Not the most romantic of dates, but Creeper isn't the most romantic of guys.

"I've never, uh, played laser tag." Bryn stutters losing a bit of her smile.

"You've never played laser tag?" Creeper and I exclaim in sync. "It's settled then," he continues.

"Okay." Bryn looks up at me. "Em you should come with us!"

"Oh, I don't know about that." This is their date, not

mine.

"Please?" She clasps her hands together and bounces up and down in her seat.

"If it's okay with Creeper."

"It's fine with me." He crosses his arms with a self-certain grin.

"Yay!"

"Looks like we're going to Woohooz," I conclude. Third wheel, here I come.

23 | Laser Tag

-Charlotte-

I thought that a high school was the biggest collection of crazed hormones on an unending sugar high, but I was wrong. Woohooz takes the cake. I'd take a hundred-gun barrels pressed to my head over the screeches emanating from the collection of video games in the center of the giant building. The number of things that could go wrong here are uncountable and my sense are overloading with information. This can either be a spy's dream or nightmare. If I weren't stuck with Em and Zack I could hide in the crowd easier than a missing phone.

A kid no older than eight years runs past our small group smashing Em's feet in two different steps. She immediately hops from one foot to the other while Zack and I move to her aid. We work like a well-trained team, yet it's all based on lies. If I never broke my cover this could be an incredible friendship. Until we move away, or when I break things off with Zack.

My pace matches that of Em while I follow their steps toward a dark side wall highlighted by slime green cracks and a starry eclipse emanating into the word *Lasertron*. From the back of a long, winding line I can see that the wall sinks into itself creating a cave with two doors to the left and right. In the center of the cave, there's a large black desk with stormtroopers from *Star Wars* on either side of it with guns held diagonally across their chests.

Zack reclines against the line barriers with his arms crossed against his chest and smirks at the kids in line ahead of us. Three little boys jump from side to side excited pointing to a small TV screen with a list of names and numbers. The tallest of them claims the title of Spiderman for team red and the second tallest is quick to say he'll be on red team as well. However, the shortest of the three grins deviously and says, "If you're going to be on red I'll be on green. No way I'd wanna be on the same team as Joe!"

The second tallest, Joe I'd assume, crosses his arms mirroring Zack and scrunches up his face. "James, that's mean. I didn't want to be on your team anyway."

"*Sure.*"

"I don't!" He protests stomping his foot down. When James continues grinning at him, Joe turns to his taller brother and starts a conversation about football. Even though he's left out, James keeps up his silly appearance by poking Joe and making fun.

Em giggles at their antics and I'm quick to join her. Even though all three young boys have the same appearance, black hair and ocean blue eyes, their personalities are starkly different. The tallest is clearly the leader with Joe being his adoring brother-maybe even twin-and James as the rebel. Zack nudges me and puts his arm around my shoulders. "They're cute, aren't they?"

I nod my head feverishly, as to get into character. "They're adorable! One's just like a mini you."

"Oh really?" He rests his head on my shoulder. "The tall one?"

"No silly! James." I point at James who is now reaching his hands to Joe's shorts trying to snatch them downward, but Em intervenes before any trouble can arise.

"Hello there." They look up practically in sync and

smile at her, though James' is slightly stretched. Em leans down so that she's looking right into their eyes. "Which team are you on?"

"I'm on green." James grins then jerks his thumb at his brothers. "But these two bozos are on red." Em giggles again at his word choice.

"I'll be on green then." She ruffles his hair with her fingers which makes him grin wildly then pull away. "They're cute." Her eyes remain on the buzzing boys even as she stands back up and talks to Zack and me. It's clear she doesn't feel nearly as comfortable anymore with us dating, but she's still doing her best to keep things normal.

The doors slam open followed by excited voices flowing from the room with their owners close behind. Kids are still jumping up and down reminiscing about their best shots and ducks. Two run out pretending to have guns in their arms. Weary parents smile after them, but don't bother to restrict their happiness.

Once about a dozen people have exited the *Lasertron* area, the employee lets our group in. The three boys in front of us only grow louder with their chatter as we get closer. They're bouncing so quickly the scanner has a hard time reading their wristbands. Eventually the employee gives up with a shrug and smiles as they skid through the turnstile stopping short of the door. There are fifteen of us in line that cram into the small space between the line area and *Lasertron* entrance, but we're quickly joined by another small group who sprint through the line.

"Hey, Brynnie dear!" Clarisse's sugary voice purrs as she scoots in next to me with Kade next to her.

"What are you doing here?" Em asks. Her voice is a hole cut deep with scars that vibrates with the slightest bit of fear. Zack steps closer to her so that they're bodies are barely touching in support, but I hold my ground.

"Laser tag silly. Unless you'd like another photoshoot."

Kade draws her back by squeezing her hand; this isn't the time or place. If it were I'd have her pinned down in an instant. Well, either Zack or I would.

We're lead into a narrow room with rows of vests lining the walls. A few of us reach to pull on our vests, but are stopped by a rather large employee who's been worked past his max as told by the stains under his armpits and halfway closed eyes. Even his words come out bored, "We're going to watch this video then you can go ahead an' put on the vests."

The lights dim and we turn our attention to a small flat screen on the far wall. A sci-fi *zoom* screeches into our ears then a robotic voice narrates the words appearing on the TV. Don't play if you have joint problems or muscle problems, yada yada, if you're old then don't do it. When the robot states that those of pregnancy shouldn't play there are clearly a couple of shoulder nudges and "That means you!"s but for the most part it's pretty boring. Half the fun is taken away when it's made clear we aren't allowed to run or have physical contact, but I listen closely to the shooting part; you can hit shoulders, chest, and back. Easy targets.

When the video finally ends Zack helps me pull a vest over my head and places the attached gun in my hand. I grin at him and help Em while he puts his own on. Clarisse and Aubrey are staring pointedly at us with an easy to translate expression. Their friends are over their feud, but they can't seem to give it up. I laugh slightly as the ultraviolet light illuminates their blue skin.

The best part so far are the three little boys who manage to keep the entire scene animated with their sound effects and silly banter. They stick their tongues out at one another from opposite sides of the room even though they're too old for that sort of thing. It's as though time froze for them leaving their innocence.

BEHIND THE COVER

Mr. Overworked guides the red team into the battlegrounds as the red headquarters are on the far end of the room and green on the near then returns to us. "Do y'all know how this works?"

James nods his head so hard I worry it might fall off, but the man continues with his speech anyway. "To charge up your vests just walk by one of the two charging stations that display the scores. Your base is that big structure which you should defend and try to target their base. You can also find your scores on the tops of your vests." I look down to my vest and see a bunch of zeros. That'll change soon enough.

He leaves us at our stations for a few silent moments before a *durrrrough* erupts from our vests alerting us that they've been charged. I speed walk away from our base and team into a mess of neon green and red structures all the while ducking and rolling to avoid being seen. Every now and then I catch sight of a red vest but refrain from firing as to keep from giving away my position. Eventually I find myself in a position with a clear line of sight to the red base. I position my gun so it rests evenly from my eye to the target. With two fingers digging into the rapid-fire buttons my score jumps from zero to thousands. My vest comments great shot repeatedly until the robotic voice booms from the ceiling. "Red team you need to defend your base. Your base is under attack!"

I immediately stop shooting and wait for the new red traffic to clear before resuming. For some reason, my vest starts to vibrate then click in defeat signaling an end to my rapid fire. I squirm around to find the oldest of the three boys with his own gun trained on me. My lips twist into a smile as I duck away behind a green blockade, but disappears the moment I realize I've stepped right into his trap. His brother is on the other side now draining my points away. My gun may be out of power, but he doesn't know that. I point my gun at him for a moment, then spin around the blockade and sprint back to my base making sure to keep away from the glaring eyes of Mr. Overworked.

Once my vest is recharged I choose the upstairs route and climb up a ramp but am cut off by a wall of red. Seeing Brandon in the center halfway tempts me to stop and take them out however I keep in mind that their points are worth exponentially less than their base. When turning a corner I thud against another body. "Zack!" I exclaim in my best Bryn voice.

"Hey, I'm going right you go left, okay?"

"Sounds good." He'd really make a great partner. Maybe one day if we're still in touch I can give him a few recommendations. Then again, maybe not. I keep reminding myself of "Spy One-Oh-One."

My vest starts to ring before I can make it back to the red team's base. The robotic voice sounds stating, "Green team victory! Check your vests for the high scorer." Not surprisingly my vest lights up letting me know that I was in fact the high scorer.

My toe studs against something soft as I make my way back to the exits and my hands fly up to my mouth in surprise and to keep me from gagging. A blonde clump of hair curls around the tip of my shoe and I back away before gulping down my terror. I hold two fingers to her throat, then her wrist, but there isn't a pulse. I stumble backwards in horror as my eyes meet her empty brown ones. Dizziness clouds my mind but I somehow manage to snap a few pictures before the gravity of this situation hits me.

Clarisse is dead.

24 | An Assembly

-Emily-

A wave of milk slops over the side of my bowl as I move my spoon aimlessly around my cereal. I should eat, I know I should especially after skipping dinner last night. But every time I attempt to take a bite my throat closes in disgust.

My mom watches me out of the corner of her eye. She's been holding back, but I can visibly see the pressure of what she wants to say building inside her like a ticking time bomb. As she scuttles around the kitchen, I dump my cereal into the sink and wash out my dish. "I'm done."

I move to go upstairs, but my mom puts her hand on my arm. "Your bag's already in the car, let's go." Not ready for an argument, I nod my head and follow her into the garage.

The car groans to a start, almost as reluctant as me. When we pull up into the school parking lot, Mom doesn't stop out front like normal. Instead, she parks the van and turns over to me. "We need to talk."

"Mom, can't this wait until later?" I gesture toward the school. "I have class."

"Nice try. I know school doesn't start for another half hour." I slump back into my seat, not even bothering with the buckle. My mom's attempted grin falls across her face.

"And I've waited long enough. Which would you like to talk about first? The predator or yesterday?"

"Predator?" I scoff in disbelief. Booklover321 was not a predator. A predator is an old man stalking young girls on the internet. "It was a stupid girl thing, that's all. Don't you remember high school? It's like the upgrade to writing on the bathroom wall."

"I'd hardly say that." Mom sighs, and shakes her head. "Now we need to decide how to handle this, because what we've been doing hasn't been working."

"What exactly have we been doing?"

"Exactly! Nothing. And that's what we're figuring out." My mom nods her head as though to give herself some confidence. "Who do we need to talk to? Who deals with this stuff? Your teachers? Principal? Police?"

"Police? Gosh, Mom no." My eyes widen in horror. We can't bring the police into this. "What are they going to do? Arrest her from the grave?"

"Emily—" I interrupt her by opening my door and swinging my legs to the side.

"I've got to go. See you later." Unbuckling my seatbelt, I hook my backpack over my right shoulder.

"This conversation is not over." I wish I could shut the door to this conversation, but the best I can do is slam the car door.

It's funny, of all the people I'd ever wish this upon, it would be Clarisse, but honestly? It's not all that it's chopped up to be. Her death feels like it's somehow my fault. Had I not been the cause of all this trouble, maybe this wouldn't have happened. Today I put on a bright blue sweater with white slacks and pulled my hair up into a loose ponytail with a goal of sending cheeriness from my appearance into my personality.

On my way to class I notice the overall lack of students in the hallways and quicken my step. In the main hallway, a collection of arrows all point to the gym with a diagram of seating arrangements based on grade. I discover the "missing" crowd on my way up the stairs as I'm enveloped in the mass of sophomores.

"Em!"

"Emily!" I somehow manage to hear my name through the cacophony of voices and turn to see Bryn and Creeper sitting at the very top of the risers. I make my way up to them where they saved me a seat.

"What's going on?" I ask.

"No clue," Bryn replies. I search her for any differences, but she looks the same.

"Probably something to do with Clarisse," Creeper states. During a normal assembly, guys are jockeying around as girls gossip about the latest news. In some ways, today is no different. The boys are still bragging about the soccer game last night and girls are whispering as fiercely as ever. Except, in between plays from the game are mumbles about Kade and Clarisse. Every giggle that reaches my ears is based around Clarrise's last moments. A sick feeling takes hold of my stomach. It isn't until Creeper squeezes back that I realize I'd been clenching his hand and I pull away.

The lights dim causing the crowd to quiet. Our principal steps onto the stage with a wall of vice principals around him like sentries. "Hello, students. Now that you're all filed into place, let's get down to business."

"To defeat, the huns," Creeper sings into my ear fishing for a smile.

"A tragedy has taken place, we lost one of our sophomore students; Clarisse Galders. We'd like to honor her memory with a short video followed by speeches. Without further to do, here's the video."

Clarisse's school picture flashes from the projector to a wall of the gym. It's supposed to be a fact that everyone has bad school pictures, but Clarisse disproves it. A dark feeling settles across the auditorium as everyone comes to the same realization: she's really gone. Even those that didn't know her hold solemn expressions.

It continues showing some videos of her on the volleyball team, diving for a ball. Then one of her laughing in the middle of her friends. Next the screen transitions into her tenth-grade picture fading into the graduation speech she gave for junior high school. Her teeth were really white, I'm not sure how I didn't notice that before. Maybe I was too concentrated on her butt showing from beneath her cut off jean shorts or wondering how her teachers let her get away with a transparent white t-shirt. They show a picture of her from every year of junior high and it's interesting to see how she'd changed. Mostly she gained more makeup with fashion trends going in and out of style.

Suddenly, it all changes.

She's no longer a snotty popular girl driven by hatred.

She has glasses and braces and a goofy smile.

Most of all, she's arm in arm with mini me.

A tear slides down my cheek but I don't move to catch it. The video comes to an end with a spliced picture of all the stages of her life from tenth grade to kindergarten pulling at me in ways they shouldn't and a polite applause fills the room. Still I don't move. My life has been separated into B.B. and A.B. Before Ben and After Ben. I tried so hard to forget the before, but one picture brings it all back.

A row of teachers give their speeches going on about what a wonderful student and great classmate she was, but they aren't really saying anything. Yet everyone remains quiet throughout the duration. Everyone seems to have a unified understanding of what's going on.

Our principal asks if there's anyone who would like to give their own speech and the sophomores collectively turn to Kade and her old group. His face remains stone still however, and the principal awkwardly claps his hands together. "Okay then, I guess that's that. Oh, one other thing. You may see some detectives around the school and please let them do their job. If they ask any questions I'm sure you'll be quick to accommodate them. Thank you, and you are released to your second periods."

Everyone stands to leave, but I stay seated.

"Are you okay?" Creeper leans down as if he's going to put his hand on my shoulder but he doesn't. Instead he holds his hands out if I need support.

"I—" I shake my head. "I think I'm going to be sick."

25 | Brothers are the Best

-Charlotte-

I lean back until my chair starts to bend and stretch my legs out in front of me. The detective narrows her eyes; she isn't impressed. Since I was the first to find Clarisse's body I'm the first person they'd have to question and Detective Miller wasted no time bringing me into her makeshift office.

Everything about Detective Miller screams unimpressed. From her lazy eyes to tight lips to crossed arms. The second period bell rings and she grimaces as though she never stepped foot in a high school before. Then again maybe she hasn't. Maybe she was trained at home all her life. Of all people, I should be the last to judge considering my special education. I make a mental note to never end up like her.

"So, Miss...?"

"Richards. Bryn Richards at your service as my principal commanded." Her hands flip down while the rest of her body tightens as I reach into my pocket. "Relax, I'm just grabbing a piece of gum." I wave the minty green box in the air using the box as a distraction to activate my earpiece. "Want some?"

"No thank you."

"Suit yourself." I plop a piece onto my tongue and

begin to smack it around obnoxiously. Funny how the smallest sources of irritation can serve as such major distractions.

"Can you tell me *exactly* what happened? Please include every detail no matter how small it may contribute to the case." She speaks slowly moving her mouth as though sounding out words for a second grader.

"Sunday my friends and I went to Woohooz to play laser tag." I move my mouth equally slowly to mimic her. "Clarisse and her friends show up just as we're about to go inside. Everything was normal, Clarisse threatening anyone and everyone and the guys making dirty jokes, then our teams separated and her team went inside. Our team went inside later. I didn't see her again until after the game ended." I conclude with a loud *pop* of my gum. A yawn sighs through my ear. Looks like sleeping beauty finally woke up.

"And how did you find her? Did you see anything or-" Her eyebrows jump up and down. Normally I'm not one to encourage the changing of one's body lest it be for a case, but no one likes a unibrow. "Anyone?"

"Let me think." I rub my chin as the sound of Nick preparing his cereal crackles in the earpiece. "I saw a lot of people. Like, a lot. I saw Zack, he's my boyfriend by the way, and Em, but they were already out of the room." I make sure to nod my head up and down just like I did when stating my, well, Bryn's name, so that it comes across as the truth. "Oh, I saw her boyfriend, he's really a d-"

"We can do without the commentary," she interjects with a steely voice. Honestly Detective Miller could use some pointers on interrogating. It doesn't take a genius to figure out that teenagers will talk to someone they trust over an ice queen.

"Okay then, I saw her boyfriend, then walked over to my hiding place where my boyfriend is-"

"I thought you said he was already gone?" She shoves the recording device in my face and I push it right back at her. There's no need to be rude.

"I thought you wanted me to tell you the part where I found her. I saw my boyfriend, then he left, then the game ended, *then* I found her."

"How did you know where she was?" I scoff at her bluntness.

Even laughter gurgles out of Nick along with some of his milk and he comments. "Wow, we've got a real winner here, don't we?"

"I didn't. I was trying to leave when she was blocking my path." My statement comes out as a sort of huff in annoyance. "Am I done yet?"

"Do you think you are?"

"I'll see you later then." I spin the chair around as I stand up.

"Sit back down."

"Touchy," Nick says. "I've got an idea, are you up for a good laugh?"

"Yes ma'am." I sit down with my elbows resting on the table.

"I'll take that as a yes. Three." I roll my eyes but smile in anticipation. "Two." Detective Miller's eyes widen in curiosity. "One." Bells screech. Water sprays. Lights flash. Everything's so hectic it takes me a moment to realize this is Nick's doing.

I halfway bow and tip an invisible hat at Detective Miller. "And a good day to you."

Her jaw clenches as I stride out of the room into the mess of students.

I'm convinced there's a sort of magic in high school that draws friends to each other or it would be impossible for Em and Zack to end up at my sides as quickly as they do.

BEHIND THE COVER

Em passes me a concerned yet comforting expression and Zack squeezes my hand while we make our way through the crowds and blaring alarms. "Owww, I regret it already," Nick whines. I cackle in response; I'll have to thank him later.

"How was it? Are you okay?" Em asks anxiously.

"Oh, it was no biggie." I skip on my toes rearranging my face into a smile. "Just had to tell her what happened and she was *super* sweet." Em and Zack exchange a look with uncertainty clear in their eyes. "Don't worry about it."

"If you say so." Zack says.

Technically I should go over to my second period, Spanish, but I doubt my teacher will look for me assuming I'm still with the detective so I stick with Em and Zack.

Everyone shuffles around in their zig-zagging class lines like bees who can't sit still. About one third of them spend their time complaining about the cold with sour expressions while another third are gleefully chattering on about how happy they are to skip that physics test. The final third is posting all about this strange turn of events on social media. They can be easily distinguished by whatever odd facial expression is the current trend.

"Do you think there's really a fire?" Every agent knows the number one rule is to not get emotionally involved in a case, yet Em's voice tugs away at my heart. Through everything she's bounced back, yet the quivers in her voice shine through the cracks of her shell. It's said that eyes are the map to one's soul, but I'd say it's the voice. Anyone can learn how to blink the right way or stare in the proper direction, the voice one the other hand, can't be trained. Some people can change their voice to create music like Ben or become a crazy voice actor, but no one can control the truth it holds in its slight tremors, just ask a boy going through adolescence.

"I thought I smelled something in the cafeteria

earlier." Zack grins with a wink. Em and I roll our eyes simultaneously. "I'll be willing to bet it was that new old lady, the one whose hair is always falling in the spaghetti?"

This earns a laugh from Em which makes me giggle, as Bryn of course. A hand taps my shoulder and I fight the urge to flip the hand behind me and to the ground. Whatever I was expecting, whether it be fellow students, teachers, Detective Miller or even some enemy agent, I was not expecting to see Nick.

"What are you doing here?" I hiss at him while keeping a grin plastered to my face.

"You turned off your earpiece, I was worried," he whispers back, then raises his voice. "Hello Zack, Emily."

"Nick, dude nice to see you again." Nick holds out his hand and Zack grabs it then pulls him into one of those weird bro hug things guys do. When exactly did they meet? I giggle at the surprise cutting into Nick's face when the air is knocked out of him.

"Yeah, nice to see you again, uh, dude." It takes all I have not to crack up, but we are siblings and even more importantly we're partners. I decide to step in and save him.

"This is my brother, Nick." I introduce him to Em. "He's my ride."

She smiles softly at Nick. "Nice to meet you."

"You too." He blushes. Oh. My. Gosh. Nick Richards is blushing. Because of a girl no less. No freaking way.

I jab my elbow into his side and whisper. "Might want to rub some of that drool from your chin." His jaw snaps shut and he rubs his chin before glaring at me. "Two to zero," I sing in his ear.

"Two?"

"One point for saving your butt, another for embarrassing you. I mean that was gold."

"What are you two whispering about?" Em asks with a

raised eyebrow and amusement glimmering in her eyes.

"Me, obviously," Zack states throwing his arms over Em's and my shoulders. "Even the toughest of guys can't hold up to my image."

"Oh contrary." Nick clicks his tongue. "We were speaking of the beautiful young woman to your side."

"Aw thanks, little bro," I coo.

"The other one," he shoots back and I glare. "Two to one," he whispers.

"No way! That's not a point," I argue, pushing my hands against Nick while nonchalantly pushing him in Em's direction. We turn our heads nearly in sync back to the conversation at hand with Em and Zack.

Em's staring down at her toes with an equally bright red blush heating her cheeks. Her mouth starts to move but stops just as quickly. Who knew Nick was such a tongue twister?

Zack looks between the two of them with confusion blurring his eyes. The tension between him and Em grows with every encounter. It's only a matter of time before someone messes up. Except, now there's a new variable: Nick.

My smile dampens for a moment when I realize what I have to do.

The bell rings and the principal pulls out his speakerphone revealing that it's safe for us to return to class. Go figure.

At this point I've missed both first and second period. All that's left would be lunch, but Nick's here already and coach cancelled practice tonight so I decide to go straight home. Once we're in his precious car where no one will hear us I take a deep breath then blow it tersely through my tightly drawn lips. If it were anyone else I would walk sugar coat it, but with Nick I can give it to him straight and he'll understand. That's one of the things I really appreciate about him.

"Nick, do you remember the plan?"

"Yup." He pops the "p" sound without taking his eyes off his controller.

"Well, for the plan to work do you remember how Zack and Em have to blow up?"

"Yup again."

I sigh, he just isn't getting it. I'm going to have to go in for the tackle. "Do you like Em?"

"Nope." His voice is as normal and steady as always.

"Oh really, are you sure about that?" He stops fiddling with the remote and puts the car on auto pilot. Nick shifts in his seat so that his body is completely facing me. I expect to see a joking glitter to his face, but not an ounce of humor could be found in his hard eyes. His back stiffens as he places his hands on my wrists and locks eyes with me.

"I promise you, I do not like Em. That is simply impossible." Nick's voice is firm and cuts into me inexplicably.

"Okay." I was right: Nick really is the tongue twister.

"It's impossible."

"How so?" My eyes flicker upward as a single explanation floats across my mind. An hour ago I would have thought it impossible, yet here it is coming right from his mouth.

"I like someone else."

26 | Number One

-Emily-

A steely hand grasps my wrist and I shudder backwards in response. I look up to find a dark glare. "Emily Parker?"

"Yes?" I ask, but I already know who this cold woman is from Bryn's earlier description.

"I'm Detective Miller, can I have a word with you?" I nod my head and collect my backpack in case our discussion goes past the end of school. Creeper passes me a confused look but I jerk my thumb toward Detective Miller and his lips form an "o" in understanding.

We walk to the principal's office where his usually messy desk has been cleared for a notepad and recorder. Upon further inspection, I notice the principal's personal items appear to be shoved carelessly to the side of his desk with a slight crack running across one of the pictures of him and his son.

Detective Miller sits across the table from me and I quickly follow suit. Suddenly my terrible posture crawls into the back of my mind and I snap my back straight, fold my shaking hands in my lap and cross my ankles to the side of my chair. This is the closest I've been to being called to the principal's office for a misdeed and my nerves are sparking. I haven't even said anything yet Detective Miller is scribbling away in her little notebook.

"What's your name, how old are you, and describe your family?"

"Emily Parker, almost sixteen, and I live at home with my mom." My voice quivers, she clearly already knows my name. Maybe she's just trying to calm me down.

"Just your mom? No dad or siblings?"

"My sister died and my dad, uh, left." I look away. What does this have to do with anything?

"I'm sorry to hear it. Your dad just left?" She narrows her eyes and pauses writing for a moment.

"Yeah," I shift uncomfortably, "I don't see how it has anything to do with the case and it's personal so I don't want to talk about it."

"Okay then. Please go over the events of that night."

"Where should I start?"

"Wherever you feel would be best." Rather than a kind tone, Detective Miller's voice comes out snappy and abrasive. Who spit in her breakfast?

"Well, Zack, Bryn and I were all going through the gates to play laser tag at the Woohooz *Lasertron* when we saw C-" I gulp down a bitter taste in my mouth. "Clarisse and her friends come in line. I don't remember much of the game; I'm not the best at laser tag and was more of a defensive player. In fact, I didn't even know anything had happened until Cr-I mean Zack and I were waiting outside the room for Bryn and she came out with a sick look on her face. She went over and told the guys in charge something, then we were all rushed out of the building. Bryn then told us what she saw, and well that's about it."

"About?"

"That's it." I gulp again though my throat is drier than the Sahara. "That's all I can think of."

"Uh huh. What was your relationship with Clarisse?" When she asks, she sets down her pen, leans on her elbows and pushes the recorder close to me. As badly as I want to back away, I clear my throat and answer her question.

"We used to be friends when we were younger."

"And what happened?"

"I don't really know." I've been wondering about this quite a bit lately. "She just started to become really cold to people. When she started bullying this one kid, I left her group to hang out with him."

"Why would she become 'cold' toward you? What did you do?" Each of her words cuts into me digging deeper and deeper at wounds I hid long ago. Physically, I can take anything. Emotionally, I don't know. My mom gets it out through tears and writing; I've found dozens of her letters addressed to my dad but never sent. What do I do? I hide it. Life is better without dwelling on the past, yet somehow it keeps catching up to me.

"I don't know! Okay?" I snap tersely. My insides squish around like they've been turned to slime then harden as they explode out of me. "I don't know why I wasn't good enough. I don't know why everyone in my life decided they needed to leave me. I don't know what I did to them. I couldn't tell you why Clarisse hates me after we were so close. I haven't a fricken clue why we were finger painting together one day and the next she decides to catfish me." I look down at Detective Miller only to realize that in my rant I had stood up with my arms slashing around. I sit down and focus on inhaling, then exhaling. It wasn't until after the texting she found out about Kade and my kiss.

Detective Miller waits a few seconds. Apparently, I was the bomb, not Mom. Her eyes flash to a box of tissues, but she needn't worry: my eyes are as dry as my throat. I expect her to comment or say something addressing my rant, but she doesn't. Not really. Instead she says, "Catfish?"

I heave a sigh. The kind of sigh that carries with it your

voice and thoughts and feelings. Detective Miller remains still, but I can see a slight recoil in her expression. "You clearly already know Clarisse and I aren't friends anymore, but I didn't know how deeply she hated me until a few weeks ago.

"An anonymous user started messaging me on Instagram and we became really close. I told her *everything*. Apparently, that wasn't a great idea."

Detective Miller raises an eyebrow. "Interesting. Do you have any proof?"

"Don't suppose you know where the internet is," I retort.

She ignores my comment, but writes in her notebook. "Am I supposed to believe that you don't have any negative feelings after this?" I blanche.

"No, I definitely wasn't feeling one hundred percent kumbaya around the campfire with her, but I never would have hurt her. With my experience, I've learned to try to get back doing literally nothing."

"Uh huh, 'literally nothing.' So, not, like, figuratively nothing?" She smirks rolling her eyes almost like Bryn.

"I promise. I didn't k-, well that is to say mur..." I trail off. I can't even say the words.

"I've heard about a certain blue dye prank," Detective Miller changes the topic and I attempt to express how grateful I am through facial expressions. "Did you know anything about that?"

"Personally, I had nothing to do with it." I avoid mentioning Bryn and Creeper's names, but Detective Miller catches on.

"However, you know who did it." She leans forward to the point that if I moved about a foot closer to her our noses would touch. "Listen, any information could help. I don't think you did it."

"You don't?"

She snorts in laughter, "first off, you couldn't even say kill. Second, you might be able to fake that, but you're worse at lying than my five-year-old nephew." I'm not sure if I should be offended or relieved.

"So, I can go?"

"I said *I* don't think you did it. The rest of the officers and community investigating this case still holds you at number one suspect."

"Oh." The room is silent as I tangle a hair band through my fingers on my lap. My chin drops down to my chest as I consider my options, then realize there really aren't any. There isn't anything I can do unless I could figure out who really caused Clarisse's death. The fact remains, do I really want to know?

Detective Miller interrupts the silence with a sigh. "If you tell me who placed the blue dyes in the showers I'll let you go, okay?"

I nod my head but it takes a minute to form words. "It was Bryn and Zack. But I promise you, they didn't do it. They wouldn't ever, and I mean *never* do anything like this. They're great people, I trust them with my life, and anyone else's for that matter."

"Thank you, Miss Parker, you are free to leave." I trip over the chair as I hurry to the door.

The sound of my sneakers slapping the floor echoes in the nearly empty halls as I sprint to the auditorium for Drama. I slow only when a teacher passes. Today was the first day I was going to get to act so naturally today's the day I miss Drama.

I reach out to grab the handle of the door but am startled by the bell ringing signaling the end of school. An irritated groan that comes out more like a growl escapes my lips while students stream into the hallways. First come the nerds who sprint with a fear of social interactions followed by those who have to catch a bus.

After most of the class has cleared out, I enter the drama room to find Creeper and Mr. Matchen having a conversation. When Creeper notices me he excuses himself with a smile and comes to meet me.

"Follow me, there's somewhere I'd like to go," I say before he can even open his mouth.

I've only returned a few times since my first visit, but Mr. Matchen has been cool about it, encouraging even. I never thought I'd be showing Creeper this, but today's been full of revelations.

He raises his eyebrows at me when I open the closet door. I shove his shoulder as if to say *shut up* even though he didn't say anything. "Sit here and close your eyes," I instruct, and for once he does as I say without any side comments.

Even though I'm sure his eyes are closed, (I waved my hands in front of his face with no reaction) I step behind a divider to change. He must hear the swishing of the dress, but remains quiet. For that, I am thankful; otherwise I might lose my nerve.

Once I'm sure the dress is completely zipped up and on properly, I double check myself in the cracked mirror, then spin his chair around so that he's facing me. "You can look now."

I attempt to gauge his reaction, but his face stays constant aside from his eyes running from my toes to my head. He spins his pointer finger in a circle so I twirl around until I stumble to a stop falling into his waiting arms. "I figured you'd do that." He says into my hair.

"Of course you did," I mutter. "What do you think?"

"You look beautiful. People may say the sun is billions of miles of way, but I'm pretty sure the star is shining right here."

I blush at his words and step out of his arms. "Thank you. You have no idea how badly I needed to hear that after today."

We both sit down on the floor with a respectable distance between us and he looks at me with concern. "Are you okay?"

"Fine. Today was just...difficult." I shake my head and my ponytail slaps into his face like a whip. I pull my hands into my hair and tug out the ponytail holder so that it falls over my shoulders.

"What happened?" He looks at me with fierceness governing his expression.

"Basically I got two things out of my interrogation with Detective Miller. One: while she doesn't think I'm guilty, and two: everyone else does."

"Guilty of what?" He looks genuinely confused, maybe things aren't as bad as I think.

"That I-I mean." I clear my throat. "That I am the cause of Clarisse's death."

"Oh heck no. Heck to the no." He holds out his hand, but I don't take it. I can't. Creeper pulls it back after a second and I pull my arms around myself trying to become as small as I can. If I'm small I'm a smaller target and not as much can hurt me. I know the logic is flawed, but it's always calmed me in the past. "What was the second thing?"

"If people are already convinced I'm guilty, we need to prove my innocence. We need to find out who really did it." Creeper nods in approval. "We need a spy."

27 | Preparations

-Charlotte-

Two days. It's been two fricken days I've waited. I've been patient, I haven't even brought it up. But no, he just has to hold it over my head. Sure, I may have *hinted* that I'm dying to know who the girl is, but I haven't outright said anything. I've waited long enough.

Just look at that self-certain smirk as he slurps on his tomato soup while fiddling with some new gadget. He's clearly attempting to irritate me. I stare at him with my eyes narrowed to laser pointers until he takes notice and stares back equally hard. My eyes dry out then tear up, but I keep them open. Red creeps around the rims of his eyes as tears flow freely down his cheeks. I'm about to give out when his eyes flutter shut. "Darn it!"

"You'll never beat me at a staring contest." I flip my hair over my shoulder with a sweet smile just the way he hates it. "3-1."

"3-2," he corrects me.

"How'd you get an extra point?" I mentally go over the past three days. Nothing really happened. Detective Miller finished her investigations, and has vacated the school to review the evidence and go crush other children's souls. Em's been recovering with her smile growing a little stronger each day. Zack and I had our first official date at the movies, though it was pretty boring as far as dates go. The bracelet he got me was nice, I suppose. My reports have been blank. A few minor details here and there from the bugs in her house pertaining to Mr. Parker, but mostly quiet. That's okay though, today will change everything.

"I've held you in suspense for nearly an entire week." This time he puts down his little wand and tools signaling he's ready for an actual conversation.

"I knew you were doing it on purpose." I smile smugly. "But it's not suspenseful or anything. I could care less. You liking a girl? Why would I care?"

"Charlie?"

"Fine. You get the point." I concede then straighten in my chair. "Now who is she?"

"You like challenges, right?" He asks instead of answering my question, but he knows exactly how to distract my attention. I'll let him, for now.

"You know I do."

"Instead of simply telling you who she is, I'll answer five of your questions about her."

This could be even better. Rather than getting the name of some random girl off the street I can get real details about her.

"First question: do I know her?"

"Yes." I know her? He promised it isn't Em, did he meet anyone else at school? Or maybe it's one of those girls we seem to see every other day at the cross light. I'm going to have to make a list.

His eyes sparkle and he flashes a toothy smile down at his lap. I can just imagine him daydreaming about her like he does his latest invention. Only instead of getting a clouded over look, it almost seems that his senses come to high alert.

"If you could describe her in three words, what would they be?"

"Two questions already?"

"I'll save the rest for later, but I need this to tide me over after your cruel restraint of details."

"Okay then." Nick pauses and does his little thing where he bites his lip and rubs his fingers together. I can see the moment he comes up with the words when his entire body seems to tense up then relax as though a jolt of energy runs throughout him. Paramount. Assimilating. Nova."

"Interesting words." I quickly jot them down. "I wouldn't expect anything less. Certainly not beautiful, funny, and kind or anything."

"She's all of those things as well." He stops to rethink that statement. "Normally she is. Maybe more of an occasional thing. But that's not what I like about her."

"You chose to like her?" I raise my eyebrow at him; that's nowhere near as romantic.

"She's the last person on earth I'd choose to like. Trust me."

"If you say so." I fold the paper gently then tuck it in my pocket. I get the feeling that if I were to forget he wouldn't remind me. The dishes clatter as I drop them into the sink, but Kriss got plastic once Nick started messing around with the dishwasher for maximum cleansing. He's even set up an entire contraption so that once we drop the dishes in the sink they'll clean themselves (he got tired of dish duty).

I sling my backpack over my shoulder on my way to my bedroom pausing for a second to give Nick time to clean up his equipment and follow. Sure enough, his clomping feet match my pace a few steps behind me.

According to my bugs, Em, Zack, and I are flying down to San Diego which is why it's time to move on to the next part of my plan. If I can push Zack and Em tomorrow I can start the true high school friendship phase with Em which will result in optimal results with Ben and Em together and feelings running high. This is going to be an emotional weekend.

"Which shirt do you think shouts depressed but trying to be happy?" I ask Nick holding up to two shirts.

"Blue. The grey is just depressing." I nod my head in agreement and hand it to Nick.

I'm beyond ready for the warm California sun over blistering Boise wind. This trip should be a nice vacation other than the case, but I plan on having everything wrapped up and sealed in a file by the end of this long weekend. Maybe even before so I can try out beach soccer or casually run into some Cali agents, they're supposedly at the top but I plan on changing that.

"The Bryn attire is a good look for you, you should consider implementing it in your daily routine," Nick comments holding up a knee-length skirt.

"No thanks, after this case I'll have had enough skirts to last a lifetime. Do you know how hard karate is in a mini skirt?" I discard his choice in skirts and grab a pale pink sun dress instead.

"Speaking of, how's the case going? You haven't given many details of late."

"Other than the dead girl you mean?"

"Other than that." We laugh even though there's nothing funny about Clarisse or her death. It came as a twist, even for me. "From your scans, it appears that it was a delayed reaction from a drug that caused her death. I couldn't find the exact drug without DNA tests, but oddly enough it looked like Leukemia."

"Like, the cancer?"

"Exactly. Her lymph nodes and liver were swollen, she recently suffered from a bloody nose, the amount of weight she'd lost in the past few hours was more than she could have if she'd tried, and there was an excessive amount of sweat." He shakes his head. "I really am starting to feel bad for the girl. I can't imagine going through what she did; it was basically an accelerated form of Leukemia or something similar."

"Wow." I stop packing to pay attention. I prop my elbows on my knees and run through the conditions in my head. "You're right. I wasn't focused on her, but now that you say it I can remember all those things. She also had these little red dots on her arms. She'd covered them up on her face with makeup-though it was all weird because of the blue."

"Sounds about right. Do you have any idea who'd do this?"

I rock back and forth on my bottom and pull my knees under my chin in thought. "Everyone at Simplot seems to like her, and even those who don't wouldn't do anything like this. I mean, Kade's still around and he'll definitely get revenge on whoever did it."

"What if he did it?"

"Kade?" I scoff in disbelief.

"Last I saw about thirty percent of murders are committed by their significant other."

"Kade," I mull over the idea. Perhaps he hadn't been the most loving boyfriend ever, no spark in his eyes, but he stood by her all these years. It's not like he'd have incentive. "I don't think so."

"Okay. Just an idea, I think we should keep investigating this, I don't want something to happen to you."

"Aw, look who cares."

"Pfft, Kriss would never leave me alone again if you decided to go get poisoned."

"I can feel the love radiating off you." I return to packing and carefully place the DB under my clothes. I pop open the fake bottom of the suitcase and add in some wigs and disguises; you never know what you might need. I finish with a bag of makeup and the womanly essentials.

"In all seriousness, I feel like there's something more than what we know going on. So be careful." I nod my head. Isn't there always something more going on? Besides, when am I ever not careful? "I'll keep investigating what's going on. Can you please share your plan with me now?"

"Sure. Tomorrow I'm going to wait for Zack and Em to do some couple like thing, or possibly trigger it if it gets too late into the day, then act all depressed for a while. Just long enough for Em to want to have a deep heart to heart conversation for us to make up with lots of tears and smiles and hugs and girly crap like that. I'll have gained all information I could possibly want from Em and will move on to Mrs. Parker if necessary. I'll set up surveillance and it'll be smooth sailing from there. I should be finished by the time I'm back." I wiggle my eyebrows. "Then it's your turn. You get to retrace all the data I have to find him.

"Sounds fun." He lays back on my bed wrinkling my sheets and plays with a spring in his fingers. It bounces up and down until it flicks past his finger flying into a picture of Kriss, Nick, and me then rebounds at my face where I catch it between my finger and thumb.

I walk over to the picture and wipe off a layer of dust. It's a normal picture, Nick's holding a giant turkey leg to his lips and I'm wearing a pair of Minnie Mouse ears while Kriss has one arm pointing at the Cinderella Castle and the other holding the castle, but the story behind it is not. It was the first mission Kriss ever took us on, only because it was a reasonably safe case and it would be at Disney World.

While I don't know all the details, I remember it had something to do with revolting turkey farmers threatening to inject poisonous pesticides into the chicken legs. It turned out the entire thing was nothing more than a hoax and we got free passes to Disney World so everything worked out in the end.

I put the picture back with a sigh. Maybe we'll get to do a family case again.

"Hey Charlie? Do you ever think about our dad?" Nick asks flippantly, still messing around with his spring. Even though his voice is as light as ever, I know he's dead serious. "I mean, with everything going on with Mr. Parker, it just seems like it should've come up by now."

Our father is a topic that isn't painful as neither of us ever met him, but is a curiosity that I know Nick longs to know. "Sometimes. Have you been trying to hack Kriss' computer again?"

"No," Nick scoffs as though the idea is ridiculous, but after I harden my eyes he concedes, "Okay maybe I was."

"If it's as classified as Kriss says I'm sure that it's of national security. Otherwise she would've told us," I say, just like I've said every other time. "If he was good enough for Kriss, then he had to have an awesome death. I can only imagine the mission."

"Yeah, I can only imagine," Nick murmurs. He puts the spring in his pocket and stands up. Noticing my pointed look at the wrinkles, he attempts to smooth out my bed again. "I'm going to get back to my new soldering tool, they really chose the most inefficient way possible."

"Not the most inefficient way." I respond. "I mean, they could've used a snake. Those things are really unpredictable."

Nick shakes his head. "Goodnight, Charlie."

"Night, Nick."

28 | Trouble Ahead

-Emily-

I twirl my pencil around my fingers as Creeper goes on and on about his soccer game. Now and then I throw in an "uh huh" or "yup" or gasp dramatically. He's not catching onto my subtle hints. Thankfully Mrs. Hobs interrupts him by starting class.

"Today you will be taking a quiz." She smiles sweetly at us inducing a sense of unease. "Hopefully it will teach you something important."

She pops a stick of gum into her mouth then reclines back in her chair with the latest pop hits sounding from her computer.

Creeper groans, "Why is she so hard on us? Her grading is way too difficult and all of these assignments, ugh."

I laugh at his annoyance. Mrs. Hobs is one of those teachers that everyone either loves or hates. Creeper falls onto the hate side whereas I'm leaning toward love. She's always energetic, though that may come from all her coffee, and acts young. Not like those teachers who think they're "hip" and try to talk slang while texting on their flip phones. Sure, she may grade us harshly, but we're sophomores. It's about time they picked up the pace a bit. My writing has improved more in these past few weeks than it has in the last couple *years*.

The stack of quizzes makes its way to my table group and I begin. Her quizzes are notorious for taking the entire class period.

As I'm writing my name down, a lanky boy with glasses stands straight up and says, "A B C D E F G, H I J K L M N O P, Q R S, T U V, W X Y and Z."

A few more people stand up and repeat the sequence. *What the heck is going on here?*

I quickly read the instructions:

Read ALL the instructions before starting quiz.

Easy enough. The questions range from state your ABCs out loud to write a story about your worst enemy. The quiz is more like a packet; five pages long, single space, front and back.

I finally reach the last question and chuckle quietly to myself. It says:

STOP! Ignore all the previous questions and pretend to continue taking the quiz.

Should I help Creeper who's helplessly trying to multiply 5860 by 2413? He gives up and moves onto the next question. After he completes fifteen jumping jacks, his eyes meet mine in confusion. "Are you too chicken to do it? I'd enjoy watching Emily Parker receive a failing grade."

"We must have gotten different tests." I shrug.

"Not cool," he replies before continuing with the questions.

Rather than watch Creeper fail, I scroll through my feed on Instagram, bracing for any more comments. One of the best parts of social media is that everything is temporary and fast. You wouldn't even know about my video and pictures.

A slime video is interrupted by Creeper clearing his throat and I look over. His hands are folded in the shape of a ring box. "Emily Parker, will you marry me?" His hands open to reveal a drawing of a ring.

I tap my chin as though to consider his proposal when a boy I don't recognize steps up. "No fair! I was going to ask her!"

"Boys," I sigh. "Let's not fight amongst ourselves. I'm going to have to say no on both accounts."

"Good, I wasn't sure how I'd break the news to Bryn," Creeper jokes and winks at me. I'm glad we can joke about it now. "I'm such a heartbreaker."

"Perhaps someday young Padawan."

"I'm afraid the student has already surpassed the master." He bows and returns to his seat.

When I finally look away from him I notice that the entire class is staring at us. The stares range from jealous glares to Mrs. Hobs' smirk. I duck down in embarrassment.

Mrs. Hobs stretches her arms and legs before standing up. "I'd say that's enough time, who's done?"

Only six or seven of us slowly raise our hands and she shakes her head. "Fine. Everyone skip to the last sentence."

A couple of people groan while others laugh, Creeper nudges my arm and whispers, "You couldn't've let me in or something?"

I shrug with a smug smile. "Now that wouldn't be any fun, would it?"

He rolls his eyes and lightly slaps me in a playful manner.

"Yes Aubrey?" Mrs. Hobs replies to a raised hand.

"What exactly does this have to do with, like, *anything?*" Annoyance rings through her voice. I scan her face in search of anything that may hint to her feelings. There a few lines under her dark eyes and her cheeks have lost their blush. I almost want to comfort her, we both lost a best friend, but then I couldn't know what she's going through.

"I wanted you to take this quiz before I handed back

your six-year-old stories. Most of you lost half of your points because you simply didn't follow all the instructions." My hands begin sweat as I'm reminded of the assignment.

At first I'm nervous when I see my paper covered in purple writing, then I see the score; 98%! Relief floods through my body. I turn to high five Creeper, but only see his downtrodden expression. He got a 64%. Our eyes meet for one awkward, embarrassment filled moment before he fakes a smile and his too-cool-for-school attitude returns.

The bell rings, releasing us from class, but we both linger a second too long. Mrs. Hobs walks over and says, "I'm sorry Zack, you have great potential, but there were a few major things that were missing."

Creeper grunts in response then sweeps up his papers and leaves for Chemistry.

I speed after him until we're walking side by side in silence. What do I say? He's embarrassed, and I don't want to make things worse.

For all of Chem I try to figure out how to help Creeper. Unfortunately this class period consists of him being unusually quiet aside from the occasional "pass the beaker." Whenever someone walks by his smile tightens as he laughs or does something to make things seem normal. With these observation skills, maybe I don't even need a spy to solve the death of Clarisse.

Class goes by surprisingly quickly between thinking about Creeper and our lab on acids and bases. I'm surprised when the bell rings, releasing us to lunch. Luckily Creeper was paying attention to the time and already cleaned the beakers while I prepared the supplies for the next class.

As we walk to the cafeteria Creeper stops and pulls me against a wall of green lockers. "Okay, spill. What's going on?"

"What do you mean 'what's going on'? Nothing's going on." I feign innocence, though I'm not completely acting. *I'm* the one who should be asking 'what's going on?' not him.

"I mean why were you staring at me like a hurt puppy?" He laughs. "I was feeling like *I* was the science experiment."

"Oh, I, uh, in English we got our papers back, right? Then you seemed really sad, so I wanted to make you feel better. And in chem I tried to think of something and, is there anything I can do to make you feel better?" I trail off from my jumble of words.

"Emily, I will never understand how your mind works." He shakes his head. "What am I going to do with you? I wasn't upset about my grade, I was mad about *yours*."

"Huh?"

"Your writing was amazing. You totally deserved a good grade."

"I thought a ninety-eight was a good grade." That's not what I expected.

"After all those marks and the expression I thought...well great job!" He rubs his neck.

"Thanks." I smile and we continue walking.

"You know." He looks at me out of the corners of his eyes. "If you ever want to cheer me up you could kiss me. That'd probably do the trick."

"Creeper!" I gasp. "You have a girlfriend!"

My hand moves to slap him, but he ducks. "My name's Zack. And it's just an idea."

I try to slap him again but this time he catches my hand and pulls me into him. He's about to throw me over his shoulder when I hear a sharp gasp, followed by "I told you so!"

Creeper and I turn to discover Bryn and Aubrey. Bryn

must have been the one to gasp since her hands are covering her mouth and her eyes are tearing up. Meaning Aubrey is the one who said, "I told you so!"

The last couple seconds replay through my head. What was an innocent (*mostly* innocent) interaction that would look horribly different to her?

Me. In Creeper's hands. Sailing toward his face.

I can't even blame her for running away.

"Bryn! Wait!" Creeper and I shout at the same time.

"Stay here, you don't need to make things worse with your big mouth," I yell at him over my shoulder. He glares at me, but doesn't move.

I chase after Bryn but am quickly out of breath. She huddles next to the French portables. I sit next to her, but she scoots away. "Bryn, please at least listen." I suck in a deep breath. "You have every right to be mad at me from what you saw. Zack was just goofing around. You know how he gets. It's not like we were making out or anything."

Bryn glares at me. "What am I supposed to think? Is it normal for 'friends' to be holding each other preparing for a kiss?"

"I'm-"

"No! I gave you a chance to talk, now listen to me." She sighs. "Why didn't you tell me you like each other? If you two could have *told* me you liked each other, I would've been totally fine with my two best friends dating. I would've been sad for a while, but who cares as long as I have the two of you? Now it's clear you don't even trust me. The worst part of this is that Aubrey was right."

"Aubrey was what?" My voice catches in my throat, my chest clenching.

"You know, I'm really starting to wonder who I can trust." The meaning of her words slowly sinks in.

"Bryn, wait!" I call out, but she walks away again. This time I let her.

29 | Perfect

-Charlotte-

Nick pulls into the parking lot to drop me off. I look through the windows to see Simplot High School with a constant flow of students shifting in and out of buildings like a parade of ants, yet I remain seated. Oddly enough, it's started to feel like a home. My soccer team waves at me as they walk by the car. Aubrey rolls her eyes and flips her hair. Even the everlasting stench I've come to find comfort in. This is my first mission on my own. Sure, Nicks' my assistant partner, but I'm going to be on my own at San Diego.

For a few minutes, I sit in Nick's car thinking things over. He glances at me as the requesting permission to speak. I grant it through a nod of my head. "I'll drop off your bags at Mrs. Parker's house. You have everything you need in the trunk, right?"

"Right." I mentally check through my list of necessities. "Well, almost everything."

"What are you missing? I can pick it up on my way."

I smile at him and roll my eyes. "Nothing that important. I was going to say a hug from my brother, but if you're offering... I wouldn't mind some snacks for the trip."

"Oh." He laughs.

We both lean to the right, then the left. I throw out my arms so that each of my hands are on his shoulders and push him to the left as I lean to the right. "Let's agree not to do that again." I say solemnly.

"Indubitably." His cheeks are flushed pink with embarrassment. "To make up for it I'll grab you some snacks as well. I stick them in the second bottom of your red bag that blocks the airport scanners so you can sneak it onto the plane."

"Thanks, lil bro." I move to ruffle up his hair, but he catches my hand and pushes it back at me.

"I'm older."

"I'm more mature."

"Sure you are."

"Glad we agree." A bell rings interrupting our banter and I look to the front doors where I find Em in the middle of the crowd followed closely by Aubrey. "Looks like it's time to blow this pop stand."

"Looks like someone's keeping up with the lingo." He shakes his head in amusement. "I'll see you Tuesday, or sooner if you need me."

"Thanks, I'll see you then." I sling my backpack over my right shoulder and hop out of the car onto the sidewalk. One or two kids ogle at Nick's precious car with confused gazes probably attempting to figure out what kind of car it is. The majority of kids, however, continue to stumble around in a dreamlike phase still attempting to wake up from a sleep the never truly attained.

Without missing a step, I pick up the pace to be a second quicker than Em, but she slips away when an arm threads itself through mine. My face briefly contorts into an expression of irritation before clicking back into its grin when my eyes meet the devilishly pretty face of Aubrey. Ombre locks of hair swish into my face shining a blood red as she flips her head to a group of football players crowding the center of the hall. She looks like a tigress hidden behind innocent blush and stripes of eye liner.

I pull forward in an attempt to slip my arm away but her claws hold strong. We flash each other fake smiles in a standoff then stop walking completely. If I were Charlie I'd tell her to stalk off already, but I'm Bryn. "Hi Aubrey! Did you want to talk?"

"Hi Bryn!" Her voice is as sugary and counterfeit as my own. "I know that you and Clarisse had, like, an awkward falling out. But I *so* don't want things to be cold between us."

"Okay!" I bounce up and down eagerly. "Let's be friends then." My arm drags her closer to me and I dig my own nails into her forearm. She cringes, but doesn't say anything in response.

"Good. To prove our friendship, I'm gonna do you a solid at lunch, 'kay?" A devious glint flickers through her eyes as her smile curves upward, a look I recognize as a thirst for revenge. I had planned on sparking my plot during lunch, but this could help me even more.

"Mkay." There's some lingo for you Nick. "See you then." I wave to her and rush off to Spanish.

A quick warmup is on the board that should take less than four minutes. Now what should and shouldn't happen get mixed up more often than not. Meaning that the warm up tends to take closer to fifteen minutes for the class to complete it, and another five minutes to go over it as a class. To my right is seated a fluent Spanish speaker whose family speaks Spanish at home. The only reason he takes this class is for the extra credits. Everyone else in this room ranges from "I don't care," to "I'm too stupid to care," which results in the entire class being wasted.

The kid next to me is too concentrated on Snapchat to notice me or anything I'm doing, as usual, so I open the DB and create an outline for today's recap.

Part 1: Physical descriptions/changes.

-Emily Parker: Usual physical. Loose fitting jeans (Gap most likely), blue Adidas zip up sweatshirt with black stripes down the arms, Puma black tennis shoes with pink logo (size six).

-Zack Taylor: Usual physical (though noticeable growth in leg muscles as well as around the abdominal area likely from soccer).

-Aubrey (Ex-best friend of Clarisse): Ombre/dark brown hair. Her skin is even darker than usual (Side note that it makes her *so* pretty). Brown eyes. Five foot seven. Large hoop earrings (honestly, who wears these things at age sixteen?). Mint aquamarine shirt that cuts off to show belly button with ring (DNA?) and black leggings. Grey unmarked sandals. Plenty of makeup especially eye liner for the "swoop" (look it up on Youtube) and mascara.

-Brandon (undeserved of a last name): Light brown hair, tall-ish. Tall but not too tall.

-Kade: TBD

Part 2: Interesting facts.

-Aubrey made contact. Planned meeting at lunch (12:45pm mountain time zone). Reason: Unknown.

"Bryn." My head snaps up in sync with the DB slamming shut. My assumption of the voice belonging to my teacher is instantly discredited when I see he's still walking around attempting to help clueless students. The voice interrupts me again. "Bryyynnn."

I respond with a grimace, "Yes, Brandon?"

"What does yo mean in Spanish?" I roll my eyes. I knew he was dumb, but not this dumb.

"I." Before I can turn back to the DB he calls out again from the opposite side of the room.

"What about encanta?"

"Love." I snap drawing glances from our other classmates.

"Tú? Novio?"

"You, boyfri-" I stop with a glare. These words weren't in the warm up.

"Aww, yo encanta tú tambien." He winks at me. When he tries his accent isn't half bad.

"You just got served! Whoo you get're boy!" Caleb calls out cupping his mouth with his hands and swinging his butt in infinity patterns.

"No me gusta tú nada porque tú no eres intelligente. Tambien tengo un oltro novio." I blurt out with a perfect accent. Everyone stops to stare at me. Even fluent Snapchat kid pauses for a second with a smirk. I had to be careful to only use words we'd learned so far, so maybe it wasn't the best Spanish, but it works.

"Muy bien," Mr. Juan says clapping his hands. "Completan? Bueno." He starts to call out students to write the warm ups on the board.

Brandon raises his hand and waves it around like a little kid who needs to pee. He hops out of his seat the moment he's called on. With his ever-constant smirk he waltzes right over to the section of the whiteboard in front of me. "Looks like someone has a secret," he whisper-sings.

"And what might that be?" I snap back. Around Brandon I don't even bother hiding Charlie's irritation. Even Bryn could be annoyed by him.

"Under her beautiful exterior she's got a wondrous nerdy interior." He stops writing and spins so that his hands slap down to my desk on either side of the DB with his face inches from mine. "And I like those smarties."

"Too bad I'm *taken*." I push him away. Only, I accidentally push him a little too hard and the back of his head slams up against the whiteboard. For a moment he stares at me with a gaze of bewilderment then shakes his head with a grin.

As sloppy and difficult to read as his handwriting may be, he is the only student to get their warm up question correct. Looks like I'm not the only hidden "smartie".

Class drags by slower than Internet Explorer. One would think today we were supposed to learn about preterite forms of verbs since that is the title of today's lesson, but the only thing in the past is the class' wasted time. Caleb distracts the teacher through complaining, random slang, and messing around with Brandon.

I count down the minutes, then seconds until the bell rings and am the first out the door to a nearly empty hallway. Using the students as barriers, I practice slipping in and out of tight spaces while keeping a practice target (purple hair girl) in sight and out of a shooter's (blue hair boy) line of sight.

Purple hair girl enters the classroom right before Chemistry but we still manage to beat most of the crowd. My jaw practically drops when I see Brandon sitting on my desk with his feet resting on my chair. This boy is full of surprises, generally unpleasant ones.

Rather than attempt at a civilized conversation with him, for no conversation with Brandon is truly civilized, I shove him off my desk onto the floor. This time he allows me to push him and lands on his feet rather than head. I ignore him while I sit down and wait for Em and Zack to arrive, naturally they're the last two to walk through the door.

Our time in Chemistry is spent doing one of two things: a lab or a lab write up. Today is a lab and we have enough supplies that we're supposed to work in partners. Seeing Brandon out of the corner of my eye, I go straight to Zack. "Wanna be my partner?"

"Sure, but I think someone else was going to ask you." He signals at Brandon with his eyes and I snort in a mixture of laughter and irritation.

"You guys can fight it out," I joke, but he waits for Brandon to waltz over here. Zack looks at me innocently and I glare at him.

"I know you're dying to ask me, but words aren't necessary at this point in our relationship," Brandon says, eyeing me. He unnecessarily touches my shoulder even as I move away.

"I haven't the faintest idea what you mean." I shrug, then turn to Zack so that my back is facing Brandon.

"I would like to partner with the fair lady." Brandon bows exaggeratedly resulting in him holding out his hand like a Shakespeare character. No thank you.

Zack rubs his chin as if in deep thought. After a moment, he snaps his fingers together. "Rock, paper, scissors."

"Sounds fair to me." Brandon nods his head in agreement. They size each other up then get into their stances: Zack standing straight with Brandon sticking his butt out.

"Hold up! I'm not sure about this." I cross my arms and step in between them, but they're long gone with their focus centered on the silly game. Em holds her hand to her lips next to me.

"Rock.'

"Paper."

"Scissors."

"SHOOT!" They shout in sync. Zack's made his hand into a fist: rock. Brandon has chosen to flatten his hand: paper.

Brandon fist pumps then grabs my hand twirling me into the lab area all the while I'm shooting daggers at Zack through my eyes. Zack shrugs and turns to Em who appears to be somewhat zoned out in thought.

I rigidly pull my hand away from Brandon's grasp and hold up two fingers. "Rule number one is that you are not allowed to touch me without my expressed permission. Rule number two is that you must raise your hand before speaking." He opens his mouth to reply, but quickly shuts it and nods his head instead. I frown at the amusement in his eyes, but otherwise ignore it.

I provide Brandon with each of my commands and he follows them without a word. It's almost too quiet without Brandon speaking, then I realize it's weird not having Nick in my ear. I wonder what he's doing right now. Maybe he's finally gotten to work on Kriss' voice equipment.

Once we have all the chemicals collected, we heat them up in a mixture of water and chemicals on Bunsen Burners watching for color changes, scents, and bubbles. It's easy for the most part as we're working with vivid chemicals so we finish long before the end of class.

While I return to my seat Brandon follows me closer than my own shadow waving his hand around. Once I've settled in my seat he places his hands on my shoulders causing me to jump. "Rule one."

"You were clearly asking for a good shoulder rub to get some of that tension out." He slowly puts his hands back and I let him.

"And rule two." I roll my eyes.

"I *did* raise my hand. You said nothing about calling on me." I don't bother to complain. He isn't worth my time. A shrill bell makes me jump out of his grasp. Brandon races off causing me to fall backward in my seat and is gone before I can even glare at him. It doesn't matter, however, as I'm off to meet Aubrey.

An excuse is already formulating in my mind to slip away when I see Em and Zack already leaving without me. If this weren't a part of my job, I might be hurt. Luckily it is so I'm not.

I tap my foot impatiently and pretend to scroll through my phone while I wait for Aubrey to show up, flashing back to the start of this case. When she finally does arrive, the first thing I notice is her change in wardrobe. She's replaced the cut off shirt and leggings with a grey hoodie and jeans sliced at the knees.

"Bryn!" She squeals, reaching to lock our arms again. Only this time I'm prepared and slip to her other side making it clear I have no interest in being trapped at her side.

"So, what are you going to show me?" I try to keep my voice excited.

"Just follow me." She grins showing her teeth. Her upper left and right teeth cut down in a way that resembles a vampire. I wouldn't be surprised if she were a direct descendent.

Rather than slide between the sweaty bodies of people and fumes, the crowd parts for her until we reach an empty hallway toward the other side of the building. I'm about to question her again when I see Em sailing at Zack's face.

Perfect.

30 | You and Your Big Mouth

-Emily-

Creeper raises an eyebrow as I walk into drama but I shake my head in response. I don't have to say anything yet he already knows this is *bad.*

Rather than sit in my usual seat next to Creeper, I sit on the opposing side of the room. I attempt to sneak in quietly since I'm late, but it doesn't take long for Aubrey to take notice of my presence.

"Look out everyone, or else she might try to snatch away your boyfriend." She stands up and states. Though she doesn't shout, her voice resonates across the room. To my dismay, more people laugh than stay silent. I thought I'd made progress in showing people I wasn't what Clarisse said; I was wrong. "Or worse, murder." My stomach drops with a sick feeling.

"Just shut up already. No one believes you anyway," Creepers snaps with his eyes aglow. My cheeks heat up in anger and embarrassment.

"Here comes the cheater to the rescue." Aubrey laughs.

Did I or did I not tell him to keep his big mouth shut?

"Aubrey," I start cautiously, "we weren't doing anything. We all know Zack can be a major flirt, not to mention *idiot*, and he got excited. Trust me, I would *never* want to kiss him. I'm not sure my health can take that kind of damage."

"Offensive much," Creeper grumbles.

"I think that you both showed the school how you really feel." Aubrey is on a roll. Clarisse may have been deadly when it came to her actions but Aubrey can kill with her words.

"Believe what you want, just don't mess with my friends." I've been trying to keep my voice even, but it rises when I think of Bryn.

"Like I had to try." Judging by the look on Creeper's face, Aubrey should be thankful that Mr. Matchen interrupts us when he does.

"Based on the many conversations over the past few days I assume you all know your individual lines. So today we will work on group scenes." He pauses and looks over his stack of papers. "Aubrey, as Clarisse's understudy you will be taking her place. Kade, join us onstage as well. Let's start with the scene where your characters meet."

"Sir." A girl name Miah raises her hand. "Shouldn't we do the play in order?"

"I see you point. However, it is the major scenes that will require blood, sweat, tears and magic to flow. These are the scenes we will work on." He lets his, what I'm sure to be inspirational, speech sink in, but my mind is on other topics. "Now get started."

Once everyone's all set, I notice the kids left in the audience are very few. As quietly as possible, I rip the corner off of a sheet of paper. I scribble down a summary of what happened with Bryn and write Zack on top of it.

"Can you pass this note along to Zack?" I ask the boy next to me. He glares and shakes his head, but after a few minutes of my pestering he passes the note to the boy next to him. Finally it reaches Creeper. I try to gauge his expression while he reads it, but his face remains a solemn mask. After reading it he passes a note back to me.

Me and my big mouth would've gotten a word in!

I glare at him and a couple of kids across our row chuckle.

On the next note, I ask what we should do. There are more giggles as his response is passed down the line causing me to sigh even before I read it.

You're the brains in this relationship, I'm the looks.

He's doing a *great* job of helping our case.

Mr. Matchen must be regretting his decision on the lead roles. We barely get through the scene before class ends.

"Miss Parker." Mr. Matchen stops me from leaving. Is he mad about the notes?

"Yes sir?"

"May I have a word with you?" I nod my head and we move out of the way of exiting students. Creeper shoots me a worried glance, so I shrug in response. "I have to admit I'm rather disappointed in you."

"Sir?" I didn't realize he'd be so upset about a couple of notes.

"Why did you audition for such a minor role?"

"I wanted to get a feel for everything before taking on more than I could handle. I mean there's been a lot going on with beginning of school homework, and tests." Not to mention I'm a key suspect in a *murder*. The disappointment in his eyes remain constant, but his features soften.

"Very well then. I'm sorry for bothering you, though I do hope you'll consider a more major part in the next play." Mr. Matchen glances around the room mysteriously. "I'm not certain I've had a more trying student than Aubrey."

We laugh together then I remember I have to meet Creeper and maybe Bryn at soccer practice. "I'm sorry sir, but I really need to get to practice. I'll think about what you said."

"Have a good weekend Emily." Mr. Matchen waves goodbye and I sprint to the girls' locker room. It's empty so practice must not have ended yet.

I wander over to the showers watching for a trail of blue, but it's as clean as a locker room ever is. The showers themselves, however, are a different story. The shower head will have to be replaced, there's no way even Mr. Clean could get out that cookie monster blue. If blood were blue, this would look like a massacre. It covers the tile and continues up the wall in splattered waves.

I cover my mouth in laughter, just imagining Clarisse, Aubrey and Kade's reactions. Then drop my hand. I would do anything to change the events of the past. Never would I wish for the death of anyone.

My thoughts remain in the showers while I venture toward the bathroom mirrors. Using the full length mirror my eyes travel from my worn-out tennis shoes to my frizzed hair. I don't look like a bad person whose mind is swirling with devious thoughts. An overly tired teenager who never moved past her awkward phase with a case of bad acne, sure. But that doesn't match the description of a murder.

A locker slams shut, startling me out of my trance. When I reach the field, practice is nearly over. I can't imagine they have more than one or two drills left. Their coach shouts something and they quickly form two lines next to a goal with Bryn and another girl stepping forward to the coach. A ball is tossed in the air and the games begin.

First, the other girl attempts to trip Bryn with her leg but Bryn jumps over it while twisting the knee so she falls. The girl lands in a push-up position and pushes off the ground like an animal. Bryn jumps up to catch the ball, but the girl shoulder checks her and grabs it before she can regain her balance. The girl offers her hand to help Bryn up, but she brushes it off. Bryn says something undecipherable from this distance and leaves the poor girl in her dust.

They continue like this until the coach ends practice with their regular stretching routine so I go watch Creeper's practice on the next field over. The guys team looks exhausted. Their legs are dragging. Their passes are slow, which their coach screams to stop hittin' the ball with their purses. No one's even trying to score.

Creeper catches my eye and winks. He steals the ball and dribbles across the field: zigzagging through player after player. Instead of shooting the ball like a normal person, he decides to show off and fake out the goalie before juggling into the goal.

Their coach decides to end practice on that play. While Creeper changes and showers with his team, I scan the fields and spot Bryn sitting under a pine tree behind a goal.

Instead of joining her, I walk over to the parking lot.

"Mom, what are you doing here?" I pass her a wary glance remembering our conversation this morning.

"I have a surprise for you." Mom drums her fingers against the steering wheel with a grin on her lips. "Check your bag in the back seat." I open the door to find my packed suitcase. Sitting on top of it is a letter. As I open it a slip of paper falls out which I discover to be a plane ticket. My eyes scan the paper and tear up:

Hi Em,

Can't wait to see you!

Love,

Ben

My jaw drops. "I forgot! Is it really today?"

"Yes!" My mom laughs. "Now go get your friends."

"They know about this too?" I ask as I move backward.

"Of course." She gestures with her hands pushing me to go faster. I start to run in Bryn's direction and hear a panting to my left.

"I thought you'd left without me." Creeper jogs up beside me.

"I can't believe you guys didn't remind me," I mutter. My smile disappears as we get closer to Bryn.

"What's wrong? If you're worried about Bryn, we'll find a way to clean up this mess. Don't worry."

"It's a little too late for that. This trip is going to be a nightmare." My hands fly up to my head, all previous excitement gone.

"It'll be fun. I get to talk this time, you had your turn." I turn to glare at him but he's already sprinting towards Bryn. I chase after him but stumble on my weak legs. I'm going to have to work out more.

Creeper must have worked on his communication skills, because by the time I reach them Bryn says, "I'm obviously going. Why else would I have stayed through this jerk's practice? As much as I may hate you two, I'm not missing out on a chance to see my partner in crime, Ben, or my favorite singers."

Creeper and I exchange a look but I still smile at her. "I'm glad you're coming."

"Did you not hear what I just said? I'm not interested in talking to you." Bryn huffs and stalks away.

"Wow Emily, you sure know how to smooth things over." Creeper nudges my shoulder.

"You have got to be kidding me," I groan.

"No, I'm actually quite serious." He winks and I push him instituting a shoving match that continues all the way to my mom's van.

I'm content to sit in the backseat with Creeper as Bryn's already taken shotgun. She and my mom continue their conversation about Bryn's class schedule and adjusting to Boise the entire ride to the airport.

The Boise airport isn't large, but the wait time is only to be reckoned with by the DMV. While we wait to board the plane, my mom goes to the bathroom leaving us with fifteen dollars to buy a snack.

"What do you guys feel like?" I offer.

"Pizza, or a cheeseburger. Anything greasy would be great," Creeper replies, making both Bryn and me grimace.

"You're *so* disgusting." It's only been one day and her voice already resembles Aubrey's. "Let's go get Starbucks or something."

"And you are such a girl," Creeper retorts.

"And that's more than you'll ever be," Bryn snorts.

"If to be a girl is to be like Clarisse, then I think I'm fine being the way I am."

"Ha! You would be a deceiving, fool hearted imbecile."

"Somebody remembers her third-grade vocab words."

"If it means I don't have to end up working at McDonalds with people like you then I'll do it." A small boy next to us gasps as his older brother shouts "Buuurrrrn!" I know then that I have to step in.

"Guys come on! I know we're not on the best terms right now, but we still need to be civilized." I try.

"That's rich coming from you," Bryn replies sharply. Creeper tries to come to my defense but I cut him off before another argument can take shape.

"Let's just go get our snack." I march in the direction of the giant Starbucks sign knowing Creeper will follow and hoping Bryn will. When I reach the end of the Starbucks line, I turn around as if I knew they'd be there the entire time. "What do you want?"

Creeper shrugs. "I'll be fine with whatever you want."

Bryn rolls her eyes before answering, "The Pumpkin Spice Latte, but hold the sugar and extra cream."

"Okay." Creeper snickers at my voice and we share a look before cracking up. I stop the moment my eyes meet Bryn's glare leading to silence until we get to the counter. A perky young lady with a voice like that of a Disney character asks for our orders and I get two chocolate muffins with Bryn's latte.

She flashes a way too cheery smile as she hands out our order and wishes us a nice day. We take our food and head back to my mom without another word. Even my mom notices something is off and doesn't attempt to hold up a one-sided conversation.

Bryn passes the time by responding to messages on her ever-buzzing phone while Creeper messes around with a loose string on his shirt. The plane starts boarding ten minutes too late just as two crazed men run up gasping for air.

"Can...we...trade...tickets...with...any...one?" The first one gasps.

"What seat numbers do you have?" To my surprise Bryn's the one to respond.

"Seats 23A and 23B. We need to sit further up front." The second one says now that he's collected his breath.

"We can trade." Bryn looks to my mom for affirmation before handing over two of our tickets.

"Thank you so much." The second smiles while the first dive hugs Bryn before they head over to their new spot in line. "I guess I'd better move to the back of the line, who wants to sit with me?"

Creeper and I make eye contact sharing a silent conversation:

Should I?

I can.

I will.

I said I can.

But you have a big mouth.

That again?

My mom interrupts us. "I will." She smiles at Bryn and they walk back to their new waiting point. Creeper shoots Bryn an annoyed look and sticks his tongue out after her.

"Really?" I ask.

"What?"

"Are you in second grade?" I shake my head as we board the plane. "Childish maneuvers like that are not going to help us get our friend back."

"If she's going to leave us over a simple misunderstanding like this, is she really our friend?" He asks. I don't reply.

Once we're all seated an announcement comes over the speakers stating that we're about to take off. Everything shakes and wobbles as the plane starts to move forward. I stare out the window at Boise's airport growing smaller as the plane flies upwards.

Creeper and I are sitting eight seats behind my mom and Bryn. Even with the conversations and movies, the tension hanging between us screams louder than anything. A flight attendant stops in the isle next to us.

"Is there anything I can get you two cuties?" She holds out her notepad looking up at us. I look down, searching for a menu.

"We'll both have a mug of hot cocoa, thanks." Creeper cuts me off and winks at the poor girl. "She's a little slow today."

"Slow?" I shake my head. "Gee thanks."

"You don't like hot cocoa? Sorry, I'll get lemonade next time."

"Hot cocoa and lemonade. You seriously think this is about hot cocoa and lemonade?"

"As much as you'd like to believe otherwise, I'm not a complete idiot. I've been trying to think of a way to convince Bryn that even though you may be infatuated with me we are not dating."

I ignore the last bit of his sentence. "And what exactly have you come up with?"

"Well, we could hack into the school's security system and show her the entire scene. Or we could bribe her with your friend Ben's money. Or, hey, we could use that money to bribe the pilot not to land the plane until Bryn forgives us."

"No, no, and definitely not." I sigh. "I need to go to the bathroom."

I push past snoring passengers, crying babies, and irritated flight attendants to the bathroom at the back of the plane. Surprisingly, it's clean. Like, cleaner than at home. I wash my hands with a vanilla scented soap then switch the water to cold and splash my face and redo my ponytail that's nearly fallen out.

With one final tug of my hair, I step out of the bathroom-right into Creeper.

"What are you doing here?" I whisper.

"Is it a crime for a guy to use the restroom?" He ripostes and I begin to stutter my way past him until he puts a hand on my shoulder. "That was a joke."

"A terrible one." I cross my arms in annoyance.

"The real reason I waited out here for you was to apologize. You're right, I'm wrong. Wow that was hard to say." He pauses and a far-off look overtakes his eyes. I snap my fingers and he jumps in surprise. Boys, they have the attention span of an ADHD puppy.

"Creeper, you there?"

"Wh-oh, yeah. I just was thinking about how we say like 'I'm' for I am, and 'he's' for he was, but we don't generally say 'I's' for I was."

I lightly slap his arm. "You're such a dufus."

"But you love me anyway."

"Of course." I say without thinking, but it hits both of us like a strike to the face. "Not. I mean of course not"

We're unusually quiet for a moment before Creeper clears his throat. "As I was saying, I'm sorry and what should we do now?"

"Well, we should start off by creating a plan to win back Bryn and show her we'd never do what she thought we did. One not including any sort of blackmail."

"Okay, like what kind of plan?"

Before I can sarcastically comment on his helpfulness, we're interrupted by the sound of something slamming against the floor then a flight attendant stepping into our little area.

"You lovers had better get back to your seats, the plane's going to descend soon." Her slangy tone isn't the only thing that perturbs me.

"We are *not* lovers," I insist.

"Uhuh, keep telling yourself that an' see where it gets ya."

A fierce blush accents my cheeks as Creeper leads me back to our row.

Our descent is much quicker and more turbulence filled than take off. The crying baby seems to sense something's different and finally manages to quiet, likewise the elderly man discontinues his snoring. A moment of relief that we landed safely is quickly pushed away by an urge to *get out*. Everyone, young and old, big and small, pushes to get to their luggage. Even Creeper reaches across my lap to stand up before I glare at him.

The speaker crackles to life causing everyone to quiet down a little bit. "Thank you for flying with Alpha Airlines. We hope that you enjoyed your flight and will visit again soon. Before I let you all leave, would a Miss Emily Parker please come to the front of the plane."

BEHIND THE COVER

Creeper and I exchange a confused look and even my mom turns around to raise an eyebrow at me.

It takes about a hundred "excuse me's" and "sorry's" to get to the front, but I manage.

The pilot himself is waiting for me when I get there. "I was instructed to ensure you were the first guest exit." He opens the door to the plane. "Have a nice stay in San Diego, California!"

I slowly turn to the door then break into a sprint, crashing into Ben's arms. We both land in his oversized pile of Snickers and laying right here, breathing in the scent of Ben's cologne and being poked by wrappers in the middle of the exit of an airplane, I feel more at home than I have in weeks.

"I missed you."

31 | Coincidence

-Charlotte-

"Should I ask?" Mrs. Parker has held back the entire car ride to the airport and through the takeoff, keeping a calm smile to cover her curiosity and concern.

"Probably not," I say kindly. "This won't last too long, I hope." Not hope, know. I have no intention of drawing this out any longer than necessary. I hadn't planned on this discomfort from withholding communication. Though, I must admit there is an undeniable pleasure in insulting Zack.

In the seat next to me, Mrs. Parker's fallen asleep, so I open the DB to page one hundred and fifty-four. I check off the first part of my plan; create drift between Em and Bryn. Now, it's time to start setting up the next part in which we have a major make up with plenty of tears and *stories*.

To my surprise, my earpiece crackles to life. "Nick?" How could he make a connection up here?

"Hey Charlie." He sounds incredibly happy. "I made the next major break in the case!"

"Do tell." With one hand, I lift my phone to my ear, with the other I softly close the DB, and use my teeth to pull away the glove.

"It's rather obvious, actually. Remember the symptoms I listed for Clarisse and her death? I also found the official medical reports."

"Found?" I interject with a grin.

"Found. Discovered. Took. Same difference. Anyway, as I was saying, her symptoms match that of Leukemia just like I thought. Even more so, in fact." He pauses as though allowing me to put the pieces together. They aren't clicking so I wait for him to continue. "There's someone else who's been involved in Leukemia in this case-"

"Em's dad!" I exclaim. My hands fly to my mouth even before the words are complete. My eyes fly across the plane, but most people are too concerned with their own lives, like Em and Zack, or are dead asleep, like Mrs. Parker. "You think he has something to do with this?" I lower my voice.

"It's too much of a coincidence not to." His voice becomes a smirk as he starts ticking things off. "First her dad becomes a Leukemia researcher with one of the most prestigious research groups in the country yet his research is nowhere to be found. Then his daughter becomes sick with the very same illness, and, come on, it's not like he picked up the germ off a random sample and passed it on to her. She dies causing him to go depression crazy and this family man leaves the rest of his family. Finally, years later, you enter the picture and come across a very mimic of the original illness in this tiny city of Boise in the most forgotten state of Idaho."

"Are you saying he created this poison?" I exhale slowly through my teeth. This is not what I wanted to hear.

"I'm not sure what I'm saying." He sighs. "All I know for sure is that you need to be careful."

Now it's my turn to smirk. "I'm always careful."

"Oh, really?" Nick's voice is sharpened by a challenge. "Shall I remind you of the past?"

"What past?"

"There was the peanut butter accident."

"I was ten!" I shake my head. "When you were that age you were still wearing diapers to bed. Try to come up with a more recent past."

"The zoo."

Memories of this fatal day throw shivers across my body. I'll never look at a penguin the same away again. Preferably, I'll never look at a penguin again period. I would need a disguise to return to that zoo.

Thankfully, a flight attendant interrupts us before I come up with a plausible excuse. With a click of her pen a smile pops onto her face. "Can I get you ladies something to drink?"

"I'll have orange juice." I think back to Em's house when Mrs. Parker would have sparkling water with her cookies. "And she'll have soda water with a lemon on the side, please." Sometimes it helps to have a spy's mind.

"Sure thing." She tosses us a few bags of pretzels and peanuts before continuing on her way.

I look over to Mrs. Parker who's still asleep. Rather than wake her up, I pull down the trays and divide up the bags. When I casually glance over my shoulder, I catch sight of Em making her way to the bathroom with Zack on her tail. I get up and follow them after allowing a few seconds of a safety cushion to pass.

Em must be in the bathroom since Zack's standing outside. Not wanting to make contact, I flatten myself into an area between the bathroom and seats. Zack whistles a light tune for a moment, but stops at the squeaking of hinges.

While I can't hear exactly what is said, it isn't hard to guess from their voices. Em's is a muffled shout until Zack chuckles and she backs off. They quiet down so I decided to test a new feature on the earpiece that Nick claims it will amplify sounds. Just as I increase the volume, a flight attendant pushes her cart into me and Nick shouts in my ear. Through a second of chaos, I manage to save every glass that was falling. What I didn't manage to save is my head smacking against a wall.

"That's gotta hurt," Nick snickers in my ear. "Only a few hours in and you're already falling apart without me."

"Shut up," I hiss through my teeth. Since there hasn't been a chance to readjust my earpiece, Nick's voice still comes across as a screech.

Zack and Em's conversation starts up again, so I hurry back to my seat in irritation; that was a complete waste of time.

32 | Shop Till You Drop

-Emily-

Ben and I finally release each other after complaints from other passengers begin to arise.

"I can't believe I'm here. We have a lot to talk about." I glance down at the Snickers. "After we share some of these. By 'share' I mean you watch while I get my much-needed comfort food."

He smiles in response and takes my hand as his guards take my Snickers. I'm halfway tempted to warn them to be careful with my babies but decide that might be a bit much.

We wait for the plane to empty and the rest of our party to disembark. Just having him here next to me is more than good enough. Sometimes, I think, it's hard to know how much you missed something until you get it back.

Bryn comes out first, followed by my mom. They share a quick hug with Ben, though he keeps his hand fastened in mine like he can't physically remove it.

When Creeper steps out with both his and my luggage he nods tersely at Ben.

"I'd assume you're the famous Ben?" Creeper asks and holds his hand out, shifting a bag onto his arm.

"I am and you're...Creep?" Ben awkwardly takes the hand.

"Zack."

"Well," Bryn claps her hands together. "As much as I enjoy moments filled with hatred and broken relationships I would love it if we could get to our luggage and even the hotel." She pauses before walking towards the baggage claim. "Ben, it was lovely meeting you in person."

"You as well." Ben smiles back.

As we follow Bryn's lead, Ben mouths: I thought she was the happy one.

I grimace and repeat, "We have a lot to talk about."

For now, any troubles are gone as long as I'm with Ben. The best friends united again.

We don't need to worry about picking up our bags, Ben explains, since his people will take care of them. In response Creeper grins. "Sweet dude!" And proceeds to attempt an elbow high five combination with Ben.

Bryn doesn't look nearly as elated. "Could I maybe wait for mine? I have some...things I'd rather get back as soon as possible."

"I guess you can stay if you really want to. Would you like one of us to wait with you?" Ben offers.

"That's okay, I can take care of myself. Thank you though."

My mom puts up her hand. "As the mother placed in charge of you I'm going to stay. No arguing."

My mom's stubbornness causes us all to laugh and Bryn replies with a quick "Yes, ma'am."

Waiting for Ben, Creeper, and me outside are not one, not two, but three limos. I had been expecting at least one, but three is a little over the top.

Creeper's eyes bug out when we walk up to them. "My lady." Ben holds open the door for me and I graciously step in.

"This is for us? Bro," Creeper shouts.

"Wanna ride with us or on your own?" Ben asks.

"A limo all to myself, or share with two other gross teenagers? I'll take my own." With that he hops into the limo in front of ours.

The door slams shut on Ben's side and we start moving past the star struck visitors. Now that we're finally alone, I notice some of the smaller things that have changed about him: the extra inch of his hair, tanned skin, even his voice has grown the slightest bit deeper.

"I missed you so much."

"Wasn't exactly easy for me either." He pulls a can of sparkling cider out of the mini fridge as well as a Snickers and holds them out to me.

I open the Snickers bar and automatically hand him half of it.

"What are you most excited for?" Caramel coats his teeth while he talks.

"I'm just glad to get to see you again." I smile with equally caramelly teeth.

"So, you aren't excited about the party tomorrow?"

"What party?" My head snaps up until our eyes meet.

"Oh, just a welcome party for you with a couple of my personal famous friends and a little singer by the name of Shawn Mendes."

I squeal so loudly it's a miracle we don't get in a wreck. First, I hug him, then I sit back in thought.

"What's wrong?" He asks, genuinely concerned.

"When did you say this party is?"

"Tomorrow night."

"Tomorrow? Ben what's wrong with you?" I throw my hands in the air. "You only give me one day to prepare for *Shawn Mendes*?"

He grins in response.

"I don't have anything to wear!"

Ben looks me over. "Were you planning on going nude this entire trip? Besides what you're wearing now would be fine."

I look down to find myself in a pair of ratty jeans and an old sweatshirt. Boys. "Thanks, but I would seriously appreciate nicer attire than sweats and jeans."

"I figured you'd say that." He sighs and puts down his cider before gesturing out the window. "I brought you here: Fashion Valley. The finest shopping in all of California! At least, that's what Krystal claims."

I all but plaster my face to the limo's window trying to get a good view of the shopping complex. Hundreds of tan and white-walled stores separated by California's signature palm trees and pearly tile set in intricate patterns produce what resembles a miniature city. Everything calls to a California oasis with open air and structured plant life. Even the balconies' dining areas create a sense of natural relaxation integrated with modern day complexity. This might be a rare occasion of Krystal and I agreeing.

Our limo pulls up behind Creeper's. As we walk through the entrance Creeper saddles up to me. "Brings back memories, eh?"

I laugh and softly punch his arm earning a questioning look from Ben.

A man in a suit walks up to Ben. "How many would you like to be positioned, sir?"

"As many as you deem necessary, although I would prefer the utmost discretion."

"Yes, sir." The polite uniform strides back towards the limos and Ben sighs.

"I almost forgot about them," I comment.

"I'm sorry," Ben glances down. "There are definitely some downsides to my life, but I couldn't risk any of you getting injured."

Back when Ben was first becoming popular, a multitude of reporters and fangirls would swamp him. On one such occurrence we were coming out of a theatre. As always, Ben was courteous, but the longer he passed out signatures the bigger the crowd became. Eventually the reporters came too. After about a half hour Ben announced that he need to go but appreciated their support. In response, the crowd only closed in on us pushing closer and closer. They pushed hard enough to make me fall, but that didn't stop them as they ran me over. One reporter's camera cord got caught on my ankle while I tried to stand up causing me to fall beneath halfway onto the street and half on the sidewalk. When someone stepped on my knee wrong it twisted and tore some minor ligaments. I'm obviously fine now, but it was the cause of my quitting soccer and I believe Ben feels guilty to this day.

"Let's get shopping." Creeper claps his hands together like a kid in a candy shop.

We advance past countless stores, palm trees, and most of all people. This place is packed, which is incredible considering how large it is. Ben leads us up an escalator to the second level of Fashion Valley. I can tell Creeper's trying to play it cool with his hands shoved in his pockets, but with the way he keeps flipping his head from side to side I'm amazed that his sunglasses haven't flown off. It's not every day you get to walk around one of the most impressive shopping complexes in the country with your best friends.

"Bryn was very...different than I expected," Ben comments thoughtfully, then snaps his fingers together. "Maybe it's part of entering my presence."

"That, it is not," Creeper says through gritted teeth.

"Sure it isn't."

"Maybe your ego is so inflated from all of the attention your fans give you you're too pigheaded to think something on this planet isn't about you."

I can tell this is really a major blow to Ben, but his smile remains constant as he calmly says, "You're the one with an ego from what I've heard. And you sound a bit jealous to me."

"Jealous?" Creeper snorts. "What would I be jealous of?"

This is *not* how I wanted these two to meet. "Guys, chill. We're here for shopping. You can sort out your boy problems later."

They both grumble in response, though Ben ends up smiling next to me with Creeper glaring at Ben.

Ben knows me all too well, and firsts brings us to H&M. I stroll through the store occasionally stopping at a clothes rack or table and throwing a shirt or jacket into Ben and Creeper's arms. Ben's still the ever-perfect star with his pearly smile whereas Creeper is still tying, and failing, to play it cool.

"You've been great assistants, but you can't follow me in here." I grab my clothes and step into the changing area. "Go shop. Bond over weird guy sweaters and jackets or whatever it is guys like."

They look over at each other: disgust evident on both their expressions. I leave them in this state and slide behind a curtain. First, I try on a blue skirt with a red sweater. *Why is it so hard for them to get along?*

The folds in the skirt bounce up and down as I turn. Cute, but a little too short for my taste.

I put on some white capris with a loose-fitting blouse. *Maybe Creeper's the problem...I mean, look at what he did with* *Bryn.*

Much better! This outfit goes straight to the keep rack.

Lastly, I have a pale sundress with a white flower design. The mirror in my dressing room isn't big enough to see the dress so I step outside towards the tri-fold mirror and twirl around in front of it. This dress looks good.

I'm embarrassingly caught admiring myself by Ben and Creeper who walk up behind me clapping.

"Guys." I blush. "Stop it."

"Why? You look great," Creeper says simply.

"I am buying you that dress and you had better wear it whether you're a 'dress kind of girl' or not." Ben clasps my shoulders with his hands and turns me so I'm facing them. "Understand?"

"Yes, sir." I giggle at how dramatic they are.

"Seriously Em." Ben pulls his arms back and sweeps a wave of hair behind my ear. "You look amazing. Maybe you just grew more beautiful while I've been gone, but I'm declaring no more. We don't want a bunch of boys to be after you."

"Please! As if. Besides you and Creeper are more than enough guys for me."

"Thankfully most of our school is full of idiots," Creeper adds, making us all laugh.

"Well, I should probably go change out of this."

"Oh, right. We'll just...go out there then." Ben awkwardly looks down and begins to shuffle away.

Creeper smirks. "Don't have too much fun without me."

"I wouldn't dream of it." I laugh and quickly change back into my sweats. A man waiting outside takes the skirt and sweater while I keep the capris, blouse, and dress, walking to the cashier where Ben's waiting. "Where's Creeper? You didn't scare him away already, did you?"

"No, he just went to grab us some snacks." We step forward in line to the cashier.

"Why hello! Will this be all for you?" A cheery girl asks.

"Yes. Thank you." Ben flashes her his pop star smile and I see her melt inside.

"Are you one of our rewards members?"

"No, and we're okay not being one. Thank you though." Ben's smile tightens.

"Haha, okay then." She starts ringing up the clothes and casually says. "I always think it's so nice when boys go with their girlfriends shopping. Mine would rather die than be caught dead in a store with me."

"Oh, we're not-"

"She's more like my-"

"You see-"

"We aren't dating."

"Okay then." She rings up the rest of our purchases foregoing any future conversations.

"It's kinda funny." Ben looks at me.

"Hmm?"

"How people think we're a couple."

"Oh. I guess so. It's annoying to me."

"Really? I think it's much more amusing."

"Of course you do." I grin. "Because you wish it was true!"

"What? No, I don't. Now that is ridiculous."

"Someone has a crush." I nudge him like we did when we were younger.

"You said it, so maybe you're the one with a crush." He nudges me back with my bag.

"That doesn't even make sense!"

"Hey, you didn't deny it."

"Deny what?" Creeper interrupts, handing Ben and me pretzels.

"Just her undying love for me."

"Ah, but I'm afraid as of this year she has a new one." Creeper counters, equally sarcastic.

"And who might that be?"

"Why me of course."

"Guys." I try to interject.

"Now that's interesting, but I'd beg to differ. Like you said, I'm an egotistical famous pop star and you're merely a creep."

"Ben!" I shout.

"I think you just provided an argument against yourself."

"Let's ask the fine lady then," Ben concludes.

"Let's. Emily, do you have a crush on Ben or me?"

"None of the above. I don't have a crush on anyone, okay? Now get over yourselves, please." Ben and Creeper look at each other before crack up laughing. "What? What is it?"

"Em you are so adorable when you get annoyed," Ben explains when he collects himself.

"And you *are* easy to annoy," Creeper adds with a wink.

"I'm sorry, I can't do this anymore Zack. This has been great but my career is in singing, not acting. I feel too guilty."

"I am so confused, could one of you please tell me what on earth is going on?" I plead. This only causes them to laugh harder as they lead me over to a table. dfcThe embarrassed blush in my cheeks becomes an angry red.

"Em, do you really think I would let any old guy hang out with my best friend without checking up on him? Much less one nicknamed 'Creeper'?" Ben starts.

"Imagine my surprise when I'm practicing soccer at home and my mom starts squealing about some singer on the phone."

"We had a great conversation about past records, girlfriends, schools and such-"

"It was very intense," Creeper finishes with a somber nod.

"We've been in touch ever since. You really do have good taste by the way, Em."

"Uh, thanks, I think," I reply, more than a little confused.

"Actually, it's her terrible taste in clothing that introduced us." Creeper winks.

"Hey, I was having a bad day!" I attempt to defend myself. I grip the bag harder, trying to think of some way to get out of this embarrassing situation.

My phone buzzes with a text from my mom asking if we're almost done here. "Hey Ben, Bryn and my mom are already home. Is it okay if my mom shows herself around?"

"Oh yeah, of course. Just give me a sec to let my parents know." He pulls out his phone and sends a quick text. "There. It's all taken care of."

"Thanks Ben. Though I'm still mad at you-both of you."

"Awe, come on Emily, we all know you don't have it in you to be mad at us for long." Creeper says and throws his arm over me.

"Is that a challenge?"

"Only if you make it one."

Ben and I share a look. "What's that supposed to mean?"

"I don't know. What does it mean?"

"And you wonder why I'm annoyed so easily." I sigh, exasperated. We finish our pretzels and make our way back to clothing stores. "Ben, what stores have dresses worthy of Shawn Mendes?"

"I thought you didn't like anyone." Ben teases.

"Shawn is an exception, obviously."

"Actually, I saw some cool stores earlier if you want to try one of those out." Creeper suggests.

"Sure!" I say and we let Creeper take the lead.

We walk in silence other than the crowd surrounding us. Eventually all the expensive clothes and beauty I could only dream of blends together. I suppose when you live in a city full of stars they start to lose their shine. In our "small town" Ben is about as famous as it gets. Here he must feel almost normal.

As promised, Creeper shows us into a store of glamor. No matter where I look there are sparkles and silk. I don't even know where to start, but Ben and Creeper appear to be in their natural habitat and reverse our former roles. They start weaving through rows of dresses occasionally asking my size or color preference. Still I stand frozen. I'm afraid to touch any of these expensive dresses. Luckily for me Ben and Creeper make their ways back in my direction. Both their arms are filled with dozens of dresses. Shiny dresses. Sparkly dresses. Velvety dresses. Ben even went so far as to grab a dress made of a spongy material. *As if!*

"Em, your arms are completely void of clothes," Ben observes.

"That's okay, we've got plenty for her to try on." Creeper smiles.

"True."

We head over to the dressing rooms and I again kick the boys out. "Which should I try first?"

Ben starts to pull out the horrid sponge dress causing Creeper and me to gasp in horror. "Dude. You've gotta be joking. I would buy that with the sole purpose of burning it. Free the world of such a disaster."

"Hey! Miley Cyrus wore it to the last event we were at, and I figured it must be in right now." His eyes squint as he runs a finger across his jawline. "Though I haven't been allowed to pick out my own clothes for ages."

Creeper and my jaws drop even further. "Miley and I don't exactly have the same...style. If you grabbed anything else based on her choices, please return it while I try this on." I grab whatever is on the top of Creeper's stack and step into a changing room. In contrast to Ben, Creeper has excellent taste in clothing. I instantly fall in love with the pale green dress that folds inward at the waist with a low-cut neckline and flowing sleeves. When I put it on it hangs funny near my arms and was cut for a different body shape. All the same, I step out of the room to show Ben and Creeper.

"You look great!" Ben claps his hands together.

"Ben, you really have no fashion sense whatsoever." Creeper shakes his head.

"I know," Ben sighs melodramatically.

"It's a great dress but the cut and shape are all wrong." He sorts through his collection. "Try this one."

I take the red dress. Again, it's gorgeous, but it's just not right. We sort through the rest of the dresses the same way, although Ben thinks they're all perfect.

"I'm just not a dress girl." I shrug, finally stepping out in my normal clothes.

"I refuse to believe that." Creeper crosses his arms. "It's the dresses that were wrong, not you. Let's look together this time."

The three of us march through the store with a unified purpose. Even the clerk can't keep a smile off his face at our determination. After about twenty suggestions by Ben, I can't help but feel that there isn't any more store left to search.

"I give up," Ben says. "I thought this would be a quick, fun trip to make up for missing back to school shopping, but this is ridiculous."

"I think you're-"

"Just five more minutes," Creeper interrupts.

"Fine," Ben and I concede. In a brief moment of eye contact Ben and I share a lifetime of laughter and understanding. It's just a dress.

Creeper scours around looking almost like a dog with a duty.

Ben checks his watch and I know five minutes have passed, yet he's too nice to say anything. Another five minutes pass and Ben checks his watch again before shoving both hands in his pockets. He opens his mouth then closes it, resembling the actions of a fish. As enjoyable as this is, I decide to help Ben and say, "Creeper, I think it's time to go. We can get that violet dress, it was pretty, right?"

Rather than reply, he gasps. His eyes focus on something to our left and he gradually steps towards it.

"Are you even listening to me?" I ask.

"Yeah, sure, just come look at this." His voice has a tone of awe.

Ben and I exchange a glance then follow Creeper's steps. I follow his eyes with my own and understand.

A single dress rises above the rest on a display. The upper bit is a snow-white color highlighted with sparkles. The white dissolves into an icy blue as the front falls down to knee level though the back part of the skirt waterfalls down to the ground growing into a deep blue. "It's really pretty!" Ben comments.

Creeper and I smile at his hopefulness. "I think this is the one," Creeper says, and I nod in agreement. He places his hand on a passing worker. "Could you please bring us this dress in a size four?"

"Of course." She scurries away only to reappear a minute later with the dress in hand.

"Thank you." Creeper takes it.

When I step outside even Ben's jaw drops a little. I do a little twirl and see the back side is a crisscrossing pattern cutting across an open back.

"Perfect," Creeper whispers, and he's right. It is perfect.

"So, we're done?" Ben asks.

"We are done," I confirm. I take off the dress as quickly as possible and we purchase it. "Do we need to find you some suits as well?"

"No, I had mine packed." Creeper answers.

"We should go to my house. I bet your mom and Bryn are wondering what's taking us so long. I'm getting hungry."

"Sounds good," I say, still cradling my dress.

Ben calls one of his men in suits who escorts us back to a limo. We snack on more Snickers and sparkling cider on the ride to Ben's new home. Creeper bugs the driver for a while about secret limo compartments and DVD players he's sure there is. After a while he finally gives up and turns back to us.

"Emily, I believe I have won our challenge."

"What? No you didn't. I'm still annoyed, it was really rude!"

"And funny," Creeper retorts.

"Trust breaking."

"Friendship proving."

"Low handed."

"Interesting."

"Rude." Ben laughs breaking our intense exchange of words.

"Okay, it was a little rude," Creeper gives in. "But we're all good now and it'll be something we'll laugh about in the future. I'm already laughing."

"I'll give you that, but I'd prefer it if you didn't spend your time trying to trick me."

"We won't. It was a onetime thing," Ben promises.

"I don't know about that..." Creeper smiles and I hit his shoulder.

"You are so violent," Ben exclaims.

"It's all her." Creeper stabs his finger towards me.

"What? No. Nu-uh. It's all you!"

"You're so cute when you're annoyed."

My cheeks heat up to an angry red as both boys smile. As annoying as they are, I can't stay mad at them for long. Especially considering how much time they just spent finding the perfect dress for me.

The house we arrive at is smaller than Ben's old place in Boise. His front and backyards, however, are so large I can't even see the neighbors. When the limo comes to a stop my door is opened by none other than Edwin.

"Miss Em, it's a pleasure to see you again."

I smile and reply, "It's nice to see you as well."

Creeper and Ben hop out and we enter Ben's house together. It might not be as big as in Boise, but it's more than I could ever imagine buying. An elegant wooden staircase spiraling upward first meets my eyes, and to the right a hallway leads to a dining room. To the left is not a room, but a large fountain with water flowing from musical notes at the top. It appears to be made of marble in contrast to the dark wooden floors. The water flows from the fountain to a marble water way protruding from the walls continuing throughout the house creating a natural river sound.

Creeper must notice it as well because he first walks over and dips his fingers in the stream. "Ben, this is incredible," I comment.

"Thanks, I was pretty proud of the design." He smiles shyly and looks down.

"Wait, *you* designed this?"

"Yeah." His voice grows more excited. "It flows through most of the rooms and even goes into another giant waterfall in the pool room."

"You have a pool?" Creeper looks like he just hit the jackpot.

"I do. However, it would probably be best if we ate dinner then went to our rooms."

"You expect me to be hungry after a giant pretzel and unlimited Snickers?" Creeper shakes his head incredulously.

"I didn't mean to assume-" Ben starts.

"Yes," I interrupt. "Of course, you are."

"You know me too well." Creeper winks and heads into the dining room without another thought.

"Shall we?" Ben holds out his arm and I take it.

Ever since I saw Ben in the airport my smile has been impossible to take away. Until now that is. My expression drops faster than the Persian Empire. At least my smile isn't the only one to fall. A pair of bright blue eyes lock with my own and convey an expression of pure hatred.

"Hi, Em." Her silky voice reminds me of a cat: smooth to cover its inner evil.

"Hi, Krystal," I reply and plaster a removed expression on my face. Ben walks over to her and gives her a quick hug during which she passes him a quick kiss on the cheek then checks to make sure I saw. I try to keep my expression calm, but she sees past it and smirks quietly.

Creeper pulls the chair out in front of me. "Thanks Creeper."

Before I can sit down, however, he takes my spot. He looks up and winks at me. "What, did you think I pulled this out for you?" I lightly punch his shoulder. "See, I told you she's the violent one."

Laughter trickles around the table and I realize that my mom and Bryn are here as well. The food is brought out before any sort of conversation can start. Edwin marches in with three giant metal pizza trays which hold my favorites: Hawaiian, Chicken Ranch, and Bacon. Creeper dives in and grabs one slice of each.

"Thanks Edwin," I comment at the same moment as Ben. My mom, Bryn and Krystal soon follow suit. Creeper makes the unfortunate decision of thanking Edwin while eating. Crumbs spew from his mouth in my direction. "Ew!"

"Sowrry." More crumbs fly out as he talks drawing a glare from me. Bryn and Krystal giggle while Ben shares a disgusted expression.

Once we've helped ourselves to a proper amount of food, Ben speaks again, "I suppose this is a good time for introductions. You all already know Em, and next to her is her friend Zack." He rests his hand on Krystal's. "This is Krystal, my girlfriend, and that's Bryn next to Em's mom." We awkwardly wave to each other and continue eating. The introduction really wasn't necessary aside from Krystal's benefit.

"Ben, where are your parents?" My mom asks.

"They're on their own dinner date after which they'll clean up some loose ends having to do with the party tomorrow," Ben replies.

All three pizzas quickly vanish from view. I can't help but notice that Creeper ate eight slices. He burps contentedly after finishing up his last piece causing Krystal, Bryn and I to grimace in sync. Bryn and Krystal seem to notice each other's' mutual dislike toward me and turn to each other. "Oh my gosh!" Krystal exclaims in her screechy voice. "I *love* your nails!"

"Mine? Oh, thanks." Bryn blushes and turns her nails as though looking at them for the first time.

"Did you do them yourself?" Krystal continues.

"Uh, yeah. It was this really neat design I saw on YouTube. I can show you if you want," Bryn offers.

"That would be great." Krystal smiles, looking almost human. "What about tonight? Ben promised I could stay with you guys. It'd be some great girl bonding time. Em could even join us." Her voice loses some excitement when she mentions my name, but it might be the nicest thing she's said to me.

"Sure!" Bryn grins at her newly found friend. Everyone turns to stare at me.

"What?" I ask confused.

Bryn shakes her head as Krystal rolls her eyes. "Are you in or not? Duh."

"I think I'm out for this one." I pause and add belatedly, "Thanks though."

"Let's go then," Bryn says.

Krystal stands up, kisses Ben again whispering in his ear and leaves with her arm interlocked with Bryn. My mom gives me a concerned look, but excuses herself as well once I shake my head.

Creeper burps again. "Whelp, I guess I'm done too. Mind showing me to my room?"

"Of course." Ben nods his head. We probably didn't need Ben as a guide to follow Bryn and Krystal's squealing. Their room is next door to mine, with Creeper right across the hallway. Ben's is on the opposite side of his house from the guest rooms, but he assures me that there's an intercom linking us together. Creeper thanks Ben and wishes me goodnight with a quick hug then we part ways.

My room is slightly smaller than back home, but this one has a walk-in closet. The bed is softer though the walls are desolate of any decor. With my current state of exhaustion, I could sleep anywhere, and sleeping here will probably feel like a dream come true.

I sit on the bed and trail my fingers over my suitcase which had already been brought in. The bed squishes next to me as Ben sits. "Are you going to tell me what's going on?"

"Hmm?" My finger swirls round and round in an infinite pattern.

"Em, something's wrong. I can't help if I don't know," Ben sighs and places his hand on mine.

"Lots of things are wrong. But even more things are right. I think. Right now I'm just confused."

"Maybe I can unconfuse you, but to do that you'll have to give me a hint of what's going on."

"Okay." I lay back on the bed. Ben doesn't push me to talk, but lays down next to me with our fingers still interlocked. "Okay, okay, okay." I lean my head on his shoulder and breath in the scent of his cologne only it's mixed with something different now. Something more feminine than masculine. "You smell good."

"Thanks." He sniffs my hair. "And you smell like sweat." I laugh and lean into him so that his chest rumbles against my ears.

"Ben, I hate you for leaving."

"I know."

"But it wasn't all bad. I met Bryn and Creeper. They were amazing friends. The homecoming invite went off without a hitch. Kind of." I pull back so I can look into his eyes and he stares back into mine with an equal intensity. We stare for a good thirty seconds before he blinks. "Anyway, Bryn and Creeper were happy dating each other. Only, Creeper has this thing where he throws me over his shoulder and Bryn saw him doing that. Aubrey convinced Bryn that we were about to kiss and now Bryn's all mad at us. She's been mad for an entire day. The whole idea of Creeper and I liking each other, it's so, so, so absurd."

"Maybe not as absurd as you think," Ben says softly.

"What do you mean?"

"Well, I thought you both liked each other. You do act like a couple, and the way Zack looks at you with that throwing thing he does, it wouldn't surprise me." I snort at the idea of Creeper and me together. "Okay, maybe it is absurd. Give her time Em, it's only been a day. She seems like a good girl, and soon she'll realize how crazy it would be for you to date Zack." I nod my head. "Remember that whatever happens, you'll always have me."

"That's all I really need, right?" We share a smile and I sit up straight. "Do you wanna know what else has been bugging me?"

"What?"

"Krystal." Ben doesn't respond immediately, which I appreciate. Instead he places both hands behind his head and blows a stream of air through his lips while he thinks.

"Life's grey."

"Grey," I repeat and raise an eyebrow at him.

"Yup. You, Emily Nicole Parker, are a very black and white person. You see good and bad. Me leaving was bad. Meeting Creeper and Bryn was good." He thinks again about how to explain. I hold my tongue in an attempt not to protest and break his train of thought. "Think about this: if we were dirt poor and on the streets and starving to death, would it be good or bad for me to steal for us to survive?"

"We can't know because we're not in that situation." I shrug my shoulders as he laughs in exasperation.

"You are incredible Em, in a good way. Let's try again. Remember when we had that soccer game and there weren't enough cars for everyone to get home? What we had to do was put an extra kid in each car. Technically it was illegal since there were more people than seats and seatbelts, but we needed to get everyone home. We couldn't leave a kid at the fields alone. Was that good or bad? Black or white?"

"It's good, I mean the positives outweigh the negatives," I quickly reply. My eyelids are starting to get a little droopy; it's been a long day.

"How can it be good if it takes bad to achieve the good?"

"It's..." I pause. I understand what he's trying to say.

"It's grey," he finishes. "And that is exactly what Krystal is."

"No, she isn't. She's all bad. She's been a complete jerk to me ever since I met her."

"To *you*. As soon as I moved here she's been the nicest girl ever. Not just to me, but to everyone. I've watched her, and-" He cuts himself off. "Em, I've got to tell you something."

"Hmm?" I look up at him, but the rest of my body falls down into the bed. Eventually my eyes close as well. The covers of the bed pull over me and I wiggle into a comfortable position.

"Goodnight, Em." Ben whispers and kisses my forehead before I fall into the darkness of sleep.

33 | Backstory

-Charlotte-

I swear we've watched every bag go around this conveyor belt twice yet mine is nowhere to be found. I disguised the bag to make it through the usual glance over by airport security, but if someone were to take it I would be in some seriously deep water. My carryon had only been supplied with the DB, gloves, and a bug or two. That's not nearly reaching the basic requirements. Plus, all of my clothes are in there.

"What color did you say it is?" Mrs. Parker asks again. Her bag had been one of the first to appear.

"Red with a strip of neon green duct tape in the middle." Just as I say this a flipped over bag passes us. The bottom is black, but when I turn it around the red becomes visible. "Thank goodness." A sigh of relief blows through my lips.

"Is that it?" Mrs. Parker asks, ending in a yawn. Seems like the sleeping pills are still taking effect.

"Yup." I grin, then skip over to the exit where a limo is waiting. Without a second thought, I climb in. Probably a bad decision without checking for a bomb or anything first, but Mrs. Parker is already stepping through the other door.

She rests her head against the window with her eyelids fluttering shut. Even as her personality is kind and energetic the tired wrinkles tell a different story. The ride is quick and quiet leaving each of us to our own thoughts. Nick even remains statically silent. I almost worry about him, then the oh-so-familiar Cheeto chomping returns.

The house is large with great attributes, especially in the water department. Ben's done nicely for himself, though I'd expect nothing less from what I've heard.

"Miss Bryn." A staff member (butler?) bows at the doorway. "It's a pleasure to make your acquaintance."

"Likewise." I smile back at him with my own little curtsy. For a second he looks slightly taken back as though he isn't sure if I'm earnest or mocking him. Then he returns my smile with a grandfatherly expression and leads Mrs. Parker and me into the mansion.

As he walks, he slowly slouches further and further forward while his knees click with every other step. What's left of his frosty white hair is neatly combed to the side and his suit is without a wrinkle. It's clear he takes pride in his work, no matter how much it's taken from him. There must be a reason beyond money for him to continue working here, and from the way he fondly looks upon Ben's pictures I'm willing to bet I have a good guess.

We stop at a kitchen and dining area where a sugary sweet scent causes me to go weak at the knees. Sure enough, a girl of raven black hair turns towards us with a platter of cookies fresh from the oven. Her cheeks pull up into a smile when she meets my gaze, "Mrs. Parker and...Brynna, right?"

"Uh, just Bryn," I gently correct, "and you are?"

"Ben hasn't told you about me?" She giggles lightly and tugs away her oven mitts. As she pulls off the cookies, one splits halfway revealing a gooey center and melted chocolate under the crust. They look perfect. "I'm Krystal: Ben's girlfriend. It's a pleasure to meet you." Instead of holding out a hand she offers the plate of cookies.

Ben might not have told me about her, but Em did. I wait for Krystal to take a bite of a cookie first. "Thanks."

"Sure thing." She grabs a carton of milk at the same time Edwin, the butler, provides three glasses.

The cookies are delicious. They're the kind that melt in your mouth so quickly you have to wonder if they were ever fully baked. The milk balances out the burning rich chocolate chips. Countering Em's words, Krystal doesn't seem to be evil. Although she makes a mean cookie. I'll keep my guard up, but she seems nice.

"These are wonderful, Krystal." Mrs. Parker comments as I reach for two more. Nick would be *so* jealous.

Krystal blushes. "Thanks, it's a family recipe. My grandma passed it down to my mom who taught me."

"That's lovely." Mrs. Parker's voice becomes distant and I process the sound of male and female voices arguing. I feel like I'm intruding in someone else's life when the argument grows hotter and the words cut through walls sharper than daggers.

Krystal clears her throat uncertainly then takes her cookies down the hall. I follow Mrs. Parker's lead along Krystal's footsteps. It's not long until we find a collection of identical looking white doors individualized by paper slips with each of our names on them.

I stow my bags away under my bed where no one will bother them. Next, I enter the room titled "Em." It looks identical to mine with blank walls, twin sized bed, one door leading to a closet and the other a bathroom. I don't spend too much time observing as I quickly move on to the task of bugging her room. On her bed rests her suitcase we grabbed earlier, so I decide to test some of Nick's new threaded recorders. They sew right into the sleeves of a shirt or waistline of pants. If one were to closely examine the stitching, they would be able to note the difference in colors. For the most part, however, it's invisible. Nice job Nick. Speaking of, I have an idea.

"Hey Nick, are you there?" I neatly fold Em's clothes and return everything to its original position.

"Always." He yawns. Not the I just woke up yawn. More of an, I'm overtired yawn. Probably working on a new invention.

"Please switch my earpiece to recording." It beeps in my ear and I assume the task is complete. "Thanks. Now get some sleep, you sound exhausted."

"You have no idea."

"Sick too," I add, but turn down the volume before he gets the chance to reply.

Mrs. Parker's room is the next one over. I knock gently so as not to wake her if she is still asleep. Thankfully, she isn't as told by the slapping of her slippers against the hardwood floors. She opens the door revealing a slightly larger suite than either Em's or mine, "Bryn, come in."

"Thank you." I sit on a couch opposing her seat on the edge of her bed.

"To what do I owe the pleasure of this visit?" She smiles at me still a little tired resulting in further confusion.

"I actually had a few things I wanted to talk to you about. Well, Em's dad if that's okay."

"Her dad?" Her face drops the instant the words leave my mouth. I attempt to backtrack, but she holds up her hand to silence me. "What do you want to know?"

"Well, Em told me that he left, but not much else. I'd wanted to help her, maybe by hearing more about his past or something, but now I see how rude this sounds."

"No, not at all. It will be good for me to talk about it anyway." Rather than fog over, her eyes sharpen with memories when she looks back into the past. "We were married in college, but we waited to have Em until I was finished with my degree. He still had another four years until he got his doctorate." I nod as though processing this information, but I knew this already. "Even while going to college and working he always made time for the girls and me. He said we were his number one job."

"That sounds wonderful," I murmur and she nods in agreement.

"It was." Her lips tilt into an expression I can't decode. "After college, he was offered an incredible job as a microbiologist. This was his-*our*-dream, but he turned it down. He told me he'd found something better. Though he had to work a second job with the research position, we all supported him.

"I wasn't concerned until he started coming home angry for no apparent reason. When I asked, he'd say there was extra stress at work and continue with a smile for us girls. Then Maree was diagnosed with an aggressive form of leukemia-the very thing my husband was researching. His long hours soon became late nights. Then no nights at all. As hard as we all tried, Maree lost the battle about ten years ago. She'd be fourteen now. I'm sure Em told you this." I nod my head and place my hands on hers for support. "He couldn't take it. He'd lost one of his girls, so he left. I haven't been able to find him since." She chuckles darkly. "I'm sorry, Bryn. I had only meant to say, 'he was kind and loved us' but I suppose either you're a good listener or I'm a large talker."

"Don't apologize." I say quickly with a squeeze of her hands. "I'm here if you need someone to talk to. I've lost a person I was close to myself, so I know firsthand that it's best to just get it out."

"Thank you." Mrs. Parker pats my hand before removing hers to rub at her moist eyes. "Now if you will excuse me, I think I'd like to be alone for a while."

"Of course." I softly shut the door behind me. A wetness drops onto my finger as I wipe my own eyes. Not for the story, necessarily, I already knew most of it, but for what was left out. He couldn't have created this poison. It would destroy what's left of this broken family. And if he did, there's no way on earth I'm letting Em or Mrs. Parker know that.

34 | Trapped

-Emily-

Sun streams through the window as I open my eyes. For once it isn't the heart wrenching sound of an alarm waking me. When I glance over to a clock I'm surprised to see the time's nine thirty. Normally, it's impossible to wake me before noon without school. Then I realize there's a time change; in Boise it's really 10:30am.

I remember yesterday as well as if it were, well, yesterday, but any events after dinner are a dreamlike blur. I remember coming into my room with Ben, but the rest is a confusion of dreams and reality.

I glance back at the clock 10:00am after briefly closing my eyes. Today I'm meeting Shawn Mendes. Just the thought of this makes me want to scream in delight, but instead I use the energy to hop out of bed and change into a t-shirt and leggings.

A breeze flows into my room bringing with it the scent of bacon and toast. I follow the smell back to the kitchen expecting to find Creeper and Ben chowing down. To my surprise, only Ben's parents and my mom are sitting at the bar drinking coffee. I can't help but notice my mom sits between them as a bridge in the conversation.

As I turn to leave Ben's mom's eyes flash across the room landing on me. "Emily! It's spectacular to see you again. Ben talks about you all the time you know."

"Thanks Julie," I say then yawn. "You wouldn't happen to know where Ben is, would you?"

"They're in the basement." Ben's dad answers. "First, eat some breakfast. I get the feeling that today's going to be an exciting day." He gestures to the left of me.

I turn my head to find a buffet of fruits, eggs, pastries, and best of all: bacon. My plate is quickly filled to the point of food stacked on top of each other. When I look back the parents are in an animated conversation about cars so I sneak out the door before they can pull me in.

It takes me a few trials and error to find the doorway leading to the basement, but at long last I finally do. Even now Ben never ceases to amaze me. The basement floor is carpeted in turf with walls like those of an indoor soccer field. To my left and right small goals are dug in the walls. Straight across the field a white door blends into the wall. I only see it because of the pounding music accented by Creeper and Ben's voices coming from behind the door.

"For the last time." The room grows suddenly quiet. *"You are not a fricken ninja!"* Creeper shouts. A few giggles escape my lips.

"What is going on here?" I exclaim opening the door.

It looks like a rainbow exploded. Green, blue, red and yellow blur together across the floor with splats of each color riddled across the walls. The distinct scent of paint fills my nose, but this scene still doesn't make sense.

Both boys look up from their crazy positions on the ground and grin at me. I shake my head. "I knew Creeper would be a bad influence on you."

"I've been wanting to do this for a while now, but figured you were much too lady like to participate." Ben shrugs-at least he attempts to without moving his hands and feet.

"More like I have the common sense not to ruin everything around me. What exactly is *'this'*?"

"It's Twister with paint mixed in. As anyone with common sense would know," Creeper answers and winks at me.

"Wanna join us?" Ben offers. A dash of dark blue paint has dried above his left eyebrow and a green stripe running down across his eyelid combined with the sparkle in his eye and bouncy tone of voice reminds me of when we were younger. I almost want to say yes.

"How about I watch while I eat this delicious smelling breakfast." I lean back against the wall while pulling out the plate of food I've kept hidden behind my back.

"Food." Creeper shouts and jumps out of his position to run to me. Without Creeper's support, Ben topples to the ground before popping back up and pumping his fists in the air.

"I win!"

"But I got bacon, so who's the real winner here?" Creeper snatches all eight pieces of bacon of the plate and shoves them into his mouth along with a strawberry cream pastry.

"Gross," I grunt in response. Ben's eyes widen after Creeper finishes the entire plate with the exception of a piece of toast I snatched before it disappeared into Creeper's black hole of a stomach. Once every crumb is gone, Creeper groans in content.

"We should probably clean this up." Ben looks around their mess.

"That would be an excellent idea. I'll leave you to it then." I turn to leave.

"Emily," Creeper whines behind me. He attempts to widen his eyes and pout his face.

"What?"

"Don't leave me! I suck at cleaning." He pauses and his face dissipates into a smirking grin. "Unless you can go get me more bacon. Then you can leave."

"I can leave and return with bacon or stay here." I rub my chin. "I think I'll just stay here."

"Yay!" Creeper pulls me over to where Ben's already pulling paper up from the ground. We each grab opposite corners of the paper and roll it to the center of the room. Each layer of paper has a fainter color of paint until there isn't any left. Luckily the floor was left unscathed. The walls, on the other hand look like a kindergarten art class passed through.

"So how do we clean the walls?" I ask hesitantly.

"Oh, don't worry about those. My parents plan on repainting this room and adding texture, or something like that. We can just leave it and the painters will deal with it." Ben wipes his hands off on his worn-out jeans then brushes his hand across his forehead. A surprised expression lights his face when his hand crosses the paint plastered on his face. "We should go clean up."

"I agree." With the rolled-up papers stuffed between my arm and my hip I pull open the door for Ben and Creeper.

"I can carry those for you," Creeper offers. I flick my eyes to his asking what the catch is.

"It's okay."

"No. I insist. I'll take the papers." He holds out his hands. When I don't hand them right over he snaps the papers from my hip.

"Hey!" My first reaction is to slap him, but then Ben's comments on our violence come back and I restrain.

"Already fighting like a married couple." Ben chuckles while shoulder checking me into Creeper. And he says *I'm* the violent one.

"In his dreams." I jerk a thumb in Creeper's direction.

"Meh." Creeper shrugs.

"Zack whatever your middle name is Creeper!"

"Going all Mrs. Creeper on me aren't ya." Creeper winks.

"You are so annoying." This time I don't hold back and slap him as hard as I can.

"You hit like a girl." He smirks.

"Why thank you."

"You're welcome, Mrs. Creeper."

"If you say that one more time I will kick you where only Mrs. Creeper should." I threaten and they both laugh. "That's not a joke."

"I know."

Ben looks up at Creeper. "What is your middle name anyway?"

"Now that, my friend, is the world's best guarded secret." Creeper winks and swings into his guest room.

"Only until I figure it out," I yell after him. His door slams shut in my face leaving Ben and me outside my room. "You should go wash up as well. Like your dad said," I deepen my voice, *"Today's going to be a big day'."*

"You talked to my-oh never mind." He starts to leave then turns back. "By the way, I love your new hair style."

My hands naturally fly up to my head and pat down the tangles leftover from sleeping. "Yours isn't too bad either." I gesture at his paint covered hair. We laugh as he walks off to his room.

I glance in a mirror and Ben was right; my hair *is* a rat's nest. Taking my time, I brush my teeth and comb out the tangles in my hair. I wash my face, but hold back on makeup as that'll come when I prepare for the party. In my closet is a small collection of sweatshirts, leggings and jeans, but I'm in the mood to dress up. Then I remember the outfit Ben got me yesterday. Perfect.

I could do my homework right now or I could procrastinate. As appealing as the second option sounds, I know I'm going to be helping Creeper finish his homework at the last minute. Sighing, I pull my backpack onto my bed and get to work. Since the class average on the essays was below a sixty-five percent, Mrs. Hobs is allowing everyone to edit their papers to receive a higher grade. There are only a few minor changes I need to make to get one hundred and five percent. Most of the edits are on the paper about my sister.

As I suspected, my paper has positive commentary until my final story. At first her comments are grammatical errors and silly mistakes since I couldn't bring myself to edit it. Then her comments decrease until they disappear completely. I skim through the story without really reading it. Mostly I just correct punctuation errors and even a few spelling mistakes. When I highlight a sentence containing my dad and sister's names, Google Explore pops up with a collection of pictures from my Drive.

The first picture is of my dad taking Maree and me out to ice cream. My dad's hand wraps around me as he sneaks a chunk of cookie dough out of my cone. I always got cookie dough just so he could steal it. Maree's orange sherbet drips down her bowl onto my dad's head as he looked up at the beautiful little girl sitting on his shoulders. Her energetic smile could light up anyone's day. In the background, I recognize a woman with her back turned standing next to a sign for the zoo. I haven't been in the zoo forever! I'll have to drag Creeper and Bryn along with me.

The next picture was from Maree's third birthday; she's blowing out the candles on an Elmo cake with Ben, my dad and me standing behind her. We all have little cone shaped birthday hats on as she insisted her birthday was a celebration of all of her and that includes us. Dad has one hand on my shoulder and the other on Ben's with a loving look in his eyes as he stares down at the three of us. Even before Ben's rise to fame his parents didn't get along with each other very well. Anytime shouts and screams erupted through their walls or glass clashed Ben entered our family without question. I forget that Maree was like a sister to Ben as well. I click past the picture.

Light gleams off the award resting in my dad's grasp slightly blurring the image. It's impossible to miss the admiration pouring off of my mom who's standing right next to him. His eyes are filled with love. I don't understand how someone could go from completely love to disappearing without a trace. It doesn't make sense. How could he just leave us like this?

My vision blurs from tears I didn't realize were collecting. As I blink to clear them I see the picture as a whole and my complete attention is stolen by a familiar figure in the background. A loud gasp escapes my lips as I lean in to get a better view of the lady.

It's impossible! Bryn couldn't have been at my dad's award assembly, and there's no way she'd be that old. The hair is a different color, brown, but the vibrant blue eyes and expression of the lady's face are a mirrored image of Bryn. Obviously, it isn't Bryn, but it's someone who looks a lot like her. An older sister or even mom?

I'm pulled away from my thoughts by my bed flattening on both sides of me. "Oh, hi."

"Are you okay, Em?" Ben places his hand on my forehead. "You don't look well."

"I'm fine." Am I fine? I'm probably a little sick-definitely delusional.

"Em-"

"She's fine," Creeper interrupts Ben. "I love your new outfit by the way."

I look down. "Thanks." An irritated sigh comes from my doorway. I turn my head to find Krystal messing around on her phone with newly painted nails.

"Are we going to go or what?" Krystal grumbles.

"You ready Em?" Ben's eyes are still full of concern as he helps my stand up out of bed and guides me out of the room.

"Of course, but what are we going to do?"

"That's a surprise." Ben looks at Creeper then Bryn.

"What are you talking about?" Krystal voices my thoughts.

"Do you know what a surprise is?" Creeper asks sarcastically.

"I meant what is this surprise that most of you seem to know about."

No one answers our question. Instead, they continue walking with silly grins on their faces. Ben stops, making Creeper run into him and, in turn, me run into Creeper. I quickly right myself as Creeper asks, "Here?"

"Here." Ben throws open the door and flips his arm inside the room. "Ladies first."

"Thanks, Benny dear." Krystal smiles and strides into the room. Since Creeper is slow to move, I follow Krystal.

We jump in unison as the door slams shut. "What is this?" I exclaim.

Ben's muffled voice comes through the door. "All of us agree; it's time for you two to get over your petty mutual dislike."

"That's putting it mildly." I mutter.

"You're staying in here until you make up with each other." Ben finishes.

"*What?*" Krystal and I shriek in unison. "What about the party?"

"There's a tape explaining further details," Creeper adds. The sharp clomping of shoes against wood echoes in my ears.

Krystal paces six steps to the left then spins on her heel and walks right back across the small room. A pale light showers down from a single bulb sticking out of the ceiling with our environment reminding me of a doctor's office. Even Krystal doesn't look good in this lighting.

"Could you quit it? I'm trying to find this tape. Not to mention you're creating a draft." I glare at her in annoyance.

"The tape is right there, dummy." She reaches down at her feet and picks up a small black box.

"Well how was I supposed to find it with you stomping all over it?"

"I wasn't stomping."

"You were too." Before she can protest even more, I grab the box out of her hands. "Can't wait to hear this."

"Only if it gets me out of here."

"Self-centered much?" I mumble under my breath.

"What did you say?"

"Nothing at all. Let's just listen to the recording." She crosses her arms and slumps to the ground next to me while pursing her blood red lips shut.

Rolling the cheap piece of recording equipment around in my hands, my finger slides over the triangular play button. I shift my legs into a more comfortable position as static noise announces the beginning of the message; it feels like a story time.

"Krystal, Em, first off, I would like to beg you not to kill me when you get out." Laughter crackles in the background so I assume Creeper was recording with him. "Now, I'm tired of you two fighting. Em, you've been my best friend for as long as I can remember. You mean the world to me." Then why can't he drop this diva? "But Krystal is my girlfriend. I'll be the first to admit that it was initially all for show. Once I moved here our relationship grew. I was finally willing to find someone beyond you, Em. Krystal was there all along, but I had limited myself to you and me. Even you will admit that if I hadn't moved, you'd have never met Zack or Bryn."

"And what a tragedy that would be," Zack cuts in.

"Shut up, dude," Ben snaps, but his voice sounds much more joking than hateful. "Krystal is an intelligent, caring, supportive, beautiful girlfriend. I think she would be an incredible friend to you." I snort in laughter earning another glare from Krystal. "Krystal, that goes for you as well. Em was there for me before anyone knew my name. She's one of the kindest people I know. Perfect in her own way." Now it's Krystal's turn to snort in laughter.

"I'm not okay with the two girls that I adore, hating each other. Seriously, it's a major stressor."

"Don't have to say that twice," Zack mumbles.

"You two aren't allowed to leave this room until you start to get along. Once you both can prove you are at least friendly you may press the button next to the door calling for my presence. Until then, I will be preparing for tonight's party. Hopefully, you will be in attendance."

"In other words: good luck! And don't forget my English essay Emily," Creeper adds.

"Some friends they are." Krystal rolls her eyes. "Does Zack expect you to do, what, his essay for him?"

"They're better friends than you could ever be," I'm quick to retort.

"Puh-lease! I could out-friend you any day!" She stands up trying to tower over me.

"Ha! Now that I would like to see." I stand, matching her height. "Miss spoiled brat playing normal for a day."

She narrows her eyes but doesn't reply. Instead she lays back down and closes her eyes. I lightly tap her with the toe of my shoe and she opens one eyelid. "What?"

"We're supposed to be finding a way out, not messing around on the floor."

"They won't let me miss the party, so I might as well catch up on some beauty sleep." She pops open her other eye and looks me up and down in disgust. "You on the other hand they should have no problem leaving at all."

I look back at the small recording device. I'm finally with Ben, and he locks me in a room so I can't hang out with him. *Correction*: he locks me in a room with my least favorite person in the whole world. Sure, it sounds all elegant and learned when he talks about looking past our small little worlds to expand our horizons, but he's not the one forced into the situation. Boys are infuriating. Actually, the girls in this situation are infuriating as well. People are infuriating. I should just become a hermit trapped inside my room left to my own small-minded thinking without people trying to break in. A groan of irritation slips through my lips as I slump down across the room from Krystal.

"Are you seriously giving up already?" Her voice is dripping with a derogatory tone as though she's encountering a broken-down toy. She rolls her eyes again. Honestly, she rolls her eyes so often it's a wonder they don't roll right out of her pretty little head. "And here I thought you were supposed to be a smart, hardworking, perfect, idealistic school girl. What. A. Joke." She smirks and looks back at the device. "It's a wonder that you ever made any friends. Actually, I take that back. Ben and Bryn are incredible and it's only a matter of time until they see past your facade. Zack, might be terribly hot, but is a blithering idiot who has no idea about anything beyond 'bro' and 'dude.' Besides, anyone who would be willing to crush on you clearly has terrible judgement."

I *snap*. "You have got to be kidding me. My facade? A wonder that they'd be my friends? I've had it with your attitude. You've been a brat since the moment I met you. Not once have you said a kind thing to me. You do not deserve a boy as incredible as Ben. He likes you so, so much. Even if you're a jerk to me you had better *never* break his heart. Understand me? Otherwise I'll break you." She opens her mouth with a fire in her eyes but my heart burns stronger.

"Don't you ever dare insult one of my friends again. Zack has been there for me when Ben couldn't be. Bryn is the most energetic, positive and fun girl to be around. Somehow, she's the first person I'd turn to in a time of trouble. Just because you can't be human enough to find a friend doesn't make it okay for you to tear mine down." I'm not sure when tears started to spill from my eyes, but angry hot streams of salty water are leaking down my cheeks. Immediately I expect a retaliation from Krystal in the hiatus of my tirade, but she sits there in absolute stunned silence.

She finally has the sagacity to snap her mouth shut. The fire in her eyes has been distinguished, replaced with a grey tint and a single tear draws a crooked line of mascara down her cheek. For a moment, I forget that she's nothing more than an actress and scoot over so I'm sitting next to her. She leans her head on my shoulder and I lay my head atop hers. A slight smile steals its way across her lips as she hiccups in sheepish laughter. "They're probably watching this, aren't they?"

"Of course they are." I snap at her. "I mean, of course they are." My voice grows quiet.

When she raises her head, it bumps mine causing us both to grimace in pain. "Sorry." She whispers. Her icy blue eyes meet mine then lower down to her lap. "I never say this, but," she mumbles the last part too quietly for me to hear.

"Please speak up. I hate it when people mumble." My mind flashes back to when Ben revealed his big exit.

"I was wrong. There I said it, you happy?" Krystal kneads her hands together in her lap to the point that her knuckles are turning beet red. "It was just a natural thing, ya know? I mean, here I find this perfect guy: smart, great singer, funny, not to mention totally and completely cute. The catch? He's constantly with this other girl. A girl he loved more than even his own parents. How was I supposed to compete with that? So, I tried to scare you away. Sorry about those news articles too, I really shouldn't have done that."

I gently place a hand over hers. They're still shaking until I pull them tight. "I-I don't know what to say. I'm supposed to believe that you were cruel to me because you were jealous? Of *me?*" I ask incredulously. "I'm pretty sure no one has ever been jealous of me. Like you said, I'm merely an ugly school girl."

"You think I'd be intimidated by an ugly school girl?" Krystal scoffs. "No one scared me, until I met you that is." I don't reply and she finally makes full eye contact with me. "Can we forgive each other and be friends?"

"Uh, no." Does she really think it will be that easy? "I'm not just going to completely change my mind and forgive you and be all whoop-di-doo magical fairy tale ending. No."

"Oh."

"I am okay with starting over though. Maybe I can't promise all will be forgotten, who could forget an 'accidental ripping of jerseys'?"

"That was pretty bad." Krystal admits, and even I want to giggle at the horrid memory. "But I'll take what I can get. Thank you."

"You're welcome." I glance back towards the recorder and then the door. "How do we get out of here? Push the button and hug it out?"

"Wait, are you just saying all this to get out?" Krystal narrows her eyes at me.

"No! Of course not. But there's no way I'm missing out on meeting Shawn Mendes!"

"*Oh-my-gosh* Shawn Mendes is coming?" Krystal squeals.

"Yes, and I need to meet him. Meaning we need to get out of here." Taking a chance, I slide over to the door and push the button. One second passes. Then another. Nothing.

"Um, this is *so* not okay. If Shawn Mendes is out there without me I'm am going to pulverize Ben."

"That, was the best thing you have ever said."

"What do you expect from a girl smothered in mascara trapped in a room with her kind of mortal enemy?" She looks back over to me.

"Glad I opted out on makeup earlier." I sigh. At this rate there won't be nearly enough time to properly prepare for the party. Assuming we get out of here at all.

"Girly, I am going to get you all prettied up for this party. You are going to be a star. Not as much as me, because, well, duh, but still." She grins. I have to hold my hand back to keep from slapping her: old memories die hard.

"Sounds like my girls are going to shine bright tonight?" A familiar voice sneaks into our room before I can argue.

"Ben!" Krystal and I shout in unison.

35 | The Beginning of the End

-Charlotte-

A sweet scent enters my nose punctuated with bacon the moment I enter the house. Beads of sweat linger on my forehead so I grab a towel from the bathroom on my way to the kitchen. Upon pulling away the towel, I discover two devious grins.

With a pool of syrup dug into a stack of pancakes I slide onto the stool next to Ben, "what did you do?"

"Us?" Zack asks attempting to swipe some of my bacon.

"No, the bacon." I swat his hand away with a glare. "Obviously I was talking about you."

"We're innocent little angels." Zack puckers up his lips and widens his eyes. I catch the laughter bubbling up inside of me remembering I'm supposed to be mad at him. I transform the laughter into an annoyed glare.

Ben shakes his head. "You are way too excited about this."

"I'd *pay* to see this."

"To see what?" I ask, confusion leaking into my voice as I grab a piece of toast.

"Em and Krystal locked in a closet together." My jaw drops. I grab their arms and pull them in some random direction hoping I'm getting closer to Em and Krystal.

Zack slips out of my grasp and points at the opposite hallway so I let them take the lead. The white hallways still smell like new paint without a single scratch. If not for the scent of breakfast, one could almost think this house was unoccupied. There are a handful of pictures displaying Ben and his mom or Ben and his dad, but never all three of them together.

It isn't long before Ben stretches his arms out in front of us drawing our mini adventure to a halt. "We're here."

I cock an eyebrow in disbelief. "Oh really?"

"Really darling." Zack winks at me pulling a disgusted sigh from my lips. He gestures to a black box covered in buttons. "Ready?"

With a roll of my eyes, I push him out of the way and push the button myself.

"Girly, I am going to get you all prettied up for this party. You are going to be a star. Not as much as me, because, well, duh, but still." Krystal's voice comes from the box. Ben and Zack spent a lot of time setting this up.

"That sounds like they've made up, right?" Ben asks, drumming his fingers together against the door.

"I'd say so," I confirm. When Zack nods his head in agreement I jerk the door open allowing Ben to fall into the room on top of Em and Krystal.

They practically devour him in a hug which he gladly returns. Zack and I share a look of disgust as he mimics his finger being shoved down his throat. Once they finally release each other, Em meets my eyes. I expect to find the same timid brown as usual, but instead they're fierce like never before.

"What do we do now?" She asks, brushing herself off.

"In an hour my mother should collect you, Krystal, and Bryn to prepare for the dance tonight." Ben holds up his fingers creating air quotes. "Girl bonding time I believe she called it? Anyway, before then you need to have your dresses on. Everything else will be prepared for you."

"Sounds cool." I spin on my heel to return to my room, but am stopped by a hand on my shoulder.

"Bryn." My eyes trail behind me to meet Ben's, "I would *highly* recommend you take a shower or bath beforehand."

I sniff my sweat-darkened armpits exaggeratedly. "Oh, all right." I ran for over two hours, but never made it past Ben's backyard. At least, I think I didn't.

Leaving them to figure out their own messes, I turn and jog down the hallways back to my room. I follow Ben's advice and stroll beyond my bed and bags to a second door leading to a bathroom. The entire bathroom is a cream white color with a walk-in shower and the newest appliances. Next to the sink is a selection of shampoos, conditioners and body washes. I move past the overwhelming fruity scents to vanilla and scoop them into my arms. The tile shower sparkles in the light as though it's never been used before, then again, it probably hasn't.

There are three separate knobs for the shower, but no labels so I twist and pull at random. After about thirty seconds I drop the bottles in my arms in irritation. No matter how hard I pull or how far I twist nothing's happening. I've faced bombs that are easier to decode than this shower. A single drop falls from the shower head as though to mock me.

"Gah!" I growl of aggravation escapes my throat.

"Sounds like someone needs my help." My feet skid across the tile as I jump in surprise. To save myself from a possible concussion I flip back from my hands to my feet and press my finger to my ear. "It also sounds like I startled *the* Charlie Richards!"

"Keep dreaming Nick." I roll my eyes in annoyance. Anyone would be startled at a random voice shouting in their ear as they're about to get in the shower.

"I think that deserves a point." His playful voice gives away his good mood. Glad to know he hasn't burnt the house down without adult supervision.

"I think not."

"Then I'll do something that will."

I raise an eyebrow. "Go on."

"I can help you start the shower." Nick laughs at my misery as I groan yet again.

"Fine," I concede. "Just hurry up; I have a lot to do today."

"What? Like dress up?" His tone turns mocking and if it weren't for a cover, I would agree with him. "Pull the bottom knob all the way out while twisting the second one to the right. Then the top one controls temperature. Make sure the plug at the bottom is open too."

I follow his instructions releasing a steady stream of warm water. "How did you know-oh the contacts, right." The answer to my question becomes apparent as a light flashes in the corner of my eye. This morning I had decided to test out Nick's new video contacts. Now he can see everything I can see; I'll have to be careful with what I look at. "Well now I'm going to get in the shower, so please turn off the video stream."

"Nothing I'd want to see anyway." His voice becomes flustered drawing giggles from me. I can only imagine how red his cheeks are burning. "Do you want to talk though? I'm rather bored."

"Not enough inventions to mess with?" Heat spreads from the back of my neck to my heels as water pours down my back.

"I'm not in a position to tinker at the moment." If I can have a conversation two states over in a shower, I'm sure he could tinker all he wants. Meaning he must not want to.

"Oh really?" I slip the shampoo from hand to hand allowing myself to take pleasure in wasting someone else's resources. Eventually, I pep-talk myself into finishing up. Once I'm covered by a fluffy pink robe I bend over to brush my hair out. "You can turn the video feed back on if you want. It's safe now." A green light in my left eye confirms he does in fact want to.

"Wait," Nick gasps, "that's how you do the loopy towel thing on your head? Your *hair* goes in it?"

"Duh," I smirk into the mirror before returning to my room and collapsing on the cushy bed. A knock sounds at the door drawing me from a light sleep. Groggily, I rub my eyes. "Yes?"

"Are you ready to go prepare for the party?" Krystal's voice breaks through my door.

"Uh, not quite." I look over to my suitcase overflowing with clothes. "I'll be out in five minutes."

"'*Kay* girlie!"

I hope out of bed, twist into my dress, and pull my hair into a soggy ponytail. I'm out the door in four minutes. Krystal's face lights up when she sees me, then cringes in confusion, "I've never seen someone look so great in a yellow dress before."

"Really? Thanks." The top layer of the skirt flares up as I do a little twirl. I'd found this dress in Kriss' closet ages ago, and she let me keep it since it doesn't fit her anymore. The straps folding over my shoulders intertwine down my back in a spindling pattern reuniting around my waist. Though the neckline isn't plunging, it isn't cute little girl either. While the first layer of the skirt falls mid-thigh, the second and third overlap like petals towards my knees with a creamy white color. I'd never seen anyone look as good in a yellow dress either.

"Ooh and I have the perfect pair of shoes to go with it! These silver flats will bring out the jewels." She stares down at my feet. "It looks like we're about the same size. Eights?"

"That'll fit." I nod in confirmation. We walk down the hall past the guest rooms. Music pours out of Zack's, shaking his door like he's at a concert and I shake my head: silly boy. "What about Em?"

"She's already down there with her mom and Mrs. Adams." Krystal explains, "they left while you were getting ready."

"Makes sense." Light milky liquid coats my eyes from closing them too long with contacts in. I rub against them, but it doesn't help.

Krystal guides me down the hallway and past the kitchen to the main living room which has been reorganized for our makeover session. The chairs were pushed against the walls with mirrors and desks in front of them. In the center of the room is a table topped by boxes of makeup and jewelry. Beneath it are dozens of shoes. They've even managed a sink set up with warm water and towels.

Em is seated in a cushioned chair in front of a mirror with both her mom and Ben's mom behind her chatting while they curl her hair. Krystal plops down in the chair next to them and crosses her arms with her legs extended out onto a desk. Rather than sit next to her, I continue to the other side of the room where the hairdryers are plugged in.

A squeal emits from Krystal's mouth louder than the hairdryer causing both Em and me to roll our eyes over our shoulders. Our eyes meet for a moment. Hers are full of regret, confusion, and even a little, anger.

"I said periwinkle blue, not sky blue!" Krystal throws her hands up then wrings her hair in irritation. "Sky blue will totally clash with my dress."

A snicker pulls at my lips as I turn off the hair dryer. My eyes glance upon the periwinkle blue eyeshadow resting atop the center table, so I bring it over to Krystal.

"You're a lifesaver," she cries out.

"No problem." I spin the chair next to her, then sit down. "It's time for me to get my makeup done too."

"Ooh I'll do it for you." Krystal hops up and clasps her hands together. "Your skin, is like, perfection."

"Great, and I can help with your makeup after mine."

Krystal giggles excitedly and clasps her hands together. "This is going to be so fun."

"So fun," I mimic under my breath at the same time as Nick.

The only way I make it through hours of primping and prodding is with the help of Nick's unending commentary.

All the while, Mrs. Parker and Mrs. Adams keep a steady conversation going. It feels like they've sensed the tension between us girls and are trying to smooth it out. I wish I could tell them they don't need to worry, that everything will be resolved tonight, but I can't exactly go around giving away my plans.

Just after Krystal finishes pinning my curls in place, Ben and Zack call into the room requesting admission. Krystal yells back that they're going to have to wait for our "royal" entrance.

"Okay, but the party's going to start without you then," Ben warns.

"Wait!" Em slips out of her chair. A cloak covers her dress, but with her white icy blue headband and white eye shadow, it's not hard to guess the color scheme. "I don't want to miss a single moment."

Krystal rolls her eyes. "You won't. All you'll miss is helping set up."

"Are you sure?" Em raises an eyebrow, clearly not completely over her grudge. "Either way, it can't hurt to help." She shrugs away her cloak at the same moment the doors slide open.

Ben's and Zack's jaws drop in sync. Zack's eyes run up

and down her body while Ben is more discreet with locking his view on her face when she turns to meet them. I lightly chuckle at their awestruck expressions. Any boy would be left defenseless at Em's dress showing off her figure. The light blue melting into white gives her the appearance of a snow queen balanced by her soft smile.

Her princes recollect themselves enough to step to her side and offer her their arms. "Allow me to escort you." Zack grins.

"Or me, it is *my* party after all." Ben steps closer to Em. She looks back and forth between them before clicking her tongue.

"I can escort myself, thanks though." Em walks right past both of them leaving the boys in her dust.

I whistle lightly. "She's got you guys wrapped around her finger."

"What?" Zack crosses his arms and turns away stubbornly. "No she doesn't."

Ben just shrugs with a sigh. At least he admits it.

"I'll believe it when I see it." Krystal pops her lips in satisfaction before placing her lip gloss in her purse. She shrugs out of her own cape to reveal a sparkling golden dress and jumps out of the chair. As she walks over to Ben, she links her arm through mine dragging me with her. "Looks like it's time to face the music."

"Is that a musician pun?" Ben takes my place in Krystal's elbow. Zack offers his but I push it away with a snort.

"What do you think?" While Krystal's heels clop against the wood flooring, my flats are quiet as a mouse.

"When it comes to you I don't know what to think." Ben shakes his head. He smiles almost as much as Em. If I didn't know better, I would have guessed they were related.

"Perfect." I wink drawing laughter from everyone.

BEHIND THE COVER

Through Ben's double glass doors, I get a window of a view of the party. Lights scattered everywhere, tables overflowing with food, a dance floor set up. Unfortunately, the window closes before I even get the chance to experience it.

Nick comes into my ear. "Charlie, I need you to do something for me." He pauses, but continues too quickly for me to respond. "Go around to the side of Ben's house to the second driveway. I have a surprise for you."

I throw the back of my hand against my forehead, mumbling that I forgot my bracelet, and growl quietly, "This had better be good."

I pull up at my skirt and jog outside through the front door. Dozens of cars worth more money than I will ever own are lined down the street. A crowd of people enter the party through the left gate, yet I go the opposite way to the right where the road splits into two curves. The further I get from the main entrance, the fewer cars there are until I find a single black van.

"Go in there." I follow Nick's instructions and open the back door to the van. Within seconds I'm pulled into the back of the car and into a pair of arms.

"Nick, what are you doing here?"

36 | Plot Twist

-Emily-

All of this, for me. Every candle flickering its way against the breeze. The gentle stream of chocolate flowing up until it peaks as a waterfall cascading down into a bowl surrounded by a table of fruit and marshmallows. A dance floor displaying beams of light separated by the makeshift ceiling decorated by varying colors of glass resting upon four poles. Even the crowd quietly chattering about the latest fashion trends and upcoming movies is here because of me.

Rather than push me through the doorway, Ben grabs my hand and Creeper rests his chin on my shoulder. "Don't worry, you look incredible. Way hotter than any of those crazy singers."

Ben's face crumples in annoyance, but the expression passes faster than it appeared. His hand tightens in mine, then opens pressing a crinkled rectangular shaped object in my palm, before releasing it. Opening my fist reveals a melted bite sized Snickers, which forces my lips into a lopsided smile. How did I ever deserve these boys?

"You ready?" Ben smiles hopefully at me. His eyes sparkle in anticipation bringing out the storm I'd grown to know and love.

"I am." They hold out their hands in sync, and I place both of mine in theirs. Stepping through the doorway with our steps in time, we enter the party. Eyes jump toward us and remain steadfast full of curiosity at this mysterious friend of Ben.

I look over to Ben for visual cues, but he's already grinning away. Zack pulls me in one direction, to the dance floor, as Ben pulls me at the chocolate fountain. I shrug out of both their grasps making my own decision to relax at a table cloaked in cream colored cloth and candles. Time had dragged on for an eternity today, yet the sun is barely winking goodnight as it meets the earth's edge for a final farewell of the day.

Creeper nudges my shoulder and flicks his eyes to the dance floor, requesting permission to leave without muttering a word. I nod my head in approval and he strides away dusting himself off as though to prepare his dance moves. My fingers graze my lips gently as giggles tug away at my face. Then I remember the layers of lip gloss and lipstick and move my hand away. Sure enough, a pink smudge runs along the edge of my pointer finger matching the table cloth.

A sigh weighs down my breathing; even fancied up I can't help but to make a mess of things. At least Ben can visit with his friends. He's remained loyally by my side even though I see his attention wavering between the crowd and me.

I muster up a brave smile and turn to Ben. "Would you like to introduce me to your friends?"

"Yes. If you want to that is. Tonight's all about you."

"I want to." My voice wobbles up and down as my head nods. Even as his expression doesn't hide an indecisiveness, the desire to show me off to his friends wins.

The conversation grinds to a halt when we walk up leaving only the music to overcome an awkward silence. A self-conscious heat trickles through my cheeks at the impeccable makeup and appearances of those around me.

"And who is this?" The voice in question though female, is deep. Almost resembling a catlike purr.

It isn't Ben or me that answers; it's Krystal. "She's a friend of mine, and really good friend of Ben. Her name's Em, I'm sure you've heard of her." Krystal's tone may hold a light ring to it, but brings back memories from our previous encounters. She inconspicuously wipes a napkin at my hand and flips her hands backward rubbing the smeared lip gloss away from my cheeks.

"Hello." I hold out my hand, only to realize that none of them have any intention of returning the favor. They look me over in a way I can't quite understand, then nod slightly in what I hope to be approval.

"As lovely as this conversation was, I need to show Em around." Ben grins at them, and they wave goodbye.

"Who were they?" I ask once they're out of hearing range.

"No clue." Ben shrugs. "Probably some models Krystal met a photography shoot or something like that."

I chuckle lightly. "Who do I get to meet next? Do you by chance know them?"

"I do in fact." Ben grins at me. "But I'm going to allow you to be surprised." He leads me to the dance floor where my eyes instantly find Zack.

He has a girl on each of his arms locking their eyes and hands on him. I shouldn't be surprised-not really. Zack by his first appearance is a funny, handsome man. I'm sure things between him and Bryn are on hiatus at the moment if not completely frozen. Yet his eyes flash to meet mine and he passes me a wink reminding me that he's still there. He's still the person who dyed half the boys' soccer team blue to avenge me. I wave slightly at him, causing him to reach up with both of his arms in an attempt to wave back. Ben joins me in shaking my head as the two girls stumble over themselves bringing Zack to the floor in a heap of laughter and mismatching parts.

We continue squeezing through the dancers until we reach the center of the dance floor. Ben grabs my shoulders and looks straight into my eyes, "Stay here without moving a muscle. Don't even turn around."

"Yes sir." I whip my hand to my eyebrow in a mock salute.

Ben's bangs flip back and forth as he shakes his head, then he makes his way back through the crowd.

The dancers stop rigidly as Ed Sheeran's *Shape of You* is replaced by a moment of silence. Then, a pleasant scratch of guitar chords shifting sounds through the speakers. Within seconds I recognize the song as *Stitches*. I've danced to this song millions of times at home, surely I could manage just as well here.

Before I'm able to test my theory, however, Shawn's voice echoes around the party growing louder and louder with each word. Soon, it sounds like it's coming from directly behind me. I've never heard speakers as clear and realistic as these, I'll have to ask Ben-

"Emily?" The song continues, but my heart does not. I slowly turn to see my unreachable celebrity crush staring right back at *me*. Sure, I knew he was going to be here. But the actuality of him being right next to me, just, *woah*.

"Yes." My voice jumps all over the place, and I clear my throat with a blush.

"I heard you were a fan." He smiles kindly, lighting up my world brighter than any of the stars above us. His brown eyes look down into my own.

"You could say that." My knees grow limp. My common sense is screaming to stop. I'm a strong self-respecting girl who doesn't need a man. *True. But...*I'm also a girl who knows an opportunity when she sees one. "Would you like to dance? This is one of my favorites."

"Me too." He laughs sending bells through my ears. "I'd love to."

Shawn holds out his hands and I take them excitedly. The sparks I'd been expecting jump across my skin, but they're exactly as I was expecting. Nothing more, nothing less. Even when he places one hand on my waist it feels just like my dreams. When he twirls me, my world spins around until I'm nearly sick with giddiness. As the song draws to an end, he pulls me closer to him while keeping a respectable distance.

"Thank you," I whisper.

"No, thank you." Shawn replies, never dropping his perfect smile. A smile I recognize all too well. As incredible as those last few minutes were-and trust me, they were Incredible with a capital I-they weren't magic. Not for him or me. My crush had been crushed within a single song. I'm sure I'll always have an uncontested admiration for him, but there was no spark between us.

Yet, I don't feel disappointed.

Shawn wraps his arm around my midsection as the speakers crackle to life. "Can everyone hear me?" Ben's voice rebounds all around louder than any of the songs. Everyone quiets until it's as quiet as it's gonna get. "I'd like to present a song I wrote for someone special: my best friend, Em."

A few people turn and stare at me, but most keep their eyes trained on Ben who I now find sitting at a piano on the stage in front of the dance floor. He tests out a few notes, then switches into a lower key pressing down each note slowly.

Everyone knows your name,

BEHIND THE COVER

Yet you always think you're the same.
When whispers come around,
You're the favorite topic to be found,
But you keep strong holding a mask to your face.

Every word is a cut,
Every sentence a weapon.
People say, actions speak louder than words.
But I say, I say,
Words cut deeper than actions,
And thoughts cut deeper than words.

So keep holding strong,
You've never let me down.
Now give yourself a round,
'Cause you're the strongest of them all.

I say, I say,
Words cut deeper than actions,
And thoughts cut deeper than words.

So don't give up,
You're my queen, my dear.
Keep on fightin' for yourself.
'Cause there ain't no one else.
Yeah, there ain't no one else.

Ben trickles his fingers down to the edge of the piano holding the final note until he's covered by applause. At first, I'm too awestruck to join them. But as soon as my brain catches up to everything going on, my clapping is louder than the rest. A coldness slices down my cheek and I reach up to discover tears forming in my eyes. "Excuse me." I smile at Shawn, placing a kiss on his cheek. A goodbye and thank you all mixed into one.

Ben's words were made for me. His voice caught my soul in a way nothing else ever would. Watching sweat form across his forehead in concentration told stories of how long he'd practice to perfect these lines.

I run from the dance floor to meet Ben behind the stage. He looks at me questioningly, but I don't bother with an answer beyond jumping into his arms with a hug. His sweaty hair is indeed plastered to his forehead, but his hands are as strong as ever around my back.

"You liked it?" A tremor of uncertainty cracks across his voice making him sound years younger than he is.

"Like it?" I laugh in disbelief. "I love it, Ben. Almost as much as I love you."

"Love?" He echoes. His fingers intertwine into each other. "Em-"

"Not *that* kind of love."

He breaths out a sigh of relief. "Oh thank goodness. I didn't want to be the first one to break your heart. I'm supposed to be the guy who stitches it back together again."

"Though your song did remind me of something rather important." I pull away and scan the crowd to find Zack crisscrossing his way by people in a search for us. A wave of my hand draws his attention over here.

"What might that be?"

"That I need to prove myself with Bryn. She saw the wrong actions, but she completely ignored my words, and who knows what thoughts she has." I summarize my thoughts throughout Ben's song.

"Not what I was expecting, but cool." Ben nods his head in approval.

Zack throws his arms over Ben's and my shoulders. "Well it was exactly what I was expecting. Let's go find our girl."

We divide and conquer the entire area of the party, but reunite inside the back doors to Ben's house, each of us shaking our head in defeat. "You don't think she's inside, do you?"

Ben texts his mom, but she hasn't been in there either.

"The only place left is the pool, garage, driveways, or streets." Zack runs his hand through his hair. "You don't think she left, do you?"

"No," I say tersely. Both boys jump a little at my alarming tone. "At least, I hope not. Let's look out front together."

Ben leads us through his front door to a line of cars surrounding his street. We walk in the opposite direction to where the line thins out. At the very end of the street is a lone black van.

Zack jogs over in front of Ben and I and grabs at the handles. "I really don't think that's a good idea," I warn him. "Why would Bryn be in there?"

"Because this," he leans down and picks up a bracelet. "Is something I got her."

"Oh," Ben and I mumble in unison.

This time, neither of us stop Zack from opening the doors. As they slowly move to the side a gasp escapes my throat. "Bryn?"

She *and* Nick stare at me like deer caught in headlights. Inside the van are dozens of levers and glowing buttons. But worst of all, are the videos playing on the many screens. Videos of me at my house. At Ben's house. At school. Even a video of Shawn and me dancing. "What is this?" Daggers coat my voice.

"I-it's, an, er, science project," Nick squeaks.

"No, it isn't." Zack crosses his arms hardening Nick with a stare. Bryn glares right back at Zack, but without her usual ferocity. Ben and I exchange a confused glance.

"It's our van." Bryn shrugs.

"I see." I allow Zack to do the talking as my throat is almost too dry to breath. "Mind telling us why Emily's life is on display?"

"I'll tell you." Bryn and Nick hold an argument through facial expressions. Nick clearly loses leaving Bryn with a resigned look. For a winner she doesn't seem very happy. "After you shut those doors."

Ben and Zack slam the doors shut, and I say, "Enlighten us, Bryn."

"For starters, my name isn't Bryn." Neither Zack, Ben or I know how to respond, so we keep our mouths shut and ears open. Nick attempts to cut in again, but Bryn-or whatever her name is-silences him with a glare. "We don't have a choice."

"Whatever, you get to explain to Kriss, though." Nick slumps back in his chair.

"My real name is Charlie, and I'm a spy."

37 | Hello or Goodbye

-Charlotte-

For a second, I wonder if they didn't hear me and come up with four different stories to exchange for the truth. Then their expressions change drastically. Em's jaw drops and as she attempts to speak the confusion only becomes more evident. Ben glares at me and places a hand reassuringly on Em's shoulder for support. Whether that support be for her, or him I couldn't tell you. Zack, however, continues his icy gaze.

"And?" He probes as though my last statement was an everyday revelation.

"This was my assignment." I look right back into Zack's grey eyes. "I was assigned to go through Emily Parker, to get to Mr. Parker."

"My father is gone," Em speaks up. Her voice is hollow as though everything has been carved out except for an empty shell. "He left us, and trust me, he isn't coming back. If you find him, or even *think* you can find him think again." Cold laughter jerks out of her throat.

"How. Dare. You?" Ben snarls. He attempts to jump at me, but Zack catches his flailing arms before I have the chance to flinch. Lucky boy.

"How dare I what?" I snap back. Not in anger, more in defense. Sometimes the best offense is a good defense. "Try to find her father and complete my first mission? Maybe try to meet some people along the way?"

"So all of this." Zack slides his hands around gesturing towards Em and me. "Was, what, a charade? A game to keep you occupied?"

"No!" My voice cracks. Fire flames at my throat. They jump in surprise, even Nick twists in his chair. "Beyond Nick, you were my first *friends*. I've broken every rule a spy could break for you guys. Heck, I'm still breaking them. Do you know how hard it was for me to pretend to be mad at you guys for all of that time?"

"Wait," Em interjects, "you mean you weren't really mad?"

"No, of course not." I fold my arms across my chest.

"That's a relief." Zack and Ben pass their own versions of death glares to Em. She shrugs in response. "Bryn, er, what was your name again, Charlie?"

"'Charlie'? Isn't that a boy's name?" Zack snorts.

"Isn't Creeper a plant from a deserted island?" I retort just as quickly. "It's actually Charlotte, Charlie's just a nickname."

"Fine, *Charlotte* then." Em clears her throat. Ben's finally given up on his attempt to pound me, so he slumps back next to Em keeping a constant glare at me. "She may have lied, totally deceived us and lost our complete trust in her, but she's still our friend. I hated fighting with her, and our times together may have been based on false information, but that can't all have been faked. She can't be that good of an actress."

This time Nick's the one to laugh. "You'd be surprised. One time she convinced me she was really an alien adopted into our family." Three heads snap toward Nick as though they'd forgotten he was there.

"And what's your real name?" Zack demands.

"Nick. No trickery here."

"You wouldn't believe how terrible he is at lying," I explain. Nick opens his mouth to argue, but closes it again realizing he has no argument. "Anyway, do you guys forgive me?" I turn my tone light so that it sounds like my Bryn voice.

"Forgive you?" Ben scoffs. "You've got to be joking."

"Well, I apologize, and there won't be any more secrets." Maybe a few, but they needn't know. "And you're my best friends like Em said. I couldn't imagine losing you all." I look at them imploringly. Nick had always told me I suck at apologies, but it's not like I have much practice. Zack and Ben don't move an inch.

"We need to discuss something first," Em states. Nick and I nod, moving to the front of the van so they can talk. While I could listen in on their whispers, I'm not sure I want to.

"What were you thinking?" Nick whisper screams into my ear.

"I was thinking that they could provide information, and- I look down. Weakness had never been a strength of mine. "They deserve to know. Haven't you been working on that mind wiping serum?"

"Sure, I've been 'working on' it, but that doesn't mean it's complete." He tries to look angry, but I can tell I'm breaking him.

"Sounds like you have a challenge then, don't you?" I cock a half smile and he finally grins back at me.

"Oh alright, but you're still explaining to Kriss." He holds out his hand and I take it. "I think I earned a point for this mess, not to mention the information I discovered."

"What information?"

"Guess you'll have to wait and find out." Nick winks at me. I groan, but am glad to have him on my side. Through it all, he's the one I can always trust to be there for me. If he weren't, then I'd know I really messed up.

We scroll around our screens aimlessly and even fall into a staring contest before Em, Zack, and Ben return. "We'll forgive you," Em starts.

"On one term," Ben continues.

"That you will discover the true murderer of Clarisse," Zack concludes.

"I will." I nod my head earnestly. Before I get the chance to express my gratitude, Em's arms are around me pulling me into a breathtaking hug.

"Let's not fight again, okay?" She breathes into my ear.

"Okay." I hug her back then push her away. "Now go enjoy the party! I saw a certain Shawn Mendes looking awfully cute out there."

"Oh, yeah, he's nice." Em shrugs then leaves the van with Ben by her side. Ben glances over his shoulder at Nick asking if he'd like to join them and Nick speeds out like a bullet. Zack, however, remains rooted with the same expression and tense position as before.

We glare at each other until he allows a slight smirk to overtake his face causing me to smile right back. Zack slides into Nick's seat and starts to trace his fingers around the buttons. He accidentally presses one causing the screens to turn black. Rather than apologize, he shrugs and continues tracing.

"So, what are you still doing here?" I drawl, "Need to spew some more gas?"

"As nice as that sounds, no. I needed to ask you something."

"Shoot, though not literally." Zack rolls his eyes mimicking me.

"How much of it was an act? Did you really have a crush on me?"

"Don't flatter yourself." I watch his eyes light up in realization.

"Meaning we were never really dating." I nod my head in confirmation. "Great. Now I have a follow up question; did Emily ever say anything about me?"

I take my turn in rolling my eyes. "Just ask her out already."

"So, she did?"

"I didn't say that." Zack runs his hands through the back of his hair in irritation and slams one down on a keyboard. Thankfully, nothing happens. "But I have noticed how you two make googly eyes at each other. Rather disgusting actually."

"Hardee har har. Thanks anyway, Bryn." Zack doesn't bother correcting himself as he stands up to leave the van.

When the doors slam shut a final time tonight, I let out a breath of relief. I dodged a bullet, but who knows about the fire.

38 | Kade

-Emily-

A book slamming against my desk startles me from a light, sleep like phase. I rub my eyes and look upward without moving my head itself. Aubrey's tight, dark curls fall over her cheeks as she leans down next to me. "Looks like someone's tired," she coos. Except, she doesn't know the half of it. Unless she's a spy too, you never know these days. "Must not be sleeping well with all that guilt on your conscience." She winks and whips her hand over her shoulder bouncing her curls along with it.

I'd argue, but no matter what I say it comes across as even more guilty. Aubrey smiles, yet her eyes appear to be looking beyond me. After glancing over my own shoulder, the answer becomes blatantly obvious; Zack is now free. Word of "Bryn" and Zack's breakup spread like wildfire over the long weekend placing them both at the top of the single category. Before school this morning girls were smirking over Bryn's loss, commenting on how stupid she was to let him go. All they needed was a new event to forget about Clarisse.

Creeper begins to smile back at her then locks his grey eyes with mine. The mix of blue and green swirling across the rim outside his pupils remind me of a planet hidden behind an eclipse. As Aubrey attempts to say something,

Zack walks by her and says, "Nice try Aubs, but I don't waste my time on girls who waste their time on eyebrows." He shrugs and sits down next to me. "Guess I'm just not an artist."

"Guess not," Aubrey repeats, then struts off to her table of girls.

I watch her with laughter tweaking at my throat, but hold back. No point in creating extra drama. My first instinct is to thank Creeper, but as I turn to do so, he rests his hands on my arms. "Are you doing okay?" His voice has lost all traces of flirty intentions replaced by seriousness.

"Of course. I'm fine." I offer him a grin to prove it, but Zack shakes his head.

"Uhuh, I don't believe that for a second." He trails his fingers through his dark hair spiking the front bit.

Our conversation grinds to a halt as Miss Hobs slams the door shut behind her. True to her word, she's ensured every student arrives five minutes prior to the bell. Zack gives me a meaningful look that clearly intends to communicate the message of *we'll continue this later.* I pretend not to notice and keep my eyes trained on Miss Hobs waltzing from table to table plucking phones out of the hands of unsuspecting students.

I've already placed my phone in the cell safety area (a small basket in the middle of our table) but Creeper insists on making it difficult. "Are we going to go through this again?" Miss Hobs narrows her eyes at Creeper.

"I guess so." Creeper looks around the classroom, drawing further stares the longer he takes. "What exactly is it you're looking for again?"

"A phone that I know only too well." She looks down in his hands. "And there it is."

"What, this little thing?" Creeper dangles it back and forth between his thumb and pointer finger. "You could've just asked."

"And ruin our little game? Never." Miss Hobs shares the same mischievous expression as Zack more often than one would expect. She quickly scoops up his phone placing it on top of her stack like the crowning jewel. "You have two choices at this point," Miss Hobs starts as she relaxes back in her throne like office chair, "we can start the *Antigone* unit, or the *Macbeth* one. Being the kind-hearted soul that I am, I'm leaving the choosing to you. If you want to do *Antigone* raise your hands."

A few hands raise, but most continue to ignore her. Creeper looks over to me and keeps his hand down after looking at my own.

"Now all you *Macbeth* people, your turn." I'm the first to shoot my hand into the air with Creeper as a close second. Eventually more hands pop into the air as people realize they don't have any more choices. "Looks like we're doing *Macbeth*. The books are in the back, and today I'd just like for you to read through as much as your table group can get through. Tomorrow we'll start watching clips and go over an introduction to the story."

Creeper slides out of his chair. "I'll get the books."

"My hero," I drawl, just like Charlie. He raises an eyebrow in amusement before grabbing our books.

At the beginning of the year, we had two other people at our table group. A girl, who eventually drifted off to Clarisse's group, and a nerdier boy who left after the drama with Zack and Charlie. Now it's just Creeper and me. "Have you ever read the play before?" I ask as Creeper places the book in front of me.

"What do you think?" Creeper doesn't sit down, rather he stands opposite of me on the other side of the table. He leans down, resting his head on his hands.

"No?"

"And she wins the golden cigar."

"What generation are you from?" I smirk, delicately

lifting a torn cover and thumbing through pages until I reach the first scene.

"Can't accept the fact that I'm more mature?" He uses my own line against me. A laugh transforms into a cough of disbelief coming out of my throat. Something flashes in his eyes that I can't place.

"Please, let's get to reading." Creeper nods his head in agreement, but continues to stare into my eyes. I look right back at him, refusing to be the first to glance away. Every second feels like an hour, but change flickers across his eyes like a constant variable. Eventually they settle on a soft glow with his pupils growing almost as large as the irises themselves.

A hand slaps across the back of Zack's neck pushing him forward. Once I realize what's happening, I barely have time to shift my head backward and catch him in my hands. Zack rubs the back of his neck as we both turn up to find Miss Hobs smirking at us. "I do hope Mr. Taylor here isn't distracting you, Em."

"N-no." I blush and face my lap after pushing Creeper as far from me as possible.

"While I do think you would make an interesting couple, I'd prefer you did *something* beyond staring at each other's eyes all class long." She continues.

I peak up to see Creeper grinning back and turn my head away. "Sorry, I forget that I'm so addicting. I'd say it won't happen again." He pauses growing only all the cockier in his tone. "But we all know I can't guarantee that."

"Good luck with this creature, Em." Miss Hobs leaves to check on another group not giving me a chance at defense.

"Now." Creeper turns back to me. "Where were we?"

As his face moves closer to mine, my hand whips in front of it pushing him away, "*Macbeth*."

"How boring." Nonetheless, he opens his book and finally reads along with me.

I have to stop Creeper every other sentence to explain a definition or pronunciation, but we manage to get further than any other group as far as I can tell. Creeper even appears to become interested in the story as we get deeper. He especially seems to have a thing for the three witches and their mysterious chanting. The best part has to be his voices for each of the characters that make me laugh too hard to read properly.

By the time the end of class rolls around, we both groan at having to close our books. I safely tuck mine into a pocket of my backpack where I know it won't be injured. Creeper, on the other hand, stuffs his copy into the general pocket pushing it deeper until he notices my glare. Sheepishly, if Creeper were to ever do something that could be described as "sheepishly," he pulls it out and returns it more delicately. I nod my head in approval at the same moment the bell rings.

Creeper guides me down the hallway clearing a path for both of us until someone grabs our arms pulling us to the wall just outside the flow of traffic. We glance over to discover Charlie which causes Creeper to pull away instantly. "What do you want?" His voice may not be as cold as in the van, but it certainly isn't warm either.

"We need to talk." Charlie sounds excited, but concerned at the same time.

"We need to get to class," Creeper counters, appealing to my academic side.

"Trust me, this is way more important than Chemistry. It's not like you're going to be absent, and the teacher never counts tardies." Charlie tugs me away against the flow. I don't resist, but don't help her either.

"That's amusing; you expect us to trust you," Creeper snickers at her, reaching out to grab my arm.

"It has to do with my side of the deal," Charlie offers.

"Why didn't you say so?" Creeper and I follow her footsteps while the crowd thins out. She slips between bodies as though they aren't even there until her hands latch on the arm of someone in a black hoodie and basketball shorts. With his hood pulled up and back to us, I can't recognize him.

A gasp of shock escapes my lips as Charlie shoves him into the janitor's closet holding the door open long enough for Creeper and I to make it through before slamming it shut. After locking it with a pair of keys, she switches the lights on.

A second gasp threatens to escape when I see black hair spiking out of the boy's hoodie and a set of dark blue eyes: Kade. Most surprising is the way he's looking at Charlie. Not with desire or disgust. His expression is a combination of joy, concern, and most of all fondness. "What does he have to do with anything?" I ask, shifting my gaze to Charlie. Does she think Kade *killed* Clarisse?

"Do you know why Nick was in San Diego?"

"To spy on us?" Creeper answered in a snarky voice.

"No, he'd been attempting to track a code signal that was the same as mine. Only, it had been blocked until a few days ago. When he finally decoded it, he discovered something interesting," Charlie's eyes flicker at Kade for a reaction, but he provides none so she continues. "This tracking signal belonged to a student at our very own Simplot High who happened to stop at Em's house every day. Nick checked my cameras to find him hanging around your backyard-"

"Wait." I stop her and narrow my eyes. "You have cameras at my house?"

"Among other things." She waves her hand dismissively. "But you're missing the point. Kade here has something he's been hiding something, and I think it's about time we find out what."

I hadn't noticed Kade's hands had been tucked behind him until he brings them out to a slow clap. Hanging off his left hand is a half-secured hand cuff I can only imagine Charlie put there. "Good job, I'm glad you finally figured it out." Then he turns to me. "I've been waiting to talk to you for a long time, Emily."

"We've talked," I snort in annoyance, "like all those times you and Clarisse picked apart my outfits, or better yet, my self-esteem."

Kade shakes his head. "Stubbornness must run in the family."

My jaw drops as my hands start to shake. "What do you mean?"

"Charlotte said it's time to explain what's going on, and I for one, agree." Charlie shifts her head to the side at the sound of her true name as though trying to solve a complex equation. "Emily, you should know that I deeply apologize for everything I've done to you. I never wanted to bully you, but it was how I could protect you."

"You call that protection?" Zack sends daggers at Kade from his body language to his voice.

"Trust me, Clarisse had much worse plans. It was my job to keep those plans from happening while remaining in her trust." Kade doesn't flinch for a moment. His cocky attitude is infuriating, but I need to know what he's talking about. "There's something no one knows about Clarisse; she had schizophrenia. That's a serious mental condition, and for a simple time conserving definition, it means that in her case she constantly had voices in her head which can cause unwarranted violence and superiority. It's enough to drive a person mad.

"There was one thing that kept her sane, and that was you, Emily. When you were younger and closer friends, her voices would quiet when she was around you providing almost a normality to her life. It was the first time she was really able to thrive. Until you shifted away from her to Ben. That's when everything got really bad. The voices turned against you putting thoughts into her head that weren't her own. She gave voice to those thoughts and placed them into the minds of others. I soon realized that the best way to keep you safe, was by assisting her."

My jaw drops as my head spins. All of this? Is anything in my life real? "It was all my fault?"

"No." Creeper steps next to me and places his arms around me. "It isn't your fault. You didn't know, don't you dare think for a second any crap this guy says is your fault."

"I couldn't agree more, this isn't Emily's fault." Kade nods.

"What about her death?" Charlie presses, keeping to the point.

"That, is the second part of my story." He grins at me and gestures at the ground. "Emily, my dear, you may want to sit down for this." I follow his instructions after Creeper lays out his sweatshirt on the ground and we sit together. Charlie remains standing with her back relaxed against the wall. "Back when your father was working on a cure for Leukemia, he discovered something else. Rather, he *created* something else. A disease that was far worse than Leukemia. One day he brought home traces of this disease, let's call it Milex for the moment, and your sister Maree became sick. Luckily, after working with Milex for so long, he was able to make an antidote." I open my mouth to disagree, but Charlie shakes her head at me. I let him continue. "Maree was saved, but with a great cost. Milex became known to his research group after your father presented his research. Unfortunately, not everyone there had the same goal.

"One member was working for a gentleman by the name of Tai Trinskie. Since the discovery of Milex became known to Tai, he has hunted down every last sample of Milex he could find. Your father realized that Tai couldn't use Milex without the antidote, unless he planned on infecting himself. The only solution your father had was to go into hiding taking Maree with him. Otherwise he'd be placing your entire family in danger. That's where I come in."

"Hold on." I shake my head. "That-this isn't right. My sister is dead and my father would never come back to us." My throat is drier than sandpaper and I have to rest my head against Creeper's shoulders for support against the clouded vertex of confusion spinning around.

"Ah, so you think. Your father had to disappear without leaving any traces, which is why he could never contact you. It's also the reason he hired me. My job was to keep you and your mother safe at all costs. Still is in fact." He winks at me and Creeper pulls me closer.

"This is too much." A tear slips down my cheek. It burns not of sadness, but of fear. Fear that he's wrong. Or even worse, fear that he's right. After all this time, it's impossible, isn't it?

"I'm sorry, I hadn't planned on telling you this way." Kade sounds apologetic for the first time since I met him "But someone took matters into her own hands." He turns to Charlie. She shrugs and comes over to kneel next to me. I feel the weight of her hand against my back.

"He's telling the truth." Her words drop like a bomb. There's no way she could know whether or not he is, but the conviction in her voice convinces me otherwise.

"Give me proof." I finally decide.

"Of course," Kade reaches into his hoodie pocket and presses a picture in my hands. It's the same one I have of my dad, Maree and me getting ice cream at the park. The only difference is that my dad's messy scientist handwriting is scribbled across the back. *Stay strong little monkey, I'll see you soon.*

I look up at Kade, my eyes now dry. *My sister's alive. My dad isn't gone.* "I believe you." My voice catches as my brain struggles to keep up. "Now finish your story."

"Tell us about Clarisse's death." Charlie adds.

"Tai thought his scientists had created the antidote, but he needed a test subject. Of all the people at our school, Clarisse was the most isolated. Your dad and I think they suspected Clarisse as being his second daughter. They kidnapped her and injected her first with Milex then with their antidote. At first, she seemed fine so they let her go after a memory swipe. Clearly it didn't work as well as they thought."

"Clearly," Charlie repeats. A silence falls upon us and I remember where we are. Could I really return to school after this? Forget school, could I really return to life after this? Nothing is what it should be, but maybe expectations are wrong. I'd dreamt of the day my father would return, but that dream had faded into the past. Now everything has changed. Yet only one question sits on the edge of my lips.

"What do we do next?"

39 | Boot Camp

-Charlotte-

Three pairs of eyes turn to me in expectation. I ponder Em's question for a moment. If Kade is telling the truth, which I believe he is, this is much bigger than anything Nick or I could ever have expected. Em's question still rings in my ears, what are we going to do? A smile sneaks across my lips as the answer becomes clear. "First, we make it through school. Then you all meet at my house for training, deal?"

"Training?" Zack repeats, as everyone else nods their heads in agreement.

"You didn't think I'd let you guys in on this unprepared, did I?" I wink at them and unlock the janitor's closet.

"I wouldn't say unprepared," Kade smirks, crossing his arms over his chest. I smirk right back at him ignoring a familiar twinge at the back of my mind.

"Yeah, Zack seems to have a pretty good handle on things," I retort. Em covers her mouth to stifle her giggles and Zack flicks his chin upward.

"It's about time you noticed." The bell rings, causing Em's face to go ashen. I bet she's never skipped class before. As the crowd outside grows in strength, I slowly push open the door and allow everyone to exit the room.

"My house, after school," I explain. Kade disappears into the flow with a slight nod of his head, a moment later I catch sight of him high fiving with a pair of his popular guys.

Zack pulls Em to his side to guide her through the hallway in her dazed state. A cloudiness is covering her eyes as her face continuously changes from one expression to the next. It suddenly dawns on me what this means for her. Her family just doubled in size, it could almost feel like they were brought back from the dead.

"Can I help?" I offer, admittedly late.

"I just-" Em stumbles as her shoe catches on the ground. Zack and I jump forward to catch her keeping her upright. "Need to sit down. Let's go to the cafeteria."

We move with the flow of students without pushing Em too hard. She looks like she could break down at any moment in time, maybe I should give her a break. It's a lot to process.

We sit at our usual table, but don't bother with food. I don't think either of them could eat anyway. Plenty of odd glances come our way at the sight of Zack and I sitting together as if nothing had happened. Over my shoulder I catch Kade's eyes in time for him to wink mysteriously at me. Aubrey has taken Clarisse's old seat at his side and is giggling gleefully. She looks over at us and lifts her fingers to her lips when she sees Zack then waves over to us. At this scene, Kade grins and whispers into Aubrey's ear causing her to fall into a heap of giggles.

Em snorts in disgust and turns away from them. "So tonight, what exactly are we doing?"

"I'm going to train you." I lean closer to Zack and Em and raise my eyebrows. "In the ways of a teenage spy."

"Spy?" Em and Zack say in sync, but their voices differentiate them from one another. Em's is anxious still in shock whereas Zack is all excitement.

"Yup." I shrug then lean back. "It's the least I can do."

"Awesome!" Zack fist pumps, jumping up from his bench slamming against the table. He falls backward jumping around on one foot while pulling his knee to his chest yet his face remains a gleeful grin. At long last Em finally cracks the slightest hint of a smile.

"Can I text Ben?" Em asks, grabbing her phone from her pocket. I nod my head in confirmation; if he's going to be in Boise for a week, I might as well keep him close as possible until Nick finishes his amnesia solution. "Great, he'll love this kind of thing."

Zack snorts in laughter, earning a glare from Em. "I'm sure he will."

"What's that supposed to mean?"

"Oh, nothing." Zack's eyes twinkle as light reflects across them. Within a matter of sentences, he's done something I doubt I could ever do: he brought Em back to her usual self.

"No, tell me." Em leans her head ever so slightly toward him with a piercing expression.

"Only that I'm interested in watching a polished singer attempt physical activities."

Em starts to glare at him, but changes her expression into a joking sneer, "Yet he was beating you at Twister."

Zack places the back of his hand against his forehead, "I'm offended you'd think I'd *lose*. I was trying to save his fragile self-esteem, clearly."

"I'm sure," Em mutters in time for the bell to cut her off.

Normally I'd split away from them to go meet Nick, but today I stick by Em's side as they continue to the drama theatre. I grimace at the sight of Kade and Aubrey strolling in arm in arm. It couldn't all be a lie with all the details he knew, but he's a darn good actor.

We sit in a row of bleachers further back in the theatre, not saying much while the other drama kids talk up a storm. The first five minutes pass without any sign of the teacher. I raise my eyebrow at Em in a questioning manner, but she shrugs in response. "It's kind of hit or miss with Mr. Matchen. Lately he's been showing up daily to get a move on with the play, but I haven't seen him today."

Zack shifts in his chair so his arm is resting next to Em's, but she pulls her away with a sly look. "If he doesn't arrive within the next five minutes, let's agree to skip class and go start training." His excitement draws a smile across my face, and Em quickly agrees to his deal.

An obnoxious voice calls out, "Brynnie!"

I turn across the room to the stage where Kade and Aubrey are sitting with their legs dangling off the edge. Aubrey's waving her arm back and forth from her direction to mine and back again in a beckoning motion. I return to face Zack and Em who both possess mischievous grins resembling monkeys. "Go on," Zack says, "*Brynnie.*"

"I hate you," I mutter under my breath. I hop up and climb over the rows until I reach the two of them. "Yeah?"

"Kadey here was just telling me about how you were so helpful with the Em situation." Aubrey rocks back and forth before grabbing my hand and jerking me up onto the stage next to her on the opposing side of Kade.

"Oh really?" I look at Kade. "What exactly did you say?"

"You know, how you pretend to be Em and Zack's friend only to bring Zack back to our side." Kade winks at me again, but with a knowing look. With a shake of his head he flips his black hair away clearing a direct bath for me to note an imploring flashing in his eyes. I ignore it, but don't understand it.

"That, right. Because I totally did that."

"Yup!" Aubrey nods emphatically. "*So* smart. Can I tell you a secret?"

I nod my head and widen my eyes in my Bryn acting, but Kade knows the difference and smirks. "Of course."

"I've had literally the biggest crush on Zack since, like, the fifth grade." I gasp and cover my mouth.

"No way!"

"Yes way!" She looks across the room at him and Em talking with a smitten expression. "I just wanted to check that things with you and him are like...totally over."

"We are indeed." Especially considering we were never an actual "thing."

"Awesome." She gasps comically, only she doesn't mean it to be funny. "Oh my gosh, he's coming over here. Do I look okay? Like is my makeup smeared." Her mascara is in fact clumped across her eyelashes and her drawn on eyebrows have started to fade. Still, I shake my head with a wide grin as she combs her fingers through her hair.

Zack and Em walk over to my side. "It's time to go," Em says coldly staring right at Aubrey.

"See you guys later." I wave at Kade and Aubrey then jump down next to Zack.

"Oh." Aubrey trails her fingers along her arm. "Zack, do you have to go too?"

"Yup. The three of us have important business to attend to." Shut down.

Nick is waiting out front so we climb into his car and pull out of the parking lot. Nick turns fully around removing his hands from the wheel and Em screeches in horror, "what are you doing!"

"Oh, did I mention I'm the behind the scenes guy?"

"What?" Em shakes her head. "Please put your hands on the wheel." She clutches at Zack's arm.

"Now, you can hold off on that-"

"Zack! Now is not the time for flirting." Em stops him with a glare.

"Actually, flirt away." Nick doesn't bother to help Em at all with her terror. "Charlie is a field agent, but I'm the technological genius. I invented this car, including its self-driving functions."

"Woah," Zack exclaims leaning over the seat to get a better look at Nick's console while Em breathes a sigh of relief.

"It's best to just go with Nick, he isn't the greatest at communication." I laugh in response to Nick's glare.

He 'harrumphs' in irritation, but doesn't say anything. We pull into our driveway and walk through the open front gates. A small ball of fear is crouching in front of our door with his hands covering his face in an attempt of protection. Numerous small red beams light up his back like a Christmas tree from hidden weaponry already trained on his unaccepted entrance.

Ben is shaking with his lips moving silently in what I can only imagine to be his final prayers. Nick and I share a look before scanning our irises into the lock opening the door and deactivating the defenses.

Em runs up and engulfs Ben in a hug, he hugs her back double checking that she's okay. "Am I okay?"

"Yeah, I mean, your dad and Maree." He twists his fingers behind her back. "That's a lot."

"Yeah." Em looks over his shoulder into our house. "Let's talk about it later. We've got training to do."

Nick and I lead them through our front door to the living room and exit the house again through the kitchen into a portion of our backyard that has been transformed into a training course from when I was in training. "Welcome to spy boot camp."

40 | A Note

-Emily-

Sweat drips from my brow into my eyes bringing with it a sting of mascara. I rub away, only making it worse. With a groan of irritation, I give up and return to the challenge at hand. So far Charlie and Nick have pushed us through ridiculous physical activities including everything from balancing on a single wooden board across a dirty pool to dodging water balloons filled with JELL-O.

I'm tasked with remaining hidden from one of Nick's drones flying around an obstacle course created by randomly positioned trees. It had been a group activity, but Ben was the first out, followed by Zack as he was found laughing at Ben. When discovered, a heated green laser burst in a direct path from the drone to their chests. The laser isn't hot enough to seriously burn us, but I noticed darker marks on Zack's t-shirt outlining his body soaked through from sweat.

Now it's down to me. A whirring passes two trees back. At the beginning of this game, I gladly would have slipped across the yard to the other side, but it's been almost an hour. How long am I supposed to endure this? Part of me thinks Charlie is trying to keep my mind busy, and I appreciate it. The other part thinks she and Nick are just having a good laugh at our expense.

My foot slips in a muddy spot, as I lean back against the tree. The whirring snaps to a stop before starting up again even faster. I regain my balance in time to run around the tree meeting the laser. As expected, it tinges slightly against my skin, but only for a second.

"Nice job, Em." Charlie walks out from the tree I was just behind slowly clapping.

"How did you get there?" I gawk at her; I hadn't had a clue she was there.

"Practice, lots and lots of practice." She grins. "I'd actually expected Zack to be the best at that, but you out skilled him by far. You could have the makings of a good field agent. Or a lucky one. Both are equally valuable."

"I wouldn't exactly say I'm lucky." My shoulders pull up in a shrug and I rest each of my hands on my forearms.

"Right, the family thing," Charlie comments, looking down at the lifeless drone. She bends over and picks it up twisting its wings with her fingers nonchalantly. "I'm sorry about that, I honestly had no idea."

"But you think Kade's telling the truth?" We both look over to a punching bag set up on the patio where Kade is pounding his fists back and forth in a rhythmic pattern.

"I do." Charlie nods her head thoughtfully. "But we're still going to collect proof."

"And we're going to stop this Tai figure and save my dad and sister," I finish for her. She grins at me showing off her white teeth.

The sun shines against her hair highlighting red shards against her blonde curls, and I notice her eyes have changed colors. Her entire disposition has changed from go happy to a smirking confidence. "Precisely. Unfortunately, I would like to ensure you don't all die along the way. Hence the training." She spreads her fingers out and waves her hand across her backyard.

"Makes sense," I agree, my breathing finally relaxing.

A screech of pain creates cause for birds to take off from the trees like a hurricane. The edge of Charlie's lips crawl up mischievously as she takes off running toward her house with me close behind. Perhaps not "close" but I can at least watch the mud flick up from the back of her heels until she slows to a stop in front of a sand pit. I heave in behind her to discover Ben sitting cross legged in the sand cradling his arm.

Zack's standing above him glaring down with his hands on his hips. His shirt has mysteriously disappeared revealing short scars swiped across his chest. He catches my gaze and winks. I ignore him and kneel next to Ben who has managed to keep his shirt on.

"Are you okay?" I reach to hold his arm, not that I know what I'd do if it were injured.

"Fine, it's just tweaked since *someone* doesn't know how to pull his punches." Ben sends Zack a meaningful look.

"Oh yeah, sorry, guess I don't know my own strength." Zack pulls his fist into a ninety-degree angle flexing against the sun.

Ben groans sharing a look with me. "Is all of this really necessary? Tai sounds like a crazy man, how much damage could he really do?"

A loud slap crunches against the patio from Kade's gloves falling to the ground. He marches over in what would appear to be a menacing approach, if not for his ever-present smirk. "Tai is crazy, but he's a crazy man with an army of followers."

"Why would anyone follow him?" I ask, dumbfounded. "Don't they realize they'll get sick too?"

"Exactly." Kade's eyes twinkle at me. "If they're on his side not only will they have an antidote, they'll also be able to have a say in the changes they want to bring about."

"Changes?" Zack raises his eyebrow.

"Why else would Tai want Milex?" Kade shrugs simply. Zack whistles and twirls his finger in a circular motion around his ear.

Charlie stares at Kade with a hard expression, she clearly thinks there's more than what he's sharing, but before she can ask about it, he takes off running. "Time to get back to training."

"No." Ben shakes his head, a slight terror accenting his eyes. "I refuse to participate in another drill that involves Zack beating up on me." Zack looks around at us innocently.

Charlie chuckles, "I was going to suggest we move on to the mental portion anyway."

As we enter the house through a door into the kitchen, Zack picks up his shirt and whips it over his shoulder. I walk by his side and whisper, "I'd appreciate it if you'd put that back on. Or better yet, a sweatshirt."

"Am I too distracting, Emily?" He stares down at me an odd mixture of joking and intensity.

"I just prefer modesty." I turn away from him to escape his trapping presence. "You're starting to smell, so deodorant wouldn't be terrible either."

Zack bursts out in heaves of laughter pushing his chest in and out. After only a few hours he's tanned more than I do in an entire summer. "Emily, you are adorable."

"Thank you. Now how about that shirt?" He appears to be on the verge of further laughter, but obliges and follows my directions.

Charlie stops at a bar in the back of her kitchen near a fridge, cabinets and pantry. We seat ourselves on the chairs as she grabs some snacks and water to tide over our hunger. Zack and Ben greedily smack away at the apple slices violently dipping into the peanut butter, but manage to leave a few slices for me.

Once their hunger has been appeased, Charlie whispers something and Nick comes down the stairs with a computer resting delicately in his arms. He rests it in front of me sliding open the top. Ben leans over my right shoulder and Zack my left as the screen lights up with a single white start button flashing in the center of the screen.

"Press any button when you're ready to begin," Nick instructs without details.

Zack immediately pushes the spacebar changing the screen to black before lighting up again. A series of numbers stream across the screen and I attempt to commit them to memory. I keep track of every odd one hoping Ben is on the same brainwave as me. After twenty numbers total have passed, the screen blanks displaying the start button again.

"What were the numbers?" Charlie asks, placing her energy drink in the sink.

"Three, five, eight, four, one." Zack ticks off on his fingers, only to have a confused expression overtake his face. "Or maybe it was zero."

Charlie blurts out, "Fail." And turns to Ben and me. "What about you?"

Ben and I make eye contact for a split second, and I know he remembered our old trick. "Three."

"Five," he says.

"Eight," I continue.

"Four." Ben and I go back and forth like this until every number has been properly restated. Nick and Charlie nod in approval, slightly impressed. In celebration, Ben and I crash our hands together in a perfect, yet painful, high five.

"Now for the real test, what animal crossed the screen?"

"Huh?" Zack, Ben, and I scrounge up our faces in confusion.

"You know, the penguin halfway through on number nine for its second-time round," Nick explains.

"No way," Zack groans leaning back on his stool only to realize there is no back. His hands flail down to catch himself just in the nick of time.

Charlie laughs then leads us into our next memory and observation exercise. We move on to codes and puzzles until our brains are as sore as our muscles. School ended six hours ago, and my mom will soon be expecting me home. I rarely hang out with friends past ten.

Nick guides us to his car, but Charlie stops me on my way into the passenger's seat. "Don't tell your mom about what you learned today, okay?"

"Okay, but why not?"

"It's a lot of shock, and we need to figure things out first," Charlie explains, but a second understanding is left unsaid: she doesn't want her cover blown.

In the back seat, the three boys are vying for space, shoving each other back and forth. Nick drops off Kade first, then Zack who blows me a kiss on his way inside his house. Lastly, Nick stops in front of my house where Ben is staying with me.

"Thank you," I say.

"It's no problem, see you tomorrow for round two of training?" Nick asks. His voice is hopeful, and it's only now I realize he must not see many people. If he's the inside brains of an operation, he can't get much human interaction.

"Of course," I reply. Ben gives him a tight smile, clearly still in pain from today's session.

When we get into the house, my mom's left a note on the inside of the door letting us know she's already in bed and hopes we had a good day. I smile quietly at the thoughtfulness of her note, not to mention the revelations that had been made. A strong urge to tell her all about it crawls up throughout me, but Charlie's warning is still fresh in my mind so I shove it back down.

Ben already knows the way to the guest room, but I walk with him anyway. It's on the opposite side of the house from my room, toward the kitchen. He smiles at me, stopping in the doorway, "Em, do you want to talk?"

"Not really." I shake my head. I just need to think. "I'll let you know if I do."

"Good." A yawn slips through his mouth. "I love you, Em."

"Love you too, Ben." He pulls the door softly shut between us, and I retire to my own room.

I throw my school backpack on my bed resulting in my phone tumbling out onto my covers. A paper scratches against my palm as I twist it around in my hand to view my notifications. Tape holds a tiny envelope to the front of my phone, and I carefully remove it as to not rip apart the paper.

A gasp of shock draws my breath away when my eyes run straight to the signature: *Love always and forever, Daddy.*

Without wasting another second, I frantically read the letter:

My Dearest Emily,

I apologize I couldn't deliver this myself (I've had to entrust Kade with the responsibility as I'm certain you have learned), but it is of not only my safety, but Maree's as well. As strong as my desire to see you may be, it is still my responsibility to keep our family alive and our world safe, which would be broken by my presence being revealed to you at such a time. However, I have deemed it safe for us to meet at the park tonight, at ten pm. I can't wait long, so please be timely.

Love always and forever,
Daddy

Teardrops drip from my eyes to the wrinkled paper stretched into my tight fists. I hadn't seen this handwriting in years, yet it is as familiar as my own. My phone screen flashes on showing the time to be ten fifteen. The aching in my limbs begs me to remain in the comforts of my bed, but are quickly banished by the thought of seeing my dad again.

I tuck my phone into my back pocket along with the letter, and tug on an extra sweatshirt. As I pass by my mom's room, I consider leaving a note, then decide against it. I won't be gone long enough for her to notice.

A brisk wind nips against my cheeks when I open the door, but it's soon to my back. It pushes me harder and harder as though we're sprinting to the same goal. Thoughts blur across my mind so quickly it feels like I'm fishing for concentration. What if Maree's there? What does my dad look like now?

The park soon comes into view, but it's vacant. I slow my pace to a casual walk as I enter the park and walk over to the swing set. Odd that he'd choose such an open place, we'd never gone to another park, so it'd have to be this one. Only, there aren't any trees or fences to hide us.

I grab my phone out of my pocket and check the time as I sit down on a swing and gently begin to dig my feet into the bark. Ten twenty.

A crunch sounds behind me.

I turn my head with a grin of expectation lighting up my face, but it instantly vanishes as a bag is pulled over my head engulfing me in darkness. Simultaneously, my hands are jerked behind my back and brought together until a plastic zip tie digs into my wrists. I open my mouth to scream but foul-smelling breath blows against my nose. "If ya wanna live, you're gonna keep that pretty lil moutha yours shut. Got it?"

41 | Emergency

-Charlotte-

"I need to talk to you." Nick slams my door shut.

"Funny, I was about to come talk to you." I set my book down next to the bump in my bed caused by my legs. "You go first."

Nick drags my chair over next to me and sits down. "Obviously, I watched the video you recorded from Kade's story, and it makes sense logically. There are still the issues of how he and Mr. Parker became associates in the first place as well as what could have caused Tai to want Milex, but Mr. Parker's actions make more sense now than before."

"That's about where I am." I pull my legs up to my chest and wrap my arms around them going over the past few days in my head. "Only, I'm not sure what to do with Kriss. She's supposed to come back in a few days, and I'm nowhere near ready to explain how four people know about my mission. Especially Kade, I can't wait to hear how he found out."

Nick shrugs. "Maybe he learned about you the same way we learned about him. If not, I'm sure you'll discover his true actions. If you need help with Kriss, I'm glad to provide backup."

I look up and smile at him warmly. "Thanks Nick, that means a lot to me. Do you think there's a chance of that amnesia concoction being complete by then?"

A twinkle alights in his eyes at the challenge. "I can try, assuming nothing crazy distracting happens in the next few days." His features change becoming more concentrated. "Why did you tell them anyway?"

I purse my lips, pushing a slow stream of air through them, "At the moment it seemed like the right thing to do. They deserved to know, and if we learned about Em's dad I'd have to tell her. It was clear that they'd caught us, and I'd rather them think we're spies than peeping toms. The latter would result in me failing my first case." I scowl down at my light blue comforter and tug at a loose thread. "If it were really that wrong I knew you'd stop me."

Spurts of laughter jump raggedly from his mouth. "Do you really think I could stop you?"

I rock back and forth with a heated red blooming across my cheeks. "I don't know, I guess I always expect you to at least try if I do something life threateningly wrong."

"Hopefully." Nick jerks his head up and down. The blond highlights of his dark brown hair remain from the previous green streaks catching my eye. "What will you do if the amnesia works?"

The tips of my fingernails find their ways beneath my teeth as I gnaw down anxiously. "I'm not even sure where we're going from here. My plan is to make contact with Mr. Parker leading to Tai, but I wanted your help in figuring out exactly what to do. After that, assuming everything worked out and we got Em's dad and sister back, we'd just blame everything on Kade."

"So Kade is your fallback plan?"

"Indeed. Have you found anything out about him?" I rub my chin thoughtfully.

"No more than before. Once Kriss is back with her computer, I can use it to search more databases, but I'm highly restricted at the moment. I knew I should have invented my processor before she left." He shakes his head in mock disappointment and I click my tongue against the roof of my mouth.

A silence overtakes us before a grin creeps back onto my face. "Did you see Ben attempting the obstacle course?"

"I'd never miss it. Especially when you managed to pit Zack against him. The natural competition merely acts as an invigorating agent in pushing them to work harder."

"It was entertaining. I doubt they'll actually have any need to use such skills, but it can't hurt to be safe."

"Would you place them in harm's way?" Nick asks suddenly, his eyes darkening as he tilts his head to the side.

I don't respond immediately letting his question worm its way around my head. Would I? It would depend on the circumstances. If it were one of them versus the world, I'd choose the world. If it were one of them or me, I'd choose them. If it were one of them versus Nick, I'd choose Nick. I will allow them to participate in missions that are void of all danger, and if it were of necessity I would force their participation in danger. I care for all of them, with the exception of Kade, and will protect them. In answering Nick's question, I roll my head from my right shoulder to my left then pull my shoulders up in a shrug. "I'm not sure."

We're interrupted by a loud alarm ringing throughout the house. I snap to face Nick who's fallen off the stool and is attempting to right himself. While rolling my eyes, I grab his wrist and pull him through my doorway. He reaches to his tablet sliding through apps until opening the security app. A notification of an invader flashes across a live video feed of Ben banging against our front door.

With a touch of a button, the alarms silence and front door unlocks as Nick and I reach Ben. "What's going on?" I ask allowing irritation to thread itself through my voice.

"It's Em-" Ben pants, trying to collect himself. "She's gone." I roughly pull Ben through the doorway as Nick restarts the security system.

"What do you mean *'gone'*?" Nick holds up his fingers as air quotes.

"So Em and I got home and went to bed, right? Well, two hours ago I heard the door slam shut, so I got up and searched her house only to find she'd left. I assumed she went outside for a walk or something."

"And you didn't look for her?" I cut him off, throwing my hands into the air.

"No. I texted her, and she replied letting me know she'd be back soon. Only, like I said, that was an *hour* ago and now she won't reply." Ben looks up at me pleadingly, his usually model like features bent in worry and sweat. The paparazzi would have a field day.

"Okay, come with me." Nick gestures with his arm over his shoulder and I help Ben up as we follow him.

Nick guides us into the basement laboratory where Ben's jaw drops at the inventions. He tightens his arms around himself as though terrified of touching anything. If it were my first time down here, I would be too. Sometimes I still am.

Stopping at a desk topped with screens, Nick powers on the bottom computer and types in a password hidden from sight. As the screens slowly light up, numbers and letters spill across them. Nick's hands fly across the keyboard jumping to the computer mouse every now and then until a map unifies the screens causing them to act as one. A light blue line of tics curves through the streets and houses.

"This is Em's locations throughout the past two and a half hours using the data from the PW." Nick explains, bringing his pointer to our house on the screen where Em's dashed line begins.

"PW?" Ben asks, keeping his eyes glued to the screen.

"Pants wiring," I explain. "It's a tracking wiring that I sewed through the seams of Em's jeans." Ben steps back, a look of fear on his face combined with anger.

"Even though a discussion on boundaries is warranted, please just tell me she's okay right now."

Nick guides the pointer from our house through the streets to Em's where it's a mess of blue lines that we really can't decipher. It is clear, however, that she left her house an hour ago as Ben explained. Her path wasn't far, continuing down the street to a park, where the dashes disappear.

"Her pace is shown by the color of the dashes." Nick explains, "Here, where I was driving her, it's the darkest. When she was at home it's the lightest because she was stationary or walking. Before her trail ends at the park, it looks like she was running, so at least we know she wasn't in a car."

"But why does the trail just stop?" I look closer at the screen. "It's slightly faded, so she isn't there anymore."

Nick shakes his head. "The few explanations I can think of are that she unbuttoned her jeans or somehow entered a data impeding device."

"The only way to find out is to go to the park," I determine, and leave the room to Nick's car. They're only a step behind me, and we rush over to the park.

I sprint out of Nick's car into an empty park that is nearly pitch black without the sun to light it. A quick scan of the playground's bark shows numerous scuffs and holes in the bark under the swings, so I run over there. Laying on one of the swings is an envelope. Ben and Nick catch up behind me as I tear open the envelope revealing a typed piece of paper that they read over my shoulders:

We have your friend, Emily. She will be the next victim unless you trade her father for her. More information to come. Don't try to find her, or us.

42 | Circuit Fixing

-Emily-

They don't talk, but I assume there are two captors. One to drive, the other who keeps grabbing at the bag over my head to make sure I can't see. We've been driving for what feels like an hour. Then again, it's hard to tell with fear pulsing through me. My dad wouldn't meet me this way; it has to be a set-up.

We drive over yet another bump and sharp turn causing my head to bang against the car door. As I flip over to the side, the zip tie cuts deeper into my wrists to the point blood is seeping out of the cuts. I don't know if they're armed or not, so I follow their instructions of remaining silent. Fear causes shivers to run down my spine with every movement.

The car jams to a stop as I hear a blaring horn of a train whistle in front of us. If I could contact Charlie or Ben, they might be able to tell where I am based on the time sequence and train tracks. Choice words wisp beneath the driver's breath as he drums his fingers against the steering wheel. Behind my back, I twist my hands to gain some slack, but it results in further twinges of pain. A sharp slap against my shoulder stops me immediately.

"Don't cha go'n try'n escape now, y'all wanna see your pa don't cha?" I bite against my lips. "Y'all can reply now. No one could hear ya even if ya cried."

"I-" My voice comes out muffled from the pillow and nasally from not talking. "Where are you taking me?"

"Like I said, to see your pa," he snickers from the seat in front of me. Disgust spreads through me. The car reeks of body odor and cheap take out.

"Are you working with him?" My voice quivers making me sound much younger than I am.

"In a way," the driver says. His voice is more polished with a hint of a British accent telling of a possible learned man. "I suppose we are working *with* your father. It is to be determined if we are working *for* him."

"You're just tryin' ta confuse me." The first snorts in a mix of annoyance and laughter. "Y'all got nothin' ta say girlie?" I have plenty to say, but nothing of appropriate terms. The train blares its horns once more before we resume driving. One of them turns on the radio, and Ben's song comes through the speakers. "Hey! Don't cha know this boy?"

I nod my head. "Yes. I do." Then I realize I probably shouldn't tell them anything.

"Nice voice for a newbie." He turns up the volume and attempts to sing along to *Sparks* with a whithery voice. I cringe when he shoots for a high note and blatantly misses.

"Please silence that grater you call a voice," The driver says through clenched teeth.

"You're just jealous." Yet he stops, thank goodness, and allows the radio to do the singing for the rest of the drive.

As we pull to a stop, the change in momentum makes me lurch forward, pushing against the driver's seat. One of them opens my door and clenches my wrists, his hand completely wrapping around it with bulging fingers. I attempt to walk along with him willingly, but he makes it difficult by dragging me with an uneven pace matching his limp.

A dampened mothball scent fills my nose as the ground beneath my feet raises by an inch switching from grass scattered dirt to hardened carpet. The Brit stops us with a string of hushed words just as the door slams shut behind me.

"Okay little lady, we're going to take off the blindfold and cut the zip tie, but you have to be good. No funny business. Otherwise they go right back on." His accent quivers in and out as he seems to be making a decision.

I nod my head in agreement. "I've never been one for jokes anyway." The singer snorts.

"Nice one. You're not too bad." His hands move away from my wrists. The plastic digs deeper into my skin for a moment before loosening and I hastily remove the zip tie. I feel around the back of my head until my fingers find a double knot with my hair twisted in and out of it. I have to tug for a while, but it finally slips away freeing my vision.

Momentarily, the hotel lights are too strong for my eyes. Once I adjust, I look at my captors. The Brit is stretching his back like a cat with his hands reaching forward with interlaced fingers. His blue and white checkered shirt is neatly pressed with only a few creases while his dark hair is neatly combed to the right. It's clear he isn't an athlete from the stick-like figure he possesses and paled skin.

I turn to view the second man. While he also entertains a sickly pale color, that is where the physical similarities between them end. Rolls of fat extrude from his midsection matching his bulbous neck. What would be a jolly grin on most people comes across as a non-impressive sneer putting his yellowed teeth-or lack thereof-on display.

Yellow stains drip down from the pits of his arms like buttery stalagmites. "Time ta get a movin on."

His hands shove into my back forcing me forward. I stumble a bit, but find myself and keep my pace between them. Even if I tried to escape, they'd have me caught the first step. A man, stops and smiles tightly with an appropriate nod. He offers a cart for bags but the Brit politely declines hustling us over to an elevator. "Nice job."

The elevator softly whirs accompanied by fatty's whistling. Brit and I share a glare, but fatty doesn't seem to notice. A sigh of relief escapes my lips as the door open on the fourth floor and the Brit leads us out. We continue down to a room where they already have a key.

The room appears to be like any other hotel room, a desk in the center surrounded by twin couches near a kitchen area. Past the bathroom is a bedroom with two twin beds. Fatty jumps onto the nearest bed causing the sheets to flare out in a wave like motion. I look over to Brit in a questioning manner, and take a slight flick of his eyebrows as and okay to get on the other bed.

I relax, almost falling asleep. My eyelids droop down. "Did you drug me?" I yawn.

"Nope," the fatty sneers, "your body's just catching up ta all the excitement. Not every day y'all are kidnapped, should be feelin' special."

"Oh yes, real *special*." I roll my eyes dragging out the word. Bryn, er, Charlie has had an influence on me. Though I doubt that one day of training helped. If anything, it tired me out.

The Brit slides open his bag and pulls out a sleek new laptop that powers on with a quiet purring. His fingers zip across the keyboard in time with his eyes flitting from spot to spot on his screen. For the most part, his expression remains calm and cool without a hint of feeling.

BEHIND THE COVER

I roll over on my bed to glance at the alarm clock resting on the table next to one of those old hotel phones. Two am flashes in red beams. I doubt anyone even knows I'm gone yet.

"So whadya like ta watch?" Fatty presses the power button on the remote opening the TV to the hotel's station. I shrug in response, biting my lip. "Guess it's my choice then. Let's see what we got here." He skips past the children's stations and sports. The screen pauses on a game of golf long enough for him to mutter, "Who even considers golf a sport?"

"I have a friend who golfs." We even have a golf team at school, I think.

"Doesn't make it a sport." His thumb presses down on the button causing the channels to automatically flip through.

I get out of the bed and stride over to the window to get an idea of where we might be. The Brit's eyes remain on me, but he doesn't say a word. Through the window I see a sort of sandy garbage dump next to a parking lot. I strain to see further, but everything blurs into a tannish brown color.

"Here's the one, come back 'ere girlie." Fatty points at my bed, and I follow his finger, shaking slightly. His tone may come across as his joking sneer, but I have no intention of getting on their bad sides. "Now this is a classic, *Seinfeld*." My dad used to love that show, always quoting it and making bad jokes that I never understood. After he left, mom stopped watching it as the old tapes disappeared along with the rest of his stuff.

I turn my eyes to the TV, but don't really watch. My brain is too mixed up between trying to concentrate on escape and overly tired.

Suddenly, the Brit jumps up. "Take off your pants."

"What?" I stutter, my jaw dropping. I cross my arms protectively over my body and glare at him. There is no way I am taking off my pants for this creep.

"Go to the bathroom, put on these." He throws a pair of black leggings at me. "And bring me your jeans."

I lean down to grab the leggings that fell before me, and watch fatty and Brit exchange a silent conversation through questioning looks. I hurry into the bathroom and slide out of my jeans pulling on the leggings. My mom had never been a big fan of leggings, so I've rarely worn them without a skirt. They are really comfortable and I don't have to wiggle and jump around to get them on.

Brit and fatty stop their conversation as I return from the door. I chuck my jeans at Brit, and relax back against the wall with my arms crossed and an annoyed expression. Brit grabs my jeans, lays them out on the ground, and starts slicing a knife through the belt. While my first reaction is to screech at him to stop ripping apart the seams of my pants, I keep my mouth shut. He finally stops after making seven neat slits, and tosses them back at me. "You can put them back on if you want." I gawk at the beltline, but know better than to lecture a man with a knife.

"Whaddya do that for?" Fatty smirks at my expression as I gnaw my teeth against each other.

"This." Brit points to a blue thread in my jeans. "Is how some pesky little teenagers have been tracking us."

Fatty gawks at the string hanging out of my jeans. I twirl it between my fingers flashing the wiring against a ray of light. I can only imagine how Charlie got it in there. The string looks exactly like a thread aside from where he cut through revealing a silver tint.

"May I go change back?" I ask, clenching the fabric.

"Of course." The Brit smiles, returning to his computer. "We should be safe from unwanted visitors now."

BEHIND THE COVER

My stomach clenches at his words as I return to the bathroom. I pull my now looser jeans on and use the leggings as a belt tying them around my waist. The edges of my jeans fold over as they start to slip over my hips, so I fold the leggings over again and tie them through the belt loops. A full-length mirror rests next to the door displaying my reflection. Not exactly my best fashion day.

As I twist around to see my backside, a spark emits across my stomach. Light flashes against the mirror catching my eyes. My finger touches where the flash occurred, heat flaring. I turn again until the light returns. Using the leggings and toilet paper, I reattach the metal threading in my jeans until it's a flickering circuit. Unfortunately, no matter how I connect it, it doesn't stay put with a consistency. An idea pops into my head, so I press the tips together then pull them apart in a pattern I can only hope my friends interpret.

"Girlie, it's time to go." The fat one's voice screeches through the door. He doesn't bother to knock before throwing open the door. His eyes trail up and down my body with a sick expression. "You kiddies an' your weird styles."

I look down to my waist to double check the leggings are covering my poor circuit fixing. They guide me out of the hotel, and we're back on the road with my zip tie and bag.

43 | Set in Stone

-Charlotte-

I pass the crinkled paper to Nick for him to run an analysis. Ben stomps over to my bed, then to the doorway and back again. His face remains grim, though his eyes flash the storyline of his thought process. After finding the note at the park, we returned home in hopes of finding further tracking on Em, but the only thing she brought with her is the jean bug.

Lazily, I drag my finger around my tablet screen tracing the ever-pending loading circle of Em's location. It's been lost since she was kidnapped from the park. The breeze from Ben's strides whips my curls across my forehead. I turn to him indignantly. "Could you stop already? Unless you can march faster than the speed of light, you aren't helping."

"Sorry," he mumbles and sits on the floor next to my bed. "Have you gotten anything new?"

"Don't you think I would have told you?" I retort, glancing back at the screen.

"I don't know! After meeting you, I'm not sure I know anything." Ben's face contorts into a grimace. His eyes flare darkly and lips pull down into a frown. "Ever since you came in town, I've been lost. Now Em actually is lost."

"I've been in town this entire time. The only one who left was you." My voice comes out snarky. Ben recoils, my words struck home. I roll my eyes in exasperation. "I'm not saying this is your fault, even if it totally is, all I'm trying to say is that it isn't my fault." It's completely my fault, but once I rescue her it cancels out, like physics or something.

"Is there anything that can help?" Ben looks up at me beggingly.

I glance at the doorway Nick just disappeared through. "Unless you have a secret tracker or communicator with Em, nope."

A coat of dust has settled across my bookshelf and my fan creaks from not being used. My clothes are unorderly with corners sticking out of drawers in my dresser. Once I would have been disgusted at the appearance, but since school started, and the mission, it's become an unnecessary usage of my time.

Ben grasps at my carpet twisting a piece around his finger until it starts to come out of the floor. As it stretches and unravels, he tries to return it to its original position, but it's too late. Once you place yourself in someone's life, neither of you come back the same.

Just as I'm about to trade my locating app for the DB, the circle pauses as though having connection errors. It flashes green for a moment before a map encompasses the entirety of the screen. On Nick's computer monitors in the basement, it was easy to decipher the different parts of Boise. This tablet, however, contains a much smaller display making the intricate map difficult to read. A blue path highlights its way in twists and turns before coming to a flashing dotted end at a Marriott Resort.

I kick Ben with my toe while my fingers twist the screen around to make it clearer. He jumps up rubbing the back of his head ready to lecture me before noticing the screen. The next moment, he's leaning over my shoulder eagerness flowing off of him.

"Nick!" I shout at the same time Ben gasps.

"I need paper," Ben says, furrowing his brow in concentration. I supply him with a pen as well as my nearest school notebook and he starts to write.

"What are you doing?" Circles and lines dot his page accompanied by his name and Em's.

"It's a code," Ben scribbles out a circle replacing it with a dot. "At least, I think it is. Em and I haven't used it in years."

"What's it say?" I attempt to read his nonsensical writing without success.

"O." Ben pauses, looking over his writing. "K. She's okay!"

While a gleeful grin lights up Ben's face, Nick appears standing in the doorway, hunched over trying to catch his breath.

"Come look at this," I call, pointing at the map.

"Wha-" Nick gulps in air as he walks over and grabs the tablet. With a nod of his head and pinch of his fingers I can see the answer in his eyes. "I know where Emily is."

"To the car," Ben shouts, stabbing his finger forward while running through my door.

"I think we should take the van for this adventure," Nick counters.

"I agree with Nick." I doubt they've seen the van, and it's better equipped.

While Nick and Ben rush into the van, I stay back and collect a selection of items, my DB, gloves, contacts, among other things, and meet them out front. My eyes catch on the movement of Ben reaching over Zack to honk his horn, but I sprint across the lawn and dive into the car grabbing Ben's hand before he gets the chance to alert the entire neighborhood to our presence.

"Are you dense?" I ask, glaring into Ben's confused blue eyes. His hands squirm in mine, but I don't release him until he mutters an apology. "You should be. Don't do anything without asking us first."

"Oh." Ben looks down at his lap.

"You already did, didn't you?" I sigh, rolling my eyes. He nods meekly keeping his vision down. "Well out with it." Why do *I* have to be the adult here?

"So, Zack has been texting me, like, *all* night. He's been super worried about Em. Apparently, they've been texting before they go to sleep, but she didn't reply." An expression of disgust passes over Ben's face. "I let him know we're on our way to go rescue her and that she's okay."

"He's going to meet us there?" I conclude, grabbing the side of my chair as Nick swerves around a pothole.

"What? No." Ben shakes his head. "He didn't say that."

"You really are dense." I drop my forehead against my hand in a pitying manner. "Zack. Likes. Em," I say slowly, as though talking to a kindergartener.

"Duh," Ben agrees.

"Meaning he's going to meet us there."

"Oh."

"Yeah." I smirk, and turn to look out the window. During the day, Boise could be mistaken for millions of cities. At night, the real Boise comes out to play. Lights dot every horizon like dozens of Christmas trees displaying their best wardrobes. Getting lost downtown is as beautiful as a big city while the outer rims reveal a starlit sky mapping out a guide from the sunset to moon. The sky is truly a painting.

The van jumps up and down as the roads transition from smooth to rough. We exit downtown heading toward the Boise river roaring in the quiet night tethered by an empty greenbelt.

"Duh-bee-duuh-bee-duuuh." I quirk my eyebrow up as I turn to the front of the van. "Dun, dun-bee-duuuuh."

"Uh, Ben?"

"Mhmm?"

"What're you doing?" I laugh slightly at his blushing cheeks illuminated by the glare of Nick's screens.

"Singing our theme song, obviously," He attempts to scoff.

Nick pulls into the drop off area of a Marriott, and opens the van door for me to leave. Ben moves to exit, but thinks better of it and rests back against his seat. "I'll have my earpiece on at all times. If I find them, I'll let you know before entering." Nick nods in understanding, and I leave the van.

There's a small crowd meandering about the lobby. According to the table, Em wasn't on ground level. A polite looking man stands behind the help desks with his hands holding down the pages of his book he's absorbed in.

"Excuse me?"

He snaps straight, but manages to keep his finger in his book holding his reading position. "Sorry about that, I've been waiting for good old Maxxy to figure himself out for a while now." He gestures toward the book, and I smile politely, not really caring about some fictional character. "How can I help you?"

My story slides off my tongue as if I were Shakespeare. Well, a *spy* version of Shakespeare. "My best friend and I are staying here with our dads for some speaking event, but I totally forgot what my room number was, and I was, like, wondering if you could be, like, the best and remind me?"

He squints down at me, before a look of understanding crosses his face. "Ah, I've been waiting for you." The man reaches into his pocket and grabs an envelope identical to t he one from the park. "Don't worry, I didn't read it. I was given specific instructions to give it to a lovely young girl accompanied by two boys, on the assumption she could provide a keyword."

"Keyword?" I repeat.

"Yes, keyword. Do you know it?" His eyes light up with energy.

"Do I get a hint?" I bite my lip in thought.

"Oh! Righto! Sorry, forgot about that bit too." He lightly slaps his head with his hand and chuckles to himself. "Keeping a dollar everything"

I look at him blankly, then smile at the obviousness of it. "Kade."

"Indeed! And here is your prize." The man reaches over the desk flailing his voice and arm like a gameshow host.

"Thanks," I toss over my shoulder as I speed walk outside to find Ben and Nick. Most likely Zack at this point as well.

Nick parked his car at the McDonald's to the east of the Marriott, so I pick up my pace to a jog and cross over the street barely noticing the lone car looping around the intersection. Probably drunk. Probably dangerous. Probably not my concern.

"Nick, open the door," I speak into my earpiece as I approach the van. When the door slides open, my eyes widen in surprise. I left the vehicle with two boys, now they've doubled in number.

Nick and Ben remain in the front two seats, but the back has been invaded by Zack and Kade himself. Whereas Kade looks as awake as ever in black jeans and matching black hoodie, Zack is exhausted. His body is drooping downward though his eyes remain frantic and crazed through a pair of glasses.

"Where is she?" Zack's voice comes out hoarse. Tired mixed with fear will do that.

"Not here." I shrug and shove Kade over so he falls into the back of the van. If I were to lose my cool, all three of the boys, not including Kade, would lose everything. Em must be alive if they left a letter and not a package.

"They weren't there?" Kade asks, righting himself.

"Nope, they were long gone. Must have known we were coming, somehow." I narrow my eyes at him. It's awfully convenient he appears as they disappear. His name was the codeword. "Anyway, they left this." I wave the letter in front of them.

Zack snatches it out of my hands and tears the back open. He clears his throat and adjusts his glasses before reading aloud:

The trade will take place today, 5:00pm sharp, at the place where this all started.

Where this all started? H&M? The bowling lanes? This Tai figure seems to know more about this than anyone else. I can't wait to get my hands on him.

"Who knows what they're talking about?" Nick asks logically.

"The mall," Zack says.

"No." Ben shakes his head flicking his bangs from side to side. "Sorry Zack, but I don't think that's what they're talking about. Charlie explained it earlier to me."

"Then what?" Kade asks coldly.

"How can we trust you?" Ben responds, an equally icy tone of voice. Instead, he leans over and whispers into my ear. I nod in agreement.

"Ben's right. He knows the place."

"Fine." Kade blows a stream of air through his lips. "Don't tell me. What's the plan?"

"Yeah, what are we going to do?" Zack asks. The paper bends beneath the pressure of his fingers as anger seeps into his tone.

BEHIND THE COVER

Everyone collectively turns to me. "Why are you all looking at me? Oh, right. Here's what we're going to do." I grab Nick's tablet and diagram my plan as well as detailed explanations. Kade offers one or two changes, but for the most part everyone agrees and it's set in stone. "For now, we're all going to get some sleep. Keep quiet, and skip school."

"Sounds good to me," Zack yawns, but his eyes explain they have no intention of allowing him sleep.

As we begin our ride back, I pull out the DB and turn to page one hundred and fifty-four. I bit against my lip, turning my decision over my mind examining pros and cons. This is one part of my plan I had chosen to keep to myself. With a series of taps, the message is typed and sent. There's no going back now.

44 | Here We Are

-Emily-

My mom is probably freaking out. She always checks on me and make sure I'm doing okay. I've never not been there. It's nearly three in the afternoon, according to the radio, and we've spent the entirety of our day driving. Fatty and Brit haven't spoken much aside from fatty singing and Brit commanding he stop.

I've attempted to send a few more messages, but I don't even have confirmation the received the first one. If Ben isn't there, I know they haven't. A shiver shakes across my back when a thought glances my mind. What if I never see them again? I've been assuming I'm going to escape, or they'll get tired of me and drop me off, but is that an option for these people? If they're working for a lunatic who's already murdered a teenage girl, they surely wouldn't hesitate to do the same to me.

My throat catches, so I clear it before speaking, "What are you doing with me?"

"You're my lil bargaining chip," fatty says from the front seat. "One Parker for another."

My jaw locks as I process his words. "You're trading me for my dad?"

"Exactimundo." He laughs at himself, then turns the music up.

My dad? He's sacrificed everything over the past ten years, and now he could give it all up for me. Unless, I stop it from happening. If I could escape they'd lose their bargaining chip. "I can't escape, so could you just take the bag off already? My air flow is getting stuffy."

"Maybe I enjoy watching y'all sweat bullets down ya neck."

"Take it off," The Brit interrupts suddenly.

"Fine, fine. I'm just messin' with her." A breath of fresh air flows up into my face as the bag is slowly loosened and removed. I blink against the sunlight and glance out the window in anticipation. Disappointment soon follows. While the hills are visible against a grey-blue sky, the only other recognizable feature would be the cow farms stretching as far as I can see. "Nice view, huh?"

"Sure," I mutter twisting around to look behind me. A few neighborhoods are in our past. Unless we're going to Oregon, I have no clue where we are.

A yawn acts against my lips, though I slept hours earlier. The Brit smiles in his rearview mirror. "Might as well rest up, you've got a big day today."

Seems like every day has been a "big day" lately.

I look around the car for something of use, but to no avail. Perhaps Charlie could have escaped with the mess of take out leftovers, magazines, and napkins, but I'm not Charlie. All I can do is send a message and cross my fingers that Ben will decipher it. I twist my leggings around adjusting them until I can manipulate the jean string with my fingers secured behind my back. As I push and pull creating tiny sparks, fatty sniffles his nose.

"Do y'all smell that?" He takes a long whiff and licks his lips. "Smells like a barbeque." He must smell my burning toilet paper. "Speaking of such, I'm starving.' Can we get food?"

"We got food an hour ago," Brit replies, sharply.

"I know that, I'm always hungry." Fatty's face bulges over his shoulder as he looks back at me. "You're hungry, are'ncha?"

"Sure." If we stop, they'll have to unlock the doors and there's a chance of running out. If I can make it into the restaurant, then I can alert the authorities as to what's going on.

"What do you want?" The Brit groans, sliding open a window now that we're beyond cow land. He rests his elbow so it's halfway hanging out of the car.

"I'll have a double patty cheeseburger, large fries-" Fatty starts until Brit cuts him off.

"Not you, the girl."

"Whatever there is will be fine." My words quiver. I've only got one shot at this.

He pulls over into a town, turning through neighborhood after neighborhood until we reach a small collection of businesses and fast food stops. The Brit pulls the car into a Jack in the Box drive through. "Hamburger work for you?"

"Cheeseburger." Irritation fills my chest as I realize we won't be going inside.

The Brit's voice becomes kinder as he yells into the speaker ordering four cheeseburgers and large fries. We start to continue forward, but fatty leans across Brit to make sure they don't forget our sauces.

As the next window slides open, a tired face leans out with a tray of waters. I move my head to the side until I'm in her direct line of sight, but she looks past me either too tired to care, or focused on something else. I send another message to Ben using my jeans while she returns inside to retrieve our meal. This time, I shake my head frantically when she looks my way and her expression changes to one of surprise. Before she can do anything, however, Brit puts the pedal to the metal driving out of Jack in the Box.

Fatty sorts through the food handing Brit his cheeseburger, and grabbing his own meal then passes the bag back to me. My burger is squashed from sitting at the bottom with a few stray fries. "I'm going to need my hands to eat this." I wiggle my wrists to my side, still tied together.

"That's right." Fatty wipes his greased over ketchup hands on the sides of his pants, and reaches over to me. Brit slams on the brakes causing my momentum to continue into Fatty. I hold back gags as he uses a pair of scissors to snip away at the zip tie. "There ya go. Don't try goin' an' escapin' or anything."

"Of course not. Why would I ever want to escape?" I ask sarcastically.

"Hey! We've been good ta ya. Just look at the food." He eyes mine with hunger.

"Oh yes, because kidnapping is such great treatment."

"We didn't have a choice," he mumbles. "It's for the best. You'll see. Once everything's all righted out, we'll have control an' everything'll be great."

"What are you talking about?" I raise the cheeseburger to my lips.

"Well, ya see," fatty starts.

"Shut up." Brit glares over at us. "This is our business, and ours alone. Not hers."

Fatty turns an angry red at being bossed around. He slumps back causing his entire seat to shudder under his weight.

I eat my food as though I haven't eaten in years, yet my stomach growls for want of more. I was hungrier than I previously thought. As I turn over thoughts in my head, each one is shot down for different reasons until my eyes begin to droop. Eventually, I allow them to drop shut.

A hand shoves at my shoulders. "Wakey, wakey."

"Five more minutes," I groan, turning over onto my side until something stabs into me. My hand reaches until it clasps around a metallic flat rectangle and I jerk awake. Memories of my situation flash across my mind causing a glare to pull at my lips. "Alright, I'm up."

"'Bout effing time." Fatty snorts. He jumps out of his side of the car, shifting the weight so that it tips from side to side. My door flies open, but any chance of exit is blocked by his bulging body. "Let's go," he mutters gruffly, clenching my forearm in his hand.

I stumble out of the car tripping over my numb legs. Once I've finally started moving at his pace, I stop equally quickly with a gasp hidden behind my mouth. *What could we be doing here?*

My question is answered at the sight of Nick's van.

45 | Questions

-Charlotte-

Ben hums lightly through his lips until Zack "accidentally" nudges his shoulder. Rather than apologize, he groans, throwing his hands in the air behind his head. "Where are they? Kade said they'd be here ages ago."

Over the past few hours, Zack's only grown more restless awaiting not only Kade's arrival, but Em's father as well. I place my hand on his arm, a motion I've noticed seems to calm him, as Ben moves further away from the pent-up anger.

"Mr. Parker has never been the most timely of people," Ben offers assurances where I cannot. "I'd be willing to bet he's just falling back into old habits. Always one to make a grand entrance."

"I'd take you up on that bet if I had anything of value to match yours," Zack returns the tone to his usual joking, "rich boy." A smirk crosses Ben's expression as Zack's snide comments have become the very foundation of their friendship.

"Oh, really?" Ben cocks an eyebrow upward. "Nothing at all?"

Zack and I exchange a look as the meaning of ben's challenge becomes clear. I lean back against a tree stretching in expectation of what's to come.

"You wouldn't be referring to Em, would you?" For a moment, Zack's voice is soft before he clears his throat. "Or my pride?"

Ben opens his mouth with a quiet smirk dancing across his lips, but a buzzing in my ear captures my attention. Nick's voice comes from the van parked outside Em's house. "They're entering the backyard now." Without a further explanation of which *they* he might be talking about, his mic switches off.

I gesture at Ben and Zack to quiet down with my hands in response to which they both take a seat in the tree. Crunching leaves announce the quickly approaching arrival of our featured guests. They stop for a moment as the forest seems to silence itself in anticipation, before breaking into view. Two gasps catch behind me at the sight of a taller, more distinguished man leading his prosaic companion with Em tightly held beneath browning fingernails.

"Em!" Zack leaps down off the tree landing with a loud thud, not caring about consequences.

I reach for the collar of his shirt, catching him while he attempts to run by me. The stately man tuts his tongue against the roof of his mouth as he draws a weapon from the inner pockets of his coat. Em cringes as the metal of a new gun presses into her neck.

Though Zack has stopped fighting against my grasp, a growl escapes his throat.

Zack casts his eyes in my direction, flashing in the final rays of sun, as though to ask for permission. I dip my head down allowing him to speak. "Em?"

Em gulps against the gun, but smiles in response. She slowly raises her hands in a thumbs up position.

The man holding her groans while the other passes him the weapon and reaches his now free hands out toward us. "I do believe it's time for some pleasantries. You may address me as the commander of our operation."

I can't help it; I snort. "Excuse me?"

His eyes flair in aggravation. "Oh, I'm sorry. It was my natural response to the ridiculous proposal."

I watch the gears slowly tick in the disgusting man whose grip has loosened the smallest bit. The "commander of our operation" however, is quick to comprehend my words. "You're a smart one, aren't you?"

"More like I happen to have a lick of common sense." I shrug innocently. "Now, how about we reveal our cards? Otherwise I have a feeling this will go on for ages. You hand over Em, and we'll hold up on our end of the deal."

"Do you take me for an imbecile?"

I turn my head to one side, then the other. My hand flourishes toward Em and her current capture. "Him, yes." I look back at the other man. "You are yet to be determined."

"My, my." He shakes his head in amusement.

"Cut the crap already!" Zack bursts out. "I'm done with this bull crap. Give me my friend or I'll take her from you." He lunges forward again, but the man is quick to flip Zack onto his back. I expect him to reveal another gun from his pocket, but this time he pulls out a syringe.

"I've been looking for a new test subject." The world pauses for a second. Leaves still in the wind behind me, and two shadows halt for a split second in front of me.

"Wait." I step forward cautiously, training my eyes on the syringe and gun. "That isn't what we came here to do."

"Quite right." The man twirls the syringe between his thumb and pointer finger. "Now where is your portion? Or else I fear I'll merely have to confiscate yet another of your *lovely* gang. I can't return home empty handed."

The shadows step out of the darkness behind the two men. The first belongs to Kade who is quick to wrap his arm around Em's captor's neck and flick the gun away. I recognize the second from pictures Nick sent me in his research of Em's dad, with a few minor changes. His hair was just as wispy and crazed as before, only paler falling just short of grey. His eyes held wrinkles created from laughing but are mirrored by dark circles. Even his figure has hunched over from the weight he's been carrying for so long.

Mr. Parker adjusts his glasses, pushing them to the bridge of his nose, "I believe you're looking for me?"

Tears flow freely down Em's cheeks, but the type, I will never know for sure. "D-dad?" Her voice cracks. She runs into his arms as though the scene around her has disappeared, leaving her alone with her long-lost father. The moment should be touching, and it would be, if it weren't for the syringe still directed at Zack's neck. I seem to be the only one still phased.

"Is it a deal? The daughter for the dad?" I cross my arms cocking an eyebrow. The man looks around until a smile snakes its way across his face.

"Drop the syringe, and I'm yours," Mr. Parker says gravely. Em shakes against his chest, grabbing his shirt in her fists. I look over to Ben whose face has become a mask of confusion.

"Indeed." The syringe drops into a small pile of leaves as Mr. Parker gently pulls the screeching Em away from him and into Kade's now empty arms. "Nice doing business with you." He tips an invisible hat in my direction twittling a whistle. His friend lets out a rambunctious laugh shaking his pot belly.

For a second all of us teenagers exchange a glance, then collectively sprint after the men. Only, before we can get there, the trees appear to move in and out of their own shadows until dozens of people emerge.

"What the—" Zack mutters, stopping alongside the rest

of us. The only one who manages to continue is Kade who is right next to Kriss. And next to her, is Miss Thomas, red lipstick and all.

I know I should do something, but the scene unfolds before me like a Marvel movie. The pair of women is quick to neatly tackle the men while simultaneously grabbing their weapons. Kriss provides a well-placed punch to the forehead causing Mr. Dignity to collapse unconscious while Miss Thomas shoots pot-belly with a dart gun.

"Nice to see you, kiddo." Kriss wipes her hands against each other. "Seems like we have a lot to catch up on."

I glance around at Em and Ben resting in Mr. Parker's arms with Zack standing nearby holding Em's arm in his hands like he's terrified she'll be gone if he ever lets go. At the two unconscious men under Kriss and my employer. At the syringes scattered across the ground. "Seems like it."

46 | Answers

-Emily-

I'd never seen so many people crying.

Even when Maree had "died," or Dad left, all tears were kept in the closet away from the confused little six-year-old. Yesterday, however, it was a cry fest. My mom arrived just after Charlie's-what would I call them? *Agents?*-left. Surprisingly, there wasn't an ounce of shock on my mother's expression. Instead, she slowly stepped into our kitchen with her eyes trained on my dad. Her steps were slow and deliberate. If not for her sparkling eyes, her actions would be mistaken as malicious. All doubts dissipated the moment her hands reached my dad's. Then the tears came.

Whereas my mom is a quiet, pretty crier with silent tears slipping from the corners of her eyes, Dad's entire body shook with sobs of joy. Ben and I were quick to join the embrace, but my eyes remained dry. Not from lack of *want* to cry. Only because there was nothing left. I didn't have anything left to give, it felt like everything had been taken away then returned. Except, unlike most returns, this one had been used and changed.

For a second, I was lost in the moment; my brain was attempting to comprehend the puzzle placed before it. The characters fit the setting, but the timing was off.

The clearing of a throat interrupted our tearful reunion. "Sorry to interrupt," Charlie said, not sounding the least bit sorry, "but Nick and I really need to get going."

I glanced at Nick standing awkwardly with one arm gripping his elbow, confusion clouding his eyes. "Yeah, sorry guys, but we do."

My mom stood up, brushing herself off while keeping one arm around my shoulders. "Of course."

Charlie nodded in Ben's and my direction then reached up to her ear with her pointer and middle fingers. Her head bobbed up and down as she listened though her expression remains constant and unreadable. After a few moments of uncomfortable silence, Charlie removed her fingers and turns to us. "I'd like to invite you all over to dinner on Saturday, *er*, Kriss would I suppose. There are some things we need to get in the open."

"*Some?*" Zack repeated incredulously. "I'd say *everything.*"

Nick shrugged. "That works too."

With that, they left, followed quickly by my dad. He had a few things he claimed he needed to take care of, but he'd meet us at Charlie's house. *With* Maree.

For the past three days, Charlie and I have been noticeably absent from school with Creeper bringing home work for me. Lately, he's been acting timid. Or maybe kinder. I'm not sure what exactly. Just different. Everyone's been different around me as though walking on eggshells. Maybe they're afraid I'm going to go make another stupid decision and get myself captured again.

Ben's spent his time with my mom and me, but had to return for some major issue with the new album yesterday. He made me promise a dozen times over to tell him everything that happens in the meeting today. Through all of our speculations this week, we still are rather clueless as to what is going to happen. While Charlie and I have been texting, she's been left in the dark as much as me. Even if Nick knows anything, Charlie claims he's making her wait until our meeting today as well. I can only imagine her wrath he's had to put up with.

Zack nudges my shoulder, breaking me from my thoughts. "Emily?"

"Huh?" I stretch back against the side of my bed, accidently scattering a pile of homework we'd been attempting to work on before I zoned off. "Sorry, what did you say?" I ask sheepishly.

"Are you ready to go?" His eyes are wide with concern. Soon he'll have wrinkles around them just like my dad if he doesn't blink.

I turn on my phone glancing at the time. I must have zoned out longer than I realized; we were supposed to leave five minutes ago. "As ready as I'll ever be."

He reaches down to fix the papers I messed up, but I grab his hand pulling him through the door. For a moment, Zack doesn't react. Then he closes his hand around mine with a comforting warmth I'm sure I'll be needing.

My mom raises an eyebrow at our intertwined hands passing us a smile. A slight blush accents my cheeks, but I still shake my head. *Now isn't the right time.* I wonder if it will ever be the right time for an *us*.

The connection between my mom and me has only grown in the absence of Dad, but we've never had to communicate it. She resolves her problems internally by thinking over them. As much as I'd love to help her, I also realize it's more helpful to leave her on her own. Even during the car ride over to Charlie and Nick's house, she says nothing beyond the usual pleasantries to Creeper allowing the radio to fill our silence. I quickly change the radio so that it's on a different station than it was during my kidnapping. The memory makes me shiver.

As we pull up in front of their gate, Creeper tightens

his grip on my hand he's yet to release. I smile gratefully at him and squeeze back. As we enter the gates, a clicking echoes in my ears like the innards of a clock snapping into place then releasing. Before we can raise a hand to knock, the door slides open to reveal Charlie.

She moves to the side and gestures inside with her arm. "Come on in." We step into the house, but no further allowing Charlie to step ahead of us. When passing my side, she nudges my shoulder winking at Zack and my hands. I chuckle in response pushing her back, but the shoving match is over before it begins. Charlie guides us into a room cut between a mini kitchen bar and living room where dad, Kade, Nick, and an older agent I had seen take out my captor are seated.

Mom slides into the couch next to dad exchanging a quick kiss as Creeper and I sit down on the floor in front of them. Dad ruffles my hair with the slight twist of his hand. Having him here still feels so surreal.

The lady stands up from her seat between Kade and Nick, motioning for Charlie to take her place. Once everyone is situated, she starts, "Welcome to our home. My name is Kriss. No need to introduce yourselves, I already know all of you." She winks at us in the same manner as Charlie.

Dad and Nick chuckle lightly as Zack starts to loosen his grip. Charlie groans in frustration, "I don't think I can take it any longer. *Please* tell me what's going on."

"Sorry kiddo." Dad holds up a hand causing Charlie's head to snap towards him with a glare. "But we've got one more member who had to use the bathroom."

"You mean, me?" A gasp flies out of my throat and I'm off the ground faster than I've ever moved before. I sprint across the room, but it's not fast enough. Not until I reach Maree's arms. I lean my head down into her shoulder. Last time I saw her I was nearly a foot taller, but now she's only a forehead shorter than me. "Nice haircut, sis."

A mixture between a laugh and sob pushes its way out of me. "Haircut? The first thing you decide to say to me is a comment on my hair?"

"I always was the girlier of us." Maree winks, stepping away while keeping her hands on my shoulders. We turn our heads almost in sync appraising each other; her hair has either transformed from chocolate dark brown to sun kissed blonde or she dyed it. Aside from the obvious height difference, she's grown into herself losing any previous roundness becoming a shapely young woman. Certain features have remained the same, our shared nose and almond colored eyes, and in those ways, we will never be lost to each other again.

She brushes her fingers across her forehead pushing away slanted bangs. "Your bangs aren't too bad either." We laugh together and I drag her over to our parents where she shares a hug with mom, then takes a seat on my side unoccupied by Creeper.

"Two beautiful Parker girls?" Creeper grins. "I think I'm in heaven."

"Ah, you must be Zack." Maree raises her eyebrows stretching the freckles dotted across her cheeks. "I'd say it's a pleasure to meet you, but, quite frankly, it isn't."

"Good choice. If only I'd have been as wise as you," I groan lightly.

Charlie clears her throat with a glare. "Now that everyone is here. Let's get on with it."

This draws laughter from all of us as Kriss steps forward once again. "Is everyone here caught up with Tai and Milex?" She pauses, allowing all of us to nod our heads. "Good. Between the two men we've taken into custody and Mr. Parker's testimony, we've built a solid case against Tai's organization. In fact, last night with their help we were able to infiltrate their headquarters here in Boise and capture the majority of their workers."

"What?" Charlie screeches. "You did all of this without me?"

Kriss shrugs. "You've been working hard and I say you need a break." Charlie's expression turns into a pout, but Kriss continues anyway, "Unfortunately, Tai escaped. Meaning that you will all be under close surveillance, and Mr. Parker and Maree along with the rest of the Parkers will remain in our protection."

I glance over my shoulder at my parents attempting to gauge their reactions, but they remain constant as though expecting this information. Zack, however, grits his teeth together. "Will I be able to contact my friends?"

"Of course," Kriss says. "We'll explain everything to you."

"Thank goodness." I breathe a sigh of relief. If I had to go much longer without Ben, and yes, Zack, I'm not sure I could do it.

"Now I believe congratulations are in order." Kriss pulls a hand out from behind her back-revealing sparkling cider. She pops the top off allowing bubbles to overflow onto the ground. "You all did spectacularly. Especially you, Charlie and Nick." Nick blushes and Charlie drops her pout long enough to smile in accomplishment. "My partner, Miss Thomas, and I have been working on this case for months before deciding it was the right one for you."

"Miss Thomas," Charlie repeats questioningly, "you mean the one who assigned this case to me?"

"One in the same." Kriss nods, appraising Charlie's reaction.

"This was all a test?"

"And you passed with flying colors." Kriss reaches inside her sweatshirt pulling out two pieces of paper. She hands one to Charlie and one to Nick.

Nick's jaw drops. "Is this for real?"

"It is." Kriss waves her hand at Kade. "You and Charlie are invited to the most prestigious and covert training academy, or school if you prefer, for agents in training. Kade is already in attendance and it is where not only I graduated, but Miss Thomas as well."

Charlie keeps quiet as Kriss passes out glasses of sparkling cider to us teenagers and wine to the adults. I look over to Creeper. "Can you believe this?"

"I don't think anything could surprise me at this point." He shrugs, and takes a huge gulp of his glass.

"That's true." I down my glass as well.

Many conversations are going on throughout this room, yet none are spoken out loud. My parents are communicating through touch and grins whereas Nick and Charlie are solely depending on their facial expressions twisting their lips in an exaggerated attempt at words.

Kriss stands up once again, she seems to enjoy being the center of attention. Strange, considering she's a spy and all that. "Now that everything is now in the open, it's time to say goodbye. If you come up with any further questions, do communicate with either Nick or Charlie. And for you Parkers, we'll be in touch." She glides over to the front door, "Oh, and I'm sure it goes without saying that nothing is to leave this house."

We all nod somberly and begin to stand up, but are quickly interrupted by Nick, "No!" He shakes his head. "Sorry, I meant no. Kriss you can't stop. You promised." For the first time tonight, anger flashes through Kriss' eyes.

"I haven't the faintest what you mean," She says innocently.

"If you won't tell, then I will." Nick crosses his arms defiantly.

"Fine." Kriss flips her hair over her shoulder, sitting down. "It was bound to come out anyway. I just assumed Charlie wouldn't want all of this in front of her friends."

Charlie's face contorts in confusion. "What? You can say anything you want. If it's safe and above board that is."

Nick nods his head. "It is."

We all turn our attention over to Kriss who appears to be choosing where to start. "Charlie, have you ever wondered why I have you call me Kriss instead of mother or mom?" Charlie nods her head slightly. "I've always looked at you like my child, but that isn't completely accurate. That is to say, I'm not your *birth* mother. Not Nick's either for that matter."

Charlie clenches the paper in her fist, not out of anger, but in need of support. "Go on."

"My role as an agent isn't solely out doing field work. I am also an agency mother. Whenever a child's parents are lost on a mission, they are sent to an agency mother. You and Nick lost your parents at about the same time on the same mission. The early stages of this mission as it happens. The agency assigned you two to me.

"As sorry as I am to say it, I never knew Nick's parents. However, I may prefer that to losing yours. Your mother was the fiercest women I ever knew. An awe-inspiring terror in her field only to be reined in by your father; the Sherlock Holmes of our time. On their own, they were the best of the best, but together, they were unstoppable."

"I can attest to that," Dad agrees, surprising all of us, "your father was the only one to score higher than me on the final vector calculus exam."

I look over to Charlie to discover silent tears trailing down her cheeks. "You knew my father?"

"We grew up together." My dad grins. "In fact, that's how Kade came to be my second-hand man."

"What?" Charlie shake her head in confusion.

Kriss interjects stopping my dad, "When your parents died, Kade was already in training at the academy, so he simply moved onto the campus whereas you came to live in my house."

"Wait, hold on a second." Charlie's expression morphs into horror. "So first, you're saying Nick isn't my real brother. Technically he's probably not even my *adopted* brother, but don't worry! Because we've replaced his spot with a jerk who goes by the name of Kade."

"Pretty much," Kriss says.

Charlie's eyes go wide before rolling back into her head as she faints.

Epilogue

A streak of light invades his room, growing larger as the door slides open. He groans in irritation at being interrupted, shielding his eyes from the unwanted light. He had given strict commands not to be disturbed unless it was an emergency.

"What is it?" His voice croaks from lack of use. It has been over a day since he last made human contact. It should be *another* day before he is forced to.

"We have a situation, sir." His secretary bites her lip nervously. He isn't known for his good moods. No one gets to the top by being good. "All other compounds have been shut down and overtaken."

He strokes his clean-shaven chin in consideration of what he just heard. "This is why we have a contingency plan. Was it not activated?"

"It was, sir. Except, the attack appears to be rooted in the capture of two of our own. Any chance at escape was cut off." The secretary hunches backward as though her body naturally knows its need to go into a self-defense mode. She had heard rumors of what happened in this room. Those who entered without expressed permission were few to leave. Her coworkers speculated his visitors were either shot to keep what was going on in this room a secret or used as lab test subjects. There never are enough test subjects.

"That would be why we have a plan B." He shakes his head disdainfully. "You are dismissed. I need to begin preparations and would prefer communications with my son to be private."

"Son, sir?" She bites her lip the moment the words leave her mouth. She was dismissed, given her own second chance. Yet she blew it all on two simple, curious words.

If the room were a touch lighter perhaps the vibrant shade of angry red glowing across his cheeks would have been more prominent to the secretary's sight. His tone took on a ferocity unlike anything she had ever heard before. "I said leave. It is well known a chain is only as strong as its weakest link, and I have no plans of keeping any weak links around here. As you can't handle a simple command, I'm afraid that I have discovered my newest weak link."

She backs away reaching for the door behind her, but it shuts on its own accord. Her jaw locks into place, nonetheless the screams escaping her lips echo around the room. As strong arms drag her onto a table and tie her down, she mumbles a final prayer praying for the safety of her family she has fought so hard to protect.

"Amen." No one will ever know what happened to her, but she will at last have the answers to her questions concerning the mysterious laboratory.

Acknowledgements

It would take the entirety of another novel to include everyone I owe my gratitude, but I (unfortunately) can't do that.

First, come my readers. Those who read from the dedication to these acknowledgments (or for some, the other way around). In other words, you. Thank you. Especially my family. Without you, I wouldn't even be here, let alone be the person I am today. Mom, you taught me how to write and inspired my love of reading, there aren't many gifts greater than that. Dad, you were the one who taught me perseverance and how to strive to achieve greatness, and I thank you because I hope both of those things are evident in this novel. Luke, Mark, and Michael, there wouldn't be a creative bone in my body without you three there to pound it into me. Uncle Daryl and Aunt Dana, thank you for providing an entirely new dimension to my life that I can't imagine living without. Thank you, grandma and grandpa, for all of the books you've ever bought me that have furthered my writing journey and your interest toward the end of this novel. I love you all.

A few names in this novel may sound familiar to some, and I hope that you already know how thankful I am to have had you join me on this journey-even if you didn't know you did. Brynna, Charlotte, telepathic-I mean Angela, Hailey, Krissy, Nick, Pejmon, Atiya, Vincent, Tyler, Carter, Micah, and everyone else who has made it through these crazy past couple years with me. And Kellan, thank you for pushing me to do better than I ever thought I could.

While some students such as Zack may find English a frightful subject, it has become a favorite of mine which is no small feat completed by my teachers. Mrs. Compton, I don't think I've ever been as terrified and excited at the same time as I was when I walked into your classroom that first day of seventh grade. Even to this day, I am unequivocally thankful for all you have done for me. It's largely because of you that my writing is where it is. Miss Miller, you were there to help me in ninth grade. You probably didn't realize it, but that was a year when my writing struggled and was on the verge of ending. With your help in and out of class, this book managed to continue. Miss Thompson, we were the team that survived Western Civ, somehow. I'm not entirely sure how we did it in all honesty. But you were the support that helped me at the end of this book. Becoming a supportive reader and friend to whom I will never be able to entirely express my gratitude.

I couldn't have asked for a better team at The Polyethnic. You were always supportive and created a fantastic environment beyond writing. Melissa, I'm so glad to have gotten to work with you, I have no idea how I got so lucky with finding not only a publisher and editor but friend as well. Handing off my years of work into someone else's hands was a terrifying step, but you, Alyssa, made it a great experience, even with my many questions. I'm so thankful to have had you as my editor.

Even though I've surely forgotten too many people, my original Wattpad audience has not escaped my mind. Sarah, my first and best Wattpad friend, we did it! We're living the Wattpad dream! JAS (or Lasagna according to your profile) your comments are part of the reason for this book finally being complete. Plus your ships never fail to put a smile on my face.

On the cover is my name and there will be my About the Author with my picture. But behind the cover, the gratitude belongs to the dozens of people who kept me going on this journey and continue to help. It was their hands and words that aided in creating this novel, not mine alone. It is the readers like you that make books like this a reality. Thank you.

About the Author

Alyse Palsulich was born and raised in Idaho among three younger brothers. Since learning to read at age five she has been consumed by the art of reading. Starting with Wendy Mass then moving up through Ridley Pearson to J. R. R. Tolkien and Ted Dekker, Alyse's passion only grew. At this point she decided to condense her creative world into writing which resulted in her dreams of becoming a published author and igniting a spark of reading for a new generation. Throughout her ninth grade year she wrote the book *Witches and Royalty*. Prior to this, she supported and aided author Brock Eastman with his series *The Quest For Truth* in a role entitled "Quester." With Wattpad she started writing her YA fiction series *Two Sides* which was soon discovered by Polyethnic Publishing. In her free time she can be found on the soccer field or spending time with her family and friends.

YOU HAVE JUST READ A BOOK PUBLISHED BY

THE POLYETHNIC PUBLISHING

THE POLYETHNIC PUBLISHING started out as a high school business project by then junior, Melissa Futrell. It wasn't until two years later when she launched the company after the success of The Polyethnic Taurus: Author Hop Tour in which she promoted many authors. Some of these are Michael Lackey, Michael Weekly, John I. Jones, and even New York Times #1 Bestselling Author, Karan Bajaj.
We are very honored that you have decided to buy this book and we cannot wait for you to see more of the titles we will be releasing. To learn more about us, our authors, and the books we will be publishing, visit our website at www.thepolyethnic.com.
Sincerely,
The Polyethnic Publishing

Made in the USA
Middletown, DE
16 November 2017